UNDENIABLE ATTRACTION

She rose and walked to him, halting an arm's length away. His intense virility was drawing her as if they were opposing poles of a magnet seeking their mates.

For a long moment they stood that way, motionless and utterly intent on each other. Then he raised his hands. She thought he would pull her close for a kiss, but instead he grasped her heavy braid and untied the ribbon at the end. After releasing her hair from its maidenly restraint, he raked the shining strands with his long fingers until they spilled in a silken mantle over her shoulder and tumbled halfway to her waist.

"You have beautiful hair," he said softly, his fingertips drifting across her cheek and throat in an erotic caress. The desire in his eyes was a potent aphrodisiac, releasing the hidden part of her nature as surely as he had unbound her hair. She caught her breath and her lips parted, wanting more . . .

Books by Mary Jo Putney

The Lost Lords Series

LOVING A LOST LORD

NEVER LESS THAN A LADY

NOWHERE NEAR RESPECTABLE

NO LONGER A GENTLEMAN

Other Historical Romances

ONE PERFECT ROSE

THE BARGAIN

Published by Kensington Publishing Corp.

The Rake

MARY JO PUTNEY

ZEBRA BOOKS
KENSINGTON PUBLISHING CORP.
http://www.kensingtonbooks.com

ZEBRA BOOKS are published by

Kensington Publishing Corp.
119 West 40th Street
New York, NY 10018

All Kensington titles, imprints, and distributed lines are available at special quantity discounts for bulk purchases for sales
promotion, premiums, fund-raising, educational, or institu-
tional use.

Special book excerpts or customized printings can also be created to fit specific needs. For details, write or phone the office
of the Kensington Special Sales Manager: Attn. Special Sales
Department. Kensington Publishing Corp., 119 West 40th Street,
New York, NY 10018. Phone: 1-800-221-2647.

ISBN-13: 978-1-4201-1727-1
ISBN-10: 1-4201-1727-0

Previously published in mass-market paperback in April 1998 by
Topaz, an imprint of Dutton NAL, a member of Penguin Putnam
Inc. Originally published in a somewhat different version in a
Signet edition under the title *The Rake and the Reformer*.

First Zebra Books Mass-Market Paperback Printing: April 2012

10 9 8 7 6 5 4 3 2 1

Printed in the United States of America

To Bill,
my favorite friend of Bill W.

Chapter 1

When two gentlemen are closely related by blood, they do not usually address each other with formality. In this case, however, the gentlemen in question were first cousins once removed, the younger had come from nowhere to inherit a title and fortune that the older had assumed would be his, and their relationship had been formally announced moments after they had come within a sword slice of killing one another.

Hence, it was not surprising that relations between the two were somewhat strained. Which is why Reginald Davenport, notorious rake, gambler, and womanizer, known in some circles as "the Despair of the Davenports," greeted his noble cousin with a terse, "Good day, Wargrave."

The Earl of Wargrave rose to his feet behind the massive walnut desk and offered his hand. "Good day. I'm glad you were able to come by."

After a brief, hard handshake, Reggie took the indicated chair and stretched out his long legs. "I make it a point to obey summons from the head of the family," he drawled. "Particularly when that person pays my allowance."

Wargrave's mouth tightened slightly as he sat again, a fact that pleased Reggie. Among the earl's many irritating virtues was his calm, good nature. Equally irritating was his

politeness. Rather than issue a summons, the earl left the
time and place of meeting to his cousin, implying a willingness to transact family business in a tavern if that was the
older man's choice.

While giving Wargrave credit for that willingness,
Reggie had no objection to calling at the family mansion in
Half Moon Street to see what changes had been wrought. He
had to admit, rather reluctantly, that the changes were all for
the better. In his uncle's day, this study had been a dark,
poky room designed to intimidate callers. Now it was bright,
airy, and quietly masculine, with leather chairs and an air of
settled comfort. The new owners had good taste.

Since he could find nothing to criticize in his surroundings, Reggie turned his observant gaze to his host. Whenever
they chanced to meet, he looked hopefully for signs that the
new earl was running to fat, turned snobbish, decked out in
green stripes and gold watch fobs, or showing other signs of
decadence, arrogance, or vulgarity. Alas, he was always disappointed. Richard Davenport continued to be well dressed
in a discreet and gentlemanly way, he retained his trim soldier's figure, and he treated everyone he met, from prince to
scullery maid, with the same well-bred courtesy.

Nor did he have a decent temper. Reggie had tried his
best, but he was seldom able to provoke his cousin into anything more than infinitesimal signs of irritation. Sometimes
it was hard to believe the blasted fellow was really a Davenport. Reggie himself was the epitome of the breed, very tall,
very dark, with cool blue eyes and a long face that seemed
more designed for sneers than smiles.

In contrast, his cousin was of only average height with
medium brown hair, hazel eyes, and an open, pleasant countenance. However, the young earl was the best swordsman
Reggie had ever seen, and Reggie had never liked him better
than on the occasion when Wargrave had lost his temper and
demonstrated that fact.

The earl interrupted Reggie's musings, saying, "Your allowance was one of the reasons I wanted to talk to you."

So he was going to cut his scapegrace cousin off with a shilling. Well, it was not unexpected. Reggie wondered what kind of position he might find to support himself if gambling proved too unreliable a source of income. Many shirt-tail relations of the nobility held government posts such as Warden of the Port of Rye or Postmaster of Newcastle, but nobody in his right mind would give such a post to Reggie Davenport. Even government officials had some standards.

Perhaps he could open a shooting gallery like Manton's. Or, he thought with an inward smile, he could start charging women for his services, rather than giving them away for free. Coolly he said, "And the other reason?"

"Caroline and I are expecting a child in November."

"Congratulations." Reggie kept his face carefully ex-pressionless. It was typical of Wargrave to personally transmit the news rather than let his heir find out through casual gossip. Well, it hardly came as a shock; to heir was human. Though Reggie was technically heir presumptive to the earldom, he'd always known that a healthy, happily married man eight years his junior would likely be start-ing a family. Politely he added, "I trust that Lady Wargrave is well?"

Wargrave's face lit up with a smile that his cousin unchar-itably described as fatuous. "She feels wonderful and is play-ing the piano so much that the child will probably be born with a music score in its hand." His expression sobered. "However, that news is not the main reason I asked you to call on me."

"Ah, yes, you were about to cut off my allowance before we got sidetracked on the subject of your progeny," Reggie said, his voice even more drawling than before. He'd be damned if he'd grovel for money to the head of the family.

"Ending your quarterly allowance is only part of what I

had in mind." Wargrave opened a drawer and removed a
sheaf of papers. "I decided it was time to make different pro-
visions for you. As an interim measure, I had continued the
allowance granted by the old earl, but it strikes me as . . ."
he hesitated, searching for the right word, "as inappropriate
that one adult male should be dependent on the goodwill of
another."

"It's not that uncommon in our world," Reggie said with
elaborate unconcern. He had been surprised when Wargrave
had continued the allowance after the two men had so nearly
killed each other, but the earl must have felt he had a responsibility to support his heir. The prospect of a child diminished that obligation.

"I wasn't raised in the tight little world of the *ton,* and I
daresay I shall never understand all the underlying assump-
tions. In the unelevated circles in which I was raised, most
men prefer to have something that is truly their own." The earl
tapped the legal papers. "Which is why I am going to sign
over to you the most prosperous of the unentailed Wargrave
properties. I've cleared the mortgage, so the property should
produce about twice the allowance you've been receiving."

Reggie straightened in his chair, as startled as if the earl
had hit him with the brass candlestick. Having his allowance
cut off would have been no surprise. This was.

Wargrave continued, "The estate's prosperity is due
largely to the steward, a man called Weston, who has been
there for several years. I've never met him—the one time I
visited, he had been called away by illness in the family—
but he's done an excellent job. His records were impeccable,
and he has increased the productivity enormously. Since
Weston is honest and competent, you can live in London off
the rents if you don't want to get involved with the management yourself." His expression hardened. "Or you can sell
the property, or gamble it away. Whatever you decide, this is
all you will ever get from the Wargrave estate. If you have

serious debts, I'll help you settle them so you can start with a clean slate, but after this, you are entirely on your own. Is that clear?"

"Perfectly clear. You have such a gift for expression, Wargrave." Reggie's insolence was instinctive, an attempt to disguise his confusion. "As it happens, Lady Luck has been smiling recently, so your assistance will not be required." Struggling to regain his balance, he asked, "Which estate are you giving me?"

"Strickland, in Dorset."

Bloody hell, Strickland! Since Wargrave owned only two or three unentailed estates, the news was not quite a surprise, but Reggie still felt as if he had been kicked in the stomach. "Why that particular property?"

"Several reasons. First, because it would support you most comfortably. Second, I understand that you lived there as a boy, and I thought you might be attached to the place." Wargrave bridged a quill pen between his fingers, a frown on his face. "Judging by your expression, perhaps I was wrong."

Reggie's face tightened. One of the many ways in which he failed to fit the ideal of a gentleman was in his too-visible emotions. A true gentleman would never show chagrin, or anger, or even amusement, as Reggie was all too prone to do when he wasn't concentrating. He was not incapable of maintaining a properly impassive face, but too often his countenance mirrored his every feeling. As it did now, when he would rather have concealed the complex emotions that Strickland raised in him.

"There is another, far more compelling reason why I chose Strickland," Wargrave continued. "It should have been yours in the first place."

Reggie took a deep breath. Too many surprises were being dropped on him, and he didn't like it one damned bit. "Why do you say it should have been mine?"

"The house and majority of the land were owned by your

mother's family, not the Davenports. As your mother's sole heir, legally you already own the bulk of Strickland."

"What the devil!"

"According to the family solicitor, your parents met when your maternal grandfather offered to buy a small property adjacent to Strickland," Wargrave explained. "Your father went to Dorset to discuss the matter on his brother's behalf, met your mother, and ended up staying. The Davenport land was added to Strickland, and your parents lived there and managed it as one estate. According to the marriage settlements, Strickland was to go to your mother's heirs."

Reggie swore viciously under his breath. So the old earl had deliberately and illegally withheld Strickland from his nephew—one more tactic in their long-running war.

"I had no idea, or you can be sure I would never have let the old devil get away with it," Reggie said with barely controlled fury. During all the years his uncle had condescended to give him an allowance, that money and more should have been his by right. If the old earl had been present and alive, Reggie might have done murder. A great pity that his damned uncle was now beyond justice.

"Perhaps the old earl never separated Strickland from the rest of the properties because he assumed the title and entire estate would come to you eventually," Wargrave said in a neutral voice. "After all, you were his heir for many years."

Reggie said icily, "Your generous interpretation stems from the fact that you didn't know him. I assure you that he withheld Strickland from the basest of motives. The income would have made me independent of him, and he would have hated that."

For the same reason, perhaps, the old earl had resented his younger brother, who had married a modest heiress and found happiness living with her in Dorset. That would go some way toward explaining the old man's later treatment of his orphaned nephew. It must have been a kind of revenge on his dead brother, who had managed to escape the Wargrave net.

Tactfully Wargrave busied himself with sharpening a quill and checking the ink in the standish. "The more I hear of the old earl, the more I can understand why my father refused to live in the same country with him."

"Leaving England was the most intelligent thing Julius ever did," Reggie agreed. Though he didn't voice the thought aloud, more than once he had wondered if he should have done the same. Perhaps it would have been wiser to escape his uncle's iron hand rather than to stay and fight the old man's tyranny with inadequate weapons. Well, the earl had won the game by dying, and Reggie had no desire to bare any more of his feelings before the young man who had come on the scene only after the final curtain had come down.

Wargrave looked up from his desk. "Would you prefer a different estate? Strickland is the best available property, but other arrangements could be made."

"No need. Strickland will do well enough," Reggie said brusquely.

Apparently Wargrave did not expect courtesy from his cousin. He scribbled his name several times, sprinkled sand on the wet ink, then pushed the documents across the desk. "Just sign these, and Strickland is yours."

Even furious, Reggie took the time to scan the papers, but all was in order. He scrawled his name across the deeds. As he signed the last one, the sound of a light footstep caused him to look up. A small, delicately blond young woman entered the study. Caroline, Lady Wargrave, had a dreamy face and an extraordinary talent for musical composition.

Both men rose as she entered, and the earl and countess exchanged a glance that gave Reggie a pang of sharp longing. He envied his cousin's inheritance of the wealth and power of Wargrave, and even more he envied the warmth that hummed between the earl and his wife. No women had ever looked at the Despair of the Davenports like that, nor ever would.

After that brief, silent interchange with her husband, Lady Wargrave turned and offered Reggie her hand.

The last time they had met, Reggie had been very drunk and behaved very badly, and Wargrave had damned near killed him for it. In spite of his lurid reputation, terrifying shy virgins was not something Reggie made a practice of, and he felt some awkwardness as he bowed over the countess's hand. Mustering his best charm, he straightened and said, "My felicitations on your happy news, Lady Wargrave."

"Thank you. We are very pleased." She smiled with quiet confidence. Marriage clearly suited her very well. "I never properly thanked you for the wedding gift you sent. Where on earth did you find one of Handel's original music scores? Every time I look at it, I feel awe that he actually drew those notes and wrote those words."

Reggie smiled for the first time in this unsettling visit. The young countess had written him a formal thank-you for the wedding gift, so her desire to greet him in person must mean she had forgiven his boorish behavior. Perhaps that was one less sin that he would fry for. "I came across the score years ago in a bookshop. I knew that someday I would know who it was for."

"You could have chosen nothing that would please me more." She started to turn away. "I'm sorry to have interrupted. I will leave you to your business."

"I'm about to depart," Reggie said. "Unless you had something else you wished to discuss, Wargrave?"

The earl shook his head. "No, there was nothing more." Reggie hesitated, knowing he should thank his cousin. Not all men in the earl's position would have the honesty to compensate for the sins of their predecessors. But Reggie was still far too angry about his uncle's duplicity to be gracious.

He gave an abrupt nod of farewell and left, barely aware of the butler, who ushered him from the house.

Outside, Reggie tossed a coin to the footman who had been walking his horses, and vaulted into his curricle. But after settling in the seat, he simply held the reins in his strong hands as the horses tossed their heads, impatient to be off.

Strickland. Bloody, bloody hell. He now owned the place that had been the site of his greatest happiness and most profound grief, and he had no idea whether he felt pleasure or dismay.

His lips tightened, and he snapped the reins over the horses, turning the carriage neatly in the street. He needed a drink.

Better yet, he needed a dozen.

Caroline Davenport drew aside the curtain and watched her husband's cousin depart, noting the tension in the whip-cord lean figure as he drove away. Dropping the curtain, she asked, "How did he react to the news?"

"Fortunately I didn't expect gratitude, because I received none. Cousin Reggie is not a man who likes surprises. If I had simply cut off his allowance, it would have been easier for him to accept." Richard limped to the window and put an arm around his wife's waist. "He was also understandably furious to learn that my late, unlamented grandfather had illegally deprived him of his own estate."

Settling herself against her husband, Caroline said, "Do you think that becoming a man of property will make a difference to him?"

Richard shrugged. "I doubt it. My grandfather must bear much of the blame for ruining him. Reggie once told me that he had wanted to go into the army, but the earl would not allow it. Instead my cousin was kept on a short leash, his debts paid but his allowance insufficient to give him any real freedom."

"What a horrid old man your grandfather was."

"True. But Reggie must take some of the blame himself. He's highly intelligent and almost uncannily perceptive about people. Becoming a rake and a drunkard were not his only choices."

Caroline heard the regret in her husband's voice. He took his responsibilities very seriously, and the part of him that had made an exceptional army officer grieved at the waste of Reginald Davenport's potential. More than that, Reggie was the nearest relation on the Davenport side of the family, and Richard would have liked to be on friendly terms with him. But that was an ambition unlikely to be fulfilled. "Do you think he is too old to change his way of life?"

"Reggie is thirty-seven years old and very well practiced in vice and outrageousness," Richard said dryly. "Rakes sometimes reform, but drunkards almost never do. Lord knows, I commanded enough of them in the army. Most drank until they died of either bullets or whiskey. I expect my cousin will do the same."

Caroline rested her head against her husband's shoulder. Reginald Davenport had once terrified her, but today she had seen him sober and polite, and for just a moment he had revealed a quite devastating amount of charm. There was good human material there, and she understood Richard's desire to help his difficult cousin. It was an effort likely to fail. Still . . . "Miracles do happen. Perhaps one will this time."

"If Reggie really wants to change, I'm sure he is capable of it. But I doubt that he will try," Richard said pessimistically. He drew his wife's slim form more closely to his side and forced himself to put aside all thoughts of his wastrel cousin.

He had done what he could. Hard experience had taught him that there was only so much one man could do for another.

Chapter 2

It was a bad day even before she awoke; whenever Alys had the nightmare, she was out of sorts for hours. Thank God, it came only two or three times a year.

In the nightmare she was always just outside the French doors, hearing the drawling voice ask with bored malice, "Why on earth are you going to marry a bossy Long Meg like her? Ten feet tall and all bones. Not exactly the sort to warm a man at night, and with her managing ways she'll keep you under the cat's paw for sure."

After a brief pause her beloved would reply, not defending her, not mentioning the love he had eagerly proclaimed to her face. "Why, for money, what else? She'll do well enough. Once I'm in control of her fortune, you'll see who rules the roost."

The words triggered the familiar nausea and the shattering pain that had driven Alys to fly from the only life she had ever known. But this morning she was in luck. Before the dream could continue to her nadir of degradation, something tickled her nose. She sneezed, a sure way of waking up when one is near the surface of sleep.

She opened her heavy lids to see a radiant nymph of dawn. The shining vision perched on the bed had guinea-gold curls, a flawless heart-shaped face, and eyes of a guileless cerulean blue. The sight of Miss Meredith Spenser, Merry to her intimates, had been known to gladden the hardest of hearts. While Alys's heart was by no means hard, it took a great deal to gladden her at this hour of the morning. The sight of a young lady looking so ruthlessly cheerful, so early, was not enough.

Before she could do more than glare balefully at her ward, a soft furry object fluttered across her face. Alys sneezed again. "What the devil . . ." She heaved herself up in the bed. "Oh, it's you, Attila. I warn you, cat, the next time you wake me up with a tail in my face, I'm going to find a dog to feed you to."

Dividing her scowls impersonally between Merry and the cat, Alys pushed her heavy hair from her face. The braid she used at night had come untied as she tossed in the nightmare, and now her hair was down around her shoulders. It would require at least an extra five minutes to brush out.

"Heaven help any dog that encounters Attila." Smiling, Merry handed over a thick mug of steaming coffee. "Here, Lady Alys, just the way you like it. Lots of cream and sugar."

Wrapping her long fingers around the mug, Alys shoved the pillows up behind her and subsided against them as she took a grateful swig of coffee. "Ah-h-h . . ." she sighed as the hot liquid began to restore life to her component body parts. Her brain clearing, she asked, "Why did I want to get up this hour?"

Merry grinned, looking much less like a porcelain doll. "The planting begins today, and you charged me to be sure that you rose early."

"So I did." Alys gulped more coffee. "Thank you for waking me. Maybe I'll keep you after all."

Unabashed, Merry retorted, "You have to keep me, remember? You voluntarily agreed to take on me and the boys, and now you're stuck with us. At least until you find some demented male who will take me off your hands."

Alys laughed, a sure sign that the coffee was restoring her natural good temper. "All the males who cluster around you are surely demented, but it's always from unrequited love. My only problem is keeping them at a safe distance."

She gazed fondly at Merry. Her ward had the kind of petite blond beauty that Alys would have killed for when she was a girl. It would be easy to hate Merry if she weren't such a thoroughly nice person. The girl was also intelligent and had a worldly wisdom that was downright frightening in a young lady of a mere nineteen summers. She occupied a niche in Alys's life that partook equally of daughter and best friend, though sometimes it was hard to tell who was raising whom.

Since her guardian was showing signs of life, Merry said, "One of the farm lads left a note for you. It was addressed to Lady Alice, A-l-i-c-e, of course."

"It's too early in the day to apologize for how my name is spelled." Alys yawned again. "Besides, if they did know how to spell it correctly, they would probably pronounce it wrong, What did the note say?"

"Something about chickens."

"That would be Barlow. I'll stop by his place today." Alys finished the coffee, then swung her long legs over the side of the bed and fumbled for her slippers. "It's safe to leave now, I won't fall asleep again. Take that imbecile cat with you and feed him."

Merry chuckled and leaned over to scoop the giant long-haired tomcat into her arms. Attila was a substantial armful, a crazy quilt of stripes and white splotches. His regal expression made it hard to remember the straggly, starving kitten Alys had pulled drowning from a stream. These days he assumed that rulership was his natural due, and peasants who didn't provide his breakfast were beneath contempt. He yowled accusingly as Merry carried him from the bedroom.

Alys's head sank onto her hands as she sat on the edge of the bed, her good humor fading under the lingering depression of the nightmare. After a moment she sighed and got to her feet, pulled on her worn red robe, and went to sit at the dressing table. As she combed her fingers through her hair to loosen snarls, she stared at her reflection and dispassionately catalogued her appearance in the way that she had learned was the best antidote to the dream.

Though she wasn't the sort of woman a man would desire, at least she wasn't really ugly. Her complexion was too tan for fashion, but her features were regular and might have been called handsome if she were a man. It was just that her face, like the rest of her, was too large. She stood five feet nine and a half inches in her stockings, and was as tall or taller than most of the men at Strickland.

Having undone the snarls, she began brushing out her hair. Back in the days when a fortune had endowed her with spurious desirability, her heavy tresses had been called chestnut. Now that she worked for a living, it was merely brown, a color of no particular distinction. Still, Alys privately thought her hair was her best feature. It had grown back even longer and thicker after the time she had furiously chopped it off, and it gleamed with auburn and gold highlights. But it was basically just brown hair.

Parting it straight down the center of her head, she started on the first of two braids. After finishing them, she wrapped both about her head in a prim coronet. In the early morning sun, her most bizarre feature was clearly visible; her right eye being gray-green while her left was a warm brown. Alys had never met anyone else with this particular trait. It seemed unfair to be both odd-eyed and freakishly tall.

The thought produced a slight smile, thereby displaying her other regrettable feature. Usually she forgot the idiotic dimples that appeared when she smiled or laughed, but seeing herself in the mirror reminded her how utterly incongruous they looked on a great horse like her. Doll-like, golden Merry was the one who should have had dimples, but perversely, she didn't. Life was definitely not fair. If Alys could have given her dimples to her ward, she would have done so with great delight.

Scowling eliminated the dimples, so Alys scowled. Her dark, slashing eyebrows were fearsome even when she was smiling, and made her scowl truly intimidating.

Then she turned from the mirror, having completed the ritual of assuring herself that she didn't look as dreadful as the nightmare always made her feel. A pity that today she must supervise the planting and would wear pantaloons, linen shirt, and a man's coat. Her usual dark dresses were better at restraining the excesses of her figure, but the male clothing required by some of her work made it all too obvious that she had a normal assortment of feminine curves. Given her ridiculous size, the effect was somewhat overpowering. Not that all men were repelled. She had seen enough sidelong glances to guess that some were curious about what it would be like to bed a Long Meg. They would never find out from her.

Jamming her shapeless black hat onto her head, Alys Weston, called Lady Alys to her face and other things behind her back, thirty-year-old spinster of the parish and highly successful steward of the estate known as Strickland in the county of Dorset, stamped down the steps to begin supervising a long day of work in the fields.

The day turned out to be even more tiring than anticipated. The new seed drill Alys had bought was temperamental, to the unconcealed delight of the laborers who were only too willing to say that the fool contraption would never work. Having considerable aptitude for mechanical things, Alys got the device to perform after an hour of crawling around underneath it on the damp earth.

She spent the rest of the day covered with dirt, too busy even to stop for lunch. Merry, bless her, had sent Dorset blue vinny cheese, ale, and the local hard rolls called knobs, which Alys ate while riding to the sheep pasture to check on the health of some lambs that had been sickly.

By the end of the day, the scoffers were reluctantly conceding that the seed drill was effective. They liked it even less now that it worked. Alys was hard-pressed to keep her tongue between her teeth. It had been a continuing battle to get these taciturn males to accept her orders, and even after four years of proof that her modern methods worked, every new idea was a battle. Damn them all anyhow! she swore as she rode home, the spring sun setting and a sharp chill in the air. There wasn't another estate in Dorset as productive, nor another landowner or steward that provided for displaced workers the way she did.

Sometimes she wondered why she bothered.

When she returned to the steward's house, Rose Hall, Merry was embroidering demurely in the parlor and the boys had not yet returned from school. Alys took a quick bath and changed to a dark blue wool dress. Then she joined her ward for a glass of sherry and a quick glance through the post. As Merry laughed at the misadventures with the seed drill, Alys came across a letter franked by her employer, the Earl of Wargrave.

Frowning, she slit the wafer and opened the letter. Most of her communications were with the estate lawyer, Chelmsford, rather than the earl. She had never met either of them, of course. If one of those respectable gentlemen learned that the steward was female, she would surely lose her situation.

The old earl had never left his principal seat in Gloucestershire, but the new one was young, active, and conscientious. She worried that someday he might turn up unexpectedly.

Luckily, on his one visit to Strickland, he had given enough warning for her to decamp with the children, leaving a message that illness in the family had called her away. She left a stern warning to everyone at Strickland not to reveal her sex.

After a week by the sea in Lyme Regis, Alys had returned to find that no one had betrayed her secret, the books had been carefully inspected and approved, and Wargrave had left a complimentary letter that included several intelligent suggestions for her consideration. The man may have spent most of his life as a soldier, but he was clearly no fool. Apart from that one visit, Wargrave had left her alone to run the estate as she saw fit. It had been an ideal arrangement, and she'd hoped that matters would continue unchanged indefinitely.

Her thought must have been unlucky. Alys inhaled sharply as she read the letter. Merry looked up from her embroidery questioningly. "Is something wrong?"

Alys gave a brittle smile. "I knew I should have stayed in bed this morning."

Merry set the hanks of silk thread in her workbox and crossed to Alys's side. "What has happened?"

Silently Alys handed the letter over. Lord Wargrave wished to inform Mr. Weston that Strickland had been transferred to his cousin, Reginald Davenport. He had no idea what his cousin's plans for the property were. However, the earl had been most impressed by Mr. Weston's abilities. Should matters not work out with the new owner, Wargrave would be delighted to find him another steward's position, perhaps running Wargrave Park itself. Apologies for the inconvenience, etc., etc.

"Oh, dear," Merry said softly. "This could complicate matters somewhat."

"That is one of the greatest examples of ladylike understatement I have ever heard." Alys stood and began pacing around the room in long, angry strides.

"Perhaps it will make no difference," Merry said hopefully.

"I believe I've read of Mr. Davenport. Isn't he some kind of sportsman? Perhaps he'll live in London and collect the rents and never come down here."

"It's one thing for Lord Wargrave never to visit when Strickland is just one of a dozen estates. But if this is the only property Reginald Davenport has, he's bound to come down here occasionally. For the holidays. House parties for friends. Hunting. He may decide to live here part of the year." She came to a halt in front of the fireplace and stared at the flickering yellow flames. "There is a limit to how many ailing relatives I can invent to escape from him."

Merry frowned. "You do have a contract."

Alys shrugged as she lifted the poker from its brass stand. "A contract isn't much better than the will to uphold it. Davenport could make my life so miserable that I won't want to stay."

"Isn't it possible that he might want to keep you on? You've done wonders with the property. Everyone says so."

"Much of the hard work has been done." Alys stabbed at the blameless hot coals with the poker. "Any reasonably competent steward could run it profitably now."

"Mr. Davenport won't find anyone more competent than you, or more honest, either!"

"Probably not. But that doesn't mean he won't discharge me anyhow." Alys had heard of Reginald Davenport, though most of the tales were not fit for Merry's young ears. A rake was hardly likely to have advanced ideas of a woman's abilities.

It was so unfair! Feeling her hands curl into fists, she forced herself to relax.

Still seeking a silver lining, Merry said, "If Mr. Davenport doesn't want you, you can work for the earl elsewhere. Wargrave Park would be quite a plum."

"How long do you think his lordship's offer would stand after he learned that I'm a woman?" Alys said bitterly, her hands beginning to clench again.

"Perhaps you could disguise yourself as a man," Merry said with a twinkle. "You're certainly tall enough."

Alys glared, momentarily tempted to box her ward's ears before the girl's humor penetrated her mood. With a wry smile she said, "How long do you think I could get away with a masquerade like that?"

"Well . . ." Merry said thoughtfully, "perhaps ninety seconds? If the light was bad."

Alys chuckled. "The light would have to be very bad indeed. Men and women simply aren't shaped the same way. At least not after the age of twelve."

"True, and you have a very nice shape, no matter how hard you try to disguise it."

Alys snorted. Merry stoutly maintained that her guardian was attractive, a campaign that was more a tribute to her kind nature than her good judgment. Her comment now was intended as a distraction, but Alys refused the bait. "Even assuming that Lord Wargrave is radical enough to hire me, my supervision is needed at the pottery works. We can hardly move that to Gloucestershire. And it would be a pity to take the boys from the grammar school when they are both so happy there."

Even Merry's golden curls drooped a bit before she replied, "I think you are making a great many bricks out of precious little straw. Mr. Davenport may not come down here for a long time, and when he does, he might be delighted to keep you on to spare himself the work. All we can do is wait and see."

Alys wished she could share the girl's optimism. As she glanced at her ward, she remembered what was said about her new employer and his womanizing habits, and felt a stirring of apprehension. What rake could resist a delectable golden sylph like Meredith? The girl had good sense and morals, but she was still an innocent. No match for a cynical, amoral man of the world. It was another anxiety, and a major one.

Alys looked into the fire, her mouth tightening. As a woman alone, she had spent the last dozen years fighting convention and prejudice to build a comfortable, productive life for herself. Now, through no fault of her own, all that she had worked for was threatened.

Sight unseen, she already hated Reginald Davenport.

Chapter 3

The Despair of the Davenports groaned and shifted. After the previous night's debauchery, the shattering jolt of nausea and wretchedness that swept through him at the slight movement was not unexpected.

He stilled, keeping his eyes tightly closed, since experience had taught him that mornings like this were best approached as slowly as possible. That is, if it was morning. His last memories were too fragmentary for him to be sure how much time had passed.

After his head stabilized, Reggie opened his eyes a fraction. The ceiling looked familiar, so he must be home. A little more concentration established that he was in the bedroom rather than the sitting room, and on his bed, which was softer and wider than the sofa.

The next question was how he had gotten here. He became aware of resonant breathing, and turned his head by infinitesimal degrees until the Honorable Julian Markham came into view. His young friend slept blissfully on the sofa, sprawled in a position that by rights should give him a sore back and neck, but probably wouldn't.

Moving with great deliberation, Reggie pushed aside the quilt that had been laid over him. He started to lever himself upright, then gasped and fell back on the mattress. He had been prepared for the aftereffects of drinking, but not for the sharp pain that sliced through his ribs. As his abused body ached and protested, he tried to remember what the devil had happened the previous night, but without success.

Deciding it was time to face the consequences, he cautiously sat up again and swung his legs over the edge of the bed. The vibration of his boots hitting the floor sent a palpable shock wave through his system. He stopped moving until his brain recovered.

After a swift inventory of damages, he decided that nothing was broken, though his ribs and right arm felt badly bruised and the knuckles of both hands were raw. He must have been in a fight. He was fully dressed, his dark blue coat and buff pantaloons crumpled in a way that would make a really fastidious valet turn in his notice. Luckily Mac Cooper was made of sterner stuff, or he wouldn't have stayed with Reggie for so many years.

Mac proved his competence once again by choosing this moment to enter the bedroom, a tumbler of orange-colored liquid in one hand, a basin and a steaming towel in the other. Wordlessly he offered the towel. Reggie opened it and buried his face in the hot folds. The heat and moisture were invigorating.

By the time he had wiped down his face, neck, and hands, he was able to take the tumbler and down half the contents with one swallow. Mac's morning-after remedy was one of the valet's major talents, combining fresh fruit juice with a shot of whiskey and a few other ingredients that Reggie preferred not to think about.

He turned his head carefully a few times, relieved that it could be moved without making him sick. Then he sipped more slowly at his drink. Only when the glass was empty did he look at Mac directly. "What time is it?"

"About two in the afternoon, sir." Though Mac's natural

accent was an incomprehensible cockney and he had the wiry physique and scars of a street fighter, it pleased him to mimic the manners and style of the most snobbish kind of valet. Actually, valeting was only part of his job. He was equally groom, butler, and footman.

Yawning, Reggie asked, "Any idea what time we got in?"

"Around five in the morning, sir."

"I trust we didn't disturb your slumbers too much."

"Mr. Markham did require my assistance to get you upstairs," Mac admitted.

Reggie dragged one hand through his dark tangled hair. "That explains why I made it as far as the bedroom." Glancing at his friend, he saw signs of returning consciousness. "Make a pot of coffee. I imagine Julian will need some, and I could use a few cups myself."

"Very good, sir. Will you be interested in a light luncheon as well?"

"No!" Reggie shuddered at the thought of food. "Just coffee."

As Mac left the room, Reggie stood and removed his cravat. Someday he was going to be strangled in his sleep by one of the blasted things. He washed his face with the hot water Mac had brought, then sank into the wing chair that stood at right angles to the sofa, his legs stretched out before him. In spite of his ablutions and the change from horizontal to vertical, he still felt like death walking. He eyed Julian's cherubic smile with disfavor as the young man's eyes finally opened.

Julian sat up immediately. "Good morning, Reg," he said brightly. "Wasn't that a great evening?"

"I don't know," Reggie said tersely. "What happened?"

Julian smiled, undeterred by his companion's gruffness. He was a handsome, fair-haired young man, with a charm and future fortune that made him much sought after by society hostesses with marriageable daughters. "You won five hundred pounds from Blakeford. Don't you remember?"

The coffee arrived. After pouring a large, scalding mug and heavily sugaring it, Reggie crossed his legs and regarded his friend's clear eyes and cheerful mien morosely. It was his own fault for going about with a man a dozen years his junior, who could bounce back from a night's debauchery with such speed. Reggie used to be able to do the same, but not anymore.

He gulped a mouthful of coffee, swearing when it burned his tongue. "I remember going to Watier's. Then what happened?"

"Blakeford invited a dozen of us back to his place for supper and whist. Wanted to show off his new mistress, a flashy piece named Stella." Julian poured himself a mug of the coffee. "She took quite a fancy to you."

Reggie frowned. It was coming back slowly. He'd gone directly from the Earl of Wargrave's to a tavern and had drunk alone for a couple of hours. Then he'd met Julian at Watier's, and events began to get hazy. "This Stella—a little tart with red hair and a roving eye?"

"That's the one. She sniffed around you like a bitch in heat. Blakeford was angry enough about losing the money, but when you disappeared for half an hour and he realized Stella was gone, too, I thought he'd explode. Did she waylay you for a little side action?"

Reggie closed his eyes, letting his head fall back against the chair. "More or less." Ordinarily he would have avoided Stella, whose sensational figure was surpassed only by her stunning vulgarity. But she had chosen her moment carefully, accosting him when he had drunk too much for good judgment, and too little to be incapacitated.

His eyes still closed, he drank more coffee as the scene came back to him. The trollop had been waiting in the hall when he returned to the card game, her hot, demanding mouth and eager little hands making it clear what she wanted. His body, which had no standards to speak of, had responded immediately. A feverish, clawing exchange had followed, with only a closed door separating them from the rest of the party. Inflamed by the knowledge that her protector was in the next room, Stella had gouged Reggie's back through his shirt with sharp nails, her breath coming in little whimpering pants.

Thank God the card party was noisy enough to drown out her last hoarse cry. He must have been insane.

No, not insane. Drunk. Nothing unusual about that.

Hesitation in his voice, Julian broke into Reggie's reverie. "I probably shouldn't mention this, but you might want to be careful. Blakeford is insanely jealous of the wench. Between Stella and the money he lost, he seemed on the verge of calling you out."

"Right. You shouldn't mention it," Reggie said tiredly, his eyelids at half-mast and the invisible band across his temples aching acutely. Why did it have to be Blakeford, of all people? He was a brooding, unpredictable sort, and Reggie avoided him when possible. "If Blakeford is going to issue a challenge every time that tart waves her muff at someone, he'll have to fight every man in London."

Julian gave a nod of acknowledgment. "After we left Blakeford's, we went to that new gaming hell off Piccadilly."

"We did?" Reggie's eyes came fully open as he tried to remember that part of the evening, but he drew a complete blank. "Did anything noteworthy happen?"

"I lost a hundred pounds, and you got into a fight."

"Wonderful," Reggie muttered. "With whom, why, and who won?"

"Albert Hanley. Said you were cheating," Julian said succinctly. "You won, of course."

"Hanley said what?" Reggie jerked upright too abruptly, and his head went spinning. Swallowing bile, he slouched down again. "No wonder we fought." In most ways Reggie had a terrible reputation, much of it richly deserved, but in sporting circles his honesty was never questioned.

"You did such a good job of putting him in his place that a challenge was unnecessary," Julian said enthusiastically. "It was quite a mill. Hanley outweighs you by two stone, and he has good science, but he never laid a fist on you. It took only a couple of minutes for you to break his jaw. Everyone agreed he should pay for the wrecked furniture, since his accusation was quite unfounded."

"Did Hanley agree?"

"Don't know. With his broken jaw, we couldn't understand a word he said."

Reggie inspected his scraped and bruised knuckles. "If I defeated him so thoroughly, why do I feel as if a horse kicked me in the ribs?"

"Because you fell down the steps when Mac and I were hauling you upstairs," Julian explained. "You ended by smashing into the newel post. I was worried at first, but Mac said you weren't permanently damaged."

"Is there anything else I should know?" Reggie asked in a dangerously gentle tone.

"Well . . ." Julian cleared his throat uncomfortably. "We saw m'father at Watier's, and he gave you the cut direct."

Reggie shrugged. "No need to look so guilty. He always gives me the cut direct."

Lord Markham was convinced that Reggie was leading his heir down the road to perdition. Ironically, it was Reggie who had taught the lad how to safely navigate London's more dangerous amusements. He'd even rescued him from an adventuress called the Wanton Widow, who had decided that Julian was the perfect answer to her financial problems.

No matter. Reggie had used his influence for Julian's sake, not because he expected gratitude from his young friend's father.

Julian returned to the safer topic of the fight, but Reggie stopped listening. He leaned forward and rested his elbows on his knees, burying his face in his hands as profound depression engulfed him.

The worst deeds of a disgraceful life had always been done when he was drinking, but at least he had always been aware of his actions. He had deliberately chosen to live in defiance of normal social strictures, and had willingly accepted the consequences. That had been fine, until the year before, when the memory losses had begun. With every month that passed, the lapses came more often and lasted longer.

Now he could no longer be sure what he had done or why, and that lack of control terrified him. The obvious answer was to drink less, so he had resolved to moderate his habits. But somehow his resolution always dissolved once he swallowed his first drink.

This way of life is killing you. The words were very clear in his head, spoken in a calm male voice.

It was not the first time he had heard such a warning. Once the voice had told him to beware moments before two murderous footpads had attacked. He had dodged barely in time to avoid a knife in the back. On another occasion the voice had warned not to board a friend's yacht. Reggie had made some clumsy excuse, incurring much taunting from his companions. But a squall had blown up, and the boat sank with no survivors.

This way of life is killing you. His fingers tightened, digging into his skull, trying to erase the sick aching, the memories—and the lack of memories. He had always lived hard, courting danger and skirting the edge of acceptable behavior. In the months since the earldom of Wargrave had vanished from his grasp, he had gone wild, taking insane chances gambling and riding, drinking more than ever.

Ironically, his luck had been phenomenal. Perhaps because he hadn't much cared what happened, he had won, and won, and won. He was completely free of debt, had more money in the bank than he'd had in years.

And what was the bloody point of it?

This way of life is killing you. The words repeated in a litany, as if expecting some response, but Reggie was too drained to answer. He was weary unto death of his whole life. Of the endless gaming and drinking, of coarse tarts like Stella, of pointless fights and ghastly mornings after like this one.

At the age of twenty-five, Julian was on the verge of outgrowing his wild oats phase, while Reggie was doing exactly the same things as when he'd first come down from university. He'd been running for sixteen years, yet was still in the same place.

The depression was black and bitter. He wished with sudden violence that someone like Blakeford or Hanley would become furious enough to put a bullet in him and end the whole exhausting business.

Why wait for someone else to do the job? He had pistols of his own.

The idea flickered seductively for a moment before he recoiled mentally. Bloody hell, was he really at such a standstill? His mind hung suspended in horror as Julian's words sounded at a great distance.

Then the inner voice spoke once more. *Strickland.*

Strickland, the one place in the world that he had ever belonged. He had thought it lost forever, and then his damned honorable cousin had given it back to him. Strickland, where he had been born, and where everyone he loved had died.

It wouldn't be home anymore—but by God, now it was his, demons and all.

There was no conscious decision. He simply opened his eyes and broke into Julian's dissertation, saying, "I've changed my mind about going to Bedford for that race. Have to go to Dorset to look over my estate."

"Your what?" Julian blinked in confusion.

"My estate, Strickland. I've become a man of property."
Reggie stood, not bothering to explain away the bafflement
on his friend's face.

He caught a glimpse of himself in the mirror above the
mantel. He looked much the same as usual, with the casual,
damn-your-eyes elegance that was much imitated by the
younger bucks. Yet inside, he felt brittle and old.

He wandered to the window, and gazed down into
Molton Street. He'd had these rooms on the edge of Mayfair
for all the years he'd lived in London. The place was comfortable, entirely suitable for a bachelor. But he had never
thought of it as home.

Behind him Julian asked, "When will you come back
to town?"

"I have no idea. Maybe I'll stay in Dorset and become a
country squire, complete with red face and a pack of hounds."

Julian laughed, treating the statement as a joke, but Reggie
half meant the words. The opinionated Dr. Johnson had said
that a man who was tired of London was tired of life. Well,
maybe Johnson was right; Reggie was tired of London and
life both.

Perhaps there would be something at Strickland that
would make life worth living. But he doubted it.

The rolling pastures and woodlands of Dorset were
hauntingly familiar, though Reggie had not seen them since
he was eight years old. He remembered the bleak heath of
the high downs, too. In contrast to that starkness, Strickland
included some of the richest agricultural land in Britain.

After deciding to leave London, he had packed and left
while Julian Markham was still asking puzzled questions
from the sofa. Mac would follow later with the curricle and
enough clothing for an indefinite stay. Reggie preferred to

ride, and to ride alone. He slept at Winchester. By early the next afternoon, he was approaching Strickland, his once and future home.

Though he had ridden hard most of the distance, he slowed his horse to a walk on the long drive that led to the house. The road was lined with three hundred sixty-six beech trees, one for every day of the year, including the extra needed for leap year. At one point there was a gap in the row. Next to the blackened fragments of a lightning-struck stump, a brave young sapling grew.

He studied the sapling, wondering who had cared enough for tradition to plant that tree. The exemplary Mr. Weston, perhaps? More likely one of the local people. The Daven-ports had come and gone, but the tenants who had worked this land for generations remained.

The drive curved at the end, and the house came into view all at once, without warning. He pulled up involuntar-ily, his eyes hungrily scanning the facade. Strickland was a manor house, midway in size between the humble cottage and the great lordly mansions. Built of the mellow Ham Hill stone that was quarried locally, it was similar to a thousand other seats of the English squirearchy.

When he was a child, the summit of his ambition had been to become master of Strickland. He'd always known that as the eldest son he would someday inherit, and his goal had been to make himself worthy of wearing his father's mantle. He, too, would care for the land, would know every tenant's name, and have a sweet for every child he met. He, too, would be a man greeted everywhere with respect, not fear. And, like his father, he would have a wife who glowed when her husband entered the room.

Then, in a few short, horrifying days, everything had changed. When his uncle's secretary had come to take the orphan to Wargrave Park, Reggie had gone without ques-tion, dazed but obedient to adult authority. He'd yearned for the day when he could finally return to Strickland, until his uncle had told him in harsh, unfeeling words that the estate was not his, nor ever would be.

After that he had no longer thought of Strickland as his home. He tried not to think of Strickland at all. During the years when he'd believed he would become the next Earl of Wargrave, he had known that his boyhood home would be a minor part of his inheritance, but he never intended to live there again.

Now, in the end as in the beginning, there was only Strickland. His great expectations had vanished, and he was merely a man of good family and bad reputation, no longer young.

But for the first time in his life, he was a landowner, and in England land was the source of power and consequence. If he ever hoped to find a meaning for his existence, it must be found here. If only he weren't so weary. . . .

His mouth tightened into a hard line when he realized that his thoughts were dangerously close to self-pity. Urging his horse forward again, he tried to recall what he knew about his mother's family. Her maiden name had been Stanton, but apart from that and his personal memories of her, he could recall nothing.

Strange how children accept their surroundings without question. He had never guessed that the estate belonged to his mother. Her family must have been solid, prosperous country squires, but after the aristocratic Davenports had taken charge of him, he had buried all memory of the Stantons.

Strickland had been built in Tudor times, a sprawling two-story house with gables, mullioned bay windows, and bold octagonal chimneys. It faced south so that the sun fell across it all day long, while the back commanded a view of gardens, lake, and rolling countryside.

The fact that the house was typical didn't mean that it was not beautiful.

The really shocking realization was how little had

changed. The grounds were well kept, the house in good repair. Only a faint air of emptiness said that his parents or young brother and sister would not walk through the door and down the front steps.

He shivered, his hand tightening so hard that his horse whickered and tossed its head. Forcing himself to relax, he dismounted and tethered the stallion at the bottom of the stairs. He went up lightly, two steps at a time, driven by an uneasy mixture of anticipation and apprehension.

His hand paused for a moment over the heavy knocker, a brass ring in the mouth of a lion. He had admired it greatly as a child, longing for the day when he would be tall enough to reach it. He buried the memory and rapped sharply. When there was no quick response, he experimentally turned the knob. After all, he owned the place, didn't he? He would begin as he intended to go on, and that was as master of Strickland.

The knob turned under his hand, and the massive door swung inward, admitting him to a large entry hall with carved oak wainscoting. He passed through to the main drawing room, then stopped, the hair on the back of his neck prickling. He had anticipated many things, but not that there would be virtually no changes at all.

Everything was neat, with only a slight suggestion of mustiness. The colors, the hangings, the furniture dimly visible under holland covers—all were unchanged. Faded certainly, and shabbier, but the very same pieces that had defined his world when he was a boy. Ghost memories of his parents sat at the blind-fretted mahogany card table, laughing over a game.

He turned sharply away, stalking across the room to the passage beyond. Wasn't anyone here? There had better be, or someone had better have a damned good explanation for why the front door was open.

He circled around to the right, toward the morning room.

There he found a plump woman removing covers from the furniture.

She looked up in surprise as he entered, wiping her hands quickly on her apron and bobbing a curtsy. "Mr. Davenport! You gave me a start. You made good time. We only just heard the news, and there hasn't been time to set everything to rights."

Reggie wondered how she knew he was coming, then decided it was logical for a new owner to inspect his property. "You have the advantage of me. You are . . .?"

She was in her forties, a rosy-cheeked country woman who was polite but hardly obsequious. "I'm Mrs. Herald. You wouldn't remember, but I was a housemaid here when you were a lad. I was May Barlow then." Looking him up and down, she added with approval, "You've grown tall, like your father."

His eyes narrowed thoughtfully. "One of the tenant farms was worked by a Herald."

"Aye, I married Robbie Herald. We're at Hill Farm."

"The house is in excellent condition." Reggie spoke absently as his eyes scanned the morning room. The proportions were pleasant, and there were large mullioned windows on two walls. His mother had always particularly liked it here.

"Aye. It was leased to a retired naval captain for a good few years. He maintained the place well enough, but never bothered making changes. It's been vacant since about the time the old earl died. I've kept an eye on things, watching for leaks and dry rot so the estate carpenters could make repairs as it was needful."

"You've done a good job." Over the years, Reggie had learned the value of an appreciative word, and Mrs. Herald beamed at the compliment.

"I'm glad you think so, sir. We've done our best." She hesitated a moment, then blurted out, "We're all ever so glad to have a Stanton here again. It's not right, the way Wargrave ignored this place for so many years. The old earl never once set foot here, just took money out and put naught back in."

She blushed then, remembering that the old earl had been her new master's uncle and guardian, but Reggie only said mildly, "I'm a Davenport, not a Stanton."

"Your mother was a Stanton, that's what counts in Dorset," she said with a firm nod. "There have always been Stantons at Strickland."

Her words reminded Reggie of the way a judge pronounced a sentence. After a moment's reflection he asked, "You'll think this a foolish question, but do I have any Stanton relations?"

"The closest would be Mr. Jeremy Stanton at Fenton Hall. He was your mother's cousin, and he and your father were good friends. He's getting along in years now, but a fine gentleman." Mrs. Herald shook her head with regret. "Your mother, Miss Anne, was an only child. Pity that her branch of the family had dwindled down to just her. If there had been any nearer relations, they never would have let the earl take you away after . . ." She stopped, then decided not to continue that sentence. She finished with, "The Stantons always took care of their own."

Perhaps that's why they died out, Reggie thought cynically, but he kept the words unsaid in the face of Mrs. Herald's vicarious family pride. Aloud he said, "My man will be along in a day or so with my baggage, but I came by myself."

"Shall I be putting your things in the master bedchamber?"

A vivid image of the room flashed in front of Reggie. His parents had unfashionably shared it, sleeping together in the carved oak four-poster. It seemed wrong to sleep in their bed. "No, I'll take the room above this one. The blue room it was called, I think."

"Very well, sir. Would you like something to eat? The house is all at sixes and sevens, but my sister-in-law Molly

Barlow is down in the kitchen, cleaning and stocking the pantry. She could do a cold collation quick enough."

"Later, perhaps. Now I'd rather see Mr. Weston. Do you know if he's in the estate office, or is he out on the property somewhere?"

Mrs. Herald paused, her normal garrulity temporarily deserting her. "It's hard to say, sir. The steward is very active. Could be most anywhere."

"I'm told Weston is very good."

"Oh, yes, Mr. Davenport. There isn't a better steward anywhere," she said with an odd, guilty expression.

Reggie eyed her curiously, wondering why mentioning Weston had such an effect. Maybe the housekeeper was having an affair with the steward? Or didn't country folk have such vices? If they didn't, Dorset would prove dull indeed.

He left the morning room. As he made his way through the house, he caught sight of two girls polishing wood and scrubbing floors. They stared with open curiosity, giggling bashfully and bobbing their heads when he nodded at them. An odd feeling, being lord of the manor.

The side door led to a wide cobbled yard surrounded by buildings of the same golden-gray stone as the manor house. It was all so familiar. He glanced up, and remembered the day he'd climbed the ladder left by a man repairing the roof. He'd skittered happily around on the slates, having a wonderful time, until his mother appeared and ordered him to come down *right now.* Having no conception of what a fall to the cobbles would do to his life expectancy, he had been surprised by her alarm, but he'd come down readily enough.

He had been obedient in those days. That was one of many things that had changed when he left Strickland.

His steps led him unerringly to the estate office on the opposite side of the yard. The door opened silently under his hand, and he stepped inside. The room seemed dim after the bright afternoon sun. Behind the desk a man stood in front of a rack of books, searching for a particular volume. The fellow didn't hear the door open, so Reggie had time to study him. A lean build and very erect posture, garbed in comfortable country garments—a brown coat, tan breeches, and well-worn boots.

Reggie's eyes adjusted to the light, and he realized with a shock that he was observing not a man, but a woman dressed in male clothing. His gaze ran appreciatively down her long, shapely legs even as he wondered who the devil she was. Another of the numerous Heralds, perhaps? Hard to imagine one of that conservative clan dressed so outrageously.

He cleared his throat and asked, "Do you know where Mr. Weston is?"

She jumped like a startled hare, then whirled to face him. The woman was the tallest he'd ever seen, with wide eyes and strong, regular features. A wealth of rich brown hair was coiled into a severe coronet that glowed in the afternoon sun and gave her a regal air that even surprise could not eliminate.

Now that he could see her clearly, he couldn't imagine how he'd mistaken her for a man. Despite her rigorously masculine clothes, she was quite splendidly curved in all the right places. In fact, the male garb made her look downright provocative.

His interest quickened. Perhaps Dorset would prove more amusing than he had anticipated. The woman appeared to be in her mid-twenties and was obviously no shy virgin; her expression was forceful to a point just short of belligerence. On the other hand, she gave every evidence of being mute.

He repeated, "Do you have any idea where the steward, Mr. Weston, is?"

There was a moment of absolute silence. Then she drew a deep breath, which did fascinating things to her linen shirt, and said militantly, "*I'm* Weston."

Chapter 4

Alys stared at the stranger, frozen with shock. Of all the ill luck . . . ! She hadn't expected Davenport to arrive so soon. She had no doubt whatsoever about the man's identity—he'd entered the office with the easy confidence of ownership.

She read the London papers regularly to monitor the world she had fled, and Reginald Davenport's name was one that turned up regularly. He was a Corinthian, one of a sporting set known for racing, roistering, and raking. Now the man in front of her confirmed her worst fears.

He might have been handsome if his aristocratic nose hadn't been broken and reset somewhat less than straight. He must be around forty, his dark hair untouched with gray, but the long face marked by years of dissipation. Despite his obvious strength and athletic build, there was a sallow, unhealthy tint to the dark skin. The wages of sin, no doubt.

Her only satisfaction was that Davenport was as shocked as she was. He said incredulously, "A. E. Weston, the steward of Strickland?"

"Yes." Her one syllable was unforthcoming.

A look of unholy amusement on his face, he sauntered across the room, his insolent glance scouring her, lingering on her breasts and hips. His eyes were striking, the light, clear blue of aquamarine, and he moved beautifully, with an intensely masculine swagger that reminded her of a stallion.

He was also half a head taller than she, a fact she did not appreciate. She was used to looking down on men, or at least meeting them eye to eye. Having to look up was disconcerting.

Her back to the bookcase, Alys stiffened as he approached, her face coloring hotly. His piercing gaze made her feel as if she were being stripped naked, a pursuit in which Davenport must be highly practiced.

He halted no more than three feet away. His complexion was the weathered tan of a man who was much outdoors. He drawled, "I do believe you are a female."

Suddenly furious, Alys subjected him to the same scrutiny he had given her. Her eyes slowly scanned down his lean body, from powerful shoulders to expensive riding boots, with special attention for the buckskin riding breeches that clung to his muscular thighs. Her voice as pointed as her gaze, she said, "Gender is not difficult to determine."

He grinned wickedly. "Not usually. And if vision is insufficient, there are surer tests available."

His implication was as obvious as it was insulting. If looks could kill, Reginald Davenport would be a dead man. Alys knew she was not the kind of woman men desired, and only an arrogant rooster who pursued anything female would speak so to her. She opened her mouth for a furious reply. Years of supervising recalcitrant laborers had given the ability to wield her tongue like a lash.

Barely in time she remembered that she was supposed to placate this man, not alienate him. Her mouth snapped shut. The yearning to reply in kind was so great that her jaw ached as she struggled for control. Finally she was able to say in a level voice, "I presume you wish to see the books. Or would you rather tour the property first?"

He studied her measuringly. "What I would really like is a discussion and a drink. Do you have anything here?"

Wordlessly she pulled open the door of the cabinet and removed a bottle of whiskey and a pair of tumblers, then poured two fingers worth for each of them. She seldom drank herself, but visitors sometimes appreciated a wee dram. Maybe the spirits would help soften Davenport.

Taking the glass from her stiff fingers, he sat and stretched out his legs, as relaxed as she was tense. "I assume the late earl didn't know you were female. He would have never permitted it." He took a sip of his drink. "Does the present earl know?"

Alys sat down behind the desk. "No, the only time Wargrave visited Strickland, I made an excuse to be away." She drank some of her whiskey, needing its warmth.

"How nice to know that my cousin didn't arrange this as an insult," he murmured.

Too tense to be tactful, Alys asked brusquely, "Are you going to discharge me because I'm a woman?"

The cool gaze slid over her again. "Don't put ideas in my head. Discharging you is a tempting prospect."

"Do you think a woman can't do the job?" Alys said, fearing that she had lost this battle before it had started.

Davenport shrugged. "You are demonstrably doing it. Though I've never heard of a female steward, it's hardly unknown for a woman to run property that she has inherited."

"Then, why would you want to get rid of me?"

He finished his whiskey and leaned forward to pour some more. Instead of answering directly, he asked, "Are you single, married, widowed, or what?"

"Single, and why should it matter?" Alys was having trouble keeping her belligerence under control.

"First of all, you're rather young for the job, even if you were male. The fact that you're also single is a potential source of gossip when the owner of the estate is a bachelor."

Alys stared at him aghast. Of all the things that Davenport might have said, this surprised her the most. "A rake is concerned about *propriety*?"

He laughed aloud at the shock in her voice, humor softening his hard face. "I have the feeling that my reputation has preceded me. Is it so unthinkable that a rake should have some concept of decorous behavior?"

Alys had the grace to blush. Calling him a rake to his face was an unforgivable impertinence. Thank heaven he was amused, not insulted. She said carefully, "I can't imagine that my gender would cause any eyebrows to raise. I'm thirty, hardly a girl, and I've had this position for four years. Everyone in this part of Dorset is used to me."

"*I'm* not used to you," he said bluntly. "It's obvious from the way you talk that you're the respectable sort of female, a breed I'm almost completely unacquainted with. In the nature of things, you will be working with me regularly. I don't relish having to watch my tongue around you."

She shrugged. "After four years of working with every kind of laborer, I'm very hard to shock. Treat me like a man." She couldn't resist adding, "It will probably be safer for me that way anyhow."

His mouth tightened. "It sounds as if you expect me to pounce on every female on the estate."

She gave him a challenging look. "Will you?"

"Not when I'm sober," he answered shortly.

Alys wished that she had not let the conversation go in this direction. She hoped that Reginald Davenport wasn't the sort to leave a trail of bastards across the county, but if that's what he wanted to do, there wasn't a thing she could do to stop him.

Luckily, he changed the subject. "Care to explain how you came to be a steward, Miss Weston?"

Alys stared down at the tumbler clasped between her hands. "I was the governess at a nearby estate. The widowed

owner, Mrs. Spenser, was having problems with her steward.
I had . . . grown up on a farm, and was able to advise her.
Eventually she discharged her steward and had me take over
his duties."

"I see." His eyes watched her expressionlessly over the
tumbler as he drank more whiskey. "How did you come to
Strickland itself?"

Alys hesitated, choosing her words. "Mrs. Spenser knew
she was dying and that her husband's nephew, who was heir
to her property, wouldn't keep me on. When the Strickland
steward was discharged, she suggested I apply for the situation. She gave me excellent references, and persuaded several
of the local gentry to do the same. They all thought it a great
joke to play on the Earl of Wargrave—absentee landowners
are not much liked around here. Because of the references, the
Wargrave business manager hired me sight unseen. The estate
has done very well under my management, so there was no
reason to question my credentials later."

Mrs. Spenser had extracted a price for her aid: that Alys
would become guardian to the older woman's niece and
nephews after her death. Alys had been quite willing to take
charge of her former students. However, she preferred not
to mention them to her new employer. The situation was already quite complicated enough.

Davenport frowned at the toes of his boots, weighing her
future in the balance. She studied his expression anxiously,
but his thoughts were impossible to divine.

The silence was broken by the entrance of the groom.
Alys said, "Yes, Bates?"

"Excuse me, Lady Alys, but I think one of the plow
horses has a splint forming." His question was for her, but
his frankly curious gaze was for the new owner.

Alys said impatiently, "Apply a cold water bandage, and
I'll take a look at it later. Is there anything else?"

Bates considered for a moment. "No, ma'am." Slowly he withdrew.

"Are you consulted about everything that happens at Strickland?" Davenport asked, his eyebrows rising.

"Of course not, that was merely an excuse for him to get a closer look at the new owner. Everyone is perishing of curiosity. After all, you have the power to make or break anyone on the estate."

Alys was pleased to see that her words took him slightly aback. Good, the more he thought about his new responsibilities, the better. He didn't look like a man who'd had more than a nodding acquaintance with responsibility in the past.

With a sardonic glint in his eye, he turned the conversation back to her. "Lady Alys? From what noble family do you spring to merit the title?"

"It's only a nickname. Someone called me Lady Alys, and it stuck." Under his probing gaze, she added, "Because of my dictatorial tendencies, I imagine."

He smiled at her explanation. "Lady Alys. It does suit you. Shall I call you that, or do you wish to be Miss Weston?"

"Whatever you prefer, Mr. Davenport," she answered, doing her level best to sound like an obedient employee even though her stomach was churning. She sipped more whiskey, hoping it would have a soothing effect.

They drank in silence, Davenport frowning to himself, until Alys could stand the suspense no longer and asked, "Well?"

He glanced up. "Well, what?"

Her chin lifted at his deliberate obtuseness. "Are you going to discharge me?"

"I decided before I arrived here to make no changes until I was more familiar with the situation." He studied her with shuttered eyes. "It will be a confounded nuisance to have a female steward, but everyone seems to hold you in high regard. Since you can do the work, it would be foolish to release you for a reason that is not your fault and which apparently doesn't hinder your performance."

Alys released her breath, almost giddy with relief. She really hadn't expected such an enlightened attitude from a libertine.

Reading her expression, he went on, his heavy brows drawn together. "I will keep you on for the time being, but I want to make two things perfectly clear. First, I intend to take you at your word and treat you like a man, so I don't want to hear any spinsterish outrage about my crude language and behavior."

He waited until she gave a nod of acknowledgment, then continued, "Secondly, for the last four years you have been running Strickland, with authority for everyone and everything on the estate, answerable only to a London lawyer who never visited. For all practical purposes, you might have been the owner. Now, however, Strickland is *mine*. If I tell you to plant orange trees in the water meadow, you will do it. If I want the laborers to cut a Saxon horse into the chalk of the hillside, you will give the orders. If I want to color the sheep pink, you will order the dye."

He set his tumbler on the desk and leaned forward for emphasis, his dark face stern. "I am quite willing to take advice on estate matters, since your experience is greater than mine. However, once I make a decision, I will expect you to implement it without further questions. Your will is no longer supreme; what authority you have is derived from me. For you, it will be a change for the worse. I don't expect you to like it, but I do expect you to accept it and behave in a civil and cooperative manner. If you can't, you had better leave right now."

Alys stared into his cold aquamarine eyes, and realized that it would be very easy to hate Reginald Davenport. Before today, she hadn't had time to worry beyond the question of whether he would discharge her out of hand.

Now she had survived the first fence, only to discover that the rest of the course would be much harder.

Her new employer had gone to the heart of her dilemma with uncanny perception. For years she had ruled Strickland like a private fiefdom. Because of her position and the fact that she was an enlightened despot, her orders had been accepted, and she was proud of what she had achieved. Now he was saying in unmistakable terms that her reign was over. She was as much an employee as the youngest field hand.

Authority came very naturally to Alys; subservience did not. Unfortunately, she had no real choice. She would never be able to find an equivalent situation anywhere else.

As the silence stretched, he prompted, "Well?"

Swallowing hard to force down her resentment, she said coolly, "I can accept that, Mr. Davenport."

He smiled with a lazy charm that was a startling contrast to his prior manner. "You can accept it, but you would rather have my guts for garters." He got to his feet and looked down at her. "I don't care what you think of me as long as you do your work and don't sulk. Agreed?"

Alys also stood. After a moment's hesitation she offered her hand with grudging respect. "Agreed."

His hand was firm and hard, not soft like many London gentlemen's. After arranging to meet her early the next morning for a tour of the estate, he took the last six years of account books to the main house to study.

After he left, Alys sank back into her chair with a sigh. She still had a job, at least for the moment. Now she would consider the serious question of whether she could work for Reginald Davenport without murdering him.

Having survived the ordeal by the owner, that night Alys faced interrogation by her wards. She waited until dinner was over before announcing, "Mr. Davenport arrived from London today."

A chorus of responses overlaid each other. Meredith looked up so quickly that her golden ringlets danced. "Lady Alys," she said accusingly, "you didn't tell us!"

Her fifteen-year-old brother Peter asked eagerly, "How long is he going to stay?"

William, at seven the baby of the family, swallowed his pudding in haste and demanded, "Tell me about his horses!"

Alys grinned at her charges. All three of the Spensers were staring at her, bright-eyed with curiosity. Even Attila watched avidly, though in his case the cause was hope for a handout. "I wanted to eat before I told you because I knew there would be no peace afterward. To answer your questions, I don't know how long he is going to stay, but it looks like he'll be here for a while. He rode down on a really magnificent black stallion. He has a carriage and some hunters coming. If the hunters are half as fine as the stallion, William will be in horse heaven."

William, who had his sister's golden hair and sunny disposition, sighed rapturously. Merry, remembering Alys's concern, asked, "He doesn't mind having a female steward?"

Alys hesitated, remembering that dark, sardonic face. "He minded, but he's willing to overlook my failings in that area, at least for the moment."

Peter said wistfully, "I'd like to meet him. It's hard to imagine a real out-and-outer in Dorsetshire."

Alys regarded him thoughtfully. Unlike his blond and pragmatic siblings, Peter had brown hair and a dreamy, scholarly nature. While his ambition was the church, he tempered that with a lively interest in the doings of the London fashionable world. Like his brother and sister, Peter was remarkably happy and stable considering that he had been orphaned so young, but now he was at an age where he needed a father's guidance, and Alys couldn't give him that. It would be all too easy for the boy to hero-worship a man like Strickland's new owner.

Hoping to reduce Davenport's glamour, she said dampeningly, "He may be an out-and-outer in London, but he looks like any other country gentleman here."

Undeterred, Peter said, "He's a member of the Four-in-Hand Club. They say he's one of the best boxers in England, that he could have been a professional champion if he wanted to."

Alys sighed. Her four years as a foster parent had taught her that sometimes it was impossible to derail the direction of youthful thought. Peter was determined to be impressed.

"Is he handsome?" That was from Merry, of course.

Alys eyed the girl with misgivings. Though Meredith handled her young suitors with innate skill, she was no match for a man of the world like Davenport. Alys wished she could keep the two of them apart, but Strickland was too small for that. "No, he's not especially good-looking, and he's old enough to be your father."

She was uncomfortably aware that her words were less than the truth. Davenport was certainly no Adonis, but he had a sexual magnetism that would fascinate as many women as it terrified. Her foster daughter was not the sort to be easily terrified.

Merry propped her elbow on the table and rested her chin on her hand. "He's going to be lonely in that big house by himself. We should invite him to dinner."

"He'll be getting plenty of invitations once the local gentry know he's in residence. Davenport is a considerable property owner now, and there are enough unmarried daughters in the area to ensure instant social acceptance as long as he doesn't do anything too outrageous," Alys said cynically. "Besides, you know perfectly well that it would be inappropriate for us to invite my employer to dinner."

Merry smiled mischievously. "This is not the normal steward's household."

"No," Alys admitted, "but that doesn't mean there should be a social relationship between Davenport and us. That would be both improper and uncomfortable."

Ignoring her guardian as thoroughly as Peter had, Merry said dreamily, "I've always wondered what a rake is like."

"Meredith, such talk is quite unbecoming," her guardian said with exasperation. "I don't want Mr. Davenport pestered by any of you. Not about his horses, his sporting activities, or his social life. Do you understand?"

She might as well have saved her breath. In a quiet neighborhood like this one, a dashing stranger was bound to be a focus of speculation and interest. The only silver lining Alys could imagine was that Davenport looked too impatient and self-absorbed to waste time corrupting the boys.

However, Meredith was quite a different story. Her beauty attracted men like wasps to a jam pot. The local swains were respectful enough, but Davenport came from a very different world. Merry handled her local admirers so deftly that she might not realize that she was playing with fire until she was burned. Which meant that Alys was going to have to keep Davenport away from the girl, at the same time satisfying the man with her stewardship.

It didn't take a prophet to foresee storms on the horizon.

Reggie spent the evening working on the estate account books, spreading them across the library table. It was nearly midnight when he closed the last. He stood and stretched, then picked up his brandy glass and wandered over to the French doors. The gardens that were unkempt by day were lovely in the pale, cool light of a waxing moon. He found the landscape eerily familiar. The old naval captain who had rented the house had made so few changes that Reggie suspected he could go to his old bedroom and find it exactly the same, with books and rocks and other childish treasures.

However, it was a proposition that he didn't intend to test. He was twitchy enough already. The house was welcoming but haunted, and he couldn't turn a corner without half expecting to run into a member of his family. Presumably that feeling would pass. It had better, or he would be unable to endure living here.

He drank deeply of the brandy. Strickland might prove unendurable anyhow. What on earth did country people do in the evenings? He would perish of boredom at this rate.

In spite of his misgivings, he had the obscure feeling that he couldn't go back to his old life. Mentally he had burned his bridges when he came down here. His life was hollow at the core. The only question was what would fill that space.

Apart from brandy, that was.

Taking a branch of candles in hand, he prowled through the ground floor. The music room opened off the drawing room, and the old pianoforte still stood there in lonely grandeur. Placing the candelabrum on the shining mahogany lid, he sat down on the bench and played an experimental chord. The liquid notes hung in the air, marred by several that were sour. He'd have to get the instrument tuned.

His fingers were rusty, unused to musical exercise. How long had it been since he had played? Years. His mother had taught him music on this very instrument. He'd loved the lessons. She had once said that if he continued to learn and practiced hard, he would someday be a superb pianist.

That possibility was one of many that had vanished when he left Strickland. Still, though he took no more lessons, for years he had played when he was in the vicinity of a piano and there was no one around to hear. At some point he had stopped. Three years ago? Five? Before the blackouts had started. Why had he allowed something so important to slip away?

He lifted the lid of the piano bench and took out the piece of music on top. A sonata by Beethoven. Perhaps he had put it there himself almost three decades earlier. Once again, the sea captain had apparently changed nothing.

Ignoring the strangeness of his situation and the off notes, he began to play the sonata. Polishing his musical skills would be one way to fill empty time. Within half an hour, his fingers were beginning to remember what his mind had half forgotten.

When he finished, he lifted the candelabrum and continued on his midnight tour until he came to the morning room. He halted on the threshold. This sunny chamber was one of the most pleasant spots in the house. It had been his mother's special retreat, but he had never been comfortable here. At night and devoid of his mother's presence, the room made the hair on his nape prickle. The rest of Strickland's ghosts were amiable, but not whatever lingered here.

Scoffing at his imagination, he returned to the library and settled into the wing chair that had been his father's favorite. He was much the height and build of his father, and the chair seemed tailored to his shape. Picking up the brandy he had left, he thought about what he had accomplished today.

Based on her efficiency at making the house habitable, he had offered the position of full-time housekeeper to Mrs. Herald. Since he had not insisted that she live in, she had accepted with alacrity. Mrs. Herald had also recommended several local girls as house and kitchen maids. Reggie assumed they were all related to her, but he didn't mind nepotism as long as they were competent.

Molly Barlow, a plump, comely widow in her forties as well as Mrs. Herald's sister-in-law, had proved to be a good plain cook, so he had given her the position permanently. Within the next two days, she and her youngest child would move into the servants' quarters. Reggie had eyed her with interest, but it would be poor policy to bed his own servants. He'd have to make different arrangements, perhaps in Dorchester

Or he could invite Chessie down for a visit. He chuckled at the thought of what the county would think. Likely some of the men would recognize her, since Chessie ran one of London's best brothels. Having her at Strickland would certainly eliminate any risk that he would be acceptable to the womenfolk of the local gentry.

Amusement faded, and he ran his hand tiredly through his dark hair as his thoughts circled around to his improbable steward. He wasn't really worried about burning Lady Alys's tender ears with his language. The real danger was that he would be unable to keep his hands off the blasted woman. While Reggie found a broad range of females attractive, tall women with long legs and richly feminine figures could turn him into a softheaded imbecile. Garbed as she was this afternoon, the legs had been immediately obvious. The figure had been equally alluring.

Under other circumstances she might have been a real find, but during their conversation, he had revised his initial impression. She might not be shy, but she was certainly a virgin. Beneath her unconventional dress and occupation, there lurked the rigid soul of a governess. She had been quite unable to repress her furious disapproval of him. Not that Reggie blamed her. If he had ruled here for years, he would be equally furious at being displaced. In her case anger was supplemented by contempt for the kind of man the new owner was.

It would be much simpler to get rid of the woman, but he was reluctant to turn her out. She had reached her present position only through a lucky chance, and she was unlikely to find another such post. Which would be both unfair and unfortunate, because his review of the accounts had showed that the woman had a talent for her work that bordered on genius.

Reggie had always had a knack for figures, and had

deciphered an intriguing story from the account books. The previous steward had been fired by the Wargrave business manager for embezzlement. When Miss Weston took over, there had been an immediate jump in income simply through honest record keeping.

Then the story became really interesting. The income had increased for the first two years under Lady Alys, but the profits had been canceled by heavy capital investment. In the last two years, the improvements had paid off with a sharp rise in income. Many of the expenditures were clear from the books. However, there were some cryptic entries that he intended to ask about.

He refilled his brandy glass. Then he settled back in his chair again, thinking of that magnificent female body, and how it was wasted on a dedicated spinster. If she had been as young as her appearance suggested, there might have been some hope of teaching her what she was missing, but since she had reached the advanced age of thirty in a state of militant virginity, her attitude was unlikely to change.

Reggie sighed and rested his head against the chair back. He didn't doubt his ability to control his base instincts when he was sober, but if she paraded that beautiful body in front of him when he was half foxed, he might behave very badly indeed. And really, he didn't need any more reasons to despise himself.

Well, he was generally sober during the day, and he was unlikely to be socializing with his steward, so her virtue should be safe. However, he had had just enough brandy so that if Lady Alys were present, he might have forgotten that he was a nominal gentleman and made a most improper suggestion. Then she would box his ears, and he would need a new steward.

He chuckled and picked up the brandy decanter to carry to his bedchamber. In his present mood, it was much more amusing to imagine what might happen if she didn't box his ears.

Chapter 5

Reggie awoke to the familiar, temple-pounding aftermath of too much brandy. He had been able to put himself to bed, which meant that he wasn't as badly off as his last morning in London, but his present state was quite bad enough. Groping for his watch on the bedside table, he discovered that it was seven-thirty. He had just enough time to make himself presentable and meet Lady Alys for his tour of the estate.

Groaning, he rolled to the edge of the bed and sat there, his head in his hands as he prayed that Mac Cooper would arrive from London today. It was much harder to face the morning without Mac's skilled ministrations.

Cautiously he stood. The brandy decanter was empty, which explained his head. He must arrange for new supplies of drink before the day was over, because at this rate the cellar would soon be empty.

The morning was damp and overcast. By the time Reggie had saddled his horse Bucephalus, he was swearing silently at himself for having requested this tour. It had been a deliberate choice to ride over the estate for the first time with someone else. Alone, he might run the risk of becoming maudlin. However, it was altogether too early in the day to face Lady Alys's censorious eye.

His mood was not improved when his steward entered the stables, bandbox neat in a dark brown riding habit. The severe cut couldn't quite disguise her luscious figure, though it did conceal the distracting legs. He studied the crown of thick, glossy braids. Her hair must be nearly waist length. Like her body, it was another splendid asset wasted; the expression on her handsome face rivaled Medusa for paralyzing effect.

"Good morning, Mr. Davenport. Is there any particular part of the estate you would like to see first?" Alys's nervousness came out as waspishness, but it was hard to sweeten her tone when such a difficult day lay ahead of her. Davenport would surely disapprove of some of her innovations, possibly to the point where his tentative willingness to retain her might evaporate.

Davenport grunted a greeting as she went for her sidesaddle. He looked like a bear with a sore ear, which made it surprising when he took the saddle away from her. "I thought you were going to treat me like a man," she remarked as he saddled her mount.

He gave her a slanting glance as he tightened the girth. "That's hard to do when you're dressed like a woman."

Uncomfortable under his piercing gaze, she changed the subject. "Mr. Davenport, you will see some . . . unusual things at Strickland. There are reasons for everything I have done. I ask that you allow me to explain rather than condemning out of hand."

He turned from the horse to face her. Alys was once more uncomfortably aware of how tall he was.

"I'll add any new oddities to the list of questions I have already," he said dryly.

The comment did not bode well.

They led their horses out into the open air. Obscurely

unwilling to be touched by Davenport, Alys went to the mounting block before he could assist her. As she settled into the sidesaddle and arranged the fall of her long skirts, she felt the ironic amusement in his gaze. However, he said only, "A beautiful mare," as he swung onto his own horse.

"She belongs to me, not the estate," Alys said defensively. "I have the bill of sale if you don't believe me."

Davenport set his horse out of the stable yard at a trot. "Did I show any sign of doubting you?"

"No." She felt like biting her tongue. To hide her embarrassment, she said hurriedly, "Most of the horses in the stables are just for wagon and plow use. The estate owns two riding hacks, but nothing of great quality. I keep my mare here because the steward's house doesn't have its own stable."

Not dignifying her inane comment with an answer, Davenport put his horse into a fast canter. He rode with the effortless grace and skill of a centaur. She supposed that good riding was essential to a well-rounded rake.

They traveled in silence until they reached the grainfields. Some were already planted while others were newly plowed, and a few lay fallow. They reined in and surveyed fields quilted by neat hedges.

"As I recall, Strickland is just over three thousand acres, about half of that let to tenants and the other half in the home farm," Davenport said. "From the amount of seed you've been buying, I assume that you've improved a good deal of what was waste. How much acreage is cultivated now?"

"Almost two thousand acres, with much of the rest used as pasture."

He nodded. "You recently bought a shorthorn ram and a score of ewes to improve the stock. What breed did you buy?"

"Southdowns from Ellman in Sussex."

"Excellent choice. Some of the best stock in England."

His gaze slowly scanned the fields in front of them. "You're using a four-crop rotation?"

Alys suspected that he was trying to impress her, and he was succeeding. For someone who allegedly had spent his life in taverns and gaming hells, he was extremely knowledgeable about modern agriculture. "Yes, usually with wheat instead of rye. Then turnips, clover, and sainfoin. It's worked so well that I've been able to increase the livestock herds."

Davenport nodded again, setting his horse into motion while he asked another question. The interrogation continued throughout the morning as he inquired about the seed drill, the efficiency of the threshing machine she had bought, the oil cake she fed to the beef cattle to improve the quality, the breeding stock used for the dairy herd, the experiments she was trying on the home farm before recommending them to the tenants. His cool expression showed neither approval nor disapproval of her answers.

By noon Alys had acquired a headache and a considerable respect for her new employer's understanding. As they rode side by side down a lane toward the home farm, she commented on his knowledge of farming.

Davenport shrugged. "I was the heir presumptive to the Earl of Wargrave for many years. My uncle wouldn't let me set foot on any of his properties, but since I was likely to inherit someday, I kept an eye on developments in agriculture."

Alys glanced at him thoughtfully. He had done more than "keep an eye" on what was going on. Clearly he had made a serious study of farming and land management, fitting it in between orgies or whatever it was that had given him such a terrible reputation. She felt a surge of sympathy. Davenport had spent his life preparing for a position he would never fill. How did he feel about that? His hard profile gave no clues, but it would take a saint not to feel resentment at being displaced. Alys saw no signs of a halo.

They came to the irregularly shaped ornamental lake that

lay near the manor house. Davenport pulled his horse to a halt and dismounted. "Excuse me, there's something I want to see." After tethering the beast, he disappeared into a thicket of trees next to the lake.

Curious, Alys dismounted and tied her own horse, then lifted the long skirts of her riding habit and followed him. Her dress put her at a disadvantage in the thick undergrowth. Swearing under her breath as she unsnagged her habit for the third time, she emerged from the shrubbery into a small clearing at the water's edge.

She halted, surprised at the beauty of the place. Lush grass carpeted the ground while bluebells clustered beneath the trees, the violet hue set off by a drift of pale yellow primroses. It was a magical spot, the only sound the fluting song of a thrush and the whisper of wind in the trees. Private, too, because it lay on a cove invisible from the manor.

Her employer stood by the edge of the lake, looking over its surface as he absently twined the stem of a bluebell around one finger. Alys studied the picture he made. He didn't have the dandy's perfection of figure that she had so admired in Randolph when she was eighteen and besotted. Davenport was taller and leaner, with a whipcord grace that hinted at power even when he was motionless.

He was also disturbingly masculine. Uncomfortably Alys recognized that his virility was much of the reason she found him so unnerving. Breaking the silence to keep her thoughts from that direction, she asked, "How did you know about this clearing? I've lived here for four years and never found it."

Without turning to look at her, he said, "I was born at Strickland, Miss Weston. Didn't you know that?"

Her brows shot up. "No, I didn't."

"I'm surprised that the local gossips weren't more efficient," he said, his tone even drier than usual.

She crossed the clearing and halted beside him. "You caught them unaware. I only heard that the estate was being transferred two days ago, and you appeared yesterday. The gossip didn't have a chance to catch up."

"It will. Gossip always catches up with me."

"And wouldn't you be disappointed if it didn't," she said tartly.

His mouth curved a little. "Probably."

"How old were you when you left Strickland?"

His smile vanished. "Eight."

Though his terseness didn't encourage further questions, Alys's curiosity overcame her manners. "What happened?"

"My family died."

Not just parents—family. A brother or sister, perhaps several? Alys felt a tightness in her throat as the ghost of old tragedy brushed her with chill fingers. Eight was very young to be orphaned and removed from the only home a child had known.

She said softly, "I'm sorry."

"So am I, Miss Weston, so am I." There was infinite bleakness in Davenport's low voice.

Silence hung heavy between them for a long moment. Then he tossed the bluebell into the lake and turned to her, vulnerability gone. "I didn't know until my cousin signed Strickland over to me three days ago that the property belonged to my mother and should have come to me. Ironic, isn't it? My dear guardian told me that Strickland was part of the Wargrave estate, and it never occurred to me to think otherwise."

"Good heavens, the old earl deliberately lied about the ownership?" Alys said, appalled by such blatant dishonesty. "How despicable!"

"Despicable was an excellent word for my uncle," he agreed. "Wargrave is in much better hands now."

"Your cousin discovered the injustice and gave you Strickland?"

"What a quantity of questions you ask, Lady Alys." There was a sardonic note in his voice as he used her nickname.

She bit her lip. "I'm sorry. Curiosity is my besetting sin."

He smiled faintly. "How nice to have only one sin, singular. Mine come in scores."

"I'm sure that I can come up with more than one," she said a trifle indignantly.

"And what might the others be?" he asked with interest. "Sleeping during the Sunday sermon? Coveting a neighbor's horse?"

Well and truly irritated, Alys snapped, "I can do much better than that."

He laughed outright. "Perhaps someday you will tell me the full list of your vices, Miss Weston. I should enjoy learning what they are."

With a horrid sense of discovery, Alys realized how charming Davenport could be with a sparkle in his light blue eyes and a wide smile that invited her to smile with him. She reminded herself sternly that a successful rake would have to be charming, or he could never beguile away a lady's virtue. How alarming that she, a woman of great experience and no illusions, found herself wanting to respond to that charm with a smile of her own.

Hastily she wiped the expression from her face before her dimples could emerge. She felt obscurely that dimples would undermine the progress she was making toward convincing him that she was a competent steward.

Still smiling, Davenport lightly took her arm to guide her back to the horses. It was a casual gesture, but Alys was acutely aware of his touch, of the feel of his strong fingers through the heavy fabric of her riding habit. She quickened her pace.

He was about to help her onto her mount when he halted

and stared down at her, his eyes a bare foot from her own. "Good Lord, Lady Alys, your eyes don't match."

"Really?" she said with asperity. "I never noticed."

"Indoors the gray-green eye looks more or less like the brown one, but in this light the difference is striking," he said, ignoring her sarcasm. "A most unusual feature, but then, you are a most unusual woman."

"Is that a compliment or an insult?" she asked warily.

"Neither." He bent over and linked his hands to give her a step up to her saddle. "A mere statement of fact."

After she was mounted, he swung onto his own horse. "You've done a remarkable job with Strickland. Even though farm prices have plummeted since Waterloo, you've managed to increase the profits, and the land and tenants are in very good heart."

She was absurdly pleased at the compliment. Perhaps her job was safe after all.

They circled the manor house and rode toward the village of Strickland, but before they reached their destination, Davenport reined in his horse. His eyes narrowed at the sight of the tall brick chimney that loomed above the next hilltop. "What on earth is an industrial chimney doing out here?"

Face set, he cantered forward to investigate. Alys trailed unhappily behind him. The new owner was about to discover one of the odder features of Strickland.

He stopped again on the top of the hill, where he could see the whole manufactory. The round bottle oven with its high, circular chimney was the unmistakable mark of a pottery. In a voice devoid of inflection, he asked, "What the devil is a potbank doing on Strickland land? Didn't this used to be one of the tenant farms?"

"The site is leased from Strickland, and at quite a profitable rate," she replied, praying that he wouldn't ask more, and knowing that he would.

He gave her an icy glance. "That isn't what I asked. What is a manufactory doing here, and who owns it?"

Choosing her words carefully, Alys said, "It's held in trust for three minors."

"Oh?" His cold syllable ordered her to continue.

"This was the smallest of the tenant farms, with the least desirable tenants," she explained. "It was a relief when they sold off their equipment and stock and skipped off without paying the Lady Day rent three years ago. I combined the land with Hill Farm, and Robbie Herald works it with his own property. I leased the buildings to the pottery."

His sardonic snort made it clear that he knew she was telling less than the whole story.

"The pottery has been an excellent venture," Alys said defensively. "It provides jobs, pays a fair rent to Strickland, and is a good long-term investment for the owners. I know most landowners loathe any kind of industry on their land, but you can't shut it down even if you want to—the lease runs for twenty-two more years."

Before she could offer more arguments, Davenport's hand shot out to catch her mare's bridle. The horse tried to throw its head upward, but his powerful grip held it steady. He turned in his saddle to face her, anger evident in his clipped words. "Yesterday I said I would give you a chance to prove yourself. Will you extend me the same courtesy?"

A fierce wave of embarrassment burned Alys's face and spread down her neck. He was being entirely reasonable, and she was acting like a rabid hedgehog. For the first time she really looked at him, not as Reginald Davenport, notorious rake and disastrous employer, but as an individual. Their gazes held for an endless moment.

With jarring insight, she recognized that her employer was a good deal more—or less—than his reputation. Under the world-weary air were tolerance and intelligence that would be a credit to anyone. And he had the tiredest eyes she had ever seen.

"I'm sorry." It wasn't enough, so she continued doggedly, "I have often been unfairly judged and condemned. It is unpardonable that I commit the same injustice toward you."

He released the mare's bridle. "Considering how many years I've spent cultivating an evil reputation, I would be disappointed if you didn't assume the worst about me."

She smiled. "I am beginning to believe that you are a fraud, Mr. Davenport."

"Oh?" His dark brows rose in the sardonic expression she was coming to recognize. "In what way?"

"I am beginning to believe that you are not at all the wicked care-for-nobody that your reputation claims."

"You had best withhold judgment on that point, Miss Weston," he said dryly. Gathering up his reins, he said, "I think it's time we ate. As I recall, there used to be a tavern on the Shaftesbury road that had good food."

"It's still there, and the food is still good." Alys wondered for a moment that he would take her to a common tavern. Then she realized that it would be less scandalous to eat with her at the Silent Woman than to share a private meal at the manor. Despite his stated intention of treating her like a man, he was being careful of the proprieties.

Half an hour later, they were facing each other across a wooden table polished by years of sliding crockery and hard scrubbing. A good number of customers shared the beamed taproom and sent curious glances their way. All of the men were local and knew the eccentric Miss Weston, and they could surely guess who her companion was. They kept a respectful distance from the new master of Strickland.

Davenport polished off the last crumbs of an excellent beef and onion pie, then refilled his tankard with ale from the pewter pitcher. "Will you tell me the whole story of the pottery, or will I have to drag the information out of you a piece at a time?"

Alys finished the last bite of her own meat pie. It was time to tell the whole story, because if he had to dig for the facts, it might ruin his expansive mood. "You know about the problems caused by discharging so many soldiers after the war. There wasn't enough work to begin with. To make matters worse, the new machinery reduces the need for farm laborers."

When he nodded, she went on, "For example, the estate could never have managed without one of the new threshing machines. There simply weren't enough laborers during the later war years. Now that the machinery has been purchased and is working well, it makes no sense to go back to slower, more cumbersome methods just to create a few ill-paid jobs. Other solutions needed to be found." She gazed at him earnestly. "Besides the fact that idle men make trouble, it would be wrong to let the soldiers who defeated Napoleon starve. Wrong, and dangerous for Strickland as well."

He took a draft of ale and prompted, "So . . . ?"

"I've encouraged the creation of various businesses to provide work. There's a wood shop in Strickland village that employs eight men, and a brick and tile yard with five workers. Because there are good deposits of clay nearby, it made sense to open a pottery as well. It makes moderately priced ware that the average person can afford. There's quite a market for such things, and now twelve people are employed."

"Who manages the place?"

She took a deep breath. "I do."

The dark brows shot up. "In addition to managing Strickland? Where the devil do you find the time?"

"I make all the decisions and keep the accounts, but a foreman supervises the daily work," she explained. "As you can see from the estate books, I haven't neglected Strickland. I . . ."

He held up one hand to stop her words. "Before we go too far afield, who are the three minors who are the actual owners of the pottery? Are they local children?"

Alys poured more ale for both of them before answering. "They are the niece and nephews of Mrs. Spenser, my former employer."

"More and more interesting. Where do they live now?"

With an inward sigh, Alys recognized that it was time to confess what he would surely learn soon. "They live with me."

"You're their guardian?" he asked with surprise.

She took another swig from the tankard, her eyes cast down. "There were no close relatives whom Mrs. Spenser trusted. One reason she helped me get the Strickland position was so that I could keep the children with me."

"I see why they call you Lady Alys," he said with a mocking humor. "Managing an estate, several businesses, and children as well. You are an extraordinary woman."

"Most women are extraordinary. It compensates for the fact that most men aren't," Alys snapped, then immediately bit her tongue. With his talent for getting under her skin, Davenport made her forget how dependent she was on his goodwill. She, who had always prided herself on her control, was continually skirting explosion with him.

He laughed, his extraordinary charm visible again. "I suppose your next project is to advance beyond needing the male half of the species? As a stock breeder, you must know that will be difficult, at least if there is to be a next generation."

Alys had no doubt that his supply of suggestive remarks could easily outlast her belligerence. With as much dignity as she could muster, she reached for the ale pitcher. "I have never denied that men have their uses, Mr. Davenport."

"Oh? And what might they be?"

His hand brushed hers casually when they both reached for the handle of the pitcher at the same time. Her nerves jumped, and she dropped her eyes to avoid his gaze. His hands were quite beautiful, long-fingered and elegant, the only refined thing about him. A seductive current flowed from him that made her want to yield, so melt and mold herself, to discover the other ways he could touch, to touch him back. . . .

In a voice that seemed to come from someone else, she said, "We're out of ale. Shall we order another pitcher, or are you ready to see more of the estate?"

"More ale," he said, apparently quite unaffected by the fleeting contact between them. "I still have a number of questions. For example, the sixty pounds a year for schoolmasters, books, and other teaching supplies."

He signaled for another pitcher, refilling his tankard when it arrived. Alys was four rounds behind him, and knew better than to try keeping up. She didn't doubt that in a drinking contest he could put her under the table.

And what would he do with you there? a mocking little voice asked. Nothing, of course. More's the pity.

Trying to ignore the lewd asides of her lower mind, Alys said, "The teachers are a married couple. He teaches the boys, she teaches the girls. I require all the children on the estate to go to school until at least the age of twelve."

"Don't the parents resent that their children can't start earning wages earlier?"

"Yes, but I have insisted," she replied. "In the short run, it's better for the children. In the long run, the estate will have better workers."

"Miss Weston, did some Quaker or reforming Evangelical get hold of your tender mind when you were growing up?" Davenport asked, his dark brows arching ironically.

She blinked. "As a matter of fact, yes."

"Wonderful," he muttered into his ale. "A fanatic."

Grabbing hold of her frayed temper, Alys said with hard-won composure, "Not a fanatic, a practical reformer. You have seen the results at Strickland over the last four years. I would be hard-pressed to say precisely which reforms have produced what results, but the total effect has been more than satisfactory. The estate is prospering, and so are the people who work on it. The evidence speaks for itself."

"I keep reminding myself of that, Miss Weston," he said dourly. "I trust you appreciate that you are being treated to a display of open-mindedness and tolerance that none of my friends would believe." He shook his head. "A female steward, and a reformer to boot."

"It's your income, Mr. Davenport," Alys pointed out in an icy voice. "If you make sweeping changes, there might be a drop in the profits."

"I remind myself of that, too." He poured the last of the ale in his tankard. He'd drunk most of two pitchers himself. "What about the money given to help emigration?"

She sighed and traced circles on the table in a few drops of spilled ale. It had been a vain hope that he would overlook her cryptic notes in the account books. The blasted man missed nothing. "Three of the veterans who returned from Wellington's army wanted to take their families to America, but didn't have adequate savings to pay their passages and start over."

"So you gave them the money?" He slouched casually against the back of the oak settle, relaxed but watchful.

"Theoretically the money was loaned, but it was understood that they might never be able to repay," Alys admitted.

"And the chances of collecting from another country are nil. So you just gave it away," he mused. "Are you running a business or a charity here?"

"If you saw the books, you know that less than two hundred pounds were lent," she said, defensive again. "All of the families had served Strickland with great loyalty. One man's wife worked on the harvest crew until an hour before her first baby was born."

Under his sardonic eye she realized how foolish that must sound to a man of the world. She added more practically, "Helping them leave also reduced the strain on Strickland's resources—fewer jobs to find and mouths to feed."

"If every worker on the estate wanted to emigrate, would you have given money to them all?" he inquired with interest.

She turned one palm up dismissively. "Few people want to leave their homes for a strange country. Most of the Strickland tenants were born here, and they can imagine no other end than to die here."

She thought, with sudden piercing sorrow, of where she herself had been born, the home to which she could never return. Alys had exiled herself as surely as the three families who had gone to America. Then she wondered how much her expression had revealed, for Davenport was watching her keenly.

"Somehow, I doubt that the old earl knew about your odd little charities," he said, a flicker of amusement in his light eyes.

Relieved that Davenport was enjoying the thought of his uncle's ignorance, she assured him, "The old earl never had any idea. His man of business must have known at least some of what I was doing, but he didn't interfere since the overall profits were up."

"In other words, you gave away less than your predecessor stole."

She gave a lopsided smile. "I never thought of it that way, but I suppose you're right." After hesitating for a moment, curiosity drove her to ask, "Now that you know how Strickland has been run, do you have any comments?"

Davenport thought for a moment, his hands loosely laced around his tankard. "As you have pointed out, your results are a justification for your methods. Also, everything you described belongs to the past, when I had no say in what went on, so I have no right to criticize your decisions.

"The future, now . . ." He swallowed his remaining ale in one gulp, then clinked the tankard onto the table as he watched her expression narrowly. "That will be a different story. I expect I'll want to make some changes, but I shan't rush into them."

As an endorsement, it didn't go as far as Alys would have liked, but it was the best she was likely to get. At least he intended to move slowly.

She started to rise, but her employer wasn't finished yet. He lifted his hand to halt her. "I have only one more question at the moment. As an eager reformer, have you had everyone on the estate vaccinated against smallpox?"

Alys was startled. "No, I've encouraged vaccination, but some of the workers are very suspicious about 'newfangled ideas.' Only about half the people would agree to it, and I don't really have the authority to insist on something like that." In fact, she had railed, begged, and pleaded with the tenants, enraged by their pigheaded stubbornness.

"In that case, I will issue my first order." His gaze met hers, cold determination in the depths of his eyes. "Everyone who is not vaccinated within the next month will be dismissed and evicted. There will be no exceptions."

"But . . ." Alys gasped, torn between approval of the result and shock at his high-handedness, "you can't . . ."

"No buts, Miss Weston, or arguments about whether I have the authority." He stood and looked down at her, dark and implacable. "The cost will be carried by the estate, and there will be *no exceptions*."

Alys saw very clearly how he had earned the reputation for being dangerous. If she were younger or more timid, she would be diving under the table to avoid that stare.

He added with a hint of scorn, "If you're afraid to tell them, I'll do it myself."

Those were fighting words. She stood also, since glaring from a sitting position lacked impact. "I am not afraid to tell them, Mr. Davenport. It will be done." Meeting his gaze with her own, she said, "Are you ready to continue your inspection?"

"Quite ready." He dropped a handful of coins on the table, then crossed the taproom with long, lazy strides. As she followed, Alys remembered that tonight she would face a barrage of questions about what kind of man the new master was.

She realized that she had no idea what the answer should be.

Chapter 6

Alys spent the afternoon showing her new employer the barns, granaries, and other farm buildings. Then they started on the village workshops and small businesses. Davenport asked endless questions, keeping his own counsel about what he thought of the answers.

Now that Alys knew he was a native of the area, she could see the quiet signs of recognition from the locals. Though watchful, they appeared ready to give him a kind of acceptance that Alys had not received in all her years in Dorset.

Of course, it helped that he was male, she commented to herself acidly. No amount of time in Dorset would change the fact that she was the wrong sex to be a steward. Even many of the people who had benefited from her management could not quite approve of the fact that she was a woman.

Just beyond the half dozen acres of orchard that produced apples and cider for estate use, they came on a large patchwork area of vegetable gardens. Davenport reined in his horse. "What are these?"

"Most of the laborers' cottages have only small gardens, so I've provided extra land for those who want it," Alys replied. "A few of the more ambitious tenants not only grow food for their families, but have enough left over to sell in the Shaftesbury market."

A young woman working in her allotment looked up and saw the visitors. After a doubtful pause, she bobbed a nervous curtsy to Davenport, then scooped up the baby dozing on a blanket by the turnips and came to show him to Alys. Under her employer's sardonic eye, Alys chucked the baby's chin and admired his first tooth before returning him to his mother. As they continued on their way, Davenport remarked, "It looks like everyone at Strickland eats well."

"They do indeed," Alys agreed. "Eating well is probably the first prerequisite for contentment. In addition to the allotments, I added a second dovecote and started raising rabbits on a large scale. Most are sold to people on the estate at a price low enough that everyone can afford fresh meat several times a week. Not only has that virtually eliminated poaching, but we have enough squabs and rabbits left over to sell in the market, which covers the costs of both operations."

Davenport didn't reply, but Alys thought his nod seemed approving.

They arrived at the potbank, last stop on the tour. As they dismounted, the foreman came out to greet them. Jamie Palmer was a gentle giant of a man, Alys's oldest friend and ally, and he took his time surveying the visitor.

Davenport was aware that he was being judged, and Alys could see his hackles rising. Wanting to defuse the tension, she swiftly performed the introductions, then asked, "Would you give us a tour, Jamie? Mr. Davenport is interested in how pottery is made."

"Of course, Lady Alys."

As Jamie led them inside, Davenport gave her a slightly pained look, but followed obediently through the works as the foreman explained clay preparation, throwing wheels, and slip-casting. Alys trailed behind. Meredith worked at the pottery several mornings a week, using her considerable artistic talent to develop new china designs. This was not one of her days to work, or Alys would not have suggested the tour. The more time that passed until Davenport met the girl, the better.

Despite Davenport's doubts about having a potbank on his property, he asked interested questions about the bottle kiln, which was being carefully packed with green ware, and the willow crates for shipping the fragile pottery to market. Alys hoped that his interest would make him tolerant of the enterprise.

The tour ended in the office, where there was a display of finished products. Alys handed her employer a richly glazed round brown teapot. "This is our most popular item. We can't compete with the large manufacturers, so I decided to make things for people of moderate income—those who like having something nice, but who can't afford the fine china from places like Wedgwood and Spode."

As with everything else, Davenport drank it in, but he didn't comment until they left to ride back to the estate office. "You continue to impress me, Lady Alys. If you hadn't been born a female, you could have succeeded at anything you chose. Strickland is very lucky to have you."

Alys glowed at the compliment. It was good to be considered talented rather than merely eccentric.

Back at the estate office, she settled wearily behind the desk and waited for the next round of questions. To her surprise, her employer asked, "Has the sheep washing been done yet this year?"

She shook her head. "The spring washing is scheduled for day after tomorrow."

An amused gleam came into Davenport's eyes. "Splendid. As a boy, I always wanted to participate in a sheep washing, but I was too small. Time has cured that."

"You really want to wash sheep?" Alys said, startled. It was a messy, time-consuming chore, not the sort of thing anyone did voluntarily.

The gleam deepened. "Would you deny me one of my boyhood ambitions?"

"It's your choice, of course, but an amateur could slow the process down," she said doubtfully. "Besides . . ."

"Yes?" he prompted as her voice trailed off.

"Wrestling sheep in a river is not exactly conducive to dignity."

He gave her a sardonic look. "While I will listen to you on matters agricultural, I'm not interested in your opinions about my dignity or lack thereof."

She flushed, knowing she had stepped over the line permitted for an employee.

The awkward silence was broken by the arrival of Meredith, golden hair gleaming in the late afternoon sun and a look of misleading innocence on her angelic face. "Lady Alys, I wanted to ask you . . ." She stopped, looking at Davenport with a pretty expression of hesitation. "I'm so sorry. I didn't realize you had company."

Alys rolled her eyes, knowing where Merry's playacting was aimed. The girl had probably been watching the estate office all afternoon, waiting for an opportune moment to trip in and meet the new master of Strickland.

Davenport reacted as any normal male would, rising with warm admiration on his long face and a twinkle in his eye. Clearly he realized that Meredith's entrance was no accident, but that didn't prevent him from enjoying the sight of the visitor. Merry was delightful in blue-sprigged white muslin, her golden curls tumbling around her shoulders with just the right touch of modest abandon.

Alys made the introductions. "Mr. Davenport, this is my ward, Miss Meredith Spenser. Merry, I'm sure that you know who this is."

Her acid tone was not lost on Merry, who tossed her guardian a roguish glance before turning to Davenport. "What a pleasant surprise!" she said with a flutter of lashes.

Eyelashes that had been carefully darkened, Alys noted. Blast Meredith for flitting in like a houri! Though most gentlemen could be counted on to see the girl for the innocent she really was, Davenport's reputation was enough to put fear in the heart of any guardian. At times like this Alys regretted taking on the responsibilities of a parent.

While Alys worried, Davenport and Merry were furthering their acquaintance. After a few moments of badinage, Meredith turned to Alys as if struck by a new thought. "Lady Alys, do you think Mr. Davenport might be persuaded to take his potluck with us tonight? Mrs. Haver is roasting a nice joint, more than enough for company."

So that was Merry's main purpose in this little charade! Not just to meet Davenport, but to inveigle him over for dinner.

In the face of Alys's glower, Davenport hesitated. "I'm sorry, Miss Spenser, but your guardian has been in my company all day. It hardly seems fair to inflict me on her this evening as well."

Meredith said, "She won't mind, will you, Alys?" accompanying her statement with a speaking look.

Cornered, Alys said, "We dine *en famille,* Mr. Davenport. A bachelor might find it rather hectic."

Merry turned to him and said coaxingly, "I shall endeavor to keep my younger brothers quiet. Do say you will come."

Unable to refuse again without seeming churlish, he said, "It will be my pleasure, Miss Spenser."

After suitable expressions of delight, Merry took her leave and departed. Davenport resumed his seat and gave Alys a companionable grin. "Have you ever considered buying her a chastity belt?"

"I certainly have!" Alys blurted out without thinking. At Davenport's laughter she said in a doomed attempt at dignity, "That is a most improper thing to say."

"I warned you, no missishness. I may assist you into a sidesaddle, but I have every intention of being my normal vulgar self the rest of the time." His voice turned ironic. "She's a taking little minx, and she looks a good deal less 'minor' than your words had led me to expect."

"She's nineteen, Mr. Davenport, and has seen little of the world." Alys toyed with a Venetian glass paperweight. "Please remember that."

His humor evaporated. "I shall endeavor not to debauch her this evening. If it's any comfort, I find virgins boring."

Alys tensed, wondering if the words were intended as an indirect insult toward her. "Merry is a bright, lively girl, and very sensible except for her flirtatiousness. She was only practicing her wiles on you because she meets so few new people."

"Nonetheless, if you want an experienced rake's advice, find her a husband, and soon," he said dryly.

Alys glanced down at her hands, tensely linked on the desk. He had a talent for touching on sensitive issues. She'd invested considerable thought in the question of a husband for Merry. "I'd like to, but the choices are limited. All the eligible men in the neighborhood are mad for her, but they are either callow lads, or widowers looking for mothers for their children. She deserves better than that." Alys sighed. "Actually, I think she would make quite a splash in London if she could make her come-out there."

"The girl is definitely a diamond of the first water," Davenport agreed, "but does she have the birth and fortune to match her face?"

"That's the rub," Alys admitted. "She'll have a respectable portion, but it's not a great fortune, and her father was a

London merchant. She has no family connections that could introduce her to the *ton*."

"She may be better off doing her husband hunting here. London can be a dangerous place for the innocent." Dismissing the topic of Merry, he asked, "Whatever persuaded you to take charge of three young people? The girl represents one set of problems, and the boys will be just as much trouble in different ways. It would be a heavy burden for anyone, and you aren't even a relative."

It was none of his business, of course, but his question seemed to come from genuine interest rather than idle curiosity. She propped one elbow on the desk and rested her chin on her hand as she considered her reply. "The obvious answer is that there was no one else Mrs. Spenser trusted. She had no children of her own. In fact, she was only their aunt by marriage, no blood relation at all, but she loved them. She wanted to make sure they were properly cared for."

"If that is the obvious answer, what is the unobvious one?"

"They were my students, and I'm very fond of them. I've known William, the youngest, since he was in leading strings." Alys gave a brittle laugh. "And this is the closest I'm likely to come to having children. I would have been a fool to pass up the opportunity." She stopped suddenly, wondering what had made her reveal a deep and painful truth like that.

Tactfully restraining himself from probing more deeply into what was obviously sensitive territory, Davenport said, "I hope they realize how fortunate they are to have you, Miss Weston."

Shaking off her mood, she said with a grin, "Merry might, but the boys look on me in the light of a necessary evil. I'm always nagging them to do their studying, mind their manners, and make at least a token gesture to the proprieties."

At the sight of her wide smile, Davenport sat up and

leaned forward in his chair so he could scrutinize her face. "Lady Alys, you have dimples," he said accusingly.

Caught, Alys blushed. "I'm sorry, I can't help it. I think God made a mistake and gave me someone else's dimples."

Davenport stood, his tall form looming over her desk. "Don't apologize. They're quite delightful. Dimples are called the mark of Venus, you know."

He smiled that lazy, intimate smile, the one designed to make proper ladies forget their virtue. Alys found herself smiling back.

He raised one hand and lightly brushed her cheek, right where a dimple lurked. It was a casual gesture that some women would hate, and others find utterly entrancing. Alys was of the latter persuasion. His touch was warm, and her hypersensitive skin recorded the faint roughness of the whorls on his fingertips. It was as erotic as a kiss, and she felt a reaction clear down to her toes.

Lord only knew what showed on her face, because he dropped his hand and stepped back, his expression growing cool and detached. "If you would prefer not having me for dinner, I can send my regrets to your ward. You really should not have your employer forced on you after normal work hours."

She swallowed hard. "If you can bear it, it would be better if you came tonight. I'm afraid of what Merry might do to get you there tomorrow."

"If you're sure you don't object, I'll be over at half past six." He gave her a wry smile. "I'm sure the conversation at your house will be more enlivening than at mine."

He nodded and left the office, his head nearly brushing the lintel of the door. With a dazed mixture of alarm and amusement, Alys realized that it was not Meredith's virtue she should be worried about. It was her own.

* * *

After clearing her correspondence, Alys had just enough time to return home, bathe, change for dinner, and stop by Meredith's chamber for a serious discussion.

Merry sat at her dressing table trying a new hairstyle. She swiveled on her stool and gave her guardian a mischievous smile. "That worked very well, didn't it? The boys will be delighted to meet Mr. Davenport."

Alys sat down on the bed with an inward sigh. Clearly she had her work cut out for her. "Merry, I'm very upset about your forward behavior today. Not only did it pass the line of what is pleasing, it was potentially dangerous."

Merry laughed and pulled a handful of blond hair to the crown of her head. She turned back to the mirror and studied the effect. "How could it be dangerous?"

"Meredith, stop fussing with your hair and look at me. This is serious." When she used that tone, Alys was always obeyed. Her ward obligingly turned and faced her.

"Reginald Davenport is very different from your shy young local admirers," Alys said warningly. "If you issue a blatant invitation, he may accept it."

"We were only flirting," Merry said, her wide blue eyes guileless. "He flirts very nicely, so it seemed a good chance to practice. He's hardly likely to ravish me, is he?"

Snapping with exasperation, Alys said, "Being ravished is not the only danger. Davenport's dealings with women are notorious—even flirting with him could damage your reputation. Falling victim to his charm could damage you a good deal more. Falling in love with him would be a guarantee of breaking your heart. Can I spell it out any more plainly than that?"

Merry gave a peal of laughter. "Good heavens, Alys, I'm hardly likely to fall in love with a man old enough to be my father. He's not even good-looking."

Alys blinked with surprise. Surely Meredith could not be

unaffected by Davenport's mesmerizing aura of virility? She
tried to remember what had attracted her when she was
Merry's age, and decided that even at nineteen she would
not have been indifferent to a man like Reggie Davenport.
Of course, she would have known better than to succumb to
that kind of low animal appeal. Merry was just showing
her common sense by refusing to find him attractive. Pray
God she continued as wise.

Fixing her charge with a no-nonsense gaze, Alys said,
"Will you take my word that it is better to be careful where
Davenport is concerned? I've seen a good deal more of the
world than you, and I promise you, the man is trouble."

Merry stood and crossed to give her guardian a quick, affectionate hug. "Poor Lady Alys. We do lead you a miserable life, don't we? If it isn't William sneaking into the
stables, it's Peter trying to learn to drive to an inch, or hordes
of my silly suitors underfoot. You must be sorry you ever
took us on."

Her tone had the teasing confidence of someone who
knew she was wanted, and Alys found her lips curving
into a smile of response. "I'll admit that with the three of
you, life is sometimes too full. But without you, it would be
very empty."

Meredith gave a wise, enchanting smile that made her
seem more the parent than the child. "I promise I won't do
anything rash that will ruin me forever, but I don't think I
will be able to resist the temptation to flirt. Though Mr. Davenport is not at all the sort of man I could fall in love with,
I did think he was rather sweet."

Fascinated, Alys tried to imagine how Davenport would
react to the knowledge that a young diamond of the first
water considered him "rather sweet." Suppressing a smile,
she asked, "What is the sort of man you could fall in love
with? We've never really discussed that."

Merry frowned at her reflection. "I'm not absolutely sure

because I haven't met him yet, but I would want him to be a man of grace and charm. Reasonably intelligent, but not a great scholar or wit, or he would find me sadly frivolous." She began deftly pinning her ringlets into place. "Naturally, I must find his appearance pleasing, but it will be better if he isn't staggeringly handsome. I don't want a man who is terribly vain."

Alys leaned against one of the bedposts and folded her arms in a most unladylike fashion. "Need the gentleman be rich and titled?"

"Well, at least comfortably well-off—I don't think I would find poverty very amusing." She secured the last curl with a well-placed hairpin. "A title might be nice, but it's hardly essential." She turned to face her guardian, her heavenly blue eyes lit with humor. "If I ever did meet a nobleman, he would surely feel that he was conferring an enormous favor by marrying a girl of no great fortune or birth. I would prefer the gentleman to be so smitten that he thinks I am doing *him* a favor by accepting."

"You're a cold-blooded wench," Alys said with some awe. She wasn't sure if her ward was brilliantly clear-sighted, or merely endowed with more than her share of feminine wiles. Regrettably, wiles had been left out of Alys's makeup. Perhaps her unwanted dimples were what she had been given instead "I gather that you want this future husband to keep you on a pedestal?"

"I wouldn't mind a low one." Merry looked down at her hands, flexing the fingers as if inspecting her carefully groomed nails. "When I find the right man, I'll make sure he doesn't regret his choice." In a voice that for once was entirely serious, she added softly, "I do intend to be a very good wife, you know."

Alys gave a nod of sudden understanding. What her ward really yearned for was security and comfort. Having lost both parents and her adoptive mother by the time she was fifteen, Merry's ambitions were modest, practical ones rather than dreams of mad passion or social grandeur. Surely such a sensible young lady was unlikely to fall victim to the fleeting pleasures of a rake's casual, lethal charm.

Relieved by the insight, Alys stood. "Our guest should arrive soon. I presume you will wait here so you can make a grand entrance?"

"But of course." Merry laughed, gravity vanquished. "A new man in the neighborhood is an opportunity not to be wasted, even if he is rather stricken in years."

Even though she knew Meredith was teasing, Alys shook her head in disbelief as she went down to the drawing room to await her guest. *Stricken in years!* Davenport looked like he could outride, outfight, and outwench any man in Dorsetshire.

She hoped he didn't feel compelled to prove it.

Chapter 7

Reggie raised his hand to the knocker of Rose Hall, the steward's residence, then hesitated. He had accepted the dinner invitation because he thought that anything would be better than another evening alone in the big house, but now he wasn't so sure. Two young boys, an aspiring femme fatale, and a magnificent Amazon who despised him were odd company for a man who usually socialized with hard-drinking sportsmen like himself.

Well, too late to retreat now. He grasped the knocker and rapped firmly.

The little housemaid that answered had a face that Reggie was beginning to recognize as typical Herald physiognomy. After she bobbed a quick curtsy, she wordlessly led him to the drawing room. It was not a large house, having no more than four or five bedrooms, but it was comfortable and well-maintained. Reggie had regularly visited the kitchen as a child. His father's steward had a cook gifted at making tarts, and Reggie had ingratiated himself in the manner of all small boys.

Miss Weston was waiting in the drawing room. She rose at his arrival. Her height and natural dignity made her look like a queen, even in her extremely conservative dark brown dress. Reggie spent a moment wondering how she would look in Gypsy red, with her hair tumbling around her shoulders rather than in a no-nonsense coronet. As he bowed, he decided that she would be quite splendid.

Smiling, she said, "I thought you might like a few minutes of peace before the children join us. Would you like a sherry?"

Sherry was hardly his favorite drink, but since it was better than nothing, he accepted. As she poured two glasses, Reggie felt an insistent pressure on his shin. He looked down to see a very large, very shaggy cat twining suggestively around his ankles. With a small sound of distaste, he stepped back. The cat followed, apparently determined to be his best friend.

His hostess turned and saw his predicament. "Sorry. I thought Attila was safely out of the way. He must have been lurking under the sofa." She handed Reggie a drink, then bent to scoop up her pet "I gather that you don't like cats?"

Even for a woman as tall as Alys Weston, the beast was a very substantial armful, a patchwork of striped and white fur with great curving whiskers that framed an expression of supreme disdain. "Not much," Reggie admitted. "They're sneaky, unreliable, and selfish."

"That's true," Alys said gravely, "and they have many other fine qualities as well."

For a moment he wasn't sure he had heard correctly. Nothing earlier in the day had led him to believe that his steward numbered a sense of humor among her formidable virtues. But a suspicion of dimple showed in her right cheek; he had noticed earlier that it came out before the left one. "Perhaps I don't like cats because they're too much like me," he said with a grin.

Laughing, she took the cat to the door and dumped him, protesting, on the other side. "Go down to the kitchen, Attila. There must be something there to interest you." Closing the door before her pet could whisk back in, she turned to her guest. "So you're sneaky, unreliable, and selfish?"

"Oh, indubitably," he said, sipping at his sherry. "And I have many other fine qualities as well."

This time both dimples showed as she sat gracefully in one of the brocade-covered chairs. "What are your other fine qualities?" Then she paused, a stricken expression on her face. "I'm sorry, I shouldn't have asked that."

"Because it's too personal a question, or because you're afraid of what I might consider a fine quality?" Reggie asked as he took a seat opposite his steward.

"The latter reason, of course," she said sweetly, then looked even more stricken at her unruly tongue.

Taking pity on her embarrassment, Reggie said, "Since you are not on duty, nothing you say can be held against you. Although I must say, I prefer your insults to having you frown me down."

"Lord," she said with a guilty start. "Is that what I was doing all day?"

"Yes," he replied succinctly.

"It's because of my eyebrows, you know," she said earnestly. "Even when I'm in a good mood, people often think I'm about to bite them."

"And when you're in a bad mood?"

"Oh, then they fly in all directions."

"I suppose that looking fearsome is a useful trait, given the work you do," he said thoughtfully. "It can't have been easy to get the Strickland tenants and workers to accept your authority."

"There have been problems," Alys admitted. "It is not a simple matter where one victory wins the war. They would take orders more easily if I owned the estate, but they don't quite approve of a female steward. Still, after four years the tenants and I understand each other tolerably well."

"I can understand their feelings. I don't approve of you

myself." As she bridled, he raised one hand. "Nothing personal, but it's a confounded nuisance that the 'A' in A. E. Weston doesn't stand for Albert or Angus." He studied her gravely. "If you value your reputation, you would be wise to look for another position."

Alys froze, her sherry glass poised in midair halfway to her mouth. Then she lowered the glass, her face pale. "Are you discharging me?"

"No," he said, feeling as guilty as if he'd struck her physically. "Just giving you some good advice."

Relaxing fractionally, she said in a freezing tone, "In that case, just as you prefer to worry about your own dignity, leave me to worry about my reputation."

"As long as you work for me, your reputation will be affected by mine, no matter how blameless your behavior," he said bluntly. "When people hear that I have a female steward, they will chuckle knowingly and assume you're my mistress, especially when it's discovered that you are young and attractive."

Alys's face colored with embarrassment, and her gaze dropped. He wondered whether she was upset by the possibility that she might be taken for his mistress, or by his compliment. The latter, he suspected. Any suggestion that she was attractive seemed to throw her off balance.

She raised her head, her expression set. "I am no green girl who must always be above the merest hint of suspicion, and I am well-known in the neighborhood. It's unlikely the local people will assume I have suddenly become lost to all propriety."

"You might not be concerned about your reputation, but I am about mine," he retorted. "Believe it or not, I have every intention of behaving circumspectly. Strickland is my home now. It always has been, really." He studied his nearly empty glass as if fascinated by the remaining sherry. "I have no desire to offend everyone in Dorsetshire."

"So you'll save your outrageousness for London?"

"Perhaps." He shrugged. "Or perhaps I will give it up entirely. Being outrageous all the time is a confounded amount of work."

Reggie's tone was light, but as he spoke he realized that his vague thoughts of the last few days had crystallized into a decision. It was time to put down the roots he had always yearned for, to stop filling his idle hours with gambling and drinking and wenching. In short, it was time to grow up—before it was too late.

He looked up to see that his steward was scrutinizing him closely, as if she sensed that his words were not casual and wondered what they implied for her. Both the brown and the gray-green eyes were bright and individually attractive. Though the contrast between them was startling, it exactly suited her. As a bonus, she had the longest eyelashes he had ever seen. Whoever had nicknamed her Lady Alys was perceptive. Miss Weston was not at all like the common run of females.

While honor had compelled him to warn her off, he was glad that she showed no desire to leave Strickland. It was true that her sex was a complication, but he admired her competence and integrity, and enjoyed her occasional flashes of barbed wit.

Besides, she was the best-looking steward he had ever seen.

She broke the lengthening silence, saying thoughtfully, "I suppose that outrageousness is boring once it has been mastered. Trying to be respectable should present all kinds of interesting new challenges."

"It will certainly have the charm of novelty." His mouth quirked into a half smile. "It does seem a pity to deprive high-sticklers of the pleasure of condemning me, but there are always new young rascals coming along to create scandal-broth."

She tilted her head to one side consideringly. "You mean that you became a rake as a sort of public service?"

"Exactly so. Virtue needs vice for contrast." He smiled wickedly, wondering if he could ruffle her feathers. She was very attractive when she forgot her dignity. "Good and evil are completely dependent on each other. Even God Himself needs Lucifer more than he needs his bands of well-behaved angels who never put one wing astray."

She gazed wide-eyed into space, her expression arrested rather than shocked. "I'm not sure whether that is heresy or philosophy."

"What's the difference? Heresy is just philosophy that the establishment doesn't approve of," he said provocatively, thinking that Miss Weston had a much more flexible mind than his first impression of her had led him to expect.

Before the theological waters could grow any murkier, the door opened and Meredith floated into the room. Reggie rose at her entrance. The girl really was very lovely, not least because of the impression she gave of not taking herself and her beauty too seriously. He bowed over her hand, wondering what Julian Markham would think of her. He'd have to invite his young friend down for a visit.

Lady Alys gave Meredith a glass of sherry and refilled Reggie's, and they exchanged commonplaces for a few minutes until the two Spenser boys entered, dressed in company best and bursting with curiosity. Reggie rose to meet them. The degree of excitement on their well-scrubbed faces was a reminder of how quiet life in the country was, and how seldom new people arrived to provide diversion. If he really intended to make his primary residence at Strickland, it would be an enormous change from the ceaseless variety of London. But then, it had been a long time since mere variety had afforded much pleasure.

Peter was an attractive stripling, his brown hair a contrast to his blond siblings. The height and starch of his shirt points and the complicated folds of his cravat showed aspirations to dandyism, but humor and intelligence showed in his blue-gray eyes. Shaking Reggie's hand, he said politely, "It's a pleasure to meet you, Mr. Davenport. I've heard a great deal about you."

While Reggie wondered what that meant, William, seven and effervescent, skipped the preliminaries to say enthusiastically, "That stallion of yours is a prime 'un, sir."

"Bucephalus is the finest horse I've ever had," Reggie agreed. "He has speed, style, and endless stamina." He shook William's small hand, which was not quite as well scrubbed as the round face. "He has a chancy disposition, though. Keep your distance unless I'm around. He broke the arm of one admirer who got too close, and he won't allow anyone but me ride him."

If he had been better versed in the ways of small boys, Reggie would have been suspicious of the gleam in William's eye. However, the little housemaid entered to announce that dinner was served and the exchange slipped his mind as the group adjourned to the dining room.

While the dinner party was quite unlike any other Reggie had ever attended, it was not without amusement. Conversation was general around the table with everyone, even young William, accorded the courtesy of a hearing. Topics included local events, literature, and the boys' progress in their lessons. Despite Lady Alys's warning that a family meal might prove to be a strain for a bachelor, the young Spensers were excellent dinner companions.

Reggie applied himself to the simple but well-cooked meal and observed the family dynamics. And it was a family, even though the relationship was not one of blood. Alys was the center around which the three young people circled, gently and humorously guiding the conversation, monitoring William's table manners, listening with total attention when one of her wards spoke. The Spensers were indeed very lucky, and Reggie's respect for his steward increased again.

The meal had progressed to the sweet course when Peter overcame his initial diffidence enough to ask Reggie, "Is it really true that you once wagered a thousand guineas that you could ride a hundred and sixty miles in fifteen hours, and shoot forty brace of grouse at the midpoint of the trip?"

Considerably startled, Reggie said, "Good Lord, has that story made its way this far south? That happened in Scotland, years ago."

"You mean, you actually did that?" Peter said, awed delight on his face.

"One of my odder wagers, but not quite as foolish as it sounds," Reggie admitted. "The actual terms of the bet allowed twenty-four hours, which gave me some leeway in case the grouse were elusive."

Not content with this episode, Peter said eagerly, "And you won a midnight coach race to Brighton?"

"It was midnight when we left. I reached Brighton about four in the morning," Reggie said, bemused.

There was worse to come. His eyes round with incipient hero-worship, Peter said, "Did you really back your mistress in a race against the champion jockey, and win?"

His eyes flicking to the other members of the party, Reggie said dampeningly, "This is not the time or place to discuss my misspent youth."

Peter was mildly chastened by the reproof, but ecstatic at Reggie's implication that they were two men together, protecting the tender sensibilities of the women and children. Alys raised her brows slightly, amusement in her eyes. Remembering how fragile a young man's pride was, Reggie frowned at her, forbidding any comments.

With a suggestion of smile, she rose and suggested that it was time for William to retire to the nursery. After a brief battle of wills, which she won, William withdrew and the older members of the party adjourned to the drawing room. Reggie thought wistfully of the joys of after-dinner port, but staying at the table to drink alone didn't seem very mannerly.

Though he had intended to return home soon after dining, he found himself lingering. It had been a very long time since he had observed the interplay of a happy family, and he found that he enjoyed it. With her combination of beauty, wit, and blithe good nature, Meredith would be a sensation in London. A pity her birth was so mundane. If she were properly launched, she would have every eligible man in London at her feet.

Peter must be another source of concern for his guardian. He was on the verge of adulthood, unsure of himself, and ripe for hero worship. Clearly he was fascinated with their guest's checkered past, and asked eagerly about several episodes Reggie himself had half forgotten. Heaven only knew where the boy got his information.

The admiring inquisition was damned uncomfortable, but Reggie, whose ability to wither pretensions was legendary, found himself unwilling to snub the boy. He remembered too clearly what it was like to be fatherless.

And for the first time in many years, he wondered what it would be like to have children of his own.

Merry was just finishing a sonata on the pianoforte when the housemaid entered the drawing room with a tall, full-bodied clerical gentleman at her heels. Alys stifled an oath. She should have realized that Junius Harper might pay a call; he was at Rose Hall almost as many evenings as at the vicarage. Junius was a very worthy man, high-minded and well-educated, with a genuine interest in the welfare of his parishioners. He had been an invaluable ally to Alys in most of her reformist projects.

He was also, alas, sometimes a self-righteous prig.

Rising, Alys said, "Good evening, Junius. I imagine you have not yet met Reginald Davenport, the new owner of Strickland. Mr. Davenport, allow me to present the Reverend Junius Harper. He has been rector of All Souls for almost four years now."

Though still in his early thirties, the vicar moved with a studied dignity that made him appear older than his years, but which would suit him very well if he ever became a bishop. After sketching a bow to Alys and Meredith and nodding at Peter, he turned to the newcomer. Davenport had risen from his chair and was offering his hand.

Refusing to take it, Junius said in accents of deep foreboding, "Surely, you are not *the* Reginald Davenport?"

"I suppose so. I don't know of any others," Alys's employer said pleasantly, his hand still out.

A look of revulsion on his moonlike face, the vicar said in freezing accents, "I have heard of you, sir, and Strickland has no use for such as you."

Davenport dropped his hand, his expression hardening. Gone was the quiet, amiable gentleman who had watched the young Spensers with an indulgent eye. His face fell into the practiced lines of a sneer and his weight shifted, so that he was lightly poised on the balls of his feet in a fighter's stance. "Are you proposing to ban me from my own property?"

"Would that I could!" Junius drew in his breath, his hazel eyes glittering as his black-clad form expanded like a pouter pigeon. "Unfortunately, English law goes nowhere near far enough to the regulation of morals. However, I can say with confidence that the right-thinking people of Dorset will not tolerate your duels, raking, and debauchery. There is no place for you here, sir—you will be an outcast. Return to London at once and leave the good souls of Strickland to Miss Weston and myself."

"Leave me out of this, Junius," Alys said with alarm,

loath to have her new employer think she shared the vicar's intolerant views.

Davenport said with a cynical gleam in his light blue eyes, "If you think the good souls of the neighborhood will cut a man who has property, money, and influence, you know precious little of the world, Mr. Harper."

The vicar's eyes narrowed into angry slits. "When the full story of your licentious ways is known, even money and property will not suffice to buy your way into favor."

"You are well-informed about my licentious ways," Davenport drawled. "You must spend a good deal of time reading the scandal sheets. Hardly the most elevating material for a man of God."

The vicar stiffened at the deliberate provocation in Davenport's tone as Alys winced, wondering if the two men would come to blows in her drawing room. When Junius spoke again, there was a hint of snarl in his mellifluous voice. "I have influential relatives, sir, among the highest levels of society. Your name is a byword among them for every kind of low behavior. Your mistresses, your gambling . . ."

Davenport interrupted, saying in shocked accents, "You forget yourself, Vicar. Remember, there are ladies present."

Indeed, Meredith and Peter were watching in fascination from their respective seats. While Junius flushed at having been caught in unseemly behavior, Alys glanced at her wards and said in a voice that brooked no opposition, "Both of you out *now*."

Her wards departed reluctantly, probably to paste their ears against the door. Alys shrugged philosophically, feeling that she had done her duty. She could hardly leave her guests, for there was less likelihood of violence if she was present.

Besides, she didn't want to miss the end of the confrontation. Seeing a saint and a sinner square off together had all the morbid fascination of a carriage wreck.

Raising her voice, she said, "Can I offer you gentlemen a glass of port?"

Without waiting for a reply, she went and poured three generous glasses, thrusting two into the hands of the combatants. She briefly considered stepping between the two men, but decided that it would be the better part of valor to let them settle matters on their own. She might end up like a bone between two mongrels if she interfered. Subsiding into a chair, she took a rueful swig from her goblet.

Davenport casually sipped his port. He seemed to be getting more relaxed as his opponent became more agitated. "Perhaps you should list the varieties of low behavior for me, in case I have missed any, Mr. Harper," he said in a conversational tone. "I should hate to ruin my record for vice through ignorance or lack of imagination."

Furious, Junius spat out, "You mock me, but God will not be mocked. Do not the faces of the three men you have killed in duels haunt your dreams?"

Davenport cocked his head to one side thoughtfully. "Surely it is more than three. Let me think a moment . . ." He pondered, then said with an air of discovery, "Ah, you must not have heard about the one in Paris last year. You really must try harder to keep up, Mr. Harper. We rakes don't rest on our laurels, you know. Wickedness requires constant effort."

Alys almost choked with suppressed laughter. Her employer was the picture of calm reason, while the self-appointed guardian of public morality appeared on the verge of an apoplexy.

His teeth audibly grinding, Junius Harper said, "Would that you had been prosecuted for dueling as you deserve!"

"When even Cabinet ministers duel, it's hard to get a conviction," Davenport pointed out. "Particularly since I've never actually killed anyone who didn't deserve it."

Unable to find a suitable riposte, the vicar abandoned

dueling for another topic. "They say that you own a brothel in London."

Arching his dark brows in surprise, Davenport said, "You are well-informed, Vicar. However, it's only a partial ownership. I'm a"—he grinned maliciously—"sleeping partner, you might say."

Junius gasped at the double entendre, then said furiously, "Don't think you can kidnap our innocent country girls to supply the vile needs of your whorehouse, or ravish them so they must flee their homes from shame."

"You certainly have a lurid opinion of me." Davenport drank half of his port off. His voice was still casual, but his grip on the stem of his goblet showed increasing tension. "I don't recall ever ravishing anyone, though. I'm sure I'd remember, unless I was too drunk, and then I'd be incapable of ravishing."

The vicar barked, "You'll burn in hell, Davenport, for eternity. Does that mean nothing to you?"

"I've always had my doubts about heaven and hell," Davenport said genially. "Still, if they exist, I'll be better off in the fire, since all my friends will be there. It might even be a pleasant change after a lifetime of damp English weather."

"Bah, you are beneath contempt!" Junius shook with rage. "I despise you and your whoring, your lying, cheating ways. I—"

The rest of the diatribe was lost forever. Davenport's right hand shot out and wrapped around Junius's neck, the strong fingers tight against the nape and his thumb pressing the windpipe with carefully calculated pressure.

As the vicar gasped for breath, too shocked to fight back, Davenport's gaze locked with his opponent's, his eyes as cold and hard as his sharply enunciated words. "I do not cheat. Neither do I lie. So far, I have never killed a vicar in my blood-drenched career, but if you persist in slandering me, I will be tempted to make an exception. Do I make myself clear?"

Junius's horrified reaction must have been satisfactory, because Davenport released him, disgust on his face. After draining off the last of his port, he turned to Alys and said courteously, as if he hadn't just been involved in a near-brawl, "It is time I took my leave. Thank you for a most pleasant evening. If it's not inconvenient, I would like to meet you in your office at nine in the morning."

At her nod he set his empty goblet down and bowed twice, first with a distinctly mocking air to the vicar, and then more deeply to Alys. As he straightened up, his light eyes caught hers for a moment, but she couldn't interpret his remote expression. Would his anger with Junius carry over to her? She hoped not.

Davenport turned on his heel and left, followed by the vicar's stupefied gaze. Ever practical, Alys rose and poured another pair of drinks, this time of brandy. She took one to her guest and urged him into a chair.

A sip of brandy brought healthier color to Junius's face. He raised his eyes to his hostess. "The audacity of the man . . . ! That he should speak so to a man of God, that he actually threatened physical violence . . ." He shook his head and drank more brandy.

Alys decided that her guest would survive the experience and chose a nearby chair for herself. "Well, you did provoke him, Junius," she said candidly. "He behaved in a perfectly gentlemanlike fashion until you started insulting him."

"Bah, that rakehell is no gentleman! That you should permit such a man under the same roof as Miss Spenser . . ." He bit off his words, then continued more temperately, "For-give me, I shouldn't blame you. It is not to be expected that a respectable, godly woman would be aware of his evil repu-tation."

"I'm no cloistered innocent, Junius," she said crisply. "I

have a fair idea of what rumor says about Mr. Davenport.
However, he's my employer, and I must work with him.
More than that"—inspiration struck and a pious note
entered her voice—"remember that the Bible says 'Judge
not, lest ye be judged' and 'Who among us is qualified to
cast the first stone?' I certainly am not."

Even though she was mixing her quotes, the words were
effective. The vicar paused; his face stricken, before he finally said in a halting voice, "How noble is your spirit,
Alys, how great your charity. Once more you are right, and
I am most grievously wrong. We are all sinners in the eyes
of the Lord."

Junius brooded for a moment on his sins, but his humil-
ity ebbed rapidly. "Even the Lord would admit that some are
greater sinners than others, and Davenport must be one of
the worst."

"Perhaps he intends to reform his way of life," Alys said
seriously. "If so, it is our duty as Christians to encourage him."

A snort of disbelief greeted her statement, and Junius
stared dourly into his brandy. If William had behaved that
way, Alys would have reprimanded him for sulking, but she
could hardly scold the vicar.

She reminded herself how helpful he had been in organ-
izing the school, how he had used the church poor money
for those who truly needed it rather than lining his own
pockets, and the numerous other ways he had helped make
Strickland the thriving community it was. When the vicar
had first come to All Souls, he had been shocked to learn
that a woman was the most important person in his new
parish, and it was to his credit that he had overcome his initial disapproval and accepted her as a near-equal.

Despite his occasional self-righteousness, they had
always worked well together. So well, in fact, that he had
sometimes hinted at the possibility of a closer partnership.
Alys always ignored the hints. Quite apart from the fact

that she could not imagine a lifetime spent with a man of blameless rectitude, she knew that Junius had a very inaccurate picture of her true character, and that he would not approve of the real Alys.

Besides, while Junius's lofty mind said that she would be a suitable God-fearing partner for a man of the cloth, it was young, golden, frivolous Meredith that his eyes followed hungrily when he called at Rose Hall. Like many a man before him, the vicar's higher and lower selves were not in agreement. Alys had once given him a copy of the writings of St. Augustine for Christmas, but he hadn't seen the joke.

Junius broke the lengthening silence to say in a hard voice, "One of the men he killed in a duel was the husband of a woman who had run away to Davenport. He killed the man, then refused to marry his mistress, even though she was pregnant."

Alys inhaled, shocked in spite of herself. "She was carrying his child, he shot her husband, and he wouldn't marry her?" she repeated in disbelief.

The vicar nodded, pleased to have pierced Alys's tolerance. "That is an example of the 'gentleman' you are defending. The woman involved was ruined, of course. Davenport was cut in Polite Society, but suffered no real retribution for his wickedness."

Alys had long since learned that every story had at least two sides, but it was hard to imagine anything that would justify her employer's callousness in this case. Wondering why it was so important to her to think well of him, she said mildly, "I think Mr. Davenport is here to stay, Junius. Wouldn't it be better to hope for the best about him, rather than to assume the worst?"

He nodded glumly. "Once more, you are wise. We owe it to the good souls of the parish to do what we can to ameliorate that libertine's influence."

Intent on conflict rather than reconciliation, he missed

the sense of her words. She also wished irritably that Junius would stop talking about "good souls," since the individuals in question were very much alive, opinionated, and capable of drawing their own conclusions. A vicar might have a flock, but that didn't make the inhabitants of Strickland sheep. However, it seemed a poor moment to take him to task, so Alys bent her efforts to mollifying his hurt dignity.

Her private hope was that her new employer wouldn't reform too much. No matter how disgraceful his past, she rather liked him the way he was. And while his behavior to the vicar had been thoroughly reprehensible, there was no denying that it was also very, very amusing. If Alys was as good a person as Junius thought, she would have found no humor in the confrontation.

Her guest took his leave a few minutes later. After securing the house and checking that Peter and Meredith had retired to their rooms, Alys decided to make an early night of it herself. Spring was her busiest time of the year, and tomorrow the laborers would begin setting potatoes, one of the estate's most important crops.

But sleep eluded her as she lay alone in her wide bed, a shaft of moonlight in her eyes and her blankets twisted from restless tossing. It was one of the great ironies of Alys Weston's life that she, who was too tall and alarming to attract any serious suitors, adored men. She liked talking to them, liked seeing how their minds and personalities differed from women's. She enjoyed watching them and took great, if surreptitious, pleasure in the powerful male bodies of the laborers who worked for her.

Sometimes, like now, her rest was troubled by hot, fierce dreams of what it would be like to lie in a man's arms, to give herself as freely as the wildest creature in the forest. If Junius Harper could see her secret yearnings, he would be shocked to the core that a respectable female could be so shameless.

But she was not really respectable, though she pretended to be. As foolish and undignified as lust was, she was unable to deny its existence in her. If she had been born with half of Meredith's beauty, she might have become a great wanton.

No, not a wanton. With a romanticism even more embarrassing than her inappropriate desires, her deepest, most carefully hidden wish was to have one true love, a man who would adore and cherish only her. In return, she would give heart, mind, soul, and body. Oh, yes, most definitely her body.

It was humiliating to admit that she was as foolish as any schoolroom girl who read the kind of novels Junius deplored, but Alys refused to be less than honest with herself. Had she not been such a hopeless romantic, Randolph's casual rejection would not have been so devastating. She would never have been so hurt that she could voluntarily turn her back on her heritage.

But she *had* been romantic and vulnerable, and so she had run away from everything she had ever known. For a dozen years she had buried her passions behind a facade of rigid propriety. It was bad enough to be a wanton at heart, but she'd be damned if she would let herself appear ludicrous as well. She had no doubt that most people would find it deliciously amusing that a great horse like her pined for male attention as much as any fashionable beauty.

She reminded herself that it was only natural that her fantasies currently revolved around Reginald Davenport. On a purely animal level, he was the most attractive man she had ever met, his lean, powerful body radiating sexual authority. His dark coloring gave him a faintly exotic air, like a gypsy or a pirate, and she was fascinated by his light blue eyes, whose expression could range from warm teasing to icy mockery.

Blast it, she must stop thinking this way! Disgusted with herself, Alys tried to banish Davenport's too-vivid image. As she became more accustomed to his intense masculinity, her reaction would surely moderate. She hoped so, because even fantasizing about him held an element of danger. She might start to feel that she and her new employer shared some kindred feeling, but in truth he was a stranger, a man who had killed other men, one who was dissolute and unpredictable. She should be grateful that to Davenport she was merely an employee, scarcely more than a servant. He hardly seemed aware that she was a woman.

The thought was depressing rather than soothing.

She rolled onto her stomach, feeling the faint roughness of the sheets against her bare legs as her nightgown twisted up around her thighs. In a burst of frustration she balled one hand into a fist and pounded her pillow. It wasn't fair. *It bloody wasn't fair!* She wanted to shout her anger to the heavens, yet she was not even sure what she cursed.

After half a dozen blows, her anger ebbed away, leaving her depressed and resigned. She was luckier than most people. Having walked away from position and fortune, she had now achieved comfort and the satisfaction of work well done. She had the respect of those close to her, and the love of the three young people she had taken in. Indeed, they gave her much more than she gave them. Given all her blessings, it was not seemly to curse the fact that the Creator had deemed her unworthy of a mate.

With a sigh, Alys rolled onto her side and wrapped her arms tight around a pillow, as if it could ease the empty ache inside of her. The pillow was a poor substitute for a hard male body, but it was the best she would ever have.

Chapter 8

Reggie was in a vile humor when he left Rose Hall. Considering the pleasure he had always taken in setting people's backs up, it was surprising how irritated he was by what had happened. For all his wicked reputation, he himself would never have created an embarrassing scene on a social occasion, in front of women and young people. It took a respectable person like Junius Harper to behave so badly.

His mood was not improved when the only drink he could find in the Strickland liquor cabinet was a bottle of sherry. He was not partial to sherry. Worse, the quantity was nowhere near enough to drown the effects of the vicar. Swearing, he made a mental note to ask Mrs. Herald about the large order for wine and spirits he'd given her.

It didn't take long to finish the bottle. He considered going out to a tavern, but the hour was late and country watering holes wouldn't keep London hours. Much as he wanted a decent drink, he didn't fancy the picture of himself storming around rural Dorset looking for one.

By three in the morning, as he tossed sleepless and still angry, he was wishing he had forsaken dignity and sought out a tavern. The house seemed enormous in its emptiness, the creaks of floorboards and windows echoing through the hollow rooms and halls. Mac Cooper should arrive tomorrow, thank God. Other servants would also move in over the next few days. Surely that would make a difference.

His temper didn't improve until the next morning, when he met his steward in her office. He found her standing in front of her desk, regarding a list of tasks with a small, distracted frown. She wore a pair of well-fitted buff pantaloons, and the sight of her glorious legs cheered him immensely. As a pleasant bonus, this morning her shining hair fell down her back in a single thick braid.

After a brief exchange of greetings, he said, "Sorry to keep you from your work, but this will only take a few minutes."

She perched on the front edge of her desk and pulled the braid over her shoulder, toying with the end. Not meeting his eyes, she said, "I'm sorry about what happened last night. Mr. Harper is a very worthy and honorable man, but . . ." Her voice trailed off as she searched for the right word.

"But he's a pompous ass?" Reggie suggested.

Her mismatched eyes gleamed with amusement before she said repressively, "I was going to say that his high ideals and blameless conduct lead him to be somewhat less than tolerant."

"Tactfully put, my dear." The endearment slipped out without his conscious thought. Wondering what it would take to persuade the dimples to appear, he continued, "Is his blameless conduct a result of his high ideals, or the fact that he has never been tempted?"

This time a smile escaped her. Repressing it swiftly, she lifted her head and tossed the braid back over her shoulder. "Junius is not entirely free of temptation. When Meredith is around, he gets a . . . a hungry expression. But I think most normal human vices don't interest him."

"Sounds like a dashed dull dog to me." Reggie ambled over to the bookcase and pulled out a copy of *Every Man His Own Farrier*, the horseman's bible, and idly leafed through it.

"He is, rather," she admitted in a burst of candor, "but he has done a great deal of good in the parish. He takes his clerical responsibilities far more seriously than many men in his position."

"Naturally that responsibility includes condemning the ungodly, of which I am a preeminent example." He shelved his book, then turned and leaned his powerful shoulders against the bookcase, his voice wry.

Alys gave him a long, level look. "From what I've seen, the wickedest thing about you is your sense of humor, which is quite reprehensible."

He chuckled. "I won't deny it. Officious idiots certainly bring out the worst in me, and your Mr. Harper is a superb example of the breed." With an edge of malicious satisfaction he added, "I wonder if he has yet realized that I now control the living of All Souls. Politeness on his part would have been a good deal more politic."

Her eyes widened. "Heavens, I never thought of that. I don't suppose that Junius has, either. He received the benefice because his grandfather had some connection with the late Lord Wargrave." Uneasily she added, "Will you dismiss him?"

Her employer's smile became downright devilish. "There's an old adage along the lines that forgiveness is the ultimate revenge, and indifference the ultimate insult. Ignoring Harper will provoke him far more than ousting him from the living. He seems like the sort who would thrive on martyrdom."

Alys stared at him for a moment, not quite believing

what she heard, then gave way to the laughter she had been trying to suppress ever since Davenport had come in. She finally regained enough sobriety to gasp, "You are the most impossible man! And quite right. His influential relations would soon find him another living, and it would afford Junius no end of satisfaction to be persecuted for his righteousness."

She stopped guiltily. "I shouldn't have said either of those things. I'm sorry."

"Never apologize for telling the truth, my dear. I *am* impossible," he said with a sardonic glint. He crossed to a chair and sat down in front of the desk, stretching out his legs and crossing one beautiful boot over the other in a negligent manner that would make a valet shudder.

Alys watched him, momentarily mesmerized by the fluent, athletic grace of his movements. Her face heated at a sudden memory of her fantasies of the night before. Devoutly hoping that Davenport was not as good at reading her as he seemed to be at understanding other people, she circled the desk to sit in her own chair. "I don't think stewards are usually addressed as 'my dear.'"

"But Miss Weston is too formal, and Lady Alys is downright intimidating," he said, raising his dark brows in mock question. "What should I call you?"

"Well, not 'my dear.' That will give rise to exactly the kind of gossip you said you wanted to avoid. I suppose Alys would be all right."

"How about Allie?" he suggested.

"Short for Alys? That would be fine."

He grinned. "Actually, I was thinking of it as short for alley cat. You scratch like one."

"Mr. Davenport," she said frostily, while trying to repress a smile, "you are incorrigible."

"I hope so—I work very hard at it." His smile invited her to join him. "Try calling me Reggie. It may cure you of being respectful. It is quite impossible to take a Reggie seriously. The name implies either villainy or fatuousness."

"And of the two, you prefer villainy?"

"Of course," he said, brows raised. "Wouldn't you?"

"I daresay I would." Giving up the struggle to keep a straight face, she laughed. "In my blameless and well-organized existence, I have never run into anyone like you before. Forgive me if I don't know quite how to react."

"It's simple enough. Always tell me the truth, no matter how appalling," he said in a light tone that did not disguise the underlying seriousness. "And remember that a life without laughter is hardly worth living."

His words struck with surprising force. She had a sense of humor—what person would ever admit to not having one? She enjoyed a good joke, she laughed with the children. But it was true that over the years, laughter had always been something that came after serious work was done. It was the reward, not an integral part of life. As a child, she had been constantly drilled about her future responsibilities. As an adult, sheer survival demanded that duty always come before pleasure. Alys said, "You must think I am quite a sobersides."

"Yes—but not hopelessly so." The light blue eyes had a warm glow. "I want you to think about what improvements you'd like to see at Strickland—equipment, buildings, stock, whatever. I have some ideas, but I want to hear your suggestions as well."

"You want to reinvest the income in the estate?" she asked, her surprise all too obvious.

"Did you think that I was going to take the income and gamble it all away?" His deep voice was cool now.

Well, he'd said to tell the truth, no matter how appalling. "It was a logical assumption," she admitted. "A good part of your cherished reputation concerns gambling."

"I always gambled to make money, Allie. Now that I have a good income, I don't need to play deeply."

She tilted her head and considered that. "I usually think of gamesters as losing fortunes. But if there are losers, there must also be winners."

"Exactly, and I have usually been one of the winners." His half smile was rueful. "I'll admit there have been times when I've been badly dipped because of a long run of bad luck, or because I was too drunk or pigheaded to quit. But over the last twenty years of gaming, I've won thousands of pounds more than I've lost. That's what has bridged the gap between my allowance and my style of living. Vice isn't cheap, you know."

"How did you manage to win so often?"

"Honestly, if that's what you're wondering," he said with an icy edge in his voice.

"I didn't doubt it, Reggie," she said mildly.

"Sorry." He grimaced. "I've won so consistently that my honesty has been questioned more than once. The trick to winning is to avoid games that are purely chance. A man who restricts himself to forms of gambling that require skill should be able to win more than he loses. At least he will if he develops the skill."

She leaned forward and crossed her arms on the desk. "This sounds interesting. Tell me more."

He thought a moment. "Well, take hazard as an example. It's a dice game, and the object is to throw certain number combinations. Since some combinations are easier to achieve than others, a knowledge of the mathematical odds makes it possible for an astute player to do very well, especially if he hedges his bets."

He grinned at her expression. "Am I losing you? You may take my word for it that most gamesters have neither the ability nor the desire to calculate odds, particularly not in the heat of play. There are also games where remembering the cards that have been played greatly improves your chances." He shrugged. "I have a good memory."

And also, she would guess, excellent judgment and nerves of steel. Intrigued by this glimpse into a masculine world, she asked, "What about the turf?"

He shook his head. "Very chancy. No matter how well a man knows horseflesh, there are too many variables, both in horses and riders. I generally don't bet much on races unless I'm riding or driving myself. Then if I lose, at least I know whom to blame."

"And you don't lose often." It was a statement, not a question.

"Losing is a bore, Allie. And I dislike boredom of all things." He stood, looking down at her from his great height. "I'll leave you to your labors. Do they still do the sheep washing at the same pool in the stream, by the clump of beeches?"

She nodded. "As far as I know, the sheep have been washed there for centuries. Things don't change very fast in Dorset."

"The land might not, but the people do." Putting his hat on, he touched his fingers to the brim in a brief salute. "As I recall, the sheep have usually been gathered in by noon. I'll be there then."

After he left, Alys looked at her list of tasks for the day without seeing it. She supposed it wasn't surprising that a rake would be physically attractive, nor that he would have charm.

But who would have guessed that a rake would be so amusing?

Back at the manor house, Reggie sought out his housekeeper and with a few short, sharp words ensured that in the future there would always be an adequate supply of alcohol in the house, no matter what else was neglected. Then he went to his study and started to make plans.

For years he had wanted to breed horses, mostly hunters, with the best trained for steeplechase racing. He'd never had the means, but now his dream was within reach. Bucephalus would be the foundation. The stallion had superb bloodlines, incredible stamina and jumping ability, and speed that would do credit to a racehorse. Reggie had won the horse at hazard, playing an earl who had no talent for calculating odds.

In the short term, the existing stables would be adequate, but new paddocks and training rings would be required, and as many good mares as he could afford. In the long run . . . His pen flew across the page, estimating costs, jotting questions to himself, laying down the outlines of what needed to be done.

He became totally absorbed, and the hours passed unnoticed. It was early afternoon when his concentration was broken by the entrance of one of the housemaids, a rosy young creature called Gillie. Like all of the maids, she looked at him as if half hoping, half fearing that he would pounce on her. "Excuse me, sir, you have a visitor," she announced as she handed over a calling card.

Jeremy Stanton, Fenton Hall, Dorsetshire. The man whom Mrs. Herald had said was his nearest maternal relation. Reggie stood and stretched, then went to the front hall.

A slightly built, distinguished gentleman with silver hair and shrewd gray eyes smiled at him. "You may not remember me, Mr. Davenport, but I knew you when you were a child. I want to welcome you back to the neighborhood."

Reggie's brows furrowed for a moment. Then an image clicked into place, followed by others. "Good God, Uncle Jerry! I'd forgotten your existence until now. How do you do, sir?" He offered his hand.

Stanton shook it heartily. "So you do remember. Of

course I'm not your uncle, but"—he thought a moment—"cousin once removed. And your godfather."

"Whatever." Reggie waved his visitor into the drawing room. "It's good to see you again. Would you like some refreshment?"

"Some tea would do nicely." Stanton glanced around the faded drawing room reminiscently as he took a chair. "I haven't been here in near thirty years now. The gentleman who rented the house was a recluse and never received visitors."

After ringing for tea, Reggie went to pour himself some brandy from the new stock. As he did, another vivid image flashed across his mind, chilling him to the bone. He saw this very room, full of adults, dressed in black or wearing mourning bands. It had been before the funeral. Reggie had staggered down in his nightshirt, knees weak and head whirling. The coffins had been in a row by the windows. He had been near collapse when Stanton scooped him up and carried him back to his room, talking softly, keeping him company while he cried himself to sleep.

He shoved the stopper into the decanter with unnecessary force, then joined his visitor for an exchange of pleasantries. Jeremy Stanton had a sharp and well-informed mind, and it was a pleasure talking with him, but Reggie sensed that he was being weighed and judged. Measured against his father, perhaps? Or as a Stanton? Oddly he realized that the old man's opinion mattered to him.

He must have passed inspection, because after half an hour Stanton asked, "Do you intend to spend much time in the district?"

"Perhaps." Reggie shrugged. "I'm inclined that way, but I've only just arrived."

"We could use another magistrate," Stanton said tentatively.

Reggie stared at him. "Good God, are you suggesting I

should be a justice of the peace? I'm not qualified in the least. In fact, there are those who would say you would be setting a fox to watch the hens."

The older man laughed. "Despite your colorful past, you are amply qualified to be a magistrate. You're a principal landowner in the county, and you come of a fine old local family. Most of what a justice does is common sense and simple fairness. I'm sure you could manage that."

Reggie found himself at a rare loss for words, not sure whether to be touched or amused at his cousin's vote of confidence. Yet he realized that the idea of being a justice was not without appeal. Magistrates were the true local authorities, as involved with administering the Poor Law and fixing the roads as with judging lawbreakers. It might be interesting. Not ready to make a commitment, he said, "The Lord Lieutenant of Dorsetshire might not agree to me."

"He'll agree to whomever I suggest," Stanton said peaceably. "We're shorthanded at this end of the county, and he's been after me to find another justice for an age. I'll forward your name to him. Official confirmation should come in a few weeks."

Arching his brows sardonically, Reggie said, "Aren't you rushing your fences?"

Most men found that expression quelling, but Stanton was unaffected. With a faint smile, he said merely, "Am I?"

Reggie opened his mouth to say something caustic, then stopped. Hadn't he been thinking it was time to make some changes in his life? Becoming a part of the establishment would certainly be a change. And he was arrogant enough to believe that he would make a capable magistrate. "No, I suppose you aren't."

"Good." Stanton gave a satisfied nod before adding slowly, "I'm surprised that you didn't return to Dorset earlier. I'd almost given up hope that you would."

"You had that much interest in me?" Reggie was surprised, and moved. It had never occurred to him that anyone had cared about the departure of an eight-year-old boy.

"Of course. You are my cousin Anne's boy, your father was my friend. This is where you belong," Stanton said, as if the statement was inarguable.

Reggie was silent as he thought about that. Perhaps he did belong here. Certainly he had belonged nowhere else. "I really don't remember much about my childhood. Nothing at all before I was—oh, four or so. Only bits and pieces afterward." Which was odd, now that he thought of it. In general, his memory was outstanding. But much of his early childhood seemed swathed in mists.

Stanton's eyes narrowed. "Nothing before you were four? Interesting."

"Is there some significance to that?"

Stanton seemed about to answer, then changed his mind. "If there is, doubtless it will come back to you." Deliberately changing the subject, he said, "I was sorry you never wrote back to me, but not surprised. You were just a lad, and there were so many changes in your life. My own boys were never good correspondents. Still aren't," he added with a chuckle.

"Write back? I never received any letters from anyone," Reggie said, frowning.

Stanton looked surprised. "I sent you a letter every month for a year or so, then stopped when you never replied. I wrote to Wargrave Park, care of your uncle. You never received any of them?"

Reggie swore, his language furiously fluent. "That's another mark to my guardian's account." He explained how his uncle had deprived him of Strickland.

Stanton was shocked, and as angry as Reggie himself. "Good Lord, if I'd had any idea that Wargrave was deliberately separating you from your mother's family, from your whole background, I'd have gone to Gloucestershire and brought you home. I was your godfather, but Wargrave was much more nearly related than I, so I didn't argue when he sent for you." He made a sharp gesture with one hand. "Your father had asked once if I would become guardian to his children if something happened to him and Anne, but he never got around to writing his will. Unfortunately."

Startled, Reggie said, "You would have challenged Wargrave over me?"

"If I had known what was going on, of course," Stanton said, surprised in his turn. "You're family."

"The idea of family as helpful is new to me," Reggie said with desert dryness.

"With Wargrave as your guardian, I'm not surprised that you have a low opinion of relatives." Stanton shook his head sorrowfully. "I should have known there was a reason why you didn't write. You were always a considerate lad—your father was proud of how responsible you were. I should have tried harder to keep in touch with you."

"Don't blame yourself. Who could have expected my uncle to be so determined to isolate me?" Feeling as if he'd had enough shocks for one afternoon, Reggie stood and offered Stanton his hand. "For what it's worth, I appreciate what you tried to do. You were a busy man, with your own responsibilities and family. There's a limit to what you could be expected to do for a distant relative."

"I should have done more," Stanton said simply. "But it's past mending." He stood and shook Reggie's hand with a firmness that belied his silver hair. "My wife asked if you could come to dinner Friday night. Will you be free?"

Another image clicked into place. A round, smiling face, placid in the midst of family chaos. "I'd be happy to come. I trust that Aunt Beth is well?"

"Elizabeth has the rheumatics, which sometimes make it hard for her to get around, but she's well enough otherwise. She'll be delighted to see you again. You were always a favorite of hers." Then, with a grin, "Don't be surprised if there is a single lady or two at the dinner table."

Reggie groaned. "Tell Aunt Beth that if that's the case, I may have a sudden attack of illness that will require me to return home instantly."

Stanton chuckled. "Perhaps I can keep her in check this time, but in the future, you're on your own."

The old man left Strickland with a sense of satisfaction. Through the years he had kept an eye on the doings of the notorious Reginald Davenport. Even if only half of what was said about him was true, there had been ample reason to worry. Stanton had feared that there would be no trace of the bright, good-natured lad he remembered, that vice and dissipation had corrupted what had been so promising.

But now that they had met, Stanton was sure that somewhere inside, in spite of outrageous fortune and a malicious guardian, Anne's son still existed. Oh, doubtless the boy had done things he shouldn't have, and it was likely that he suffered from his father's near-disastrous weakness. But there was honor there, and intelligence and humor. Get him involved in the community, encourage him to find a wife . . .

Full of plans, Stanton cracked the whip over his placid horse. He couldn't wait to get home and tell Elizabeth the conclusions he had formed.

After his guest left, Reggie found it impossible to concentrate on his future plans. His godfather's visit had released a whole whirl of memories, most of them happy ones. The Stantons and Davenports had been in and out of each other's houses all the time in the old days. The youngest Stanton boy had been a particular playmate of Reggie's. James was in India now and doing very well, according to his father.

Looking back, it was obvious why Reggie had suppressed so much of his childhood. As soon as his uncle had taken him in charge, Reggie had been packed off to school. In the fierce jungle of Eton, remembering a happy past that he could never return to would have weakened him, so he had tried not to think of what he had lost. He had been all too successful. Even after the visit from Stanton, he could remember nothing from when he was very small.

His musings were interrupted by the arrival of his valet, Mac Cooper, looking dignified despite being covered with dust. "Am I glad to see you!" Reggie stood and went to the brandy decanter. Generally servants and employers didn't drink together, but the two men had an unconventional relationship. "Did you have trouble on the journey?"

"Broken axle," Mac said laconically as he accepted a glass of brandy. Then he settled his wiry frame into a chair with a sigh of satisfaction. "Quite a place you have here. Will we be staying awhile?"

"Permanently."

Mac's eyebrows shot up. "Not live in London?" he said incredulously.

"I'll want to go up to town sometimes, but I intend to make my headquarters here." Reggie cleared his throat, then added gruffly, "I know you're city bred, Mac. If you can't stand the country, I'll understand."

Mac gave him a look of intense disgust. "Did I say anything about leaving?"

"No," Reggie admitted, "but you've only been here ten minutes."

"If they have women and whiskey in Dorset, I'll manage."

"There's no shortage of either." Reggie smiled. "Including the most extraordinary female I've ever met."

"Extraordinary in what way?" Mac asked with interest.

"Any number of ways. Her name is Alys Weston, and she happens to be my land steward."

Mac choked on his brandy. "She's *what*?"

It was rare to surprise the imperturbable Mac. Reggie enjoyed giving a brief explanation of how his steward had reached her present position.

Mac shook his head in amazement. "All very well that she's good at her work, but is she pretty?"

Reggie thought of the strong, sculptured features, the tall, graceful body, the dimples he was learning to coax out. "Not pretty." He smiled to himself. "Something a good deal more interesting than that."

Chapter 9

Sheep washing was a communal affair, and neighboring flocks were included with Strickland's. As Reggie rode into the heathlands at midday, he could hear complaining sheep and barking dogs from two hills away.

He crested the last ridge and looked down at the stream that had been dammed to form the washing pool. On the east bank, several thousand sheep were crowded into a large fold as well-trained herd dogs paced menacingly around the stone walls. Close up, the anxious bleating was cacophonous.

Clustered by the pool were a dozen or so men, plus the unmistakable, willowy form of Alys Weston. Reggie swung off his mount and tethered it, then joined the group.

Alys interrupted her conversation with a burly shepherd when Reggie approached. "Mr. Davenport, this is Gabriel Mitford, Strickland's chief shepherd."

Reggie stared at the broad, muscular figure, not quite believing his eyes. Then he offered his hand with a slow smile. "We're acquainted."

Mitford nodded as he took Reggie's hand in a powerful grip. "Aye. I'll be bound I can still best you at wrestling, two falls out of three."

Laughing, Reggie clapped him on the shoulder. "Don't

count on it, Gabe. But if we still have the energy after washing a couple of thousand sheep, we can give it a try."

"Only a damn fool would want to wash sheep," the shepherd proclaimed, his dour voice belied by the amused gleam in his eyes.

"It's not the first time I've been called a damned fool," Reggie agreed pleasantly.

A small chuckle escaped Alys Weston. Hastily arranging her face to sobriety, she was about to signal the workers to their places when one of the sheepdogs came galloping up with a stick and laid it at Reggie's feet. The animal was a rough-coated female, mostly black with white paws and band around the ribs, plus a white face marked with a clownish black mask.

Reggie regarded the young dog in bemusement as she wagged her tail hopefully. "What kind of sheepdog wants to play fetch?"

Gabriel Mitford waved a disgusted hand at the animal. "A bad one. Been trying to train her. Only collie I ever had who wasn't born knowing how to herd. Couldn't even work ducks." He looked glumly at the dog, who rolled over and waved her white paws playfully in the air. "Going to have to put her down."

As if understanding that she was under sentence of death, the collie jumped to her feet and hopefully licked Reggie's hand. He scratched the shaggy head and received a lolling-tongued grin of pleasure in return. "Any chance someone might want her for a pet? She's a friendly beast."

"Hill folk don't want an animal that can't work." The shepherd waved the dog away. Floppy ears drooping, the collie headed back to the milling group of herd dogs.

Alys raised her arm and signaled the men to their positions so work could begin. Reggie pulled off his coat and boots and tossed them aside before joining Gabriel Mitford and a shepherd named Simms in the icy, thigh-deep water.

Aided by dogs, a lad drifted sheep out of the fold two or three at a time. Alys and an ancient, wizened shepherd did a quick check on heads, mouths, and ears, sending animals to a smaller fold if they needed medical attention.

Sheep that passed inspection were wrestled into the water by three muscular young fellows. It was a process the sheep much resented, and they protested long and loud as they kicked and fought their fate.

Once forced into the water, they floated easily. Reggie pulled the first one over to him. Despite their staggering stupidity, he'd always liked sheep, though it had been a grave disappointment when he first hugged one as a child and learned that the soft-looking fleece was dense and dirty.

There was a trick to flipping a sheep onto its back and scrubbing its belly without being kicked by a flailing hoof. Reggie watched Gabriel for a moment before he tried it himself. The outraged ewe managed to catch him in the ribs with a kick; he'd have a ferocious bruise there later. Still, he managed to clean her filthy underside without drowning either of them. Then he turned the animal upright and squeezed the thick wool in large handfuls, forcing out most of the dirt and grease.

When he was done, he pointed his indignant victim toward the other side of the stream and released her. The fleece got a good rinse as the ewe swam across the pool.

On the far bank she scrambled out of the water and was rewarded with a handful of hay. Then she was guided into another fold to dry in the late spring sunshine. By the end of the day, most of the lambs would be weaned by the simple fact that they could no longer identify their mothers' scents.

A good washer could clean a hundred sheep an hour, and clearly Gabriel and Simms were first-rate. It took time for Reggie to pick up the technique, but soon he was working at a creditable speed.

Within minutes of starting, he was as wet as any of the

sheep. He wondered with an inward chuckle if any of his London acquaintances would recognize him. No matter— he was enjoying himself. The work was satisfyingly physi- cal, and the result—a clean sheep—was something that could be immediately appreciated.

The workers settled into a steady rhythm with little con- versation. Every half hour or so, a pewter tankard of hot water liberally mixed with whiskey was passed to the wash- ers to help them keep warm in the bone-chilling water. All three of them partook liberally.

The second time the whiskey came around, Reggie ac- cepted it from Simms and took a deep pull, clasping the tankard with both hands so it could warm his numb fingers. Handing it on to Gabriel, he asked, "What do you think of Miss Weston as a steward?"

"Does well enough." The burly shepherd tilted his head back, draining the last of the tankard, then tossed it up on the bank. "Likes sheep."

Coming from Gabriel, that was high praise. But then, if the shepherds didn't trust her judgment, they wouldn't let her work with their flocks.

Reggie glanced up at the bank. Alys expertly checked over a well-grown lamb, expression intent, then urged it on and reached for another. Amazing that she could do such thoroughly masculine work, yet manage to look so fetch- ingly female. Those pantaloons really did the most remark- able job of outlining her shapely backside . . .

With a grin Reggie grasped the next bleating ewe, grate- ful that he was standing in cold water.

It was a long, hard afternoon for all concerned, but Alys still found time to be impressed at how well her employer took to sheep washing. Even when an ornery ewe reared up, planted both hooves on his chest, and shoved him backward into the water, he had emerged smiling as the rest of the work crew roared with laughter.

His willingness to do a hard job on the same terms as his employees had won him instant respect and acceptance. Had Davenport planned that, or was he genuinely indulging a childhood ambition? Either way, the results were worthwhile.

Toward the end of the afternoon, Simms, who was smaller than the other two washers and could absorb less alcohol, subsided into the water with a peaceful smile. Davenport and Mitford fished the drunken shepherd out and laid him by the small fire, where he snored contentedly. One of the young sheep wrestlers joined them in the stream to finish the last of the flock.

Traditionally the washing ended with a meal for the workers, and Alys had arranged for a small mountain of hearty fare to be brought to the site. They shared ham, boiled new potatoes, and warm bread, washed down by generous quantities of ale. By the time they finished eating, all the men were very merry.

Even Alys drank enough ale to feel a warm glow of satisfaction at a job well done. She always enjoyed the communal activities of farming, like sheep washing and harvesting, and today there was a particularly friendly spirit in the air. Doubtless the new owner was responsible for that. By this time he had made the acquaintance of every worker, and they were relaxed in his presence.

She and Davenport were the only ones who had ridden to the site. As dusk fell, they headed for their horses so they could ride back to the manor together. Her employer must have been freezing in his wet clothes, but he showed no signs of discomfort. Probably that was because of the amazing quantity of alcohol he had put away. Alys was impressed at how well he carried his drink.

The long ride home began in companionable silence.

Then Alys glanced back and saw the playful, incompetent sheepdog following behind, her waving black tail held high. "Don't look now," she said with a laugh, "but I think you've made a conquest."

Davenport glanced back. "More likely Gabe sent the worthless beast after us to get rid of her."

A canine smile on the clownish face, the dog loped up and fell into step by Davenport's horse. Alys barely restrained herself from commenting that Davenport was irresistible to almost any female creature. Such a remark would have been most unsuitable. But true, alas, too true.

Hastily attempting to rein in her ale-lightened spirits before she embarrassed them both, she said, "I gather you and Mitford knew each other as boys?"

"We used to swim and wrestle and stalk through the hills. He was never much of a talker, but he knew the downs and the woods like the back of his hand. Chief shepherd is perfect for him. A good life for a man with a contemplative nature."

They finished the ride in comfortable silence. As they dismounted and led their horses into the stables, the dog stayed as close to Davenport as possible. She seemed determined to prove how well behaved she could be.

The grooms had finished for the night, leaving the stables quiet except for the shuffle of hooves and an occasional equine whicker. The scents of hay and leather and healthy horses lay soft in the air. Alys unsaddled her mount, noting again how her clothing affected the way her employer treated her. When she dressed like a lady, he treated her as one. Now that she was in boots and breeches, he let her groom and bed down her own horse. She enjoyed his casual assumption that she was competent to do what any male took for granted.

After brushing down her horse, Alys emerged from the

box stall and almost fell over the collie, which made a sudden dash in front of her to rear up and plant its paws on Davenport. The dog's sudden weight jarred him backward, almost tipping him into a pile of loose hay that would be transferred to racks the next day. "Down!" he ordered.

The dog obeyed instantly, settling on her haunches and wagging her tail across the well-swept plank floor. Davenport said ruefully, "Why do I get the feeling that this beast wants to move in with me?"

Alys chuckled. "Because she undoubtedly does. Are you hard-hearted enough to turn your back on those brown eyes?" She bent to scratch behind the collie's ears. As the dog wiggled happily under her hand, she briefly considered taking it home, but discarded the notion. Attila would not like sharing the house with a dog.

Straightening, Alys realized how close she was to Davenport, only a yard away. She was struck once more by how tall he was, and how intensely masculine.

She was also close enough to see that he was much drunker than she had thought. There was a kind of haziness about him, a rakish, unsteady air that he had not shown before. He must be drunk indeed to look at her like that, with such warmth in his eyes.

She yearned to close the distance between them, to discover if that was really desire she saw on his face. Instead she started to step back, determined to put distance between them.

Then the collie, which had been sniffing curiously at the hay, struck an unexpected quarry. An enraged Attila exploded from the mound like a furry lightning bolt, claws slashing.

The dog leaped into the air with a terrified yelp, then made a mad dash for escape as the cat followed, yowling like seven demons from hell. Alys stood between the collie and the door, and the dog's solid body cannoned into her, knocking her into Davenport.

He could have steadied her easily enough if he'd been sober, but his balance was not at its best. As the hissing cat chased the dog into the night, Alys and Reggie went crashing into the hay. She landed hard on top of him, the wind knocked out of her.

She stared down, horrified by the realization that she was sprawled full-length along his lean, muscular frame. Their bodies were pressed together with shocking intimacy, and the harsh planes of his face were mere inches away.

After the first instant of surprise, his expressive lips curved into a mesmerizing smile. He was the most irresistible sight she'd ever seen in her life. She struggled to catch her breath, knowing that she must scramble up and apologize, but she was momentarily paralyzed by proximity.

Before she could lift herself away, Davenport said huskily, "What a splendid idea." Then he slid one hand behind her head and pulled her face down for a kiss.

All thought of escape or apology fled. Alys had been kissed by Randolph when they were betrothed, but her fiancé had acted with gentlemanly restraint, not wishing to offend her delicate sensibilities. Too shy to tell him that passion would not offend her, she had been left with the frustrated feeling that there was a great deal more to kissing than she was being taught.

Now Reggie was filling in the gaps in her education. She might be an aging spinster, but he allowed no quarter for her inexperience. His kiss was deep, intense, and utterly enthralling. She shivered as he explored her mouth with slow, rich sensuality. Knowing hands slid under her coat to caress her back and hips as his damp clothing warmed with the heat between them.

Though she might lack skill, Alys did her best to compensate with enthusiasm, kissing him back with all the abandon she had never dared show Randolph. Desire surged through her, searing like liquid flame.

There was a moment of shock when he wrapped strong arms around her waist and rolled over, reversing their positions. Then his long powerful frame pinned her into the yielding depths of the hay. The sweet green scents of crushed vegetation surrounded them, drenching her heightened senses with sensation.

She gasped when he pressed his warm mouth to her ear, then trailed kisses down her throat. Her hands moved frantically over his back, hungry for the tense masculine feel of his body.

He cupped her breast with one large hand, teasing the nipple to taut response with this thumb. "You've a rare talent for this, Allie," he whispered.

In a remote part of her mind, Alys knew that she was about to abandon a dozen years of blameless respectability, and she didn't care. Nothing mattered but this, the passion that promised to fulfill the dreams of her restless nights. She licked his throat, tasting the salt of his warm skin against her tongue.

He was fumbling with the buttons of her shirt when the sound of a throat being cleared struck like a blast of icy water. Alys froze, torn between pure horror at being caught writhing in the hay like a dairymaid, and raging fury that they had been interrupted.

Reggie went rigid. Then he gave a sigh of regret and rolled away, leaving her cold and bereft. The warm hand he offered to help her to her feet was poor compensation for what she had lost.

As she stood, wavering from the force of what she had just experienced, Alys saw that the intruder was a wiry fellow dressed in London style. Though his expression was carefully blank, she sensed the disapproval radiating from

him. Her face burned with shame that a stranger had seen
her wanton behavior.

Totally unabashed, Reggie steadied her with a light grip
on her elbow. "Lady Alys, this is Mac Cooper, who came
down from town yesterday. Mac, this is Miss Weston, more
familiarly known as Lady Alys." After a quick, perceptive
glance at her face, he added, "Don't worry, Mac never sees
anything he shouldn't."

He released her arm and swiftly brushed the hay from her
back and legs, his hands impersonal where they had been so
intimate. Alys supposed that his words were meant as reassurance that everyone at Strickland would not know that she
was a slut by breakfast the next day. But she would know,
and so would Davenport and his servant. That was two
people too many.

Barely managing a nod at Cooper, she turned and fled the
stable, into the safety of the night. She was halfway back to
Rose Hall before her pace slowed. Not yet ready to face her
household, she halted under a tree. She had the irrational
feeling that the marks of Reggie's hands and lips were
blazoned across her in streaks of scarlet.

The night air cool on her flushed skin, she folded down
under a tree and wrapped her arms around herself, shuddering with humiliation. Yes, Davenport had briefly desired her,
but drunks were notoriously undiscriminating. Any female
would have suited him equally well. He and his servant were
probably laughing over how susceptible she had been,
amused that she was desperate for any man's attention.

Of course, Reginald Davenport was not just any man.
The blasted fellow was so diabolically attractive that all he
had to do was stand and wait for females to hurl themselves
into his arms. She made a choked sound and buried her face
in her hands.

For a handful of astounding moments, she had forgotten
propriety, reputation, and obligations. Now, alone in the

night, Alys wondered with despair how she was going to
face Davenport in the morning.

As Reggie brushed sprigs of hay from his coat, Mac said,
"Miss Weston is an unusual female, to be sure," his voice
frosted with disapproval.

A smile still lingering on his lips, Reggie said, "She most
certainly is."

"I see you're proud of yourself," Mac said sharply.

"Not exactly that, but certainly in charity with the world,"
Reggie said lazily. "What are you so Friday-faced about?"

Mac scowled. "Miss Weston is highly regarded here.
'Twould be a pity to see her ruined because you have nothing better to do."

Reggie's face stiffened. "I doubt that she would consider
it ruination. If you were spying for any length of time, you'll
have noticed that she was entirely willing."

His valet spat on the floor. "Did you see her face when
she left? She may have succumbed to a moment's temptation, but now she hates herself. She must be thanking her
lucky stars that you were interrupted."

"I sincerely doubt that," Reggie snapped. "If I have ever
met a woman eager for ruination, it's Alys Weston."

"Why don't you just discharge her and get it over with
quickly?" Mac asked caustically. "She'd still be out of work,
but at least she'd have her reputation."

"She does her job superlatively well, and I have no intention of discharging her," Reggie growled, his temper dangerously near the explosion point.

"How long do you think she would be able to do her work
if the locals found out she was your mistress?" Max
frowned. "She'd be forced out in a fortnight. Besides, since
when have you taken to seducing respectable virgins?
You've always said that they were nothing but trouble."

His temper well and truly lost, Reggie roared, "Bloody hell, Mac, who are you to tell me what to do?" He turned to storm out of the stable.

Mac's quiet voice followed him. "Your conscience."

Reggie swung to face him, eyes glinting with fury. "You should know that I haven't got a conscience."

"You will in the morning when you're sober."

Reggie swore viciously and spun away into the night, but Mac's words pursued him. Knowing that he would be dangerous to anyone whose path he crossed, he turned away from the house and into the park, needing to work his anger off. Bloody-minded little cockney prig. How dare he lecture his employer, who had taken him from the gutter? Reggie was a trifle foxed, but hardly roaring drunk. And if there was any seduction going on with Lady Alys, it had been entirely mutual.

Entirely mutual, and entirely pleasurable . . .

Reggie had suspected that his steward might have an ardent nature under her controlled exterior, but he hadn't realized how dangerously close to the surface it lay. Though her response might have lacked polish, he would lay odds that her capacity for passion equaled that of any woman he had ever known.

Swearing softly for any number of reasons, he made his way to the lake. The moon was nearly full, and sheets of light silvered the water. He followed the shore to the thicket that concealed his private clearing. As branches slapped him in the face, he made a mental note to have the old path cleared.

His temper had ebbed by the time he made it through the thicket to the smooth water of the lake. Half of his anger had been because of Mac's officiousness, he decided, but the other half was pure frustration. His hands tingled with the remembered feel of her lithe body. Just thinking of her fiery, uninhibited responsiveness made his temperature begin to rise again.

It was on this very spot that he had learned to swim as a boy. On impulse he stripped off his damp clothing and dove headfirst into the lake.

The chill waters brought a measure of reason back to his brain. He surfaced, sputtering, and admitted that Mac, damn him, had a point. He usually did. Alys Weston might be willing, even eager, to experience what she had been missing, but Reggie would do her no favor by taking advantage of that fact. Any affair posed the risk of physical, social, and emotional damage. Remembering the dazed, shaken look in Allie's wide eyes when they had been interrupted, he bestowed a particularly scathing curse on himself.

During his lengthy career as a rake, Reggie had learned that few females could enjoy an affair without having their emotions become involved, and Allie wasn't in the small number. Besides passion, she had a great capacity for selfless love. Look at the family she had created for herself. Look at what she had done for everyone on the estate. She was a giver by nature, and would be unable to prevent herself from giving away more than she could afford to lose.

His powerful strokes had carried him the full width of the lake, so he turned to swim back. Alys Weston might be physically ripe for an affair, but she was the sort of female who needed a man she could respect, while Reggie represented everything that decent, God-fearing folk despised. If she indulged her perfectly natural desires with him, she would hate herself, and him as well. It was a curiously unappealing thought.

He rolled onto his back and floated lazily in the moonkissed water, stroking just enough to stay afloat. With Allie's looks and passionate nature, it was amazing that she had gotten to her present age unwed. Her height, forceful intelligence, and independence must intimidate most men. A waste; such a very great waste.

While he certainly lusted after that lovely body, he also liked and respected the woman inside. He had no desire to see her hurt. Which meant that he had damn well better stay sober around her, because he didn't trust himself an inch when he had been drinking. Reggie had resolved to behave himself in Dorset, yet when that stupid dog knocked her into his arms, her warm, willing body had caused him to instantly forget his good intentions.

With wry humor Reggie realized that the water wasn't cold enough to cool his rude male instincts. He had better find a topic other than Alys Weston to think about.

Distraction was provided when something splashed into the water at the edge of the lake. Automatically watchful, he floated and listened, though there shouldn't be any animals in the area that could threaten a human.

Then he identified the creature paddling valiantly toward him. The collie was ecstatic to find him, almost sinking in her attempts to wag her tail while swimming. Raising one hand from the water to scratch her head, he asked, "Haven't you caused enough trouble for one night?"

A raspy tongue across his face was the only reply. "Aren't you ashamed of yourself, having been routed by a mangy cat?"

Shame was apparently as foreign to the collie as herding instinct. The dog just tried to climb into Reggie's arms, not easily done when both man and beast were in the water. He pushed the collie away. "Come ashore before you drown, you idiotic creature."

Side by side, they swam back to the shore. The collie managed to shake an amazing amount of water out of its shaggy fur while Reggie pulled on his clammy, uncomfortable clothes, shivering in the brisk night air.

As he walked back to the house, collie at his heels, he

decided to go up to London for a few days. He had hared off so quickly that he had left some business undone. Besides, a brief absence would give Alys Weston some time to recover from her embarrassment. And if he was being strictly truthful, which he preferred to be in the privacy of his own head, he wasn't looking forward to the next time he saw her. She probably despised him just now, and with justice.

Back in his room to change, he found Mac unpacking and brushing out his master's wardrobe, unperturbed by the row that had occurred in the stable. Reggie felt a stab of guilt, remembering his uncharitable thoughts earlier. While he had helped the cockney out in the beginning, Mac had more than repaid Reggie's casual generosity. Hard to imagine anyone else putting up with Reggie's drinking, mood swings, and ups and downs of fortune. There had been times when Mac's pay had been months in arrears, and never once a complaint from him.

His valet glanced up, his eyes narrowing at the sight of the collie. "In case you haven't noticed, there's a dog following you."

Reggie took off his coat and began to unbutton his shirt. "So there is," he said with an elaborate show of surprise. "Fancy that."

Mac snorted. "What kind of dog is it?"

"A boarder collie, b-o-a-r-d-e-r collie," Reggie spelled out as he stripped off his wet pantaloons and drawers. "She's a hopelessly incompetent sheepdog. The shepherd was going to have her put down, so I decided to see if someone would take her as a pet."

Unaware of the plans for her future, the collie sat on her haunches, tail wagging, black fur matted with water, and an expression of imbecilic happiness on her face. Mac looked at her dubiously. He didn't know much about dogs, but this one seemed to think she had already found a home. "What's her name?"

"She doesn't have a name. Once you've named an animal, it's yours for life." Reggie toweled himself off vigorously, then pulled on the dry clothing Mac handed him. "I'm going to London for a few days. Anything you'd like me to get?"

"See if you can find some sanity," Mac suggested dourly. "You'll be needing it."

Reggie just laughed. In spite of everything, he felt better than he had for years. Snapping his fingers at the collie, he said, "Come on down to the library, and I'll let you watch Mac and me test the quality of the local whiskey."

With a clicking of toenails, the dog trotted after him downstairs. The collie might be a hopeless herder and not very bright by some standards, but she knew a good offer when she heard it.

Chapter 10

Having spent a sleepless night mustering her courage to meet her employer without blushing, Alys found the note waiting in her office distinctly anticlimactic. In a few terse words, Davenport informed her that he would be in London for several days. In his absence, he hoped she would think further about possible improvements to the property. Also, please see that a path was cleared through the brush to the little clearing by the lake. Yours, etc., R. Davenport.

It was as if the previous night's incident in the stable had never happened. Perhaps he had already forgotten it. As she stared at his bold, slashing handwriting, Alys wished vehemently that she could forget as easily. But how could she forget, when she could still feel the shape of his body in her arms?

Since he had been gone from London only a week, it was unlikely that the metropolis was any more crowded and noisome than when Reggie had left. Nonetheless, it seemed as if it were, as drays and peddlers and pedestrians fought for space while expressing themselves at the top of their lungs.

He arrived in the early evening. After stopping by his flat to change, he went out again to take care of business. Reggie had won five hundred pounds from George Blakeford the night before leaving London, but his opponent hadn't had the cash and had given a vowel instead. With all that he wanted to do at Strickland, Reggie could use the money. Blakeford should be at White's at this hour.

There was also the matter of Blakeford's mistress, whom Reggie had plowed that same night. If he had been attracted to the very available Stella, Reggie would have pursued her openly. But he hadn't been interested, and he felt an odd kind of guilt for having casually succumbed to the doxy's lures. Blakeford was damned possessive about his women, and Reggie preferred not to stir up trouble without a good reason. He had enough enemies without creating more unnecessarily.

Blakeford was in his usual spot at White's, making inroads on a bottle of port, so Reggie went over. "Mind if I join you?"

Blakeford nodded without enthusiasm, but did not look overly distressed at the company. Apparently Stella had the sense not to taunt her protector with her infidelities.

Reggie sat down opposite and signaled for more wine. Though they moved in the same circles, he and the other man were not really friends. Blakeford was tall and burly, a good boxer and heavy gambler with a face whose color showed his homage to port. He seemed a typical man about town, but Reggie had always sensed a dark, unpleasant side to Blakeford and preferred to keep his distance.

Unfortunately, a certain amount of socializing could not be avoided under the circumstances. Crossing his long legs casually, Reggie said, "I've been out of town for a few days and just got back. Would it be convenient . . . ?" The question hung in the air.

Blakeford nodded. "Lady Luck has been with me. Have the vowel on you?"

Reggie produced the note and exchanged it for a handful of bills. Blakeford's mood improved when he challenged Reggie to flip a coin for fifty pounds and Blakeford won. Reggie didn't mind. Tossing coins was a fool's way to gamble, but fifty pounds was not a bad tithe to pay for goodwill.

Good cheer abounding, they ordered another bottle of port while Blakeford recounted the news of the last week. Reggie carefully suppressed any indications of boredom. After he downed another bottle of port, perhaps knowing who had won or lost at whist would sound more interesting.

As Blakeford broached the third bottle, he remarked, "I never really had a chance to mention it before, but I was sorry when you were cut out of inheriting Wargrave. It must be hell seeing some upstart enjoying what should have been yours."

Reggie shrugged. That was old news by now. "I was only a nephew, and always knew I might be superseded."

"You're more philosophical than I." Blakeford grimaced, his heavy face sour. "I've been heir presumptive to Durweston for the last dozen years. I wouldn't wish the uncertainty on anyone."

Reggie's lips formed a silent whistle. "You're heir to the Duke of Durweston? That's a prize indeed."

He searched his memory for information about the duke, but with little success. Durweston was an elderly widower who lived in northern England, seldom coming to London. And when he did, he didn't move in the same circles as Reggie. "Are you concerned about Durweston marrying and getting a son, or is this another case of a missing heir, as with Wargrave?"

"The Duke of Durweston's only child ran away from home at eighteen and hasn't been heard from since." Blakeford shook his head in disgust. "Surely dead by now, though Durweston refuses to admit it."

"I've never met the duke, but I've heard him called a stiff-rumped old Croesus," Reggie remarked.

"To put it charitably." Blakeford look a deep swig of port, his face brooding. "The old boy hates knowing everything will come to me. I'm only a second cousin, but there's no one closer, so he'll damn' well have to make the best of it."

Reggie felt a surge of unexpected sympathy for Blakeford. "It's a bad business, waiting for some old autocrat to die."

It was more than a bad business; it was a postponement of real life, as Reggie knew to his cost. He sipped his port, then offered what consolation he could. "Granted, being superseded was a shock at first, but I didn't come out badly. My cousin Wargrave just signed over an estate to me as a sort of compensation. If the missing Durweston heir turns up, perhaps he'll be equally fair to you."

"No joy there. My cousin and I never got on. Besides, what is one paltry estate compared to Durweston?" Blakeford's face twisted into an ugly scowl for an instant before he said with determined civility, "Hadn't heard that you had come into property. Tell me about it."

"The estate is called Strickland. It's between Shaftesbury and Dorchester. About three thousand acres, and it's been very well managed."

"That's unusual for an estate that hasn't had an owner in residence," the other man said idly.

"Strickland has been blessed with a first-class steward." Reggie found himself smiling. "A female, and a most redoubtable one. An odd-eyed reformer who's nearly as tall as I am."

"You don't say!" Blakeford had been about to pour more port, but his hand stopped in mid-gesture. "What do you mean by odd-eyed?"

"One eye is brown, the other gray," Reggie explained. "Very striking."

"I knew a woman with eyes like that once," Blakeford said slowly. "What's her name?"

"Alys Weston."

Blakeford resumed pouring the port, his hand not quite steady. "The one I knew was called Annie. Short and round and sassy. I can't imagine her as a steward, but she had other talents," he added with a broad wink.

Something was not quite right about the other man's manner, but Reggie shrugged the thought off. Probably Blakeford had been as obsessed with his Annie as he now was with his Stella. Some men were weak that way.

His thoughts were interrupted by a familiar voice.

"Reggie! When did you get back to town?" Julian Markham's handsome young face shone with pleasure as he came up to them.

As Reggie stood and offered a handshake and a smile, Julian continued, "Have you dined yet? No? Then come and explain what took you out of London so quickly." Turning, he added, "Care to join us, Blakeford?"

Blakeford shook his head and rose to his feet. "No, I'm expected elsewhere. Good evening to you."

As he stared sightlessly at the other men's departing backs, Blakeford's mind was dominated by one horrific thought. The bitch was alive; there couldn't be another woman in England who fit that description.

Who would have believed it possible, after so many years?

Spurning the dining room at White's, Reggie and Julian Markham went to a nearby tavern renowned for its roast beef. As they settled down at a corner table, Julian commented, "I'm glad Blakeford couldn't come. He always seems angry about something. Makes it dashed difficult to relax."

After tearing his appreciative gaze from the round back-side of the barmaid who had taken their dinner order, Reggie said, "I know what you mean, but now I understand why he acts like a bear with a sore ear. It must be a confounded nuisance wondering if the missing heir to the Duke of Durweston is going to reappear and cut him out."

"That's bad enough," Julian agreed, "but I suspect that what makes it worse is that the heir is female."

"Good God, surely you're joking. Since when can a woman become a duchess in her own right? Even with baronies, that's rare," Reggie said, startled but intrigued.

Julian wrinkled his brow in thought. "I have a great-aunt who loves prosing on about such things. As I recall, the case was similar to that of Marlborough. The title was originally granted to a military hero with no surviving sons. However, he had daughters, so the patent of nobility specified that the title could pass through his eldest daughter. In the case of Durweston, there's the added wrinkle than an incumbent duke has the option of willing the title to the nearest male heir if he doesn't want his daughter to inherit. However, even if the missing heir is alive, I'm sure Durweston would pass over her, so Blakeford is worrying needlessly."

"How bizarre. There can't be another patent of nobility in England written that way," Reggie observed. "Why do you say that Durweston would consider his daughter unworthy even if she is still alive?"

Julian grinned. "My great-aunt loves scandals even more than genealogy. Apparently Durweston's daughter was betrothed to some thoroughly appropriate fellow—the Marquess of Kinross's younger son, I believe. But instead of marrying him, she eloped with her groom. If Durweston wasn't such a tough old devil, the shock would have killed him. He publicly disowned her, and not a word has ever been heard of the wench from that day to this. My aunt's theory was that she died in childbirth, and the servant she married was afraid to inform his noble father-in-law."

"That sounds likely," Reggie agreed.

Their dinners arrived then, and both men tucked into the beef and boiled potatoes. After they had finished and begun on their port, Reggie told his interested friend about Strickland, but the earlier discussion stayed on his mind.

When the conversation slowed, he said thoughtfully, "Primogeniture really is an iniquitous system. I suppose in feudal times it made sense to pass the entire property to a single heir, because concentrating the power helped everyone survive. But now it means younger sons being raised in a luxury they will never be able to afford when they're grown, so they go into the church or the army or the government and spend the rest of their days resenting being poor relations."

"And heirs kick their heels, powerless to do anything but drink, gamble, and wait for their fathers to die." There was rare bitterness in Julian's voice.

Reggie said sympathetically, "Does that mean your father turned down your proposal for managing the estate at Moreton?"

Julian scowled. "I was so sure that he would agree. I had it all worked out, the crop plan, the cost of cattle to improve the herd, income forecasts . . ." He broke off with a sheepish smile. "Of course you know that, since you were the one who spent weeks helping me develop the proposal." He shook his head in exasperation, a lock of brown hair falling loose across his brow, "It simply doesn't make any sense. I could double the estate's income, and he would also save the cost of keeping me here in London."

Ever since coming down from Oxford, Julian had been trying to persuade his father to let his heir assume some responsibility for the family fortunes. Lord Markham had steadfastly refused to yield a single shred of power. At the same time he complained that Julian was an extravagant wastrel, intent on destroying the family fortunes. If it would have helped, Reggie would have given his lordship a sharp lecture on how he was mishandling his heir, but Markham would never listen to a man whom he thought was corrupting his son.

Though Julian was fond of his father despite their differences, if the older man continued to be so pigheaded it would end with the son praying for the father's death. Having lost his own father so early, Reggie hated to see that. Unfortunately, he could think of no way to help.

Keeping his gloomy thoughts to himself, he topped up both goblets with port. "It isn't easy for a man who is aging to see himself supplanted by a young one in the prime of life, even when the younger one is his son. Perhaps especially when it is his son."

"But I don't want to supplant my father. I just want him to treat me like an adult, not a schoolboy." Julian sighed and leaned back against the oak settle. "Do you suppose if I married, he would decide that I was ready for responsibility?"

"Perhaps, though I wouldn't stake serious money on it." On impulse Reggie suggested, "Come to Strickland for a visit. If you're in the market for a leg-shackle, Dorset has its share of pretty girls."

Julian laughed. "I'd be delighted to see Strickland, and I never mind looking at pretty girls. I won't be able to come down for another fortnight, though."

"Good. I'm going to Leicestershire to buy some mares, but I'll certainly be back at Strickland by then." It would be good to have some company. Reggie was also looking forward to his young friend's first sight of the delectable Meredith Spenser.

The evening was yet young when Reggie parted company with Julian and went to take care of another piece of business. This one, however, should be more of a pleasure.

The muscular ex-pugilist who opened the door of the

discreet house on the edge of Mayfair welcomed him with a broad smile. "Good to see you, Mr. Davenport. It's been some time."

"It has," Reggie agreed, surrendering his hat. "Will you find out if Mrs. Chester will see me?"

"No need to ask, sir. Just go on up. You know the way."

Yes, he certainly knew the way. As he headed toward the stairs, he passed the open salon door and glanced in. This early, there were more females available than males to admire them. In their bright, revealing gowns the girls looked like the inhabitants of some exotic aviary. Several waved and beckoned to him while the men glanced up jealously to see who was causing such a flutter.

A saucy redhead came to the door and draped herself against the frame, cooing, "I knew this would be a good night. You came to see me, didn't you, Reg?"

Reggie chuckled and patted her bouncy derrière. "Sorry, Nan, I'm here to see Chessie."

She pouted prettily. "Some girls get all the luck." Her voice floated after him as he climbed the curving stairs.

When he knocked on the paneled door, Chessie's husky voice invited him in. She'd had a nearly unintelligible East End accent when they had met, but now she spoke the King's English as correctly as any lady born.

Her chamber was decorated with all the flamboyant richness that one of London's most successful madames deserved. Chessie sat at her dressing table, surrounded by an elegant clutter of expensive perfumes and cosmetics. When she saw her visitor in the mirror, she immediately rose and crossed the room to give him an affectionate hug. "Where have you been, you rascal? It's been an age."

Chessie had been a real dasher in her youth. Her blond hair now required assistance, and she had put on a good few pounds over the years, but she was still a fine figure of a woman. The extra pounds were soft and pleasant in a hug, and Reggie released her with reluctance. "In the country. I'm only in town for a few days, then I'll be off again."

Chessie went to a cabinet and took out a bottle of the special brandy she kept for him, and poured two glasses. After they were seated, he regaled her with a brief account of Strickland.

"So you're turning respectable. A magistrate, no less!" Glancing down at her brandy, she absently traced the rim of the glass with one finger. "I suppose we won't be seeing much of you now. I'll be sorry in a way, but I'm relieved in another."

"Oh? Glad to get rid of me?" Reggie asked with amusement.

"You know it's not that." Chessie tilted her head as if debating whether to say more. "I've been worried about you," she said slowly. "You've changed in the last few years. You used to raise hell because you enjoyed it, but now it seems more like a bad habit that's making you miserable. You carry on like a man condemned to die in the morning. If you don't change your course, sooner or later that's exactly what will happen."

"You think I can't take care of myself?" he asked in a silky voice that masked his stab of irritation.

"Not that you can't, but that you won't bother to try," she answered bluntly. "I know men as well as any woman alive, and I know when one is sending himself to perdition." Visibly gathering her courage, she continued, "Blast it, Reggie, you're drinking far too much. If you don't stop, it will kill you soon, either directly, or because you'll break your neck riding, or because you'll get into a fight and not be quick enough for once."

He finished his brandy and set the glass on the delicate end table with an audible clink. "Of course I drink too much. It's part of being an English gentleman. A really serious politician, for example, needs to be able to put away at least three bottles of bad port a night, and five or six is better."

"Yes, and it's killing a lot of them, too. But it isn't just a matter of how much you drink. What counts is how it affects you." She gave him a level look. "And it affects you very badly."

His temper rising, Reggie snapped, "You think I can't hold my liquor?"

"It used to be that you could drink anyone under the table and be as good as new the next day," she admitted. "But over the last couple of years, I think the booze has gotten the upper hand." She looked at him earnestly, willing him to really hear what she was saying. "Like I said, I've known a lot of men—"

He cut in sharply, "Several regiments worth, at least."

Chessie flushed, but she refused to back down. "Do you remember the first time we met?"

"Of course I do. A group of drunken bucks intent on gang rape is memorable." It had been at Ranelagh, shortly before the pleasure garden closed for good. Chessie had been very young and very new at Venus's trade. She had also been terrified and screaming for help, and he was the only man around who had seen fit to aid a prostitute.

His chivalrous gesture had been rewarded with a broken nose, but he had been less damaged than any of the men who had been attacking Chessie. One of his better fights, if he did say so himself. He'd won because he had been sober and they had not.

Uneasily, he shoved the last thought aside and added belligerently, "What has that got to do with anything?"

"Reggie, I think you saved my life that night. Now I want to return the favor." She spread her hands expressively. "Yes, almost everyone drinks too much, but sometimes it goes beyond a bad habit and becomes . . . almost like a disease, or an addiction, like the opium eaters. Once that happens, a man can't control his drinking anymore. He's a drunkard, and booze becomes more important than anything else in his life. It ruins his health, rots his guts, turns him nasty. Eventually it kills him."

"What a pretty picture you're painting," he said, his self-control etched with acid. "However, I assure you that I am not addicted to any form of spirits. I can stop whenever I choose."

"Have you ever tried?" she asked, her eyes grave.

Defiantly he reached for the bottle of brandy and poured himself three fingers worth. "I've never seen any reason to."

Chessie sighed. She hadn't thought he would be receptive to the idea that he was a drunkard; she had never known a man—or a woman, for that matter—who was. But she'd had to try. She and Reggie had lived together for several years after the night he had rescued her, and there had always been more between them than just business. It had hurt, these last years, to see him change. He had always had a quick temper, but in the past the clouds passed quickly and his usual good nature would reappear.

These days he seemed to be depressed or angry most of the time, more prone to use his quick tongue in caustic, hurtful ways. His remark about her having known regiments of men was an example. The old Reggie had never been unkind to his friends. Well, Chessie did indeed know men; well enough to know that there was no point in saying any more. "Did you have some other reason for stopping by, besides for a scold?"

He smiled faintly at that and reached inside his jacket for a folded paper which he handed to her. She opened it, then drew her brows in question. "Why are you handing me our original business agreement?"

Reggie lounged back in the sofa, sipping his brandy. "It's time the business was all yours. You do most of the work, and Martin does the rest. It isn't right that I keep taking part of the profits."

Chessie studied the contract with bemused affection.

Eight years before, she had been left in dire straits when her current protector abandoned her. No longer young, and tired by the precariousness of being a kept woman, she had turned to Reggie for temporary shelter.

Not only had he rescued her again, but he had suggested that she go into business for herself, and lent her the money to get started. She had built the brothel up with plenty of hard work and fair treatment for both the girls and the customers, but she could never have done it without him.

She rose and crossed to the sofa to give him an energetic kiss. "You're a real gent, Reg. A quarter of this business is worth a lot. There aren't many who would give it away for nothing."

He shrugged negligently. "I don't need the income anymore, and I've made back my initial investment many times over."

"Are you sure there isn't anything I can do to . . . show my appreciation?" Mischievously she ran a practiced hand down his lean body.

There was a flare of response in his eyes before he shook his head regretfully. "I don't think Martin would like that."

"No, I don't suppose he would," she agreed with equal regret. Martin was the former boxer who greeted guests, kept order, supervised the kitchen and wine cellar, and generally helped run the house. He was a fine fellow, her partner in more ways than one, but a bit possessive about his woman. Stirring up old embers would only cause trouble.

As Reggie stood to leave, Chessie asked wistfully, "Will you still stop by now and again to say hello? Even if you are respectable?"

He grinned, his earlier irritation forgotten. "Of course. Since most of your male guests are respectable, I shan't look out of place." He gave her a light kiss and left.

Chessie sighed after the door closed. She and Martin had

a very good arrangement, but there had never been anyone quite like Reggie.

The sun had reached its zenith and begun its downward path when Reggie woke the next morning. He lay very still, knowing that if he moved quickly he would probably be violently sick. Even the daylight glowing through his closed eyelids was a strain on his shattered nerves. His thoughts moving with painful slowness, he tried to piece together what had happened the night before.

White's and Blakeford, then dinner with Julian, but they had parted early. He started to roll onto his side, subsiding when a stab of pain lanced his eyeballs. Then Chessie, to return their business agreement. That visit he remembered all too clearly; she'd made a lot of damn' fool remarks about his drinking.

And you didn't believe her?

The inner voice that had given him bleak warning before echoed in his mind. He groaned, not wanting to think about the subject anymore. He should have brought Mac with him. Some of the valet's magic elixir would have been a godsend just now.

After dozing again, he was able to move, albeit slowly, the next time he woke up. Luckily there was water in the pitcher. Splashing his face helped clear his bleary eyes.

Wondering how he had gotten home the night before, he was starting to strip off his crumpled clothing when he spotted an unfamiliar chamber pot on a table by the door. Even in his present state, he had enough curiosity to investigate.

To his shock, he discovered that the china vessel was stuffed with banknotes. Good Lord, what had he been doing the previous night? He must have ended up in a gaming hell.

Lifting a handful of notes, he tried to guess how much money might be there, but it was too much effort.

Later, when a shot of Irish whiskey and fresh clothing had restored him to a semblance of life, he counted the money in the chamber pot. There was over a thousand pounds. He scowled at it in frustration. He would give the whole lot to know just what he had done last night. In a way, exact knowledge was unimportant. It had undoubtedly been a night of gaming and drinking like a thousand others, but he would never be sure unless he ran into someone who had been a witness to whatever had happened.

Though Reggie had always taken risks, he had done so knowing the odds and feeling himself to be master of the situation. To lose his memory was to lose control of himself in a deeply disturbing way.

As he bundled banknotes into a leather bag to take to his bank, Reggie remembered what Chessie had said the night before. His mouth tightened. Perhaps—just perhaps—she had a point. At Strickland he had drunk less and felt better.

Now, after less than a day in London, he felt like death would be a welcome release, and for reasons stronger than just the physical results of carousing. Well, he would be out of London tomorrow. He would go to Leicestershire to look at some mares, and after that he could go home.

It was such a natural thought that he wasn't even surprised by how quickly Strickland had become home.

Chapter 11

A week had passed since Davenport had left Strickland. Alys had progressed from relief to a cautious hope that he would see fit to return soon, in spite of the inevitable awkwardness. The man was certainly a disgraceful reprobate and a complication in her orderly life, but it was . . . interesting to have him around.

She was hard at work in her office, checking accounts and thinking, for the thousandth time, that Britain ought to change to a decimal money system, when Davenport reappeared. A light knock sounded at the door, and she bid the visitor to enter without raising her head.

Cat-footed, her employer crossed the room and was scarcely three feet away when he said, "Good afternoon."

Alys almost jumped out of her skin in surprise, her head whipping up and her pen spattering ink across the page. So much for dignity, she thought with an inward sigh. At least shock superseded the embarrassment she would have felt otherwise.

Davenport was his usual collected self, though amusement glinted in his eyes. "Sorry to startle you," he said mildly as he lounged against the edge of her desk, "but you did say come in. Anything noteworthy happen in my absence?"

She laid down her quill. "Everyone on the estate has now been vaccinated against smallpox, as you wished."

His brows shot up. "That was quick work. Did anyone resist?"

"Not for very long," Alys said with satisfaction. Backed by the landlord's authority, she had brooked no opposition. It had been a pleasure to accomplish so worthwhile a task.

"Congratulations on a job well done. Anything else?"

"I've been working on my proposal for improvements," she said hesitantly.

"What do you recommend?"

"To begin with, I think we should increase the livestock herds. Grain prices have been depressed since the war ended, and I don't see them getting better anytime soon. Some of the grain acreage can be converted to growing mangel-wurzels." Seeing a peculiar expression on Davenport's face, she explained, "Mangel-wurzels are a kind of beet root that makes excellent cattle fodder."

"I've heard of them, but never actually conversed on the subject." The corners of his mouth quirked up. "Come, Lady Alys, forget about their nutritional excellence and try to say *mangel-wurzel* with a straight face."

She had to smile. "You're right. It is an absurd name, isn't it?"

"Even a poet devoted to Nature would have difficulty writing a decent sonnet to a mangel-wurzel." He grinned. "Perhaps 'One of nature's major puzzles is the mangy mangel-wurzel.'"

That was too much, even for a woman of habitual seriousness. Alys gave way to laughter. "I doubt that Wordsworth could do better," she said when her mirth had subsided. Reggie's gaze on her face was warm and amused. Remarkable how intimate shared laughter could be.

Suddenly self-conscious, she rustled through the piles of papers in front of her. After extracting several sheets, she handed them to her employer. "Here is a list of new equipment we could use. Things are listed in order of usefulness, with estimated prices and notes on the advantages."

He ran his gaze down the column of neat printing. "I'll study this in more detail later. It looks plausible, though it won't be possible to buy everything at once. Anything else?"

"We need to build more cottages for the laborers. The older ones are a disgrace, damp and unfit for human habitation, and all of them are overcrowded." She produced another set of papers. "Here are the cost estimates."

He scanned the pages until he reached the last, where his lips pursed in a silent whistle that was definitely not approving. "This would be very expensive, and there are no direct financial benefits to the estate."

"But there are many indirect benefits." She leaned across her desk earnestly. "Healthy, happy people are better workers."

His gaze was sardonic. "Possibly true, but unprovable. You used a similar argument in support of your school."

"Yes, and it's as true now as it was then." Alys rose, feeling that if there was going to be a battle, she would do better standing. "Those prices are extremely reasonable. Much of the work can be done by estate workers during the quiet season, and the materials are all local."

She was just getting her wind up for a more detailed presentation when Davenport raised his hand. "I didn't say that we wouldn't do it. Again, it will have to be in stages." Then, with a half smile, he added, "I am not wholly wedded to practical return. To prove it, I'll show you what I've brought back."

Alys followed him outside and across the yard to the stables. There, in stalls that had been empty, were three new mares. "You're going to breed hunters?" she asked in surprise.

"You've a good eye for horseflesh."

She reached out to the nearest mare, a lop-eared chestnut

with powerful hindquarters and a deep chest. The mare gave Alys a friendly nudge in the shoulder. "These obviously aren't showy enough to be Rotten Row hacks, but they would do very well in the field."

"That mare may have lop ears, but she's very clever over fences and has the endurance to stay all day." Then, without a shift in his tone, Davenport continued, "I was going to apologize for what happened here last week."

Alys gave him a quick, shy glance that contained all of the discomfort she had anticipated from this meeting. Davenport was regarding her with a thoughtful expression on his dark, almost-handsome face, the light eyes inscrutable.

"I'll be damned if I can honestly say I'm sorry it happened," he continued, "but I am sorry if I embarrassed or distressed you in any way."

Alys's gaze whipped back to the mare. She concentrated on stroking the velvety muzzle. "I can't really say that I'm sorry, either," she said awkwardly, "but it mustn't happen again."

"Agreed. Subject closed?"

"Subject closed," she repeated. It had been a disgraceful episode, and she had behaved in a way quite unbefitting a lady of mature years and practiced dignity.

So why did she feel so regretful that it would not be repeated?

The day after his return to Strickland, Reggie visited the Stantons for the dinner that had been postponed when he went away. The evening proved to be surprisingly enjoyable. A round and smiling Aunt Elizabeth hugged him with almost as much enthusiasm as the collie had shown on his return from London.

Several other members of the local gentry were present, and they greeted him with amiable acceptance, as befitted someone born in the neighborhood. Over port, the men discussed local issues on the assumption that he was one of them. Luckily there were no single ladies present, though the matrons eyed the newcomer speculatively. Probably they were deciding which of the available fillies they should throw in his path.

Mindful of his resolve to drink less in general, and not to disgrace himself in front of the Stantons in particular, Reggie was moderate in his consumption of wine. Perhaps that was why he was so restless when he returned to Strickland. In the library he poured a very large whiskey, enjoying the familiar soothing glow that spread through his body. But the drink was not enough to relax him.

He glanced around the room, thinking that he really must do some redecorating. After thirty or forty years, it was hardly surprising that the place was drab. Perhaps fresh wallpaper and draperies would make the house seem less tomb-like. . . .

Exasperated, he finished his whiskey in a gulp and decided to go out. The collie, still unnamed and ownerless but ever eager for a walk, frisked along beside him. He was growing accustomed to the silly beast despite her penchant for tripping people.

The night was warm and fresh with the scents of early summer. Reggie lit a cigar and wandered toward the lake, feeling more at peace with the world. The land was like a seductive mistress, beckoning him to partake of its charms. Nonetheless, as small creatures rustled in the bushes and the hoot of an owl haunted the night, he felt very alone. Not with the frantic loneliness of London, but with a kind of sad melancholy, a sense of years wasted and paths not taken.

Without thought his feet had taken him past the lake and around to Rose Hall. The rambling outline of the steward's house had a certain elegance in the gentle glow of the crescent moon. No lights showed, for the hour was late, well past midnight.

He leaned against a tall elm that stood on the edge of the grounds, wondering if Alys Weston was ever lonely. She had her adopted family, and every person on the estate needed and respected her. Was that enough? She seemed a self-sufficient woman, so perhaps it was.

He drew on his cigar again. The tip flared with momentary brightness, then subsided to a dull glow. A faint sound came from the far side of the house. Then, oddly, he thought he saw a shape moving away from Rose Hall, a darker black in the night.

Reggie frowned and tried to make out more detail. Perhaps one of the children slipping away on some unsanctified expedition? That would probably be harmless in the case of the boys, less so if it was their nubile sister. Or perhaps it was a servant, or someone who had been visiting on one of the house's residents, or perhaps nothing at all.

He dropped the butt of his cigar and ground it under his heel, then quietly circled around the building to investigate. Less quietly, the collie pattered along beside him.

Whatever Reggie had seen was gone by the time he reached the far edge of the grounds. He said softly, "Well, dog, are you any good at tracking?"

With typical acuity the beast immediately turned away from the trail to face the house. She lifted her clownish head, ears pricked and shaggy tail still.

"Remind me not to offer you to the local hunt," Reggie said dryly.

The collie growled, a deep, throaty sound, and began moving forward. "For heaven's sake, quiet down," Reggie hissed. "You'll wake everyone in the house."

He caught the dog's collar, but she still strained toward the building. Worse, she began to bark with agitation.

Reggie swore under his breath and started to wrench her

away by sheer force. Then he detected a scent that the collie's sensitive nose had already recognized as different and wrong. The still night air carried a whiff of smoke, not the vegetal scent of his cigar but a sharp, acrid smell.

Suddenly tense, Reggie scanned the house. A faint glow showed through the windows on the ground floor. As he watched, he saw the first tentative lick of fire, followed with horrifying speed by a multitude of hungry flames. Rose Hall was burning.

Swearing, he released the dog's collar and sprinted toward the front door.

Haunted by memories of touch and vague longings, Alys had trouble falling asleep. When she did, she was seized by the familiar nightmare of rejection. *Why marry a bossy Long Meg like her? Why, for money, of course.*

Once again she fled in despair to self-destruction and dishonor, but tonight there was a change in events. For the first time she dreamed that her father sent pursuers after her. Hoarsely shouting hunters on horseback and baying hounds closed in, panting for her blood as she sought frantically for a hiding place.

Slowly her mind fought free of the depths of sleep to recognize that the barking was real but it came from a single dog, not a nightmare pack. And a man was shouting and pounding on the door. For a moment more she lay suspended in confusion.

Then she smelled the smoke. Coming instantly alert, she uttered an oath under her breath as she scrambled from the bed.

The floorboards were warm, dangerously warm, beneath her bare feet. She grabbed her robe and pulled it around her as she left her room and raced down the hall, shouting, "Merry, Peter, William, get up!"

Throwing open Meredith's door, she saw the girl sit up sleepily. "Quick, the house is on fire!" Alys said in a staccato voice. "We must get out immediately."

Merry gasped, then jumped wordlessly from her bed and pulled on slippers and robe before following her guardian into the hall. This end of the house was still cool, but smoke was spreading along the ceiling, swirling ever lower in thick, eye-stinging clouds.

The boys were emerging from their rooms. William rubbed his eyes drowsily, but Peter was alert and aware of the danger.

"Peter and Merry, get outside and take William with you," Alys ordered. "I'll get the servants."

Peter opened his mouth to protest, and she cut him off sharply. "Just do it!"

He nodded and took his little brother's hand. Alys waited long enough to see her charges start down the center stairs, then headed to the attic, grateful that the narrow steps were at the far end of the house from the fire.

She shouted a warning as she ran up. At the top of the steps, she found the cook, Mrs. Haver, emerging from her room, a dark shawl clutched around her plump shoulders.

"The stairs are safe, just go down quickly and get outside," Alys barked. The smoke had followed her up, and drawing in breath to speak made her cough.

Mrs. Haver's eyes widened in shock. Then she darted back into her room. Alys chased after her, swearing. "For God's sake, whatever you have here isn't worth the risk!"

"Easy for you to say." Mrs. Haver's voice trembled on the edge of hysteria as she lifted one end of the mattress and pulled out whatever treasure she had hidden.

Alys grabbed the cook's arm and propelled her out the door and toward the stairs. "Move, dammit!"

Not waiting to see if she was obeyed, Alys sped down the narrow, dark passage. The only other servant was Janie

Herald, the young housemaid. Her bedroom was at the opposite end of the attic, and in the dark Alys couldn't find the right door at first. She mistakenly entered two storage rooms before finding the correct one.

The little, slant-ceilinged chamber smelled faintly of the cheap perfume Janie used, but there was no response to Alys's call. She fumbled her way across the room, stubbing her toes painfully before falling onto the narrow bed.

The bed was empty, the blankets unwrinkled. Momentarily breathless, Alys's mind flashed through the possibilities. Janie had been walking out with a boy from the village. Perhaps she had slipped out to meet him?

Praying that was the case, Alys pushed herself upright and ran out of the room, her long legs carrying her rapidly down the length of the attic hall. Smoke was heavy on the steps, but much worse on the lower floor, where ravenous flames were devouring what had been her own bedroom.

Tickled by some vague memory, Alys dug a handkerchief from the pocket of her robe, then made a quick detour into Peter's room to dip the fabric square into his water pitcher. Holding the wet cloth across her nose and mouth and bending low into clearer air, Alys forced herself to run toward the inferno, and the steps that led to safety.

The staircase to the ground floor was still clear, but only just. Her left side scorched as she raced downward. She heard a hideous grinding noise, then a deafening crash as the timbers collapsed from the upper floors. A blast of hellish heat hit her, and the steps shook beneath her feet.

As she reached ground level, a cloud of sparks swirled around her, burning tiny black holes in the robe and stinging exposed flesh. The lung-choking smoke was so thick that she could see almost nothing despite the fiery glare.

She was starting toward the front of the house when she heard a wail of animal terror. Attila came flying toward her, his tail singed and smoking. She scooped the frantic, clawing cat into her arms, then turned the corner toward the front door.

There she stopped in horror. The main hall in front of her was completely blocked by smoke and flame. She whirled back the way she had come, but fire now engulfed the stairs. Her fear erupted into a scream of pure terror. She was trapped in the inferno.

She felt herself becoming dizzy as savage flames consumed the air. With no place left to run, she crouched on the floor, half fainting. Her suffocating lungs labored vainly for breath. The heat was unbearable, and there was no air left to breathe, no air at all. Her arms tightened around the cat's trembling body.

As she slid into unconsciousness, she wished with grim humor that she had seduced Reginald Davenport. Since she was going to burn in hell, it was a pity she didn't have any really enjoyable sins to suffer for.

When Reggie's shouts and pounding on the door of Rose Hall produced no visible results, he pulled off his coat and wrapped it around one arm. He smashed the neared window and unlatched the casements, then scrambled into the drawing room. From the noise and the heavy smoke, the fire was spreading swiftly.

He stepped into the main hall, and found the three Spensers racing toward him. Reggie shouted, "Merry, where is Lady Alys?"

As Peter hurried his young brother toward the front door, Meredith paused, her hair a pale halo around her face. "She went to the attic to wake the servants."

"Get outside with your brothers and stay there."

She nodded and darted away.

Reggie had been caught in a burning tavern once. No one who hadn't had such an experience could appreciate the

unbelievable speed with which fire could move. Praying that
Allie and the servants were on their way out, he started
along the center hall that led to the stairs. He'd gone only a
few steps when a woman emerged from the smoke and ran
right into him. Heavy and middle-aged, she was stumbling
and gasping for breath.

Reggie slipped an arm around the woman and half carried
her to the front door. "Where is Lady Alys?" he asked sharply
as he helped her outside.

"She . . . she went for Janie." After an endless interval
of coughing, the woman added hoarsely, "Should be right
behind me."

Reggie turned to see the flames burst through the roof at
one end of the house. The yard was lit by garish, wavering
light. A safe distance from the house, the young Spensers
stood watching the destruction of their home in mesmerized
horror.

From the direction of the tenants' cottage, Reggie saw the
dark forms of approaching people, several of them pulling
a fire engine behind them. He doubted that it would do
much good, but at least someone was thinking.

Seeing the engine, Peter turned and ran to help. Meredith
simply stood, her hand holding that of her little brother.

Reggie turned back to the house, swearing. Allie should
have been out by now with the missing servant, unless they
had been overcome by smoke. He plunged into the house
again.

Flames had cut across the center hall a bare dozen feet in
front of him. The incredible heat struck him like a weapon.
He halted uncertainly, trying to remember the layout of the
house. Was there a way around the blaze?

Then he heard a soul-chilling scream from beyond the
curtain of fire. *Allie.* His stomach turned as he realized that
she must be trapped on the other side.

The Oriental carpet in the drawing room. Instantly he

darted into the room on his right, where a thick Persian rug held place of pride. Only a few light chairs weighed it down. With a ferocious jerk on the nearest edge, he tugged it free. The carpet was small enough for one man to handle, just barely. He folded it in half, then in half again, before pivoting and returning to the flaming hall.

Going up to the searing edge of the fire, he hurled the weight of the carpet forward, keeping one fringed end in his hands. The heavy wool smashed down over the flames, creating a temporary fire-free zone. Eyes burning, he ran across between walls of flame, keeping low so he wouldn't pass out from lack of air.

Beyond the carpet the fierce, blazing light revealed Allie crumpled against the wall. Praying that she was still alive, he closed the distance between them and scooped her into his arms. Then, drawing on every shred of strength and stamina developed in an athletic life, he carried her back across the rapidly charring carpet. The walls of fire were nearer now, the flames scorching voraciously.

Lungs burning with smoke and strain, Reggie staggered through the dimly visible front door to safety. As he stumbled down the shallow steps, he thought dizzily that it was absolutely typical of Alys Weston that she would be rescued clutching a scorched and yowling cat in her arms.

Blessed coolness surrounded her. Perhaps hell was ice and not fire. Her lungs were working again, drawing in air uncontaminated by smoke.

Slowly Alys realized that she was being carried. A pair of familiar feline legs thumped against her stomach. Apparently Attila had just kicked away from her.

Her eyes stung as she forced them open. With some effort she brought Reggie Davenport into focus as he lowered her to the ground. He stayed kneeling beside her, one powerful arm supporting her in a sitting position. His soot-smudged face was only inches away, the blue eyes pale as ice.

"Are you all right?" he asked, his voice quiet against the sounds of crackling fire and smashing timbers. Swathes of black marred his white shirt.

When she nodded, he continued, "Is the other servant still inside?"

Alys swallowed and attempted speech, her voice emerging as a charred croak. "I don't think so." She broke into a spasm of coughing.

Davenport's arm tightened around her as she struggled for breath. "I hope she isn't," he said grimly. "No one else will be coming out alive."

"I think Janie might have slipped out to see her young man," Alys managed. "When I find her, I'm going to wring her neck."

"You're entitled. You damned near died in there."

"I noticed." Alys lifted a trembling hand to her face. Her thick braid had come undone, and long strands of hair trailed across her cheek. Brushing them back, she looked up to see the children's concerned faces around her.

Smiling with as much reassurance as she could muster, she tried to stand, but Reggie held her firmly against him. "Stay still until you get your strength back. There isn't anything you can do."

Alys looked toward the house she had lived in for four years, just in time to see the slate roof crash inward with thunderous force. Flames shot high into the dark night air, illuminating the men pumping water onto the blaze. It was a futile effort.

Her friend Jamie Palmer crossed the yard and squatted beside her, his face grave. "Are you all right. Lady Alys?"

She patted his arm, knowing that he was feeling guilty for not having been there to stop the fire before it could get going. The dear man was wonderfully protective. "I've been better, Jamie, but there's nothing seriously wrong."

He nodded, then went back to the fire engine. Beside her, William's voice quavered. "Wh . . . where will we live?"

Alys opened her arms, and he burrowed into them, seeking reassurance. Before she could answer his question, Davenport said, "You'll come back to the main house. There's plenty of room there, for you and your servants both."

Alys had not thought that far ahead, and she was intensely grateful to let her employer take charge. They might have only the clothes they stood up in, but at least they would have a roof over their heads.

She heard a familiar voice, and looked up to see Janie Herald hastening across the yard, her young face frightened in the uneven light. "Oh, Miss Weston, it's dreadful! Did everyone get out?"

Reggie answered astringently, "Miss Weston almost died in the fire because she was looking for you. Remember that the next time you go sneaking off."

Expression crushed and guilty, the maid began to cry. The young man at her side put his arm around her, and she turned to bury her face against his shoulder.

Alys quietly told Reggie, "You shouldn't have been so hard on her."

His dark brows rose sardonically. "Am I correct that the extra time you spent looking for her was the difference between getting out easily and being roasted like a Christmas goose?"

Alys sighed, too drained to argue. "You're quite right." His arm was still around her, and it was too pleasant a sensation to interrupt.

Reggie glanced at the young Spensers. "There's no point in lingering. Peter, collect the older woman—the cook, I think?—and help her to the house. The maid can come, too, unless she wants to go to her family, or her young man. Miss

Spenser, you keep an eye on William." Turning to Alys, he asked, "Can you walk on your own?"

She nodded and got to her feet, then almost fell when she took a step forward. For some reason, her knees were remarkably weak.

With a muttered oath, Reggie grabbed her. "Good God, woman, you don't even have shoes on."

Without so much as asking permission, he scooped her up in his arms and started back toward the manor house. He carried her easily, though she was not a small woman. When he had brought her out of the burning house, Alys had not been conscious enough to appreciate the experience, but now she was very aware of the strength and warmth of his arms. Settling her head against his shoulder, she prepared to enjoy the ride, but could not resist a faint chuckle.

"If something amusing has happened, perhaps you can share it with me?" Davenport suggested.

"I was just thinking that I've never been swept off my feet before," Alys murmured, too tired to censor her words.

He laughed. "You've probably never given a man a chance to do any sweeping."

She was still trying to decide if there were any deeper meanings to his words when they arrived back at the manor house. The housekeeper had been wakened by the commotion associated with the fire. With a few quick words Reggie arranged for rooms to be readied, milk to be heated for William, and brandy poured for the others.

Then he carried Alys upstairs to a guest room. Alys was exhausted and three-quarters asleep, but she struggled to sit up after he deposited her on the four-poster bed. "The children . . ." she said hazily.

"They're fine," he said, pressing her back against the pillows with a firm, impersonal hand. "Lie down."

Alys was used to being responsible for everything, and for a moment she resisted. She hadn't been tucked into bed since she was in the nursery. But oddly, it was easy to trust that Reggie would take care of everything, and in her present state of exhaustion she welcomed relinquishing her burdens.

Sleep claimed her almost immediately, but with the last threads of awareness, she felt him sponging the soot off her face. Surprising how gentle a large man could be.

This time when she slept, there were no nightmares.

Chapter 12

When she opened her eyes and saw the light-drenched brocade canopy, for a moment Alys thought she was home in Carleon. Then memory snapped her back to the present. Carleon was irrevocably lost. Now she was the steward of Strickland, homeless and possessing no more than a shift and a robe with burned spots. Oh, yes, she also owned a cat and a mare.

From the angle of the sun, it was late. She sat up in bed and stretched. As she did, a knock sounded, followed by Merry's golden head.

"Good, you're awake." The rest of Meredith followed into the room, along with a tray holding steaming coffee and a plate of fresh bread rolls. "Mr. Davenport said not to disturb you, but I knew that without your coffee, you'd never wake up properly."

Alys accepted the hot drink gratefully and leaned back against the headboard of the bed. "When you decide whom to marry, I will send references to whatever lucky man you have chosen. You always know exactly what a person needs."

Meredith laughed and settled gracefully into a chair. She wore a plain calico dress that didn't quite fit, but showed no signs of harm from the night's disaster.

Alys asked, "How are the boys?"

"They're fine. Mr. Davenport found some clothes for them in the village, then packed them off to school. This afternoon a seamstress is coming to take our measurements so proper things can be made up."

Alys felt a spurt of annoyance at his high-handedness, but had to give him credit for efficiency.

Merry helped herself to a fresh roll and spread marmalade on it. "He said he's sorry there aren't any women's clothes available in your size, but he found some men's things that should fit." The girl gestured at the garments in question, which lay across a chair. "He said that when it's convenient, he would like to talk to you in the library."

It was born in on Alys that Davenport had made a strong impression on Meredith. Her entire conversation seemed to revolve around his words and wishes.

A moment later another concern was laid to rest. Merry had left the door ajar, and now Attila strolled through. His lofty dignity was intact even though his tail was much less plume-like than usual.

"I'm so glad Attila is all right," Alys exclaimed as the cat jumped on the bed, then walked up to sniff at the roll in her right hand.

"It takes more than a fire to disconcert Attila," Merry said with amusement. "This morning, he showed up at the kitchen door and demanded to be fed as if he hadn't a care in the world. Some of his hair had charred ends that I trimmed off, but he appears to have taken no real harm."

"Obviously not. It didn't take him long to find out where the food is." Alys put aside roll and mug to cuddle the cat on her lap. He settled down, purring.

As she scratched his neck, Alys noticed that most of his magnificent long whiskers were gone, leaving only short stubs. "Look at the poor fellow's whiskers," she said. Those whiskers that were left were curled into tight little corkscrews.

She tentatively touched one. Made brittle by heat, it snapped off, leaving another stub. "He'll have to be careful going into narrow places until these grow back."

"Attila got off very lightly," Meredith pointed out. "If you hadn't been clutching him when Mr. Davenport brought you out of the house, he'd be in cat heaven now."

"I got off very lightly, too," Alys said with feeling. "I thought my time had come last night."

Merry's face instantly sobered. "We all did," she said, unable to suppress a tremor in her voice. "We were sure you were gone. And Mr. Davenport, too, when he went back into the house . . ." She shuddered, her brightness dimmed. In her young life, she had already lost too many loved ones.

"It takes more than a little fire to get rid of me," Alys said, moving Attila to one side so she could swing her long legs out of the bed. As her feet touched the floor, she said involuntarily, "Ouch!"

"What's wrong?"

Alys perched on the edge of the bed and examined her soot-stained feet. "I didn't pay much attention last night, but I banged my toes at least once, and the floor was very hot. Now, don't look so upset," she added quickly, "and don't you *dare* hover over me as if I were an aging relation."

"Yes, ma'am," Merry said meekly.

Alys wriggled her toes experimentally. "There's no real damage, but I would dearly love a bath."

"The water should be here any moment," Meredith said. Right on cue, a soft knock sounded on the door, and two maids carrying coppers of hot water entered.

"I'll write you two references, not one," Alys promised.

Once she was alone in the hip bath, she surrendered to the bliss of soaking soot and soreness away. She finished by washing the scent of smoke from her thick hair, then climbed from the tub with regret, not quite ready for the unavoidable world that waited outside her bedroom door.

She toweled her hair dry before combing and braiding it into her usual coronet. Then she dressed. Her employer had done a good job choosing clothing. Doubtless he was expert at judging a woman's measurements, she thought with a touch of acid. The trousers were inevitably a bit tight in the hip and much too loose in the waist, and the boots and socks were a little large, but they would do.

Reminding herself that beggars couldn't be choosers, she went downstairs. Davenport was working in the library. He got to his feet as she entered. "You look well recovered."

"I am." She chose a chair. "Attila and I owe you a considerable debt of gratitude."

"You might, but Attila doesn't. I assure you, any rescuing of that worthless creature was purely accidental," he said with a smile as he sat down again.

The black and white collie trotted over from where it had been lying at Davenport's feet. Alys ruffled the dog's furry neck. "Speaking of worthless creatures, I see you still haven't found a home for the dog."

"Last night, the collie proved that she wasn't entirely worthless, so I think she's earned the right to stay." At Alys's inquiring look he explained, "We were taking a walk last night when she smelled smoke and insisted on investigating. If she hadn't, I might not have been on the scene in time."

Alys looked into the collie's limpid brown eyes. "Thank you, Dog." Looking up with a smile, she said, "If you're going to keep her, you'll have to give her a name."

"You mean I can't just call her Dog?"

"I suppose so," she said dubiously, "but it would be better for her self-respect if she had a name of her own."

Reggie's light eyes twinkled. "In addition to your other skills, you're also an expert on canine self-esteem?"

"No, but I have opinions on everything," she said with a straight face.

Reggie laughed. "Very well. If she must have a name, how about Nemesis?"

Alys grinned. "That seems appropriate, since she seems to be your fate." More seriously, she asked, "I trust you are well? You were exposed to your share of smoke and fire last night. You could have been killed."

He looked faintly uncomfortable. "Don't paint me as a hero, Allie. It was in my own best interest to save you. With a less efficient steward, I might actually have to do some work myself."

Alys gave a sniff of disbelief. "You will do as much or as little as you please, either with me or without me." Then, curiously, she asked, "How did you manage to find me in that inferno?"

He shrugged dismissively. "I heard you cry out and knew you couldn't be too far down the hall, so I took the drawing room carpet and threw it over the flames. It created a temporary firebreak."

Alys thought of the moment when she had realized that she was trapped, and shivered. "That was quick thinking."

There was silence for a moment. Deciding that it was time to start talking about the future, she said, "I also appreciate your letting us stay here last night. I'm afraid it will take a day or two to make long-term arrangements, but we can move to the Silent Woman this afternoon and get out from under your feet."

"Nonsense. There's ample room here." He toyed with a letter opener for a moment, his beautiful long fingers graceful. "Actually, the simplest solution to finding you a home is for all of you to stay here."

Alys stared at him. For a moment she thought she detected a touch of diffidence in his suggestion. She dismissed the thought; diffidence was not a quality she could associate with Reggie Davenport. "Don't be absurd. It would be wholly inappropriate."

"Your contract states that I provide you with housing. With Rose Hall gone, there's no suitable residence on the estate," he pointed out. "All of the tenant cottages are occupied, and my housekeeper says there are no houses to let that are close enough."

Alys bit her lip, knowing he was right. As steward, she needed to be available, not miles away. Besides, the boys' school and the children's friends were all nearby. It would be extremely convenient to stay at the manor. But she was uneasily aware that she had felt a treacherous tickle of pleasure at the thought of sharing a house with her employer. Absurdly, she liked having the man around, liked talking to him.

Would like to kiss him again.

Suppressing the thought, she considered Meredith. Would a responsible guardian let an innocent girl live under the same roof as a rake?

With his usual uncanny perception, Davenport said, "If you're worried about propriety, I think that having the whole family here would rate as suitable chaperonage."

And a thirty-year-old, dyed-in-the-wool spinster certainly made a good chaperone. No rake could possibly be interested in her. At least, not when he was sober. Alys said, "I'll consider your suggestion, and discuss it with the children."

"I trust that you don't think one more night here will compromise you?"

"I suppose not," she allowed ungraciously.

He appeared amused at her quandary, but said only, "Do you feel ready to look at what's left of Rose Hall?"

It had to be done sooner or later. She nodded, and together they went outside and made the short walk to her former home.

A house looked much smaller when only stone walls remained. Rose Hall was a desolate shell, the windows blank and empty. There would be nothing worth salvaging, for the destruction was nearly total. The roof and floors had collapsed all the way through to the cellar, and smoke still curled from charred beams. Incongruously, a few flowers bloomed where the beds hadn't been trampled the night before.

Alys circled the remains of the house, picking her way around blackened fragments of wood and shattered slates. When she thought of how close she had come to leaving her burned bones among the embers, she shuddered. She suspected that for the rest of her life, her dreams would relive the panic of being circled by fire. Perhaps, if she were lucky, that would displace her other recurring nightmare.

Davenport's voice pulled her back from her dark thoughts. "How much did you lose in the way of personal belongings?"

"The usual things. Books, clothes, mementos. The bits and pieces that define a life." Alys shrugged, exerting iron control. "There was nothing very valuable kept in the house. My savings and the best pieces of jewelry Meredith inherited from her mother are in the bank at Shaftesbury. The only real loss for me . . ." She stopped.

When she didn't continue, he prompted, "The only real loss was . . . ?"

Her throat tightened. "I had a locket with my mother's picture in it."

"I'm sorry," he said gently.

His sympathy brought a quick sting of tears to her eyes. Perhaps that was why her all-too-perceptive employer changed the subject.

"Have you any idea what might have caused the fire?"

The practical question restored Alys's composure. "To be honest, I hadn't thought about it. At this season the fireplaces weren't lit. The only source of fire would be the banked coals in the kitchen, or a lamp or candle if someone was still awake."

"I doubt it was a lamp. When I walked by, I didn't see any

lights. I remember thinking that everyone must be long since asleep. As for the kitchen, it was on that side of the house, wasn't it?" Davenport pointed.

When Alys nodded, he began circling the ruins, his eyes narrowed. "The fire began at the west end of the house, probably in the cellar. I came along about the time the flames had burned through to the ground floor and had become visible."

Alys frowned. "I know that sometimes fires can start spontaneously in piles of rags or rubbish, but our cellar was quite orderly, and rather damp to boot. I can't think of anything there that might have started a fire."

Reggie absently rolled over a blackened piece of wood with the toe of his polished boot. "Do you have any serious enemies?"

"Good God! Do you really think it could have been arson?" Alys stared at Reggie, wondering if his wits were wandering.

"I don't know what to think, except that a fire has to start somehow, and this one doesn't appear to have been an accident." He studied the smoking ruins. "When I came by last night, I thought I saw someone sneaking away from the house. It could have been your hot-blooded housemaid, but when she showed up at the fire, she was wearing a light-colored dress. The person I saw wore dark clothing. If I really did see someone."

"What kind of lunatic would set fire to a house full of sleeping people?" Alys said, aghast.

"Someone obsessed by fire. There are such madmen." He turned to face her, expression stern. "But we must face the possibility that the blaze was deliberately set to injure someone in your household. Does Miss Spenser have any heart-broken swains who might fire her house from pure frustration?"

Alys made herself seriously consider the idea before

answering. "No. She has any number of admirers, but she is always charming to them. I can't imagine that any are lovelorn or unstable enough to do something so dreadful."

His brows drew together. "Was anyone so angry about the smallpox vaccinations that they might want to retaliate? I would be a more logical target, but you were the one that carried out my orders."

"There was some grumbling, but no one was really outraged."

"I hope you're right. I would hate to think that you were endangered by my actions." His gaze met hers, dark with concern. "Perhaps I'm just naturally suspicious. But—just in case—be careful. And talk to your wards about this."

"I will," she said soberly. "I surely will."

Alys had her discussion with her charges over tea that afternoon. Though each had lost cherished personal possessions in the fire, their gratitude that no one had been injured or killed kept their losses in perspective. Alys mentioned the possibility of arson, but decided not to suggest that it might have been deliberately aimed at someone in the house. Davenport's wild theory must be a result of his own colorful past. Murder by arson simply wouldn't happen in peaceful Dorset.

She half hoped that her wards would be reluctant to live in the manor house, but they received the idea with enthusiasm. "By Jove, Mr. Davenport really wouldn't mind having us here? He's a great gun." Peter gave his approval quickly, then subsided into silence, probably plotting the best time to ask Davenport for driving lessons.

William liked the idea of being so close to the stables, while Meredith got a speculative expression on her lovely face. "We would actually be living here, not just guests?" When Alys nodded, Merry said dreamily, "This house is so much better for entertaining than Rose Hall, don't you think?"

"Yes, and Mr. Davenport has insisted that we treat it as home. He has been very generous." He'd even tried to pay for the cost of replacing their wardrobes. A brisk argument had ensued, resolved only when Alys agreed to let him pay half of the costs. She continued, "He doesn't really understand what he's letting himself in for. If you plague the poor man to death, we'll have to make different arrangements. But since you all like the idea, we'll try it."

Her decision was greeted with whoops of joy. Of course the pleasure Alys herself felt was merely because her wards were happy.

After the boys left, Alys had a private talk with Meredith. Eyes dancing, Merry assured her guardian that she had no intention of succumbing to Mr. Davenport's elderly charms. He had acted in a most respectable—indeed, positively avuncular—fashion. Not quite convinced of her employer's respectability, Alys resigned herself to trusting in Meredith's considerable good sense.

The only real objections came from Junius Harper. He arrived late in the afternoon, bubbling with solicitude and indignation. Alys received him in the small salon, grateful that Davenport was away from the house.

Junius clasped her hand fervently. "I spent last night with the bishop in Salisbury, and have only just returned. You can imagine the perturbation I felt upon hearing the dreadful news! Sweet, fragile Miss Spenser . . . such danger must have been a great strain on her delicate nerves."

While Merry certainly had cause to be distressed, it was Alys who had come closest to being baked like a Sunday joint. But as everyone knew there was nothing delicate about that great, strapping Alys. She disengaged her hand. "Certainly it was a frightening experience, but at least no one took any injury."

As they seated themselves, the vicar's expression changed to one of dire foreboding. "As alarming as news of the fire was, it was as nothing to the agitation I felt on learning that you had spent the night in this . . . this . . . house of infamy!"

"House of infamy? That's coming it a bit strong, Junius," Alys said, amused by his priorities. "Would being burned alive really be preferable to a 'fate worse than death'?"

Ignoring her digression, he intoned, "I do not hesitate to tell you that I was shocked. Nay, more than shocked. *Appalled.*"

Wishing that he had hesitated to say it, Alys said with asperity, "Brave of you to risk your immortal soul by calling here."

Blind to sarcasm, Junius said, "I hope I know where my duty lies. But I must insist that you remove yourself and the children immediately. I am surprised that you did not think to go to the vicarage last night. Though I was not there to receive you, my housekeeper would have made you welcome, and Miss Spenser would not have been exposed to that rake's wiles."

The vicar's generosity was not quite enough to balance the surge of temper Alys felt at his peremptory words. "Since I was in no condition to consider alternative residences, Mr. Davenport's offer was most welcome. And need I remind you that you have no right to insist that I do anything?"

"Surely I have some right as your spiritual adviser, if not as your friend," Junius said stiffly.

Feeling ashamed of herself, Alys said in a more conciliatory tone, "I know that you've taken Mr. Davenport in dislike, but I assure you, he has been most gentlemanly. He also showed great presence of mind and courage last night. Did your informant mention that he saved my life, at great risk to his own?"

The vicar dismissed that with a flick of his hand. "Physical courage comes easily to his type. It is his morals—or rather, his lack of them—that concern me. I will have no peace of mind until you and your charges are away from here."

"Then resign yourself to having your peace cut up," she said, her eyes glittering with exasperation. "Mr. Davenport has invited us to live here, and we have accepted."

Horror showed on the vicar's face. "You cannot mean it! It is bad enough to have stayed one night in the aftermath of a disaster, but to *live* here? It is wholly unacceptable. Miss Spenser's reputation will be ruined forever."

"Between her brothers and me, she will be adequately chaperoned." Alys was quite willing to use Davenport's own arguments. "Besides, we must live somewhere, and there are no other houses available in the area."

"You could live at the vicarage."

She sighed. While Junius was not a stupid man, he could be quite maddeningly obstinate. "If it is propriety that concerns you, the vicarage would be no improvement, since your household is also a bachelor establishment."

"Surely the differences between the homes of a man of the cloth and a libertine should be obvious!" Junius said hotly.

"Of course there are differences. For one thing, Strickland is considerably more spacious," Alys snapped, struggling with the desire to give Junius a really crushing setdown. "While your offer is magnanimous, it would look very odd indeed for us to move in with you. Mr. Davenport's obligation to provide his steward with housing is at least a legitimate reason for us to stay here."

Junius swallowed hard. "If you need a reason, you can marry me. Besides providing a proper home for the children, you would also be able to give up an unladylike employment that must surely be distasteful to you."

Not only was she not the sort of woman men desired, she couldn't even inspire a decent proposal! Provoked beyond tact, Alys exclaimed, "That is the most bird-witted reason for marriage I've ever heard! Believe me, there is no need to sacrifice yourself. My wards are all delighted by the prospect of living at Strickland, and I think it will work well. As for my employment, I don't find it in the least distasteful. Indeed, I enjoy it."

"If you won't marry me, then let me pay my addresses to Miss Spenser!" the vicar said wildly. "It is unthinkable that such sweet goodness be corrupted by a man such as Davenport."

Two proposals within a minute! The vicar must be setting some sort of record. "I assure you, Junius, such draconian measures as marriage are not necessary. Meredith will come to no harm here. Your lack of faith in her virtue is most unflattering, I might add." Offering a sop to the cleric's anxiety, Alys went on, "Besides, Mr. Davenport will probably soon tire of the country, and we won't see him again for months." She didn't believe that, but the possibility might reconcile the vicar to the situation.

He stood, his movements heavy. "I see that your mind is quite made up. I will pray that you come to your senses before it is too late."

As Junius was taking his leave, Davenport entered the small salon with Nemesis faithfully shadowing his heels. His eyes took on a glint of unholy amusement when he saw Alys's visitor, but he greeted the vicar with civility, as if they hadn't come close to blows at their previous meeting.

"No doubt you are surprised to see me here, Davenport," the vicar said belligerently.

"Not at all. Since you are a friend of Miss Weston and her charges, I would expect you to call," Davenport said with perfect affability.

"I shall be calling again." Junius's tone made it a challenge.

"But of course." Davenport raised his brows. "You don't

strike me as the sort of man to flinch at entering the lion's den if his cause is just."

While Alys suppressed a choke of laughter, the vicar gave his host a suspicious glare, unable to decide if he was being mocked. Deeming discretion the better part of valor, he took his leave. After his departure Alys said, "It was good of you not to forbid him the house, even though he behaved so badly the first time you met."

Davenport gave a half smile. "If this is to be your home, I hardly have the right to forbid your guests. I'll admit I would rather the good vicar didn't run tame here, but I daresay my godless presence will reduce the number of his visits."

Alys was sure that he was right, and took a certain guilty pleasure in the thought. Junius could be rather a trial. "Were you looking for me?"

Reggie nodded. "I thought it might be useful to discuss sharing the same establishment so we know what to expect of each other."

"An excellent idea," Alys agreed, sitting down again. Over the next hour they discussed a variety of issues. Davenport felt no need to eat in solitary quiet, so dinners would be taken together. Alys did suggest that William could eat in the nursery, but was glad Davenport felt it unfair for the child to be condemned to eat alone merely because he was the youngest.

The bedrooms assigned to the guests the night before would become permanent. The young people were in a cluster in the east wing, Davenport was at the far west end of the house, and Alys's spacious chamber was in the center, flanked by empty bedrooms on each side so she would have more privacy. Although it wasn't said aloud, the location was a good guardian position since, at least in theory, Alys would hear any surreptitious night traffic. Propriety was such a silly business. Any two people wishing to misbehave together could surely find a way.

They had discussed the duties of Alys's servants and reached an amiable accord when Alys saw Attila enter the door of the salon. The cat immediately went into his hunter mode, golden eyes feral, belly tight to the carpet, hindquarters and tail quivering. Moving with panther swiftness, Attila lunged across the carpet and pounced on the collie, who was peacefully sleeping with her muzzle on her master's foot.

Nemesis jumped up yelping and whirled madly, looking for the attacker. As Alys swept the cat up in her arms, Davenport concentrated on calming his beleaguered dog. "Your cat, Lady Alys, is a bully," he said, his face alight with amusement.

"I'm afraid you're right," she said ruefully, struggling to keep Attila from going after Nemesis again. "I hadn't realized quite how much of one. I know cats don't much like other cats unless they are raised together, but I'm surprised that Attila will attack a sizable dog."

As the trembling collie pressed against Davenport's leg, he ruffled her ears comfortingly. "You're going to have to get used to him, Nemesis." He chuckled. "I have a feeling that the humans of our households will get on better than the pets."

As they laughed together, it was easy to believe that was true.

Chapter 13

Adjusting to life in the manor house proved painless. Even effervescent William recognized that the owner of the house was unused to the vagaries of children, and didn't press his attentions unless invited to.

Dinner was the only meal they took together, and it proved a comfortable occasion. Davenport tended to speak little, but watched the young people with obvious amusement. Soon everyone was relaxed and volunteering information on their respective activities. Peter screwed up his courage to ask for instruction in driving, and with dazed delight found himself the eager student of a veritable top-sawyer. William's heart was won when a lively pony, just the right size for him, appeared in the stables, while Merry quickly fell into a friendly, teasing relationship with Davenport.

After her initial surprise, Alys realized that it was only to be expected. The children had missed having a father, and if not precisely paternal, Davenport did make an excellent honorary uncle. Only with Alys did he maintain a certain reserve, friendly but not entirely relaxed. Perhaps he feared she would pursue him ruthlessly if he gave her any encouragement.

Nonetheless, he did make the effort to subvert the seamstress. When the last lot of clothing was delivered, it included several gowns Alys had not ordered, all in brighter
colors and more daring cut than she usually wore. Meredith
admitted with a smile that she and Davenport had planned
it between them.

When Alys confronted him indignantly, he pointed out
that she was no longer a governess, so why did she dress like
one? Surely there could be no need to restrict herself to navy
blue and brown when she was dining with her family. In
fact, she owed it to the people who had to look at her to
maintain a good appearance.

Half amused and half exasperated by his high-handed
ways, she kept the gowns. In her fashionable youth she had
been restricted to demure white muslins which did nothing
for her coloring. It was a pleasure now to wear rich green or
rust or gold. She thought she looked rather well. Certainly
the children thought so, and the admiring warmth in Davenport's eyes sent a glow through her entire body.

The days quickly returned to the normal pattern of work
and family. It was the nights that were difficult. Alys told
herself the problem was a strange bed, but she was all too
aware that she was sleeping under the same roof with a man
of quite overpowering attractiveness. A man, moreover, who
showed occasional signs of interest in the fact that she was
a female.

As she endured her fourth night of insomnia, she finally
asked herself exactly what she wanted from Reggie Davenport. An affair? While it was conceivable that in the heat of
passion she might throw caution to the winds, it was quite
impossible for sober, unglamorous Alys Weston to cold-
bloodedly embark on such a wanton course.

In a burst of candor, she admitted to herself that the idea
of being his mistress was enormously appealing. Yet how
could she set such an example to the children? An affair

could not be kept a secret for long, and would surely jeopardize her position as steward.

So an affair was out of the question, and there was no other possibility. Her employer appeared to enjoy her company, had even found her not wholly lacking in appeal, but he was certainly not going to marry her. If Davenport wanted to set up a nursery, there were any number of more eligible females in the area. Or he could go to London and have the pick of the crop. The very respectable fortune he had acquired would offset his rakish past, and with his personal magnetism he would have his choice of ladies who were far younger, prettier, and wealthier than she.

Alys reminded herself that if he ever did marry, he would doubtless make the very devil of a husband. However, she feared that her thoughts had a faint whiff of the fox complaining about unobtainable grapes.

As she rolled over in her bed, she faced her worse fear with brutal honesty: that in a moment of drunken indiscrimination, Davenport would take her to his bed, and find the experience too uninteresting to repeat. Even the thought brought a sick knot to her stomach. The least pain and humiliation lay in accepting that her present amiable, limited relationship was the best she could hope for.

Her logic was faultless, and there was a certain relief in having worked the matter through. Unfortunately, her stomach was still knotted with anxiety. Perhaps some brandy would help. With a sigh, she sat up and fumbled for her new dressing gown, an attractive garment in gold velveteen with braid trim.

The most convenient brandy supply was in the library. She expected the room to be empty at such a late hour, and was startled to see her employer lounging in his favorite wing chair, coat and cravat off and his feet on a brocade stool. It was a perfect picture of a gentleman at his leisure. Reggie had a book open in his lap and a half-empty goblet in his hand. Candlelight touched the tooled leather backs of the books and cast a warm glow across the room, and Nemesis snored peacefully by his feet.

Alys halted uncertainly in the door, admiring the play of light on the planes of his lean face. She was about to end her brief moment of self-indulgence and go away when he glanced up and saw her.

He gave her a lazy smile. "Come join me."

"Are you sure I'm not disturbing you?" She hung back, even though she yearned to accept his invitation. "I didn't realize anyone else was still awake."

"You're not disturbing me. It's no bad thing to have company in the dark watches of the night." He raised his goblet in a wry toast, then drank deeply. Waving a casual hand at the decanter, he said, "Have some brandy."

Usually he was impeccably dressed, but she had noticed that when he drank he became faintly disheveled. Tonight he looked distinctly rakish. She guessed that he had been drinking since she and the children had gone to bed. Still, his speech was clear and unslurred, so he could not be really foxed.

She went to pour herself a glass of brandy, and noticed that the book on his lap was in Greek. That shouldn't have surprised her, but it did. While he must have had the usual education of his class, he radiated such physical force that it was easy to forget how intelligent he was. She, who had worked with him, should know better.

Alys curled up in the wing chair opposite, legs tucked under her, and sipped her drink. The restlessness that had kept her awake dissolved, replaced by contentment. Enjoying the slow burn of the brandy on her tongue, she said softly, "You're right about the dark watches of the night. They can be very lonely indeed."

"Sometimes. Often." His voice dropped to a whisper. "Always."

His clear light eyes met hers with no trace of the reserve he wore like armor. She could not decipher the complex blend of emotions in his gaze—surely vulnerability could not be among them? —but she became acutely conscious of the fact that it was very late, and that they were alone. The tautness in her midriff changed as a more pleasurable kind of tension coiled deep within her.

"What keeps you awake late at night, Allie?" he asked, his voice soft and intimate. "Don't hard work and a clear conscience count for anything?"

His openness called for a like response. She replied, "Who among us has a really clear conscience?"

"I certainly don't." He finished the brandy in his goblet, then leaned over to pour more. "Though in all modesty, I'm sure that my sins utterly surpass yours."

She smiled faintly. "If even half the stories about you are true, you're probably correct."

"I should think that about half is the correct proportion. The question for you is . . ." He paused, an amused glint in his eyes. "Which half?"

"Would you tell me what was true if I asked?" she inquired, her head tilted and her heavy braid falling over her shoulder.

"Probably. I generally answer direct questions. Most people are too well-bred or too afraid of the answers to ask." His amusement deepened. "It would be interesting to see if you are as unshockable as you claim."

Perhaps it was the brandy, or perhaps her intense curiosity about him, but she recklessly decided to take Reggie up on his willingness to be forthright. And she might as well start with the worst. "Did you really have a pregnant mistress run away to you, kill her husband in a duel, and then abandon her?"

For a moment she thought he wouldn't answer. "A good

place to start," he said finally, "since that story is exactly half true."

"Which half?"

"The lady in question did indeed seek my protection, I did kill her husband in a duel, and we did not marry." His words were cool and precise.

Chilled, Alys wondered how he could admit to such monstrous behavior so calmly. "In what way is the other half false?"

He leaned his head against the chair back and watched her through half-closed eyes. "She wasn't my mistress, and I didn't abandon her."

Feeling irrationally relieved, she settled more deeply into her chair. "It sounds like an interesting story. May I hear the rest?"

She saw him subtly relax. Had he thought she would not believe him?

"Sarah was the sister of a school friend of mine, Theo. Since my guardian and I shared a profound mutual dislike, I spent most of my school holidays with Theo's family. Those were some of the better memories of my youth. His sister was a pretty little thing who tagged around after us."

He took another sip of brandy, his gaze distant. "After Eton, Theo's father bought him a pair of colors. We had once planned on going into the army together, but . . . well, it didn't happen. He and I continued to correspond, but I lost touch with the rest of his family. In that time his sister married, and both of his parents died.

"Then one day Sarah showed up on my doorstep, bloody and beaten within an inch of her life." His voice was coldly angry. "Her husband was a vicious devil who regularly bounced her off the walls when he was in a jealous fit, which was often. When she became pregnant, he decided she had been unfaithful to him, and damned near killed her. Her brother was fighting in the Peninsula, too far away to know what was happening. But he had told her once that if she ever needed help, she should come to me."

Reggie shrugged, his powerful shoulders flexing under his white shirt. "Since her brother couldn't protect her, I did."

Amazing how different his version of the story was from what Junius Harper had said. Alys released the breath she had been holding. "You eliminated her husband?"

"Exactly." His flexible mouth twisted. "If her husband had assaulted another woman as he did her, he could have been convicted and jailed. But since she was his wife, beating her was perfectly legal, unless he actually murdered her. There was no possibility of divorce. Violence isn't enough to free a wife of her husband."

"After Sarah took refuge with you, did her husband challenge you to a duel?"

"Not precisely." Reggie smiled unpleasantly. "He hired a couple of bully boys to murder me in an alley. When I escaped more or less unscathed, I challenged him."

Alys's goblet was forgotten in her lap, her fingers locked around the stem. "And then you killed him."

"I executed him," he corrected. "Since the law didn't offer justice, I took it into my own hands."

"And Sarah?"

"I offered to marry her if that would make her situation easier, but she said the last thing she wanted was another husband." He shrugged. "I'll admit I was grateful that she didn't accept, though I think we would have dealt tolerably well together.

"After her son was born, even her late husband's vengeful relatives admitted that the boy looked just like his father. To the outrage of the entire county of Lincoln, Sarah went back to her husband's estate and took control of the property on her son's behalf," Reggie smiled. "Last year, she scandalized the county all over again by marrying a local physician, a man quite beneath her in fortune and birth. From her letters she's entirely pleased with her life, though the high-sticklers won't receive her." He glanced at Alys. "She's rather like you—a strong-minded woman."

Ignoring his last sentence, Alys said thoughtfully, "So you let the world think what it wished, and of course it preferred the most scandalous interpretation."

"Of course."

"Is it hard to kill someone?"

He was surprised at first, then thoughtful. "If you're asking whether I enjoy killing, the answer is no. However, on the occasions when I have found it necessary, I have felt little compunction and no remorse. The world was not a better place for having Sarah's husband in it. My conscience would have troubled me infinitely more if I had attended her funeral, knowing I had done nothing to help her while she was alive."

Alys nodded, understanding perfectly. Fascinated by this glimpse of the masculine world, she wanted to take full advantage of Reggie's willingness to talk. Next question. "Have you fought many duels?"

He pursed his lips. "Between twelve and fifteen, I suppose. I've never actually counted."

"Was Junius accurate about the number that . . . were fatal?"

"The estimable Mr. Harper is quite well-informed," he answered obliquely.

"Tell me the about the other fatal ones."

His brows rose. "What a bloodthirsty wench you are."

"Not really." Alys colored. "But I am curious. Though men make such a commotion about honor, I've never quite understood what is worth killing for."

He made a face. "I did say I would answer direct questions. Once I killed a Captain Sharp fond of fleecing green boys from the country. Everyone agreed he was a disgrace, but no one did anything. A lad I knew slightly lost his fortune to the man, and shot himself the next morning. So I did something."

"What about the duel in Paris last year?"

"The French had trouble accepting defeat, even after Waterloo. Some retaliated by forcing quarrels on Allied officers. They would then choose to fight with swords, with which most French officers are extremely skilled. Several Allied officers were killed." He gave a bored shrug. "I didn't like that."

"I have the feeling you are very good with a sword," Alys murmured.

"Tolerably so," he agreed, volunteering no more.

"Were your other duels also mercy missions?"

He sighed. "Don't think me heroic. On several occasions I felt impelled to administer rude justice, but most of my duels were the result of too much drink, too much temper, or quarrels forced on me which I could not easily avoid. When one has developed a reputation, a certain kind of man feels compelled to challenge it."

"What of the other time you killed someone in a duel? Was that another occasion where you acted as justice?"

For the first time Reggie shifted restlessly. "Bacchus was the deity in that case. I never meant to kill the fellow. It was just a stupid quarrel over a woman, but . . . I'd had far too much to drink. My aim was off." His voice was very flat.

"The other deaths you can live with easily, but not that one," she said softly

"Exactly so." He gave her a satirical smile. "Are you satisfied in your pursuit of knowledge about rakes?"

"Not in the least." Alys widened her eyes ingenuously. "Surely duels are only a small part of being a rake. On another occasion you explained about gaming, but there must be a multitude of other vices to explore."

His face eased. "There are, but to be honest, I haven't tried every single one."

"No?" she said in disappointment. "How about orgies? Have you ever participated in one?"

Caught in the middle of a swallow of brandy, he choked and began coughing. In a sputter of amusement, he asked, "What do you know about orgies?"

"Very little," she admitted. "I was hoping that you would explain them to me."

He eyed her suspiciously. "You may be unshockable, but I find that I'm not. Explaining what might be called an orgy would bring a blush to my manly cheek."

She shook her head sorrowfully. "And here I thought the first requirement for aspiring rakes is an utter lack of embarrassment."

He gave a wry smile. "No, the first requirement is to not give a damn about what other people think."

"I expect that you were born that way."

His amusement vanished as quickly as it had come. "Not born that way, but I learned it early."

Wanting to erase his dark expression, she asked, "What are some of the other requirements for being a rake?"

He gave the matter serious consideration. "The one thing that is utterly indispensable is overindulgence in the fair sex."

"Discreetly put," she said with approval. "Exactly how many women must one indulge with in order for it to become *over*indulgence?"

"Ten," he said promptly.

She burst out laughing, thinking that this was the most extraordinary conversation she ever had. Her behavior was every bit as outlandish as his. "That's it? Slake your wicked lust with ten different women, and you are automatically a rake?"

"Ten is the minimum requirement, but more is better," he allowed.

"How many have you . . . ?" Alys's voice trailed off as she realized that this was a question she did not want answered.

"Once again, I didn't keep count." He sighed, his face suddenly weary. "Too many. Too damned many."

Reggie stood and went to reshelve his book, his movements betraying him as his speech had not. He still had the grace of the born athlete, but there was a precise, slightly exaggerated quality to his actions, as if moving normally required conscious effort.

Alys disliked seeing him like this, being less than he should be. Yet if he were not drunk, they would not be having this remarkable conversation. Not wanting to analyze more deeply, she asked, "What were you reading?"

He slid the book into its slot, part of a matched set of volumes bound in blue leather. "The *Odyssey*." He ran his long fingers lightly over the gold-tooled titles. "My father taught me to read Greek in this room."

"Was he a scholar?"

"No, but like many men of his education and generation, he loved the classics. He spent over a year in Italy and Greece on his Grand Tour." Reggie turned and propped his broad shoulders against the oak bookshelves. "He was a good teacher."

She had a sudden poignant image of the father and son bending over the old volumes as sunlight slanted through the library windows, the man reminiscing of his travels, the boy listening eagerly, wanting to learn and to please his sire. She herself had learned mathematics and accounts that way. Did he miss his father as much as she missed hers? His father had died. She had lost hers to anger and implacable pride, a combination as final as death.

Throat tight, she said, "I'm not surprised that you enjoy the *Odyssey*. I rather fancy you as Odysseus."

He smiled wryly. "The roguish hero who spent twenty years getting into trouble while he tried to find his way home again? Perhaps."

"Exactly. I always thought the fellow sounded rather

rakish. Just look at that business with Circe." She regarded him with affection. "Though it took you longer than twenty years to find your way home."

He folded his arms across his chest, saying dryly, "Odysseus had the incentive of a faithful Penelope waiting."

"Well, he wasn't eight years old when he left for Troy," she said reasonably. "You may have been precocious, but not that precocious."

When he chuckled, she decided to probe further. "Among all those women you've overindulged with, surely there must have been a Penelope who wanted to wait for you?"

His laughter became sardonic. "Good God, Allie, while I have known many women, I doubt that any were fool enough to want to marry me. Females are practical creatures. Even the ones who pursued me rather than vice versa were interested in one thing only, and it wasn't marriage."

Alys hoped the candlelight covered her blush. From the first moment he had come swaggering into her life, she had understood perfectly why a woman would pursue him. But there was so much more to Reggie than physical magnetism. She could not have been the first female to notice that.

"Perhaps some of them were interested, and you didn't notice since you didn't share their interest." She swirled the brandy in her goblet reflectively. "I would have thought that at least once in your life, you considered giving up raking and settling down with one woman."

His expression hardened. "Everyone is a fool for love at least once, and I was no exception. It's part of being young."

She, too, had been such a fool. The pain of first love was not something that ever quite went away. "What happened?"

"Nothing much. I met a girl and became absolutely mad about her for reasons I can't begin to remember. For a few weeks she appeared to feel the same way."

"And then?"

His expression became a self-mocking sneer. "After I

made my impassioned declaration, she informed me that while I was well enough for a flirt, she certainly would never consider marrying a man with no expectations."

Alys winced. The curtness of his tone revealed how deeply wounding that rebuff had been.

Recognizing her fellow feeling, he said harshly, "Don't waste any sympathy on me. She was quite right—I was wholly ineligible. Besides," he added with a bitter twist to his mouth, "I had my revenge."

She cocked her head. "Not, I trust, by challenging her to a duel. I suppose it would have been easy to ruin her reputation."

He gave a short, humorless laugh. "I could have, but that isn't what I did."

When he fell silent, Alys said, "You can't leave me in suspense after such a provocative statement."

"I suppose not." He sighed. "Very well, but don't blame me if this time you *are* shocked. The female in question—I won't call her a lady—captured an aging gentleman of substantial wealth. Then, after she was safely married, she indicated to me that she was available for . . . extramarital activities."

Alys watched in fascination. "And you turned her down?"

"On the contrary." His eyes were ice pale. "I accepted, then exerted myself to the fullest to ensure her satisfaction."

He fell silent until Alys asked in exasperation, "How was that revenge?"

"You're sure you want to know?" When she nodded, he continued, "Our little . . . encounter was quite unlike anything she had experienced before. She positively panted for an encore."

Suddenly Alys knew what was coming. "And you refused her."

"Exactly so." His voice was dry in the extreme. "With a few choice comments on how unrewarding I'd found her."

Alys gasped at the sheer ruthlessness of using physical intimacy to enslave a woman, then callously rejecting her. His revenge was an eerie reflection of her own worst nightmares.

It was also a measure of how deeply hurt he had been by a heartless girl's casual cruelty. "That is quite wickedly clever," she said slowly. "It was also absolutely appropriate."

"You mean I still haven't shocked you?" His dark brows arched with surprise and a certain respect.

"A little, perhaps." she admitted. "But there's a rough justice to what you did. In comparable circumstances, I might do something similar if I were sharp-witted enough."

He laughed with real amusement. "More and more, I think that your proper appearance is no more than a facade. Underneath, you have the soul of a marauder."

She considered. "Very likely you are right."

His eyes met hers, pale and clear as aquamarine, and she could feel the energy change between them. His deep voice husky, he said, "Come here."

Alys sat stone still for a moment. Earlier she had decided she could never embark on an affair in cold blood. But her blood was not cold now—it sang warm and urgent in her veins.

She rose and walked to him, halting an arm's length away. His intense virility was drawing her as if they were opposite poles of a magnet, seeking their mates.

For a long moment they stood that way, motionless and utterly intent on each other. Then he raised his hands. She thought he would pull her close for a kiss, but instead he grasped her heavy braid and untied the ribbon at the end. After releasing her hair from its maidenly restraint, he raked the shining strands with his long fingers until they spilled in a silken mantle over her shoulders and tumbled halfway to her waist.

"You have beautiful hair," he said softly, his fingertips drifting across her cheek and throat in a deeply erotic caress. The desire in his eyes was a potent aphrodisiac, releasing the hidden part of her nature as surely as he had unbound her hair. She caught her breath and her lips parted, wanting more, not knowing how to ask.

He lifted her chin with one finger. She had been uncomfortable with his height, but now she realized that he was exactly the right size, tall enough to make her feel fragile and feminine, not so tall that it took more than a slight inclination of his head to bring his lips to hers.

It was a brandy-flavored kiss, rich and heady and intoxicating. All her senses were heightened, and she was acutely aware of the pulse of blood in her veins, the subtle library scents of leather and oak, the strength of the arms that enfolded her.

They came together, and passion flamed between them, fierce and mindless. Tentative touch became crushing embrace. Ever since she had been an awkward, yearning girl, Alys had longed to learn love's mysteries. Now she had found her teacher in this improbable man, with his cynicism and mockery, his wry self-knowledge and dangerous sense of justice. She knew herself for a fool, and didn't care.

She was so sure of her desire, so totally immersed in the moment, that when he pulled back the shock of deprivation was like a splash of frost-bitter water. Dazed, she opened her eyes.

"Bloody, bloody, hell!" he swore, his hands gripping her arms with bruising strength as he held her away from him.

"What's wrong?" she whispered, bereft by her aloneness, terrified that he was repulsed by her wanton behavior.

"I said I wouldn't do this." He released her and stepped away, rubbing his temples as if trying to clear his mind.

Harshly he repeated, "I said I wouldn't do this." Then he met her gaze, his expression twisted with self-contempt. "Allie, I'm sorry. You deserve better."

He spun away, crossing the room with long strides to the French doors that opened to the patio. As he fumbled with the key in the lock, she cried out, "Where are you going?"

He glanced back at her, his face bleak. "Out. Anywhere, until I sober up." Then he disappeared into the night.

Alys sank into a chair, her knees too weak to support her. Her body cried out to continue what it had begun, and her mind was an ache of confusion. Was the statement that she deserved better a gentlemanly way of avoiding doing something he would regret in the morning?

How many? Too damned many. The rake's lament.

She did not doubt that for a handful of drunken moments, he had wanted her. But even in his present undiscriminating state, he had realized that by dawn's sober light he would regret lying with her. For a man who had known women beyond counting, there was no challenge or sport in bedding an unattractive, overeager spinster.

As the collie came over and whimpered sympathetically, Alys huddled in the chair, her face buried in her hands, her shoulders shaking uncontrollably. Though more kindly phrased, this was a rejection as painful as the one Randolph had given her.

The only comfort she could find was a fervent hope that in the morning he would remember nothing of what had transpired between them.

Chapter 14

Reggie rode all night, letting his horse have its head at every crossroads, not caring where he went as long as he kept moving. When he'd first left the stables, dizzy and on the edge of passing out, only the skill and habit of years kept him in the saddle.

Recognition of his state had led him to saddle a calm chestnut hunter instead of Bucephalus. The stallion was a lively handful under the best of circumstances. In Reggie's jug-bitten condition, Bucephalus would probably have broken his neck.

His mouth twisted bitterly. Maybe he should have ridden the stallion and hoped for the worst. Despite frustration and brandy-induced confusion, one thought stood out with brutal clarity: he was failing at his attempt to change his life.

The roads and lanes ran through fields of ripening summer grain that rippled pale in the moonlight, lined by dark hedges and shadowing trees. He and the chestnut wound their way up to Shaftesbury, across the barren, undulating downs, then south again through quiet lanes and occasional sleeping village greens. Light mists pooled where the road dipped lower. He had left without his coat, and the damp chill bit deep through his linen shirt.

As his mind cleared and a headache began pulsing in time to the horse's hooves, his thoughts were as cold as his body. He should never have invited Alys Weston and her quasi-family to move in with him. It had seemed an irresistibly good idea to fill the empty spaces of the manor house with youth and laughter, and Strickland was large enough to give him privacy as needed.

In one way the idea had worked. The young Spensers had intelligence, enthusiasm, and good manners, and he enjoyed their company. The problem was with Lady Alys. He had found her attractive from the first time he saw her, and knew that having that tantalizing body under his own roof would be a constant temptation. However, contrary to popular opinion, he was quite capable of resisting temptation—when he was sober.

All too aware of his weaknesses, he had known that he must be careful about his drinking. Self-control and judgment were the first things to go when booze went down the throat. He hadn't anticipated how preoccupied he would become with Allie's nearness. Her nearness, and her responsiveness.

It didn't help that he had yielded to the impulse to buy her something better than her governess gowns. He had known she had a good figure, but had not realized just how splendid it was until she had appeared for dinner in one of her new dresses. He had been tempted to turn her into the first course.

Oddly enough, Allie was quite unaware of how attractive she was. That must be the result of too many years where work and propriety came first. Or perhaps she had been scorned when she was a growing, gawky girl, too tall and too unusual for mere prettiness, and had never learned to see herself as the striking woman she had become.

Nonetheless, he had not thought sharing the house with her would cause problems. Unless he was half sprung, he

knew how to keep his hands to himself, so all he had to do
was restrict his serious drinking until late in the evening.
Since he was nocturnal by preference, this was no hardship.
For the first few nights he had gotten quietly foxed with
none the wiser. Except Mac, of course. Then his plan had
broken down.

A vainer man might have thought Allie had sought him
out deliberately, pretending surprise at finding him in the library, but Reggie did not number vanity among his faults. It
had been chance that had brought her downstairs at such a
late hour, a chance he should have guessed would occur
sooner or later. Short of locking her in her bedroom every
night, it would surely happen again. And next time, whatever remnants of decency he still possessed might not stop
him in time.

He thought of the shock and hurt on her face when he
had pulled away, and winced. The blasted woman was such
a mixture of intelligence, worldly wisdom, and vulnerability. He had enjoyed their outrageous discussion, enjoyed her
curiosity and open mind and lack of missishness. It was
different from talking with Chessie. While he had never had
to guard his tongue with his former mistress, she had lacked
the education and temperament to appreciate his more
oblique mental flights.

Tonight he had learned that in many ways Allie was a
kindred spirit, as isolated by circumstances, as intense and
unconventional, as he himself. There were two major differences between them. First, as a woman she had been raised
to be proper and restrained, to deny her passionate nature.

Second and more important, she had chosen to use her
gifts of talent and intelligence constructively, while he had
thrown all of his away. He was generally considered a rake,
but wastrel was a more accurate term, for he had wasted so
much over the years. So much money, so many choices.

Most of all, so much time—time that could never be recaptured.

Eventually Reggie stopped and tethered his horse, then stretched out under a tree on the dew-moistened grass. He was enormously tired and wished he could sleep, but when he closed his eyes everything began spinning and nausea threatened. He lay stark-eyed and awake, thinking of his desire to change his life and what a bad job he was making of it.

First one bird chirped, then another and another, multiplying to a chorus as dawn began to tint the eastern sky. He took a certain sour intellectual curiosity in feeling his hangover slowly develop, bit by wretched bit. Usually he slept through the process.

With the sky perceptibly lighter, he wearily got to his feet and remounted, feeling the ache of fatigue and depression in his very bones. He let the horse amble until they came to an intersection with a collection of fingerposts pointing in different directions: Fifehead Neville, Okeford Fitzpaine, Sturminster Newton.

He had read once that the absurd double names many English villages carried were a result of Norman designations being tacked onto the original Saxon. It was the sort of fact that he loved—utterly useless. In a debate at Eton he had once successfully defended the proposition that a fact should be loved for itself alone rather than for what it could do.

Turning his mount to the left, he headed toward Strickland, unsuccessfully trying to avoid thinking about Alys Weston. It would be so easy, so infernally easy, to fall into an affair with her. She was ripe for appreciation, eager for experience. For a little while, she would welcome his advances—that had been made clear tonight.

But the same quirky sense of honor that had led him to administer rough justice as required would not let him ruin an innocent. More than an innocent—a good woman, though that was a rather colorless description for someone so vibrantly, forcefully alive.

He had to get her out of the house. Some of his working capital could be diverted into rebuilding Rose Hall. After the embers had cooled, he'd checked the walls and found them to be sound. If construction began soon, Alys and her brood would be back where they belonged by early autumn.

And Strickland would be empty again.

The days were very long this near the solstice. Though the sun was well above the horizon, the hour was still so early that even the farmers were barely stirring. Instinctively Reggie was heading toward home—as a Mussulman bowed to Mecca, he always knew in which direction Strickland lay—and the countryside was beginning to look familiar. It took his tired, sodden brain time to realize that he was skirting the fields of Fenton Hall.

Still, it was a surprise to turn a corner in the deep lane and come on Jeremy Stanton on a placid gelding. His godfather was also startled, but the leathery face immediately creased in a smile. "Good morning, lad. You're out early." After a shrewd glance, he added, "Care to join me for breakfast?"

Reggie winced, wishing he could beat a retreat without being unbearably rude. He was unshaven, coatless, grass-stained, and generally must look like hell. "I'll pass, sir. I should be getting home."

Stanton's eyes twinkled. "I'm disappointed that you think I'm too old and respectable to deal with the aftereffects of a night's debauch. If you're worried about Elizabeth seeing you, she won't be up for hours. I realize you might not be able to face food, but perhaps a cup of coffee?"

Reggie hesitated, on the edge of bolting, then smiled wryly. "That's an offer I can't refuse. It's been a long night."

Stanton turned his horse, and they trotted companionably along the lane, then up the tree-lined drive to the manor house. Little was said until both men were ensconced in the sunny breakfast parlor with steaming coffee and fresh warm rolls on the table. Between sips of his beverage, Reggie clasped the mug between his hands to warm them.

Breaking open a roll and spreading it with sweet butter, Stanton said reminiscently, "Do you realize how much you resemble your father just now?"

"Certainly there's a general resemblance," Reggie agreed, "but I don't recall him ever looking as if the sexton had just dug him up in the churchyard."

"You're too young to remember, but many's the time he was here looking just like you. And for the same reason." While the words were casual, the older man's gray eyes were shrewdly observant.

Coloring under the examination, Reggie growled, "Are you trying to insult me, or my father?"

"Neither." Unoffended by the rudeness, Stanton said pensively, "Drink is one of the curses of the Englishman. We're told from the time we're mere lads that a hard head for liquor proves we're real men, so naturally we drink ourselves to oblivion, with rowdiness and ill-temper along the way.

"With maturity and increased responsibilities, most men decide boozing interferes with the serious business of life, and they reduce their libations. Some, however, drink more and more." He added a spoonful of raspberry preserves to his roll, spreading them neatly over the surface. "Your father and I drank together often. He was one of the wittiest men I've ever known. Oh, we were merry as grigs over our bottles."

He bit into his bread, chewing and swallowing before he

continued. "It was all good sport, until drinking almost ruined both our marriages."

"How fortunate that I don't have a marriage to ruin," Reggie said caustically. "If you're trying to tell me something, just come out with it. You may call me a lad if you wish, but I'll be damned if I'll sit still for a lecture."

"I don't intend to give you one," his godfather said in a peaceable tone. "I merely want to fill you in on a bit of history that you might not be familiar with."

"You're right, it's quite unfamiliar to me," Reggie said shortly. "I don't remember my father ever drinking so much as a tankard of ale."

"That's because he gave up every form of alcohol when you were a child. About four, I think."

Reggie was about to pour more coffee, but he paused in mid-gesture and shot Stanton a suspicious glance. "I told you once that I don't remember anything from when I was younger than four."

"With good reason, perhaps," his godfather said, still imperturbable. "Excellent preserves, these. Sure you wouldn't care to have some?"

Reggie had enough to digest without adding food. Scowling at his coffee, he forgot his host for a time. Abruptly he asked, "You said drink almost ruined your marriage. What happened?"

Stanton shrugged. "I woke up one morning, or afternoon actually, and Elizabeth and the children were gone. She'd packed them up and returned to her parents. She refused even to see me for a fortnight. In fact, her father's solicitor called here to discuss a legal separation."

Reggie stared at him, aghast. "But you and Aunt Beth have always been as close as inkle weavers."

"Not always, I fear." Remembered pain showed on Stanton's thin face. "When she finally agreed to talk, she told

me that she was tired of sleeping alone while I drank myself
to a stupor downstairs, she was tired of running the estate
and the house both, and she was *damned* tired of seeing her
children hide from their father because they never knew
what mood he would be in."

The thought of plump, gentle Aunt Beth swearing was as
incongruous as imagining her brandishing a sword. As incongruous as the thought that Jeremy Stanton's children
might have been afraid of him. Reluctantly intrigued, Reggie
asked, "What happened then?"

"I thought about it, and decided that my wife was a much
better companion at night than a half dozen bottles of bur-
gundy. So I told her I would stop drinking." He smiled without humor. "I thought it would be easy. Elizabeth said she
wouldn't come back until I had been sober for six months.
It took me over a year to achieve that. But in the end, I did.
I haven't had a single drop of alcohol since."

Reggie remembered how his godfather had refused a
drink at Strickland, and how he had drunk only water the
night Reggie had come for dinner. So that wasn't mere
caprice, but iron habit. "And my parents? What kind of
problems did they have?"

Stanton shook his head. "The situation was similar. Since
the crisis occurred at the same time as my own problems,
I'm not sure of the details. You were there—perhaps you
might remember some of what happened if you tried."

"What would be the point of the exercise?" Reggie said,
his voice hostile.

"There might be some relevance to your own life," Stanton said, as immune to hostility as rudeness.

"Are you implying that I can't hold my drink?"

"Since you are your father's son, perhaps not." Stanton
regarded him gravely. "You would know that better than I."

Coldly furious, Reggie yearned to curse Stanton for a

meddlesome old fool and stomp out. Something stopped
him. For the third time in a matter of weeks, someone was
talking to him about his drinking, and all three people were
in the very small handful who had demonstrated a genuine
concern for his welfare.

As the fatigue and despair of the night flooded over him,
he set his elbows on the table and buried his face in his
hands. Without looking up, he muttered, "Maybe I do
drink too much, but I haven't a wife or family. Who am I
harming?"

"Yourself," Stanton said softly.

The silence stretched. Reggie thought of the depression
that had been dogging him, and for the first time wondered
if it might be a result of drink. And while he did not have a
wife or child to lose, there was Strickland. He remembered
the last night in London, when he had gone gambling and
won a thousand pounds in some unknown way. He could as
easily have lost.

If he had been on a losing streak, might he have been fool
enough to put up Strickland as a stake? Chillingly he knew
that was possible. Voice muffled by his hands, he said
gruffly, "You're right. I should drink less."

"Possibly that would work," was the noncommittal reply.

Lowering his hands, Reggie looked up with narrowed
eyes. "Would you care to elaborate on that statement?"

"Some men can reduce their drinking, and that solves
their problem." Stanton grimaced. "I tried that. It didn't
work. As soon as I swallowed that first mouthful of booze,
I would forget—or rather, no longer care—about my good
resolutions. Then I would drink until I was unconscious. For
me the only answer was to stop altogether. There was no
middle ground."

"I have a strong will."

"I don't doubt it." Stanton's shrewd old eyes studied him.

"But strength of will might not be enough in this case. It wasn't for me."

"How did you stop if will wasn't enough?" Reggie challenged.

Stanton's mouth quirked up. "You're going to laugh at this, but the only thing that helped was prayer."

Ignoring his godson's expression of distaste, he continued, "This is something I've told no one else, but for me the turning point came seven months after Elizabeth left. First I tried to moderate my drinking. That didn't work. Then I tried stopping altogether. That would last a few days or weeks. Then, when I was sure my problem was under control, I would have just one drink. Next thing I knew, it would be the morning after and I had the devil's own hangover and no memory of the night before."

So those terrifying memory losses were not exclusive to Reggie. "What happened then?"

"I woke up in the drawing room one morning, lying in my own vomit, and knew that I couldn't stop drinking. I had tried my damnedest, and I simply could not do it. I was going to lose my wife and children forever, and without them, there wasn't much point in going on." Lines showed around Stanton's mouth, and Reggie realized that this was no easier for him to say than for Reggie to listen to.

"So lying there, too sick and miserable to stand, I prayed." The older man grimaced. "Nothing formal, mind you. Just a desperate lot of drivel asking anyone who might be out there to help me, because I couldn't help myself."

Eyes distant, he absently crumbled a roll, pulling it into shreds with his thin, parchment-colored fingers. "This is hard to describe. I don't know how long I lay there, mentally babbling, but suddenly, a . . . a sense of peace came over me. There really aren't any words for it." He started to elaborate, then changed his mind. "After that, things were different. I didn't have the same need to drink. Oh, I won't say I wasn't tempted sometimes, but it was possible to say no."

He leaned back in his chair, composed again. "Within a few months, I felt better than I had in years. I didn't miss the drink at all. Then Elizabeth came home. It took time for her and the children to really believe I'd changed, but eventually it all worked out. You've seen the results."

Yes, he'd seen the results. Reggie stood and walked to the window, his thumbs hooked in the waist of his buckskin breeches, his shoulders taut. Without looking at his godfather, he said stiffly, "I'm not sure any of that is relevant to me, but I appreciate your concern. I don't suppose it was easy to say."

"No, it wasn't," was the calm reply, "but it needed saying. Maybe, in time, it will even seem relevant."

Reggie turned to his host and took his leave. As he rode back to Strickland, he thought long and hard about what his godfather had said, and decided there was some good sense there. Reggie's drinking hadn't gotten out of hand until the last couple of years. Waiting for his uncle's estate to be settled had been the devil of a strain. During that period he had drunk and gambled and gotten himself into the worst financial straits of his life.

After his cousin Richard appeared to claim the estate, Reggie had deliberately thrown himself into every manner of what-the-hell-does-it-matter folly. Ironically, his gambling had prospered and his finances were repaired, but he'd acted like a damned fool, no denying it.

Had it not been for the uncertainty and frustration over Wargrave, his drinking would never have become an issue. The solution was clear. All he need do was stop drinking for a while, both to prove that he could, and to break the habit of overindulgence. Then he could return to his normal consumption. Stanton might not have had the strength of will to control his tippling, but Reggie had.

He thought of Stanton's talk of prayer tolerantly. No doubt when a man was of an age to see his end approaching, it was natural to take refuge in religious superstitions. Reggie had no need of such.

By the time he reached Strickland, he was feeling in charity with the world. His state of mind was immediately tested when he led his horse into the stable and encountered Lady Alys, about to start her daily rounds. Wearing a new bronze-colored riding habit, she was very tall, slim, and regal.

Allie stiffened when she saw him, then inclined her head politely. "Good morning. I was about to ride over to one of the tenant farms, but I can postpone that if you wish to discuss anything now."

He shook his head and began unsaddling the tired chestnut. "No, carry on with what you intended. I want to discuss the improvements, but that can wait until later."

She raised her brows. "I thought we had settled that."

Her glossy brown hair was once more in a neat coronet of braids. Remembering that beautiful hair loose around her face brought Reggie a sharp stab of regret for what he had foregone. "I've decided Rose Hall should be rebuilt this summer, which will reduce the money available for other projects. I'll want your opinion on what is most needful."

A pulse beat visibly in her throat. "I see."

She obviously thought he was trying to get rid of her. Well, he was, but his motives were pure. Amazingly so. Quietly he said, "I think it would be for the best."

"You needn't feel guilty about last night," she said with cool control. "You weren't forcing me."

Remembering how deliciously she had responded made his voice brusque. "You don't have to remind me. I'm quite clear on what happened. It would have been better if it hadn't."

Her face paled under its unladylike tan. "Quite right," she

said, her voice clipped. She turned and led her mare from the stables, her back as erect as a grenadier.

Reggie watched her leave with a combination of regret and irritation. Since he was being noble, he ought to at least get credit for it.

Sobriety proved far more difficult than Reggie had expected. By the second day, thoughts of drinking were becoming an obsession. Again and again he imagined himself opening the library cabinet and pouring amber fluid into a glass. He could almost taste the exquisite tang on his tongue, feel the warmth that would glow through him after he swallowed that first mouthful.

Several times he caught himself about to act out that vision. Then, fiercely determined, he turned away. He could, and by God would, do this.

It was the haying season, so he spent the morning hours swinging a scythe with the laborers, finding respite in the mindless rhythms of farm work. When the luncheons of bread and cheese and ale appeared, he left to remove himself from temptation. *It's only ale,* his longing mind would whisper. *Not wine or spirits. Quite harmless.*

So must the serpent have whispered in Eden. But Reggie had gotten drunk on beer and ale often enough to know that only the quantity required was different from drinking spirits. If he was stopping, he must stop entirely, without self-deception.

In his first afternoon of sobriety, Reggie visited a horse fair near Dorchester and bought four young horses with excellent potential as hunters. The next afternoon he began schooling them. It was a task that required patience and concentration, so it focused Reggie's mind on something other than his ever-increasing need for a drink.

Though Dorset was not first-class hunting country, there

was enough variety of terrain around Strickland for training purposes. Some of the schooling was done over the country-side, and some took place in the paddock. Young William perched on the fence and watched whenever he could. The boy had the makings of a real horseman.

Reggie also took Peter out for driving lessons. While the older boy lacked his brother's all-encompassing fascination with horseflesh, he was bright and eager to learn. Teaching him to drive was another good distraction.

Yet no matter how hard he worked during the day, in the evenings Reggie was intolerably restless, too tense to read, too bad-tempered to talk. During the hours he had once spent drinking, he took refuge in walking around the estate. The sun set very late at this season, and in the cool hours of waning light he became intimately acquainted with his ancestral home. He prowled from the high, lonely downs dotted with sheep to the rich water meadows with their ripening grain, his long strides taut and impatient.

Even walking until full dark could not subdue his tension. Invariably he would end at his private cove on the lake. There he stripped off his clothes and plunged into the water, swimming furiously until utter exhaustion made sleep possible.

By the fourth day he was feeling so irascible that he canceled a driving lesson with Peter, knowing that he would have trouble being civil. Reggie considered taking dinner apart from his new housemates, but decided not to change the routine. So he ate with the others, saying little to avoid wounding feelings with his sharp-edged tongue. The young Spensers were too well brought up to comment on his silence, but they cast occasional puzzled glances in his direction.

Alys did not look at him at all.

Even Mac was wary, as if Reggie was a volcano on the verge of eruption. Only Nemesis seemed to see no difference, and, as Reggie thought with what humor he could summon, the dog was notably brainless.

Despite his slanderous thoughts, he was glad that the collie accompanied him on his expeditions and slept on the foot of his bed.

On the fifth day, he began wondering when it would become easier, for each day was worse than the one before. Grimly he cut hay, worked the horses, walked the estate, and swam. As he returned to the manor house, he wished without hope that tonight he might sleep soundly.

It was after midnight when he reached his room, his body still thrumming with need in spite of his fatigue. *Just one little whiskey, to help him sleep. Just one. Hadn't he proved that he could go without?* No, he hadn't, not when the longing for drink was so powerful that it damned near blotted every other thought from his head.

One thing Reggie had, perhaps in excess, was strength of will, though the unappreciative might call it stubbornness. Having decided to stop drinking for a time, he would not deviate from his resolution until he no longer craved alcohol. Only then would it be safe to drink again.

Intent on his inward battle, he didn't notice that he was not alone in the room until he was ready to climb into bed. Then the sight of a rounded female form under the covers made his heart leap. If Alys Weston was willing to go this far, not a man on earth could blame him for giving in to temptation. And making love to her was one thing that would surely distract him from his aching desire for alcohol.

The thought had hardly formed when he realized that it wasn't Allie. Too short, too round. Pulling down the edge of the blanket, he exposed the soft brown curls of a dozing housemaid. As he stared at the girl, trying to remember her name, her eyes opened. An expression of alarm appeared on her small, pretty face.

Caustic with disappointment, he said, "Don't you belong in the attic with the other maids?"

She gulped, then said in a soft Dorsetshire accent, "I . . . I thought you might like a bit of company, sir."

Could Mac have thought a woman might improve his temper? The cockney had never pandered before, but Reggie supposed it was possible. "Who put you up to this?"

The girl looked even more alarmed. "No one, sir. I've fancied you from the time you came here, and . . . and I thought you might not mind."

He was briefly tempted, for the chit was a pretty little thing. He would certainly have accepted her offer if he were foxed.

But she wore a dying kitten expression that made her seem less like a lusty wench intent on pleasure than like Joan of Arc waiting for the torches. Perhaps she had come from hope of material gain. An unflattering thought. He snapped, "This is not the way to earn a better position or a higher wage. Go back to your own bed, and we'll pretend this never happened."

It was not a graceful way to reject her, but even so, he did not expect her sudden tears. Exasperated, he pulled the blanket down to encourage her departure.

She was naked. At the sight of her rosy body his resolution wavered. It had been weeks since he'd had a woman, and having Alys Weston constantly under his nose was keeping his rude male instincts at constant simmer. Then his eyes narrowed as he studied her. Admittedly the signs were not yet obvious, but Reggie was no green innocent. "You're increasing," he said flatly.

The girl stared at him with horror, as if he were the devil incarnate for guessing. Then she yanked the blanket up around her shoulders, her helpless sobs worsening.

He sighed. Obviously there was no getting rid of—Gillie, that's what her name was—until she recovered. He donned his robe, then looked around for her clothing. Her shift and dressing gown were folded neatly on a chair.

He handed her the shift. "Better put this on."

Then he turned away, taking his time rifling through his drawers for a handkerchief. By the time he gave one to the girl, she was standing by the bed in the hastily donned shift, tying her shabby robe around her. She accepted the handkerchief gratefully and buried her woebegone face in its snowy folds. Reggie sat down and waited for her to emerge from the handkerchief, curious as to why she had come.

When Gillie's sobs subsided to hiccups, he said with as much gentleness as he could muster, "Did you think that if you . . . visited me, you could pass the child off as mine?"

From the stark look in her pansy eyes, he had guessed correctly.

"Didn't you think I could count?" he asked, beginning to find some amusement in the scene. "Sit down and relax. I won't eat you."

She perched nervously on the edge of the bed. The girl probably had only the vaguest understanding of procreation and gestation. Patiently he asked, "Won't the father marry you?"

She twisted the handkerchief in her hands, not meeting his eyes. "We'd been walking out together for ever so long, and he s-said we'd marry someday. But when I told him w-what had happened, he asked how he could be sure it was his."

Another sob escaped her. "The next day he told his pa he was going to Bristol to get a job as a sailor, and off he went. H-he didn't even say good-bye." She covered her face with her hands, shoulders shaking again.

Reggie's mouth tightened. He wasn't very proud of the male sex at times like this. While he was no paragon of virtue, at least he hadn't left a string of abandoned bastards scattered across the countryside. He sat next to Gillie on the bed, patting her shoulder comfortingly. Still sobbing, she turned and burrowed against his side. He held her until she had cried herself out.

Finally she straightened up and wiped her eyes with the damp handkerchief. Her nose was red and her face blotched, but she still had a certain dignity as she said unevenly, "I'm very sorry, Mr. Davenport. It was bad of me to try and trick you, but I was that desperate. I didn't know what else to do." She swallowed hard, then said fiercely, "I won't go to the workhouse, I won't. I'll have my baby in a ditch first."

"Is the workhouse that bad?" Reggie asked.

She nodded and looked at her hands. He made a mental note. Magistrates administered the Poor Law, and it appeared that he should investigate local conditions. But that was for later. "Won't your parents help you?"

She shook her head, her tangled brown hair falling over her forehead. "They're Methodists and ever so strict. My pa said that if I ever got myself in the family way, he'd never have me in the house again. Even my mam . . ." Her voice trailed off.

"Does Mrs. Herald know?"

"Oh, no, Cousin May would never have hired me if she had known," Gillie said bleakly. "When she finds out, she'll discharge me right away."

"Where would you go, then?"

"I . . . I don't know, but not the workhouse. Maybe I can walk to London and find work there."

Reggie frowned. The only work she would be likely to find in London would be on the streets, with all the dangers that entailed. He could send her to Chessie, but he doubted the girl had the temperament of a good prostitute. After swiftly reviewing the available choices, he said, "You can stay here. I'll tell Mrs. Herald not to discharge you."

She looked up, eyes wide with hope. "You'll really let me stay until the baby is born? I swear, sir, you won't even

have to pay me. I'll work as hard as I can to have a roof
and food."

"That won't be necessary—you'll be paid for your labor."

Her eyes started to fill again. "God bless you, Mr. Davenport. I don't know how to thank you. You can't know what
this means." She laid a shy hand on his forearm. "If . . . if
there is anything I can do for you . . ."

Her meaning was obvious. Once again he was tempted,
for at least she no longer looked like she was offering herself to be sacrificed. But he knew enough of human nature
to realize that in her present mood, the girl was likely to
fancy herself in love with the first man who was kind to her,
and he didn't need any more complications in his life.

"Just don't do it again," he said crisply. "Lust is a normal
part of life, but if you want to indulge in it after the baby is
born, take precautions. If you don't know an older woman
who will explain, ask me and I'll tell you what to do."

Gillie blushed violently, but nodded. Besides being
pretty, she seemed fairly intelligent. In time she would probably find a husband. Illegitimate children were not that uncommon.

Suddenly tired, he stood and offered her a hand up. "Off
to bed now. I'll talk to Mrs. Herald in the morning." He
scowled ferociously at her. "Make sure that none of the
other maids get ideas. I might not be so tolerant next time."

Unintimidated by his expression, she gave him another
shy smile, then slipped out the door. He pulled off his robe
and climbed into bed, then snuffed the candles. At least the
girl's problems helped put his in perspective.

Alys's bedroom had been chosen with an eye to her
monitoring night traffic. Wakeful herself, she had heard
her employer come in late for the last several nights.

Tonight, half an hour after hearing his light, booted steps, she heard a different sound. Curious, she rose and opened her door a fraction, and saw a girl leaving Reggie's room. She froze, feeling ill. The moonlight wasn't bright enough to distinguish details, but Reggie's visitor was one of the maids, Gillie or Janie from the size and shape.

The girl paused in the hall, wiping her eyes as if she had been crying. Then she pattered toward the stairs that led to the attic. Alys eased the door shut and pressed her forehead against the cool panels. So he was sleeping with one of the maids. She wondered how long the affair had been going on. The girl was sniffling as if she was a virgin who had just been seduced.

Not that it was any of her business what Reggie Davenport did. Wretchedly she returned to her bed, drawing herself into a ball and tugging the covers close for warmth. She had thought there was a little understanding between her and Reggie—some laughter, a certain similarity of mind—but that must have been her imagination. If any connection did exist, it certainly did not include any interest in her as a woman. She had been a fool to think otherwise, even briefly.

Remembering how he had kissed her, she pressed a fist against her mouth, her teeth cutting into the knuckles as she fought against crying out with pain. She had been watching her irascible employer closely all week and guessed that he had stopped drinking. Now that he was sober, he clearly wasn't interested in her. He'd been drunk both times they'd kissed, and apparently the experience had been so dreadful that he was altering his entire way of life rather than run the risk of a reoccurrence.

Strong and confident in so many ways, in her sense of herself as a woman Alys was utterly vulnerable. And so she wept through the night, until she fell into the sleep of the utterly exhausted as dawn began tinting the eastern sky.

Chapter 15

The next morning Reggie discussed the pregnant housemaid with his housekeeper. Mrs. Herald clucked her tongue disapprovingly, but she was a kindhearted woman and agreed that they couldn't put the girl out when she had nowhere to go. Having borne children herself, she was also willing to assign Gillie's duties with an eye to the girl's condition.

The only other person Reggie told was Mac Cooper, who raised his eyebrows in an unusual show of emotion. "That pretty brown-haired lass? Pity her lover isn't around to horsewhip."

"I agree." Reggie was dressing for dinner, and he paused to pull on a fresh white shirt. "If it's any comfort, the young man will probably find that life as a common seaman is quite punishment enough."

Mac said with a questioning note, "You've not been drinking the last few days."

"Very observant of you," Reggie said dryly as he tied his cravat.

Undeterred, the wiry valet said, "Sobriety is no bad thing."

Reggie donned his waistcoat. "Glad you approve."

Mac put on his lofty, upper-servant expression. "I'm sure that it is not for me to approve or disapprove."

Reggie made a rude noise. "Since when have you not had opinions, you cockney fraud?"

"I never said I didn't have opinions," Mac said with a hint of smile. Then he added, his London accent thickening as it always did when he was concerned, "It's that worried I was getting."

Reggie gave his servant a hard look as he tugged on his beautifully tailored coat. "In other words, I was going to hell in a handbasket, and everyone noticed except me?"

Mac considered for a moment, then said simply, "Yes."

Reggie smiled with reluctant amusement. Mac had never been overconcerned with tact. Then he went down for dinner, glad that Julian would be arriving the next day. The household would benefit from some of his friend's easy good nature.

After his master left, Mac went through the motions of cleaning and straightening automatically. So little Gillie had been given a slip on the shoulder. Perhaps he would ask her if she wanted to go for a walk this evening. She'd be in need of a bit of cheering up. A slight smile on his face, he completed his work and headed to the servants' quarters for his own dinner.

Much of a steward's job involved moving around and keeping a watchful eye on how work was progressing, and Alys spent her morning doing exactly that. After riding up to the pastures to consult with Gabriel Mitford about when the sheep would be ready for shearing, she stopped to check on the haying.

Most of the grass meadows had been cut, the fragrant shocks piled into small stacks that dried the hay and kept it cool. She dismounted into the ankle-deep stubble to talk with the bailiff. He admitted that work was going well, adding with a countryman's caution that if the weather continued sunny, they would be finished the next day.

As Alys mounted to ride to her next task, she caught sight of her employer in the line of laborers moving steadily forward against the tall grasses. She had known that he was working on the haying, but had not chanced to see him.

Davenport riveted her attention, and not only because he was the tallest man in the field. His dark hair was tousled from the breeze, his sleeves casually rolled up, his open-throated shirt revealing his darkly tanned skin. She was struck by the beautiful image of a man and the land, and the sense that he belonged here.

Absorbed in work, he was unaware of her scrutiny. His lean body moved in a steady, graceful rhythm, his powerful arms and shoulders swinging the scythe from right to left, the mowed grass falling neatly to the side.

As she watched, the knot of misery that had formed in her breast the night before dissolved. It is said that every man is the hero of his own play, and every woman, too. Alys was the heroine in the story of her own life, and ever since Reginald Davenport had come to Strickland she had viewed him in terms of the role he played in her own personal drama. As her employer and a forceful, magnetic man, he had automatically become a leading player. He had absolute power over her livelihood, had saved her life, and, perhaps inevitably, had come to be a focus of her secret dreams and unadmitted desires.

Now, for the first time, Alys changed her perspective and tried to see how his world must look to him. Though he had not said so in words, she believed that the central drama that now absorbed him was an attempt to rebuild his life, to find some sense of connection and meaning. He had changed in small ways since he had come to Strickland. Now, by stopping his drinking, he was trying to change on a much more fundamental level.

She had known other men who routinely drank them-selves insensible. Most would have vigorously denied that they were drunkards, and only the barest handful ever at-tempted to stop, no matter how destructive their habits. Yet Reggie, a self-admitted rake, was making the effort. The desperate, angry tension she had felt in him these last days was a measure of the difficulty of what he was attempting.

She was only a minor actor in Reggie's world. His happi-ness or misery, his drinking or sobriety, had nothing to do with her. The silent battle that he was waging with his inner demons was far more important to him than she would ever be.

The thought was a curiously liberating one. Davenport was a complicated man, one who could act with both hero-ism and villainy, though he was neither hero nor villain. A man who, while not old, was certainly not young; who had the recklessness to create problems for himself, and the hon-esty to admit when he had done so. From what she had seen, he was fair and compassionate in his dealings with those around him.

He was also very much alone.

He didn't need her professional skills or her femaleness, her wistful fantasies or her regrets. What Reggie might need at this difficult time was friendship, acceptance, and un-derstanding. Those things she could give freely because, quite simply, she liked him.

She urged her mare forward and rode away, resolving to work harder at being a friend, no matter how snappish his temper. And even though he had a lamentable taste for housemaids as bed partners.

After a late luncheon at the manor house, Alys was on her way to the stables when she saw Reggie working with a tall gray gelding in the paddock. Moved by her new resolution to be more friendly, she decided to stop and watch for a while before going out for the afternoon. William was there already, his small, sturdy body balanced on the paddock fence while he watched, enthralled. He barely turned his head to greet his guardian when she joined him.

Alys had to admit that Reggie was a sight worth watching as he put the gelding through its paces. She already knew that he was a superb rider. Now she saw that he was a superb trainer as well. Rather than using his strength to dominate the horse, he worked with his mount, not against it, patiently guiding and correcting with nearly imperceptible shifts of weight and touch.

When he was done, the result would be a vastly superior hunter. It was an understatement when she commented, "Very light hands."

William nodded reverently. "He could ride Smokey without any reins at all."

When Reggie's circle-turning exercise brought Alys into his view, he hesitated, then turned the gelding to where she and William sat. Though he appeared pleased to see her, his expression was a bit wary, lacking its customary glint of subversive humor. He was probably unsure how she would greet him. They had scarcely exchanged a dozen words in the last week.

She smiled cheerfully. "From the looks of those hindquarters, I'd guess that Smokey is a first-rate jumper."

His face eased at her friendly greeting, "You're right. A little wild, but very strong over fences and with tremendous stamina." He reined in the gray by the fence so William could pat it. "He'll do for the hardest hunting in the Shires."

One could give a hunter no higher compliment. Alys said, "Are you training the new horses for sale, or for your own use?"

"For sale," he said. "This one will be worth ten times his purchase price in another year. Two of the others I bought in Dorchester will be equally good."

"And the fourth?"

"She's too small for flying country like the Shires, but will do well enough in rough, hilly counties like Devon, where cleverness over fences is more important than speed." Reggie automatically calmed the gelding when Nemesis slipped through the fence and caused the horse to sidle away nervously. "A horse that's bred for racing but isn't fast enough is a sad creature that has failed in its purpose in life. A horse bred for hunting is far more versatile. The fastest can be raced in steeplechases, and the rest are almost always suitable for some kind of hunting or riding."

"So hunters are philosophically more satisfying than racehorses?"

"Exactly." His eyes crinkled at the corners. "And better business as well."

By this time Alys was no longer surprised to learn that a rake could have a shrewd head for business. She shifted on the fence, beginning to find the narrow board uncomfortable. "If you intend to expand the horse training, you'll be needing more men for the stables."

William chimed in, a hopeful gleam in his blue eyes. "I can work as a stable lad."

Reggie smiled. "I think Lady Alys would prefer that you keep to your schooling." He glanced at her. "You're right, though, more will be needed, and soon. Do you know anyone in the neighborhood with experience of horse training?"

Alys bit her lower lip, considering. "Jamie Palmer, the supervisor at the pottery, used to be a groom. He was particularly good with young horses."

"Can the pottery spare him?"

"He would be missed," Alys admitted. "But his assistant is very capable, and I think Jamie would prefer to work with horses if he has the choice. Shall I ask him?"

Reggie shook his head. "I'll stop by the pottery myself. I'll want to know him better before offering a position." He gathered his reins, preparing to go. "By the way, did I mention that a good friend of mine, Julian Markham, is coming for a visit? He should be here sometime later this afternoon."

"No, you didn't say."

Alys must have looked doubtful, because Reggie said with a trace of humor, "Don't worry, he's one of my more respectable friends. He won't cause any trouble."

Before Alys could think of an appropriate response, they were interrupted by the sound of hooves and the jingle of harness. A smart chaise drawn by matched bays swept into the yard between the stables and the paddocks. Alys shaded her eyes with one hand to study the newcomer. "I'd say your friend has arrived."

"So he has." Reggie smiled. "Julian has always had good timing."

His eyes popping at the sight of such a bang-up equipage, William scrambled down from the fence for a closer look. Alys followed at a more dignified pace while Reggie dismounted and tethered the gelding, then came through the gate.

The driver of the chaise handed his reins over to his groom, then jumped lightly to the ground while Reggie stepped forward to welcome him. Alys examined the newcomer with interest. She had assumed that a close friend of Reggie's would be about the same age, but Julian Markham was considerably younger.

He was also quite the handsomest man she had seen in the last dozen years. Since Randolph, in fact. Even after hours of driving, his well-tailored forest-green coat and gleaming boots were elegant to a point just short of dandyism.

After shaking hands, Reggie turned and introduced his friend to Alys and William. Markham bowed gracefully over her hand. When he straightened, his gray-blue eyes widened slightly when he realized that she was as tall as he.

Or perhaps it was her mismatched eyes that surprised him, or her tan pantaloons.

Whatever he thought, he was far too well mannered to show disapproval. He said with a smile, "Reggie told me about you, Miss Weston, and of the superlative job you have done at Strickland."

For a moment she wondered if he was being sarcastic, but Julian had a smile of singular sweetness and charm. In fact, he was altogether quite adorable. She wondered whether Peter or Meredith would be more impressed. Peter would see him as the perfect London gentleman, while Merry would be hard-pressed not to consider him as husband material. Well, perhaps he was.

As Alys made a suitable reply, Merry herself appeared on the scene, drawn by the signs of activity. Smudges of dry clay marred the shapeless, ill-fitting gown that had been acquired from a maid after the fire, and her golden hair was tied back with a plain black ribbon. Obviously she had been at the pottery, working on her china designs.

Davenport said, "Meredith, I'd like you to meet a friend who has come to visit." Merry turned to greet the newcomer. For an instant horror flickered across her face. Alys almost laughed out loud even as she winced with sympathy. Meeting a handsome, elegant young gentleman when looking like an urchin was the stuff of nightmares. Luckily, Merry could not look less than pretty.

Alys glanced at Reggie just as his eyes turned to hers. For a moment they wordlessly commiserated about the painful tribulations of youth. Then he performed the introductions. The speed with which Meredith rallied and gave Julian a dazzling smile was a credit to her aplomb. Within moments the young people were chatting easily.

While William went to investigate the chaise and team, Alys gestured Reggie to one side and asked in a low voice,

"As a good guardian, I'd better find out if your friend is eligible."

"Very," he said succinctly. "Heir to a viscountcy and a substantial fortune, no major vices, and a gentleman to the bone."

"A paragon," Alys murmured. "How on earth did the two of you become friends?"

Just as she realized how insulting that sounded, Reggie grinned wickedly at her. "For the best of all possible reasons—because our friendship infuriates his father."

"I am properly chastened," she said with a laugh. "Tell me, did you ask him down with matchmaking in mind?"

A slight smile quirked his mouth. "Not precisely, but the thought did cross my mind that he and Merry might suit. A match would solve your concerns about finding a worthy husband for the girl, and Julian would be lucky to have her. Merry has far more to offer than most of the chits that come onto the London Marriage Mart."

Alys was oddly touched that he was concerned for the welfare of her wards. She glanced at Merry and Julian, who were laughing together. Obviously there was mutual attraction, in spite of Meredith's deplorable gown. The two of them looked very well together, and not only because both were exceptionally good looking. Perhaps it was the general air of intelligence and good nature they had in common.

But in a practical world, it took much more than looks, compatibility of mind, or even love, to make a marriage. "Would his family object to his marrying a girl whose birth and fortune are lackluster by society's standards?"

"They would not be enthralled," Reggie admitted, "but Julian could probably bring his parents around if he wanted to."

Alys was relieved to hear that. Of course it was absurd to speculate about a match when the young people in question had only just met, but she had quickly learned that worrying was part of being a parent, even a surrogate one.

Alys and Reggie broke off their conversation as Merry and Julian approached. Deciding that being a gracious hostess was more important than stewarding, Alys suggested, "Would you like some refreshment after your journey, Mr. Markham?"

He smiled. "Thank you, Miss Weston, I'd like that very much."

Alys collected her wards—easily in the case of Merry, who was anxious to change, with some difficulty in the case of William—and carried them off to give the men a few minutes of privacy.

As soon as they were out of earshot, Julian demanded, "Why didn't you tell me Miss Spenser was such a stunner, Reg? I would have chucked my other obligations and been here a fortnight ago." Then an alarmed expression crossed his face. "Unless . . . is she your . . . ?" He stopped, too embarrassed to continue.

"My *petite amie*?" Reggie suggested helpfully. "Nonsense. Surely it is obvious that she is a lady."

Julian flushed, looking very young. "Sorry. Of course she is."

Nemesis trotted up, tail wagging. As the collie started to rear up on Julian's immaculate pantaloons, Reggie said sharply, "Nemesis!"

The dog settled back on her haunches, tail still hopefully sweeping back and forth on the ground. "My dog, brainless but amiable," Reggie said wryly. "Don't let her climb all over you. She has enough bad habits."

"You're getting very bucolic. All you need now is the pack of foxhounds." Julian ruffled Nemesis's ears. "You'd better explain how matters stand here before I commit some dreadful faux pas. Are Miss Spenser and her brother visiting Miss Weston, are they neighbors, or what?"

Reggie entered the paddock. "They live here, along with a middle brother." As he untethered the gray gelding and led it inside, he described how Alys had come to be steward and guardian of the Spensers, and the fire that had left them homeless.

Much intrigued, Julian said, "I thought Dorset was supposed to be a quiet county! It sounds like you've had no shortage of excitement. But then, excitement follows you around. You're the only man in England who would acquire an estate that not only has a female steward, but one who is a splendid Amazon."

Reggie felt a flash of irritation. "Lady Alys is not your type," he said shortly as he uncinched the gelding's saddle.

"Is she yours?" Julian said with a gleam of speculation.

"Did you lose your wits on the journey down from London?" Reggie said scathingly as he turned the gelding over to a stable lad for grooming. "All women are my type. Or none. It comes to the same thing."

Properly chastened, Julian accompanied his friend into the manor house. He should have known that Reggie would have no interest in a virtuous spinster. Even one who was a splendid Amazon.

Strickland became much livelier after Julian Markham's arrival. Within a day the guest was on first-name terms with everyone in the household. While William continued to dog Reggie's heels, along with the real dog, Peter Spenser found in Julian a new idol, one more approachable and less alarming than Reggie. Peter immediately began to mimic Julian's manners, his neck cloth knot, even his turns of speech.

Alys suspected that Julian was a little amused, but he was young enough to remember the awkwardness of fifteen. He was also kind enough to be tolerant of the imitation. He really was a fine young man, exactly the sort she would wish for Merry.

Her pleasure was tempered by concern. Clearly Merry and Julian were attracted to each other, sharing laughter and endless conversation. Alys would have been delighted, except for the fear her ward would be unacceptable to the Markham family.

She had a brief word with Meredith about not developing expectations. Merry laughed and said that Julian was behaving with perfect propriety and had given her no reason to build feather castles. Nonetheless, Alys worried. Though Merry might not admit to having her feelings engaged, there was a suspicious glow about her.

On a more positive note, Alys was relieved that Reggie was finding sobriety less difficult. He talked and smiled more easily, and his air of tension had diminished. He did continue to push himself physically with estate work and horse training, but Julian didn't seem to mind being left to the devices of the younger members of the household. Excursions were planned to various local points of interest.

Alys went along on the first, but she disliked taking time from her work during the estate's busiest season. Also, she realized that her chaperonage was not required. A gentleman who cheerfully accepted the company of a girl's young brothers had to be trustworthy.

The subject of the assembly in Dorchester came up at dinner after Julian had been at Strickland for a week. With twinkling eyes, Meredith suggested that they make up a party to go to the assembly so Julian could see what high style they kept in Dorset.

Julian laughed. "Does that mean the waltz has come to the provinces?"

"There's a rumor that it will be introduced at this assembly," Merry replied. "But there is fear that even if one is played, no one will know how to dance it!"

"What a catastrophe that would be. I shall teach you to waltz." He glanced across the table. "That is, if you permit, Lady Alys."

"I would like to see how it is done myself," Alys admitted. "Any dance so thoroughly condemned by high-sticklers must be interesting."

In a spirit of general merriment everyone adjourned to the drawing room, even William, who had nothing better to do and was not ready for bed. Alys was thumbing through the sheet music, looking for the waltzes Merry had ordered from London, when Reggie stopped her. "Peter wants to learn also, so you'll be needed as a partner. I'll play the accompaniment."

Alys was startled. "I didn't know you played the piano."

"Wait until you've heard me before you decide," he advised as he seated himself at the instrument.

In fact, Reggie played very well. As Alys watched his long, beautiful fingers stroke the keys, first tentatively in a series of rippling scales, then confidently as he sight-read the score, she wondered when a rake found time to practice the piano. Between orgies, perhaps? Then she remembered the times, late at night, when she'd thought she'd heard distant music. So that hadn't been her imagination.

Alys joined the others and watched as Julian demonstrated the steps of the waltz. Ever punctilious, he would dance first with Merry, then Alys. Peter partnered whichever female wasn't benefiting from Julian's superior skill. Within half an hour there were two couples twirling about the drawing room, while William watched with glazed boredom.

By the time the tea tray came, Alys was exhilarated. She had loved dancing in her salad days, even if she was far too tall. It was fortunate that she was now in the ranks of chaperones, and wouldn't have the chance to make a fool of herself in public.

On the day of the assembly, Alys's path intersected Reggie's in the stables at the end of the afternoon. The annual sheepshearing had begun, and with his usual interest in trying everything himself, Reggie had participated. Alys had been otherwise engaged, so she asked, "How did the sheepshearing go?"

Reggie removed the saddle and blanket from the mare he had been riding. "It certainly requires more skill than washing the foolish beasts. Did you know that to shear a sheep's foreleg, you have only to press a spot under the shoulder and the leg will shoot straight out for clipping? Quite extraordinary."

When Alys grinned, he continued, "Yes, of course you would know that. I knew it once, but had forgotten. Gabe Mitford spent some time teaching me the basics of shearing, but it was obvious from the pained expression on his face that I wasn't up to his standards. Every time I made a cut, he winced, as if I had just ruined the entire fleece."

"Well, it's easy to do that, and wool is one of our most important products," Alys said. "Did you ruin any?"

"One or two," he admitted. "However, Gabe allowed that I wasn't doing badly for a beginner."

Reggie moved to the far side of the mare and took a handful of clean straw. As he began brushing sweat and foam from the brown hide, Alys asked on impulse, "How are you doing with sobriety?"

He raised his head and regarded her with eyes as cold as chipped ice. "I can't imagine what business that is of yours."

She felt a hot flush of color rise in her face. "None at all. I am merely an employee who has no choice but to tolerate your bad temper."

She pivoted on her heel and was heading toward the stable door when he said in a low voice, "Allie, I'm sorry. I shouldn't have snapped at you."

She stopped, still fuming, then turned back to him.

His hands lay quiet on the horse's back and his long, dark

face was rueful. "I know I've been difficult lately. I've tried to be as silent as possible to minimize the effects of my evil temper. Forgive me?"

Alys knew how hard it was to apologize; she wasn't very good at doing that herself. "Forgiven and forgotten. I've been known to be irritable a time or two myself. And I *was* impertinent."

"Then I'll cancel your remark out with an impertinence of my own," he said with a faint smile. "Wear that gold dress tonight instead of one of your dark chaperon dresses."

Her brows rose. "How biblical, an impertinence for an impertinence."

"Well, I'm much better at impertinence than I am at sheepshearing," he said reasonably.

"No one would deny it," she agreed as she left the stables. She was not entirely displeased that he had an interest in her appearance.

Chapter 16

Public assemblies were gatherings of the families of local gentry, professional men, and prosperous merchants, not the most exclusive of company. Furthermore, the low-ceilinged assembly room attached to the King's Head in Dorchester should have seemed paltry to a woman who had had a London Season.

But to Alys, the long room with its simple floral decorations was lovely. She had brought Merry here several times, but there was something special about tonight. Perhaps it was because of Julian Markham, so handsome that every female eye in the room swiveled to look at him when their party entered. Or perhaps they watched Reggie, who looked very tall, dark, and devilishly attractive in immaculate black evening garb. And of course Merry was stunning in a simple muslin gown trimmed in forget-me-not blue ribbons that matched her eyes.

Or perhaps it was Alys herself who felt special. The low-cut golden gown Reggie had requested was the most dashing garment she had ever owned. Merry had pulled Alys's thick glossy hair back into a loose twist, then let it tumble in curls down her back with one lock falling forward over her bare shoulder. Alys studied her reflection with pleasure and some alarm. She did not look like a chaperone.

She'd felt nervous when she came down from her bedchamber, but Julian and Peter had complimented her looks extravagantly. Best of all, Reggie had studied her from crown to toe with a slow, approving smile on his face. Yes, the night was special.

Alys and Merry knew almost everyone at the assembly, and the girl was immediately besieged by admirers. Alys herself was considered an Original, not at all what one would wish one's own daughter to become, but she was generally well accepted.

Tonight, however, she was wondrously popular. Mothers of nubile daughters came from all directions to offer greetings and sympathy about the fire. Then they waited expectantly to be introduced to Julian and Reggie, who were the most attractive men present, as well as the most eligible.

The attention put a sardonic gleam into Reggie's eyes. During a pause in the rush, he murmured to Alys, "A few months ago, most of these good matrons would have had their husbands call me out if I so much as said hello to their darling daughters."

"Timing is so important in life," she returned sweetly, "and now is your time to be deliciously in demand." She nodded to an approaching woman. "So nice to see you again, Mrs. Baird. Have you met Mr. Davenport yet?"

During the introductions, Mrs. Baird examined Reggie with scowling intensity, as if half expecting him to ravish her on the spot. Then she tried to probe Alys about Julian Markham's background and expectations. Blandly Alys turned the queries aside.

When Mrs. Baird withdrew in defeat, Reggie said under his breath, "That woman resembles nothing so much as a ship of the line in full sail."

Alys chuckled. "She has three daughters who are more

like frigates. Give them a few years, and they'll be in the same nautical class as their mother."

Reggie groaned at her bad joke, then escaped to talk with some of the men whom he had met in the last few weeks. Alys watched him for a moment. From the way the gentleman welcomed him, he was well on his way to being established in the county.

Then she returned to her duties, chattering with the other older women and keeping an eye on Meredith. After one dance with Merry, Julian gave a sterling example of noblesse oblige by asking the shyest, plainest girls in the room to stand up with him.

Having herself been plain and shy, Alys knew just how wonderful it was to have a young man like Julian claim a dance. Besides his good looks and exquisite manners, he had the ability to make a female feel like she was the only woman in the world while he was with her. Tonight he was giving a dozen girls shining memories they could cherish their whole lives.

The dancing started promptly at eight and would end at midnight. At ten o'clock, after a portentous pause, the musicians struck up the first public waltz to be played in Dorchester. For a dozen bars the dance floor was empty.

Then Squire Richards and his wife, who often visited London, stepped onto the floor, followed by another couple. Julian had been saving his second dance with Merry in hopes of a waltz, and now he led her out. They were both so beautiful that they drew every eye as they swirled into the waltz. Merry laughed up at her partner, her golden hair spilling back over her gauzy gown.

Alys was watching her ward fondly when Reggie materialized, taking her elbow. "Shall we show them how it is done?" Before she could refuse on the grounds of age, dignity, or propriety, he swept her onto the dance floor.

She tensed, afraid that she would disgrace herself and

become an object of derision. When she had danced in public as a girl, she was always miserably aware of her height. But with Reggie that was not a problem. Here was a man she could literally look up to. She relaxed, raising her gaze to meet his.

He drew her into waltz position, one strong hand on her waist and the other clasping her gloved hand firmly. "Good girl," he said softly as they began dancing.

"I'm hardly a girl," she murmured, profoundly aware of his nearness.

"No, for which be thanked, but you are hardly in your dotage, either." His eyes were very blue, his steps very sure, and a faint smile curved his lips.

When they had first met, she had thought him almost handsome. Now she could not imagine why she had qualified her appraisal. He was more than handsome—he was devastating. Like the shy young girls who had danced with Julian, she savored her moment of magic.

She should have known that if Reggie chose to dance, he would do it well. She didn't talk, simply enjoyed, her body pliant, her golden dress belling out behind her.

Though they had shared passionate kisses, there was a different kind of eroticism in this waltz. With only a handful of couples on the floor, there was room to move freely, to yield one's self to the passion of the music. Secure in his arms, Alys understood why the waltz was considered so improper. Certainly her thoughts were as she gave herself over to delight, feeling the slow fire of his touch stealing through her body.

Far too soon the music ended. Breathless with exertion and proximity, Alys laughed and swept into a deep, formal court curtsy before her partner, not even considering how odd it would appear that she knew how to do such a thing.

With a lurking smile Reggie bowed in reply, then led her from the floor. "Now that I have revealed that I know how to dance, I suppose I must stand up for a few more sets or be thought rude," he said with resignation.

Alys dimpled. "Very proper of you."

"That's what I was afraid of," he muttered before going to ask Meredith for the quadrille that was forming.

Alys thought her moment's frivolity was over, but Julian came over and insisted she join him. "Leave it to Reg to persuade you to dance," he said admiringly. "If I had known you could be convinced, I would have asked earlier."

Julian was a delightful partner, and she enjoyed the quadrille, though it was not the same as being with Reggie. The musicians then struck up another waltz. Wistfully Alys recognized that Reggie really couldn't ask her again. Instead he asked Mrs. Richards, and sturdy Squire Richards led Alys out.

This time more couples were willing to reveal steps practiced in secret, and the floor filled up. Though it was not like dancing with Reggie, Alys enjoyed herself again. She didn't even mind that the top of Squire Richards' head came only to her nose. The squire was a skilled dancer, and he complimented her freely on her own mastery. "Been hiding your light under a bushel, Miss Weston," he beamed.

It was the closest Alys had ever come to being the belle of a ball. It was quite close enough.

The party of well-dressed strangers arrived shortly after eleven o'clock. Three women and two men entered and stayed in a cluster by the door as they gazed around with bored condescension. The musicians were taking a short break, so the newcomers' loud, slurred voices were readily audible. All were dressed in the height of fashion, the women with a flamboyance that suggested the muslin company. Alys guessed they were Londoners who happened to be in the neighborhood, coming to observe the natives from lack of any better amusement.

After a brief examination of the newcomers, Alys turned back to Reggie and resumed her explanation of how fleeces were stored and shipped. Then, out of the corner of her eye, she saw one of the newly arrived females catch sight of Reggie. The woman's face brightened, and she started across the room. She was redheaded and floridly attractive, with a gown cut so low that it made Alys's dress seem positively puritanical.

Completely ignoring Alys, the redhead laid one hand possessively on Reggie's sleeve and cooed, "Reggie, darling, I had no idea that you were in the neighborhood. What are you doing so frightfully far from town?"

He said coolly, "I live here."

"Here?" she asked incredulously. "Amongst these rustics?"

Finally noticing Reggie's companion, the redhead made a leisurely scan, tilting her head up as if Alys's head was scraping clouds. "Good Lord, Reggie, where did you find such a strapping creature?" She giggled tipsily. "Her eyes are peculiar."

In the face of the redhead's petite, voluptuous prettiness, Alys's buoyant pleasure in the evening evaporated, leaving her feeling horribly gawky and unattractive. Not to mention homicidal as she watched the woman's provocative behavior to Reggie.

Reggie removed the redhead's clinging hand as if it were an unwanted thread. "What are you doing in Dorset if you mislike it so, Stella? It *is* Stella, isn't it?"

Stella's hazel eyes flared angrily before she smiled with dagger-edged sweetness. Slanting a glance at Alys, she cooed, "If you prefer, you can use some of the names you whispered the last time we were . . . together."

Alys had no doubt about what "together" meant in this case. Perhaps she should feel flattered that this trollop seemed to consider Alys a rival, but fury was her predominant emotion. She was tempted to stalk away. A combination of embarrassment and morbid curiosity kept her rooted to the spot. Curiosity, plus the belief that Reggie was no more pleased at what was happening than Alys was.

When Reggie ignored her last remarks, Stella said pettishly, "I wouldn't be here if I had a choice, but George has taken a house nearby. Some dreary aunt of his is dying, and he visits her regularly so she won't forget him in her will. It's incredibly tedious, but he says we'll go to Brighton soon."

"Where is George now?" Reggie asked, his expression bored.

Stella shrugged, an action that almost unmoored her gown entirely. "Outside with the carriage. He'll be along in a moment."

Her companions had drifted after her. One of the men moved forward and clapped Reggie on the shoulder. "'Lo, Davenport," he said with alcoholic good humor. "Haven't seen you in town lately."

"That's because I haven't been there, Wildon," Reggie said with barely restrained impatience. Wildon was an acquaintance, not a friend, and Reggie disliked familiarity from a near-stranger. Was he himself equally oafish when in his cups? An unattractive thought. The sooner he got himself and Allie away, the better.

Cursing the fate that had brought London acquaintances like Stella and her protector to Shaftesbury, he took Alys's arm. "Good to see you all. Give my regards to Blakeford. Sorry I missed him, but we were just leaving."

Under his fingers he felt Alys's muscles spasm. He couldn't blame her for being upset. As if Stella's rudeness wasn't bad enough, by this time they were the objects of attention of a circle of curious Dorset gentry.

Before Reggie could retreat, Stella made one last bid for attention. "Do settle a question for us, Reggie darling. On our way over, we were talking about whether chivalry is dead. Martin here"—she waved at the nearest foxed gentleman—

"says that defending a lady's honor is old-fashioned, utterly passé."

While Reggie tried to remember why he had been willing to fornicate with this coarse slut, even when he was roaring drunk, she fluttered her darkened lashes and undulated her bountiful curves. Then she continued huskily, "I say that Martin is wrong. You're a gentleman. Wouldn't you fight for my honor?"

"Why should I?" Reggie said in a clear, carrying voice. "You never did."

The horrified silence that greeted his words had a gelid quality. Except for one weak gasp, the circle of Dorset gentry might have been carved from stone.

Stella's mouth went slack with shock as she absorbed what he had said. Then her face turned murderous, all her pouty prettiness gone.

Having delivered his lightning bolt, Reggie was momentarily nonplussed. He had made his share of scenes in his life, but usually when he was so drunk that he hadn't cared what happened next. Stone-cold sober was quite a different matter.

Feeling a tremor in Allie's arm, he gave her a swift glance. Her face was rigid, as if she was trying her hardest to suppress laughter or strong hysterics. Or more likely, both. He had to get her away.

Seeing George Blakeford approach, Reggie said easily, as if he hadn't just offered deadly insult to the man's mistress, "Here comes George now. I have a hunter he might be interested in. Do you know if he'll be riding with the Cottesmere hunt this season?"

As the drunken Wildon replied, the musicians began to play. The circle of onlookers dissolved as if the interlude had never taken place, though Reggie was sure they would be discussing his comment for years to come.

Under cover of the renewed activity, Allie jerked her arm free of his grip and slipped away without a backward glance, cutting through the crowd to a side door. As her tall, slim figure disappeared, Reggie turned to follow, but before he could make his escape, Blakeford arrived. He seemed more sober than his companions, and his eyes had sharpened with interest at the sight of Reggie.

Fairly caught, Reggie spent a few interminable minutes exchanging commonplaces as Stella glared daggers. As soon as he could, Reggie made his excuses and slid away to the exit Allie had used.

The door opened to a passage that led to the garden behind the King's Head. By the light of a few scattered lanterns, he searched the flower-lined paths. He found her on a stone bench at the far end of the garden, head bowed and fingering a pale rose.

She stiffened and raised her head when he sat down beside her. It was too dark to see her features clearly, but the moonlight gave a milky translucence to her fair skin and laid subtle highlights in her hair.

In a stifled voice Allie said, "I was feeling a bit faint and wanted some fresh air."

At least she wasn't throwing things at him. Mildly Reggie said, "You? Faint? The woman who can work twelve hours straight in high summer and never tire?"

She eyed his dark outline warily, unsure why he had followed her outside. "Very well, I wasn't faint. I was furious."

"That's the Lady Alys I know," Reggie said approvingly. "Are you going to favor me with a colorful description of my morals, manners, and ultimate fiery destination?"

She had to smile. "I considered it, but try as I might, I can't quite blame you for that, that . . . bit of muslin's behavior."

"Well, you could, but I would prefer that you didn't."

The silence eased into comfort. He was only inches away, close enough for her to feel the radiant warmth from his body. "She was quite attractive, in a vulgar sort of way," Alys observed. "Since men are at the mercy of their animal nature, I can see why you were interested in . . . consorting with her, even if a bed was all you had in common."

"A bed never entered into it, actually," Reggie said with wry humor in his voice. "Tell me, does anything shock you?"

"Nowhere near enough. I should have been shocked at that appalling set-down you gave her. Instead I thought it quite possible that I would shatter into small pieces if I didn't laugh." Alys shook her head, bemused. "Honestly, Reggie, I know that she was behaving badly, but how could you say something like that in public?"

"It was easy. Appalling insults are something of a specialty of mine. They've certainly gotten me into trouble often enough." He sighed. "You must have noticed that Stella isn't a particularly nice person. And I didn't insult her until she had insulted you."

Alys toyed with the rose, its sweet, fragile fragrance scenting the night air. "I don't understand women like that."

"I don't, either." After a lengthy silence, he said quietly, "I'm sorry that my evil past intruded tonight, Allie. I know quite a lot of rackety folk, but I didn't expect any of them to turn up here."

It was a perfect opening. She asked, "I gather that the man you two were discussing, George Blakeford, is Stella's protector. He's a friend of yours?"

"Not really. We've been acquainted for years, but not friends." He chuckled ruefully. "And if we had been, we wouldn't be after Stella tells him what I said."

"Might he call you out?" Alys asked with sudden alarm.

"I doubt it," Reggie said calmly. "The man is no fool. He might spread a little slander about me, but what's another drop in an ocean?"

Alys considered asking more about Blakeford, but knew that it would look odd. Besides, it was mere coincidence that George was in the area. The miracle was that no one else from her past had ever turned up to haunt her.

Music and humming voices from the assembly sounded clearly in the night air. When the silence had lasted too long, Reggie asked, "Are you ready to go back in?"

"No!" Alys said, sounding more abrupt than she had intended. Well, he could ascribe her unwillingness to lingering cowardice. Better that than if he knew the truth. "I'm sorry, but I've had quite enough of crowds for one night. Do you think Merry and Julian could be persuaded to leave a little early?"

"I'm sure they'll cooperate. The dancing will be over soon anyhow." Reggie got to his feet. "I'll go collect them." He took Alys's hand to help her up.

His courteous gesture helped restore the feeling of being delicately female that had been shattered by Stella. Glad that he had made the effort to soothe her injured feelings, she said, "While you extricate our companions, I'll get the coach."

Amused, he said, "I can manage both. Since you're very much a lady tonight, you must accept being treated like one."

Still holding Reggie's hand, Alys looked up at him, trying to read his expression in the dim light. The air between them had weight and substance, a legacy of the melting sensuality of the waltz.

Oddly intent, he raised his other hand and touched her face with gossamer lightness, his fingertips skimming her brow and cheek, then circling under her heavy hair to brush her sensitive nape. She caught her breath, vividly conscious of his nearness, of his irresistible masculinity. Weak with yearning, she prayed that he would kiss her again.

But he was sober tonight, so of course he didn't. He would have to be drunk to consider her worth the effort. She tried not to let the bitterness of that thought destroy memories of the simpler pleasures of the evening.

His hand dropped, and he stepped back. "I'll put you in the carriage before I find Merry and Julian." His voice sounded unnaturally loud.

Silently she accompanied him toward the garden gate. Since he didn't want her, there was nothing else to do.

On the ride back to the rented house, the other two couples were noisily engaged in preliminaries to the night's final entertainment. However, George Blakeford was driving the carriage, so Stella was left alone to seethe in her fury.

To think that she had actually been glad to see Reggie Davenport! She had hoped that he could help alleviate her boredom when George was off toadying to his aunt. She had not forgotten their prior encounter, and the thought of further explorations at greater length had been delightful.

She tugged her shawl closer, as if she could shut out the memory of how he had publicly humiliated her. Davenport must be interested in that oversized rural creature, or he would never have insulted Stella the way he had. She would make him pay for that.

Blakeford was a dangerous man, and properly directed, he would avenge her. All she need do was decide the best way to inflame her lover against Davenport. She thought about it for the rest of the journey back to their inn.

George seemed abstracted, not falling on her ravenously as soon as they were alone, the way he usually did. Instead, as he ripped his cravat off, he said, "When I came into the assembly room, I saw a very tall woman in a gold dress with Davenport, but she was gone by the time I joined you."

Stella turned so that he could unfasten her gown, which was too expensive to allow a man to rip off. "Surely you didn't think the creature was attractive?" she said crossly. "She was most peculiar, far too tall and with mismatched eyes. Lord only knows where Davenport found her. Perhaps he likes women with wooden legs as well."

George's impatient hands paused in their unfastening for a moment. Resuming, he said casually, "There's no accounting for tastes. Me, I find redheads irresistible." He pushed the dress from her shoulders and slid his hands around to cup her breasts.

Now was the time to put her plan into effect, while her lover was lustful and irrational. Stella said in a quavering voice, "It was dreadful finding Davenport there tonight. I hoped never to see him again, after . . . after what he did the last time."

Blakeford spun her around and seized her shoulders, his lips a hard, narrow line. "What do you mean?"

She widened her eyes, trying to look innocent and vulnerable. If she didn't play this exactly right, George would be furious with her, dangerously so. "Remember that night you had the card party and you lost five hundred pounds to Davenport?"

"I remember." Blakeford's mouth twisted nastily. "I also remember you wagging your tail at him."

"Georgie, darling, not at all!" she protested. "I was just being hospitable, since he was your guest. But . . . but he misunderstood. You remember how drunk he was. And . . . and when I chanced to meet him in the hallway . . ." She bowed her head and shivered, as if unable to continue.

Blakeford's hands tightened bruisingly on her arms. "What happened?"

Hurt by his grip, Stella was able to produce genuine tears. "He . . . he forced himself on me, George. It was just awful. I tried to scream, but he had his hand over my mouth."

His eyes narrowed. "Why didn't you tell me about it then?"

Stella said huskily, "I was afraid of what might happen. You know his reputation, how dangerous he is. I couldn't bear to think that something might happen to you." She began unbuttoning her lover's shirt with expert hands. "I thought it best to forget the incident, but when I saw him tonight, I was frightened. He insulted me horribly, for no reason. And the way he looked at me!" She swallowed hard, then continued. "What if he comes after me again? He was so *large*. So *strong*."

Each of her words was chosen to imply subtly that Davenport was more of a man than Blakeford. Stronger, more virile, more dangerous. She understood her lover's pride and possessiveness well enough to be sure that he would not let anything foolish like honor restrain him when he was enraged. If he wanted revenge, it was quite possible that Davenport would be found with a lead ball in his back, and no one would ever know who did it. Stella savored the thought.

As her hands roved farther, Blakeford's groan became more than just fury. Raggedly he said, "I'll make him pay, Stella, for what he did to you, and to me."

He crushed his mouth down on hers. He was not entirely convinced that the slut had been unwilling when Davenport made his advance. But she was *his* slut, by God, and Davenport would pay for having trespassed.

Damn Davenport to hell anyhow. First the man had taken Stella, and then he had saved "Alys Weston's" life. If he hadn't been around the night of the fire, she would be dead and none would be the wiser.

It had been bitterly disappointing to learn that the bitch had survived. At the time he'd had no special interest in whether Davenport lived or died, but after Stella's revelation, it was doubly infuriating to think how close the fire had come to removing both problems.

Vengeance must wait a few days or weeks, until the time was right, but it would most assuredly come.

He pulled his mistress to their bed, determined to ride her with such ferocity that he would completely obliterate her memories of being touched by another man—especially a man who was large, and strong, and dangerous.

Chapter 17

The first time Julian Markham saw Meredith Spenser in her clay-smudged dress, he'd thought that she was a remarkably pretty girl. A few hours later he saw her gowned for dinner and knew she was a stunner. By the time he had spent three days in her company, he had fallen quite thoroughly in love.

Even in his besotted state, he knew it wasn't only Merry's golden beauty that he loved, but her intelligence, buoyant good nature, and calm good sense. Love was a novel and delicious sensation, and he kept it to himself, biding his time and saying nothing to Merry that might give offense. Luckily, in the country they were able to spend nearly every daylight hour together, walking, riding, and visiting local sights. Such companionship could never have occurred in London, and was a tribute to the confidence that Lady Alys had in her ward, and in Julian himself.

The confidence was not misplaced. Nothing untoward or improper had been said between Julian and Merry, but as they laughed and talked of everything and nothing, the conviction grew in Julian that she returned his feelings. He decided to speak to her the day before he would have to depart for a family engagement. While he was sure that Merry cared for him, he was not quite so confident that he wished to leave without assuring himself of her affections.

The afternoon's activity was a tour of the potbank. Julian would cheerfully go anywhere with Merry, but found it surprisingly interesting to see how clay was prepared and pottery was made. "It used to be that there were little local potteries all over Britain," Merry explained as she showed him where slipware was cast. "But now that roads are so much improved, pottery can be shipped longer distances. The industry is becoming concentrated in places convenient to raw materials, like Staffordshire."

Julian studied her enchanting profile as she lifted a plaster of Paris mold from a shelf. "You know the most remarkable things," he said admiringly.

She chuckled. "Remarkable, unladylike things is what you mean." She opened the mold for him. "See? The lique-fied clay, which is called slip, is poured into the mold. The plaster pulls the water out, the clay deposits on the inside of the mold, and voila! We have a vase or cup or whatever. Very elaborate pieces can be made this way."

"Merry," Julian said, laying one hand on hers where it held the mold, "one reason you are so special is precisely that you are un-missish."

She gave him a swift, uncertain glance, then pulled away to return the mold to the shelf. "Neither my aunt nor Lady Alys would ever permit me to be missish. Shall we go and look at the bottle oven so you can see how the pottery is fired?"

He obligingly followed her outside to the oven, which was large enough for two dozen people to stand inside when it was empty. At the moment it was half-filled with earth-enware waiting to be fired a second time. Merry pointed out objects of interest, including dainty teacups in their own protective firing container. "Those are some of my trial pieces. I'm working on designs for when we're ready to add new lines."

His gaze on Merry's face, Julian murmured, "Very pretty."

For a moment he thought he saw sadness in her deep blue eyes. Then she smiled mischievously. "An expert flirt can turn anything into a compliment." Leading the way out of the oven, she went on, "It should be full enough to fire tomorrow. After this second firing, I'll be able to decorate my samples. I'm pleased with how they're turning out. The shapes are rather good."

"So is yours," he said, admiring her silhouette in the door of the bottle oven.

A teasing laugh was his only answer.

The works supervisor, Jamie Palmer, was outside, and she waved at him as she and Julian left. They had walked over from Strickland. As they turned their steps back toward the manor house, Julian said, "Merry, I want to talk to you."

They were walking along a hedgerow. Acting as if he hadn't spoken, she picked a sprig of pale pink flowers from a lanky plant growing among the hawthorn. "This is valerian. Did you know the roots make a tea that will help a person to sleep?"

As she sniffed the cluster of pink blossoms, Julian asked, "Why are you trying to avoid talking to me?"

She stared down at the flower, not meeting his eyes. "I don't want our summer idyll to end," she said softly. "But I suppose it already has."

He cupped her chin in one hand and looked into her sapphire eyes. Shocked to see tears gathering, he said with alarm, "Merry, what's wrong? Is it that you don't want to hear me say that I love you because you don't feel the same?"

Her eyes shut as the tears spilled over. "Oh, no, not that! Not that at all."

It seemed the most natural thing in the world to take her

in his arms and hold her. Julian had known that he loved her sweetness, beauty, and gaiety. Now he discovered a tender ness beyond anything he had ever experienced. "Hush, my dear," he murmured. "If I love you and you love me, what cause is there for tears?"

Merry pulled away from him. "I never expected being in love to hurt so much." She gave a brittle smile. "Alys used to laugh at how well I had my life planned. I had decided that I would find a kind man of moderate fortune who would adore and cherish me. In return I would make sure he never regretted his choice."

She dug a handkerchief from a concealed pocket and blew her nose in a futile attempt to recover her composure. Julian found even her pinkened nose endearing.

Realizing that serious talk was needed, Julian sat down in the shadow of the hedgerow, sparing one pained thought for his fawn-colored inexpressibles. He took Merry's hand and tugged her down beside him. "Why are you finding love so uncomfortable? I've never been happier in my life."

She stared bleakly down at the crumpled muslin square in her hand. "It hurts because I can't believe we'll have a 'happily ever after.' We are too far apart in birth and fortune. Why couldn't your father have been something less lofty than a viscount?"

"I wouldn't have thought you would mind the idea of being a viscountess. You will make a very good one." He laid his hand over hers, where it rested on the grassy turf. "Since my father is hale and hearty, you should have years as the Honorable Mrs. Markham before you have to face becoming Lady Markham."

Her smile was rueful. "Julian, my mother was the daughter of a minor country squire, my father a city merchant who was reasonably successful, but nowhere near rich enough to overcome my deficiencies of birth. I will have a portion of five thousand pounds. That's quite decent by the standards of rural Dorsetshire, but I can't believe it is what Lord Markham wishes for his only son and heir."

His respect for her increased. Obviously she had been doing some clear thinking. "I don't expect my father to like it, but he hasn't the authority to forbid my marriage, or to disinherit me." Julian smiled reassuringly. "He should be delighted to hear my news, since he has suggested several times in the last couple of years that I marry. I think he wants to see the succession assured for another generation." He halted a moment. "I've gotten ahead of myself. Will you marry me?"

"I would like nothing better." As Julian began to smile, she added, "But not at the expense of separating you from your family." She swallowed hard and looked away. "That is why love hurts. I find that I care more for your happiness than my own. I . . . I know too well what it is to lose one's parents. I won't be the cause of cutting you off from your family."

Another wave of tenderness swept through Julian. Merry's generosity of spirit was vivid proof that love had deeper levels than he had realized. A lifetime with her would introduce him to kinds of loving that he could not even imagine now.

Sunlight shafted through the hedge to touch her golden hair to a halo. Her loveliness was unearthly, but her expression was such a blend of sorrow and longing that Julian could restrain himself no longer. He leaned forward and touched his lips to hers, first as lightly as a butterfly wing, then with increasing pressure.

She responded with such sweetness that he ached, longing to enfold and protect her forever. His arms went around her, and he drew her close. He'd had his share of experience with the physical side of loving, but her simple kiss moved him more deeply that the most unrestrained passion in his past.

When he found himself on the verge of pulling her down full length on the soft grass, he knew it was time to stop. He released her, his breath unsteady. "We had better get on our feet and moving, or I am going to betray Lady Alys's trust."

Her face shaken and vulnerable, Merry hastily rose and brushed her crumpled skirt. Then she tucked her hand into Julian's elbow, clinging more tightly than she usually did as they resumed walking along the footpath.

When Julian had himself under control again, he said, "Why are you so sure my family will object to you? It isn't as if you're an opera dancer."

She giggled, as he had hoped she would, but sobered swiftly. "I'm just being logical. I'm not the least bit romantical, you know. You could do far better for yourself."

Julian stopped and turned her to face him, his hands lightly resting on her shoulders. "No, I couldn't," he said intensely. "Remember that."

Having lost parents, aunt, and several homes already in her life had made Merry pessimistic, he decided. What mattered was that she loved him. All he had to do was convince his father that there wasn't a better, sweeter girl in all of England. Uneasily he acknowledged that he had his work cut out for him, but he had no doubts about his ultimate success.

Making an effort to hide her fears, Merry laid the back of her hand against his cheek for a moment. In some ways Julian was far more innocent than she. But at least she'd had her summer idyll.

In an everyday voice she asked, "How did you meet Reggie? I've often wondered. You're so different, yet you're obviously the best of friends."

Accepting the change of subject, Julian released her, and they resumed their stroll. "In a gambling hell. I was just down from Oxford, feeling very much a man of the world. Then I got into a game of whist with some deep players. Over the course of a very long evening, I lost every penny I had, including my allowance, a small inheritance I had just received from a great-aunt, and vowels drawn against my future expectations."

"Merciful heaven!" she exclaimed, shocked to the bottom of her practical soul. "How dreadful. Did you lose it to Reggie?"

"No, but he was in the game. He was playing casually and running about even, neither winning nor losing much." Julian grimaced. "As I floundered around, losing more and more, Reg watched me like an angry eagle, which didn't help me feel any less of a fool. Soon I was so far in debt that I would cheerfully have jumped in the Thames rather than confess to my father. It was the wretchest night of my life.

"I was quite drunk, of course, and must have looked desperate. I finally had the sense to drop out of the game. I was going to leave, but he told me very harshly to sit down and watch how the game was supposed to be played." Julian smiled with self-mockery. "When Reggie says, *sit,* one sits."

Merry nodded, understanding perfectly.

"I've never seen such an example of concentration in my life," Julian continued. "Reggie was so absorbed it was frightening. Over the next four hours he won everything of mine back, and several hundred pounds besides. Then he took me home with him, saying I was too drunk to walk the streets. I didn't really want to go with him, but I did, since the alternative was Markham House and a lot of explanations I didn't want to make.

"The next morning, I woke up with the devil's own hangover, and Reggie proceeded to give me the dressing down of my life." Julian smiled reminiscently. "My father is a dab hand at that sort of thing, but Reg is in a class by himself. He called me a stupid young cawker and spelled out in excruciating detail the folly I had committed. Then he asked me to promise that I wouldn't gamble again until I learned how to do it properly. After I agreed, he burned all my vowels."

Fascinated, Merry asked, "And he asked nothing in return?" Julian grinned. "He made me buy him breakfast that morning."

Merry started laughing. "That's an incredible story. Yet it sounds like Reggie. I've gotten the feeling that his reputation does him considerably less than justice."

"Very true," Julian agreed. "He undertook to give me lessons in intelligent gaming, and I have never gambled more than I can afford to lose since. London can be treacherous, and it's been a blessing to have a friend who is up to all the tricks. The irony is that my father is absolutely convinced that Reggie is leading me straight to perdition. Whenever I've tried to correct his misapprehensions, he just rants and raves."

"So your father isn't very reasonable?" Merry said in a stifled voice.

Guessing her thoughts, Julian patted the small hand curled around his arm. "Not always—but he will be about you."

Merry wished she could share Julian's confidence, but that was impossible. In her heart she believed that she would never see him again after he left the next day.

Julian asked for a private interview with Lady Alys later that day, after she had returned from the fields and bathed and dressed for dinner. She was delighted to grant his request for Merry's hand, with the proviso that there be no formal engagement before he had talked to his father. He saw that she had the same doubts as Merry about whether Lord Markham would approve.

The rest of the household had retired after an evening of music and charades when Julian broke the news to Reggie. The two men were lounging in the library, Julian sipping a glass of port, Reggie smoking a long, slim cheroot, and Nemesis snoring by the open French door. His friend's face split in a grin. "Wonderful, though not unexpected. A blind man could see what has been going on."

Julian shook his head in mock despair. "And here I thought I'd been a model of discretion." A besotted gleam in his eyes, he continued, "Isn't Merry the loveliest of creatures? And such a delightful disposition."

Patiently Reggie spent the next half hour listening to similar paeans to the young lady's myriad perfections, making agreement noises as required. Finally Julian broke off with a laugh, "I'm babbling like an idiot, aren't I?"

"Yes, but anything less would be inappropriate to the occasion," Reggie said genially, tapping ash off his cheroot.

Julian frowned at his port. "Both Merry and Lady Alys think that my father will oppose the marriage. What do you think?"

"I think it very likely," Reggie admitted, "but I imagine that with persistence and tact you can win him around. While it isn't a brilliant match, it is respectable. If you have trouble persuading your father, just take Meredith to meet him."

"A marvelous idea, Reg," Julian said enthusiastically. "Who could resist her?"

Before he could continue in that line, Reggie held up one hand. "You needn't repeat her splendid qualities. I don't think they've changed in the last five minutes."

With a sheepish expression, Julian rose and went to the liquor cabinet. He brought out a decanter of Reggie's best brandy. "Shall we have a toast to my success with my father, and to my future happiness?"

Reggie hesitated. "You must have noticed that I haven't been drinking."

"True," Julian said cheerfully, "but this is a special occasion." He poured generous measures into two Venetian cut-glass goblets and brought one to Reggie.

Reggie accepted the goblet and stared at the clear amber liquid, wary of the fierce longing that literally caused his mouth to water and his heart to beat faster. He had vowed to stop drinking until the craving went away. It had subsided in the last fortnight, but there were still times when the desire for alcohol nearly overwhelmed him.

Then insight struck. Since he'd always enjoyed the taste of alcohol, it was unrealistic to wait for the craving to disappear. To do that was like assuming that abstinence would end sexual desire. On the contrary, abstinence increased desire—he should have recognized that sooner. Not drinking was probably actually increasing his desire to drink.

Relief flowed through him. He had proved that he could stop. Now it was time to resume his normal habits.

He raised the goblet. "You're right, this is a very special occasion. May I be the first to wish you and Merry long life and every happiness?"

As Julian beamed, Reggie drank the entire glass of brandy in one long swallow. Then he hurled the empty goblet into the fireplace, as befitted a toast from the heart.

He watched the crystal shatter and spin away in glittering fragments, savoring the marvelous taste and feel of the brandy. The sweet burn tingled on his tongue, warmed his throat, then curled and soothed throughout his entire body, stilling the incessant longing that had consumed him since his last drink.

What a fool he had been, to torture himself unnecessarily for weeks. He could no longer remember why he'd thought it necessary to prove he could stop drinking.

Crossing to the liquor cabinet, he poured himself another

glass of brandy, then turned to Julian with a smile. "What else can we drink to?"

When Alys and Meredith retired early for the evening, they went to Merry's room for a comfortable coze. Alys expected her ward to be ecstatic at having won Julian's heart and hand. Instead Merry was deeply sad, convinced that when Julian left the next day his father would prevent him from ever returning. Nothing Alys said could change Merry's mind.

When Alys went to her own bed, she found herself unable to sleep even though she'd had a long and tiring day. Julian was a kind and thoroughly honorable young man; he would not have spoken to Meredith and her guardian if there was a serious likelihood that the match would be blocked. Nonetheless, Merry's conviction of disaster, coupled with Alys's own doubts, held sleep at bay.

Hours passed and Alys ached with fatigue, but her anxious mind allowed her no rest. Being a surrogate parent was so stressful that she didn't know how a real, biological parent managed to survive the experience.

Her bedroom allowed her to hear traffic on the stairs and in the halls, and eventually she heard Julian come upstairs and go to his room. She knew it wasn't Reggie; his step she always recognized.

Finally, after mauling her pillows and blanket with restlessness, she decided to go downstairs and see if Reggie was in the library. Her employer had considerable worldly experience, and surely was acquainted with Julian's father. Perhaps he could give an informed opinion on the likelihood of Lord Markham's accepting Merry into the family.

She fumbled in the dark to put on her robe and slippers, then made her way down to the library. As she'd expected, light still showed under the door. But the scene that greeted her eyes when she opened the door was unexpected, and deeply unwelcome. Alys halted in the doorway and surveyed the room with distaste.

Reggie was sprawled casually in his favorite chair, his long legs crossed in front of him. If she was right that his sobriety could measured by his neatness, he must be roaring drunk. His coat and cravat lay where they had been tossed on the floor, his white shirt and tan pantaloons were blotched by spilled liquor, and a miasma of brandy fumes hung in the air. One empty decanter lay on its side on the liquor cabinet, and another, nearly empty, sat on the table next to him.

Because the night was a warm one, the French doors were open and Nemesis lay by the sill. The dog jumped to her feet and pattered over to Alys, making whimpering sounds, as if seeking aid for her master.

Alerted by the collie, Reggie glanced up and gave a hazy smile. "Good . . . good to see you, sweet Alys. Julian had 'nough and retired. Good lad, but no 'ead f'r drink. Night's young 'n I could use a drinking companion. 'Ave . . . Have some brandy." He lurched to his feet and poured the remaining brandy into another glass, spilling half of the spirits over the tabletop.

She had seen him foxed before, but his present state went far beyond that. The superbly conditioned, athletic body nearly fell over when he turned to bring her the glass.

"I didn't come here to drink," she said coldly. "I wanted to talk about something important, but obviously you're in no state for that."

He raised the glass and emptied it himself, a drop of brandy trickling from the side of his mouth. Grasping only part of her statement, he said with pleased surprise, "Glad you didn't come to drink. C'n think of better things to do m'self."

For a drunk he moved with amazing speed as he closed

the distance between them in two swift strides. He enfolded her in a hungry embrace. The lurch of his weight shoved Alys back until she was pinned against a bookcase, the warm weight of his body pressing against her from knees to chest.

His brandy-spiked kiss aroused the same fierce response that his touch always did, and for a startled moment she kissed him back. Then he shifted his hold and murmured into her ear, "'S been hard keeping my hands off you. Anyone ever tell you what a glorious body you have? 'S enough to drive a man mad."

His words brought her to her senses. "Let go of me, you drunken rakehell," she said acidly as she planted both hands on his chest and pushed. "The only time you ever notice my 'glorious body' is when you're too drunk to care what female you're fondling. If you're randy, go find your housemaid."

He almost fell as she twisted away, but managed to retain his grip on her left arm. "Coyness don't suit you, Allie," he said reproachfully. "I know what you want, and be m . . . more than happy to give it to you." He slid one hand around her head in a travesty of the gentle gesture he had made in the garden of the King's Head.

Alys was not alarmed, not yet. As he drew her toward him again, she turned her face to the side. "You're drunk, Reggie. Just go to bed."

Since her lips were unavailable, he concentrated on what was within his reach, trailing kisses across her cheek to her ear. Then he traced the outline of her ear with his tongue. Alys gasped as he cupped her breast with one hand, sensuously stroking the nipple to hardness through the gold velveteen. Perilous warmth flowed through her, melting her limbs and her resistance.

With horror, she realized how close she was to giving herself to a man too drunk to know or care who she was.

A ghastly sense of déjà vu gave her the strength to shove him away again, this time furiously. "Damn you, get away from me!"

Taken by surprise, he staggered back into a small table carrying a globe. The table pitched over, the globe frame smashing and the colorful sphere bouncing across the carpet. Reggie managed to avoid falling, but only just, and when he regained his balance his expression was ugly.

With the volatility of the drunkard, he tilted from boozy goodwill to fury. "Don't play with me, y'r bloody ladyship. Don't you think I know why you're always twitching around me? Under that prim facade you're as hot as they come, and we both know it."

The fact that he was right was unbearable. Alys wanted to weep. She also wanted to murder him, for seeing too much, for invading her heart and soul with such careless ease.

Anger was swiftly followed by fear as she realized that Reggie was moving toward her with dangerous deliberation. Gone was the amused, tolerant man she had worked and bantered with. This was a cold-eyed, angry stranger.

She would have to get by Reggie to reach either door. She gauged the distances, and knew that she was trapped. Slowly she backed away, keeping her gaze on him while her heart accelerated toward panic. Though she was tall and strong for a woman, she was no match for Reggie if he wanted to ravish her.

Her retreat ended in a corner with bookshelves stretching away on both sides. She tensed, ready to fight.

Into the angry breach came Nemesis, who trotted between the humans with soft nervous yelps. Reggie stumbled over the collie and almost fell. "Damned dog!"

He kicked at Nemesis and landed a glancing blow along the ribs. With a howl that was as much shock as pain, the collie bolted across the room and out the French doors.

The distraction gave Alys a moment to prepare. Arming herself with a heavy volume of French plays, she hissed, "Don't you come near me!" when Reggie resumed his stalking.

Ignoring the warning, he lunged toward her. Alys hurled the French plays into his stomach, then grabbed another book, a huge leather-bound edition of the complete works of Shakespeare. She heaved it blindly. The massive volume smashed into the side of Reggie's head, then clipped his knee on its downward journey.

"Christ!" he swore as he fell to the floor, gasping from the impact. "You *bitch*!"

Not stopping to see how much damage she had done, Alys whipped past him and headed toward the door. Just short of the hall, she collided with Mac Cooper, who was racing into the library. The impact knocked her breathless, and only the servant's steadying hands saved her from falling.

She had seen little of Reggie's valet, knowing him mostly as a rather dapper, distant figure, but now his face was alive with concern. "Are you all right, Lady Alys?"

No, blast it, she wasn't! But she damned well wouldn't admit that to a stranger. "I'm fine, no thanks to your drunken master," she said icily as she struggled for breath.

Mac released her and went to kneel by Reggie, who was being violently sick. Alys started to leave, but the valet looked up and said, "Don't go. I'm going to need help getting him upstairs."

"Why not just leave him here?" she snapped. "A night on the floor in his own vomit might do him some good."

Cooper grimaced. "Not when he won't even remember what happened."

That at least was a blessing. As Alys hesitated uncertainly, Cooper waited until Reggie stopped retching. Then he said calmly, "Time for bed, Reg. Let me help you up."

Groggy and green-faced, Reggie muttered, "Don't have to help me home, 'm already there."

The valet tugged at one of his arms. Since he wasn't making much headway, an exasperated Alys went to help. Between them they managed to get the incoherently muttering Reggie up and moving.

The trip to his bedroom was slow. Halfway up the staircase, their unruly burden gave a wild lurch that almost knocked all three of them down the steps. Alys would have a major bruise on her thigh where she was slammed into the railing.

A yard from his bed, Reggie suddenly went berserk, swearing and throwing a wild punch at his valet. If it had connected, Cooper would have been in trouble, but the valet deftly dodged. Then he gave his master a short, neat clip in the jaw, using just enough force to knock him out.

By the light of the lamp burning on the bedside table, Alys saw that Reggie was dead to the world as they deposited him on the bed. "Is he like this often, Cooper?"

"Aye, though not husually so bad," the valet admitted as he rolled his master onto his back. "'E'd been off the booze for ha while, and Hi'd 'oped . . ." His voice trailed off.

Alys was interested to note that Cooper now had a thick cockney accent, quite unlike his usual genteel tones. "Why do you put up with him?"

She didn't expect an answer, and was surprised when the valet glanced up. "I stay because if it hadn't been for Reg, I'd have been transported or hung a dozen years ago," Cooper said, his accent under control again.

Seeing her surprise, he said, "S'truth, Lady Alys. I was the scrawny product of a flash house, stealing whatever I could to survive. I'd been caught and put in Newgate twice already. If I went up before a magistrate again, they wouldn't be making any more allowances for my youth."

Interested despite herself, she asked, "How did you meet Reggie?"

"My specialty was robbing rich swells who were too jug-bitten to defend themselves. I made the mistake of trying it with Reg, and he broke my arm. I started howling and begging him not to turn me over to the watch. He said that since I was such a poor excuse for a thief, I should find an honest job. I told 'im I wanted one, but who would hire a footpad? He laughed, then said that he needed a valet. If I was willing to learn, he'd take me on. And if I tried to rob him again, he'd break my neck, not my arm."

Cooper's mouth quirked wryly. "The first few months were right lively. There have been times I've wondered if I would have been better off on the streets, but it's never been dull. Reg has gotten us into some rare trouble, but he always gets us out again."

Alys gave the little cockney a hard stare. "Why did you tell me that?"

"Thought you might need reminding that Reg has some good qualities."

"You're right, mate," she said sourly. "I'd forgotten."

"But no harm was done, was it?" Cooper said soothingly. "You get some rest, Lady Alys. I'll clean up the library."

For a long moment she studied the limp, powerful figure sprawled across the wide bed. Then she left with a sigh.

Why couldn't the blasted man be a simple hero or villain?

Chapter 18

The vicars were right: there really was a hell. The prospect of fire hadn't seemed so bad, but this poisonous swirl of nausea, pain, and black, soul-deep depression was a worse torment than anything a medieval theologian could have concocted.

Reggie shifted slightly, then stilled when his head threatened to split. The only virtue to being alive was knowing that in the natural course of things, he should eventually feel better. He'd read once that drinking was the perfect puritan vice, since it carried its own built-in punishment. He thought it bloody unfair that the resolutely non-puritanical had to suffer equally.

The mists closed in again. When they rolled away once more he tried opening his eyelids, which felt as if they had been sewed shut. The glare of the light sent a spike of agony through his head and scalded eyeballs, and his empty stomach heaved.

This way of life is killing you.

He must have made some sound, because Mac's calm voice penetrated his lacerated brain. "Can you drink this? It will make you feel better."

With Mac's arm supporting him, Reggie managed to

drink. Mac's elixir was mostly apple juice this time, with other ingredients, including a small dash of spirits. His nervous stomach began to settle down.

Burning eyes still closed, he asked in a grating voice, "What time is it, and has anything happened that I should know about?"

"Almost noon. Mr. Markham left early this morning, with regrets that he couldn't wait late enough to say goodbye." A hint of irony underlay the valet's voice. "Master William inquired after you, saying that you had an engagement to ride with him this morning, but I said you were indisposed."

Reggie groaned, remembering that he had promised to take the boy up to the downs. Well, it would have to be another time. "Anything happen last night?"

"You might ask Lady Alys about that," Mac said, bland as an egg. "It's not my place to say."

Reggie's stomach lurched again as he tried to remember what might have happened with Allie. He drew a blank; the last thing he remembered was Julian yawning and bidding good night. Had Allie come downstairs? Or, God forbid, had he gone into her bedroom? *What the hell had happened?* With deep foreboding, Reggie asked, "Where is Lady Alys?"

"Working somewhere on the estate. Took bread and cheese with her and said she would be out all day."

Making a supreme effort, Reggie pushed himself to a sitting position. Then he hung his head forward until the world steadied. "Bring me some whiskey."

"Wouldn't coffee be better?" Mac suggested. "I've a pot right here."

"Then pour a cup, and put some whiskey in it."

"I don't think that's a good idea," Mac said doubtfully.

"God damn it, just do as I tell you!"

It was very rare for Reggie to take that tone, and Mac

knew better than to disagree. Within two minutes a huge mug of coffee, liberally spiked with whiskey, was in Reggie's hand. He gulped it down, ignoring the scalding of his mouth and tongue.

As the whiskey took effect, he started to feel better. He lurched to his feet and stumbled to the washbasin. Water in his face helped, though his hand was still too unsteady to risk shaving. He let Mac do that.

After two more mugs of doctored coffee, a floating calm had eradicated the worst of his misery. Ignoring Mac's worried face, Reggie changed into fresh riding clothes and headed toward the stables, trying to guess where Allie might be today. Would the sheepshearing still be going on? He couldn't remember. But he had a very bad feeling about the night before, and Mac's suggestion that he ask Lady Alys what happened boded ill.

Surely he wouldn't have hurt her, no matter how cupshot he was? She must be all right, or she wouldn't be out riding.

Physical injury is not the only, or even the worst, kind of damage.

He shook his head to chase the inner voice away, then immediately regretted the action as a wave of dizziness surged through him. He should have had more whiskey to steady himself.

What got you into this condition in the first place?

Swearing under his breath, he opened the stable door. The grooms were taking their midday meal, so there was no one in sight. As his eyes adjusted to the lower light level, his ears were struck by the sudden, earsplitting neigh of an enraged horse.

He stopped dead. It sounded like his stallion Bucephalus, but what could have set the horse off like that?

Then the enraged whinnying was joined by the high-pitched scream of a child.

William. Oh, God, William, who had always been fascinated by the stallion. Reggie had told him more than once to keep clear of the horse's unpredictable temper, but the child must have ignored the warnings.

His physical ills forgotten, he raced toward the stallion's large box stall at the far end of the stables. To the screaming of horse and child was added the ominous boom of heavy hooves smashing against wood.

Reggie reached the stall and looked over the half door to see William cowering in a corner, his small body drawn into a ball, his arms raised in a futile attempt to protect his head. Half buried in the straw on the floor was a carrot he'd brought as a present. Shrieking with a fury that made the walls vibrate, Bucephalus reared above the boy, a thousand pounds of lethal horseflesh with flailing, iron-shod hooves.

The stallion lurched downward, one hoof gouging the wall by William's head while the other grazed the child's arm. Viciously the horse reared to strike again. Reggie grabbed a pitchfork that was leaning against the wall, then charged into the stall, shouting to distract the stallion's attention from the child.

Too furious to recognize the one human for whom he had any affection, Bucephalus wheeled and struck at him. With agonized regret, Reggie defended himself with the pitchfork. He tried to do as little damage as possible, but even so, he risked ruining the animal forever.

The fork shivered in his hands as the horse's heavy shoulder slammed into the tines, drawing blood. As Bucephalus retreated a step, Reggie barked, "William, get out!"

The boy scuttled across the stall and out the door. Reggie waited until he was clear, then raced for safety himself, slamming and bolting both halves of the door. The crazed animal continued to scream and smash its massive hooves into the walls. Grimly Reggie recognized that Bucephalus might lethally injure himself even if the stab wounds were minor.

Dropping the pitchfork against the wall, he turned to William. The boy appeared uninjured, though he was badly shaken. He dragged one sleeve across his eyes to wipe away tears.

The terror Reggie had felt for the boy's safety combined with the sickness of hangover and the fear that his favorite horse might have to be destroyed. Completely out of control, he grabbed William's shoulders and shook him violently. "You damned little idiot! Do you know what you've done with your disobedience? That horse may have to be destroyed. I should have let him kick your skull in!"

Then, as Reggie's hand curled into a fist, time and space seemed to shatter into a kaleidoscope of fragments. In front of him was William, white-faced and trembling, more frightened of Reggie than he had been of the horse. Yet at the same time he was a dark-haired boy, smaller, equally terrified, and somehow the child was Reggie. The endless equine screaming was also that of a woman, and the man was not Reggie, but another man of similar height and coloring and drunken fury.

A wave of dizziness and panicky, hysterical fear engulfed Reggie, sweeping him away and shattering him on the knife-edged rocks of memory. With horror he realized how close he had come to striking William with his dangerous adult strength.

Releasing the boy, he straightened, dazed and unseeing. The scene in front of his eyes was not the stables but his mother's morning room, a place he had avoided without knowing why. It was a lifetime ago and his parents were arguing about his father's drinking, one of an endless series of conflicts. His mother was crying and saying that her husband must leave Strickland and never come back, that she would not let him hurt her children. Drunk and enraged, his father had first railed at his wife. Then he turned violent.

Reggie had been drawn by the sounds of fighting. Indelibly etched in his mind was an image in silhouette, both his parents standing in front of a window, his father's powerful arm frozen at the moment of impact as he struck his wife on the side of the head. How could Reggie have forgotten an image so sharply edged, limned in agony?

How could he bear to remember?

He had been small, three or four, but he hadn't hesitated. As he heard his mother cry out, heard the sickening thud of flesh and bone colliding, he had hurled himself at his father, shrieking his own childish fury, his fists flailing, wrapping himself around his father's leg, kicking and biting, doing everything he could to protect his mother.

Drunkenly, mindlessly enraged, his father had seized him by the shoulders, lifting him bodily and hurling him viciously through the air. That brief flight had seemed very slow, almost languid. There was no pain when he hit the wall, though he could feel the snap and stab of breaking bones before his body tumbled to the floor. His eyes were open, but he could neither move nor feel.

His spirit seemed to detach from his body, floating dreamily above the turmoil. He saw his mother scream, then fall to her knees and sweep the broken body of her son into her arms. He had believed her words when she cried out that her husband had murdered their son, for surely he must be dead to see and hear, yet be powerless to act.

Then, with a shattering jolt, he was back in his own body. He felt his mother's fierce embrace, her desperately beating heart beneath her soft breasts, and the comfort of the rose scent she wore. He remembered with excruciating clarity his mother's frantic tears, his father's anguished expression as he cried out that he hadn't meant it, Annie, that it was an accident, that she must believe he'd meant no harm.

And cruel as a blade, he remembered the fury and revulsion that filled the room. As he faded into blackness, he carried with him the horror-etched images of his parents' faces. He recalled quite clearly telling himself that he mustn't die. Though he had been too young to define it in words, he had known instinctively that death would separate his parents forever, isolating his father in an endless hell beyond forgiveness.

As awareness returned, Reggie found himself staring blindly at the stable wall, his hands knotted in front of him on the splintery surface, kneading and clawing as if release lay somewhere within the wood. In an agony of despair, he knotted his right hand into a fist and smashed into the wall with all his trained strength, striking again and again in a futile attempt to destroy the memories and the anguish and the knowledge.

The fierce pain of the blows engulfed his hand and stabbed up through his wrist and arm. Welcoming it, he looked down to see the skin ripped on his knuckles and rivulets of crimson trickling between his fingers. He stared mutely at the blood and tried to establish a fragile control over himself.

Remembering that he was not alone, he turned to William. There were tear tracks on the round face, and the boy was staring at Reggie as if he had never seen him before, bewildered and frightened by such incomprehensible adult behavior.

Reggie inhaled deeply, trying to find some sanity in his whirling, disoriented brain. Then he knelt to bring himself to the boy's level and said unsteadily, "Come here."

After a long moment's hesitation, William approached. Reggie placed one hand on his shoulder. "Are you all right?"

William nodded warily.

Holding the boy's gaze with his own, Reggie said, "I'm sorry that I was so angry. I was afraid you would be killed. Then when I knew you were safe, I went a little crazy. Stupid of me, but adults are often stupid." That elicited a more vigorous nod. Reggie continued, "Do you understand now why I said to keep away from Bucephalus?"

"Yes." The boy swallowed hard. "I'm sorry I caused trouble. I . . . I just wanted to make friends. Will Bucephalus have to be destroyed?"

"I hope not." Face set, Reggie got to his feet. "Go and get the head groom. We'll see what can be done."

William darted off, and Reggie cautiously opened the upper half of the stall door. The stallion had stopped neighing and kicking, but he still pranced about in agitation, patches of sweat and foam marring the sleek black coat. Reggie began talking softly, a process that calmed his agitation almost as much as it helped the horse.

By the time the head groom arrived on the run, Reggie was in the stall, patting Bucephalus's neck and checking the extent of the horse's injuries. The puncture wounds weren't deep, though there would be scars to mar the glossy hide. A hock was also sprained, but the horse seemed to have escaped serious injury.

Reggie left the stallion in the groom's capable hands and went back to the house. There he retreated to the library and folded wearily into the old leather-upholstered wing chair, unable to keep his thoughts at bay any longer.

This had been his father's room, his father's chair. As Reggie slumped back, eyes closed, the missing pieces of his childhood fell into place. No wonder he had forgotten everything before the age of four, and no wonder Jeremy Stanton had been unsurprised to hear that. His godfather had made some cryptic comment that doubtless Reggie would remember if there was anything he needed to know.

What had been blocked out was the ceaseless fear and fighting caused by his father's drinking. His mother had swung between hope and anger and despair, and with a child's sensitivity Reggie had known that something was horribly wrong.

Though he had adored his father, he had also feared the unpredictability of his moods. Sometimes his father was a great gun, other times he must be avoided at all costs. Reggie's habit of endlessly watching and analyzing other people's behavior, of looking for weaknesses that could be used in defense was needed, had originated then, when he was scarcely old enough to walk.

Shortly after the birth of Reggie's younger brother, Julius, matters culminated in that last fearsome brawl. Horrified by what he had done, his father had stopped drinking.

Reggie had spent a long time in bed with his injuries— concussion, cracked ribs, and a broken shoulder. He had been frightened the first time his father visited. Expression stricken, his father had patiently worked to regain his son's trust, playing games and teaching lessons and reading aloud.

By the time Reggie recovered, his father was truly sober. Anne Davenport did not insist that her husband leave Strickland once he stopped drinking, and in time the family had healed. Then had come what Reggie thought of as the Golden Age. His parents had been happy with themselves, their marriage, their family. The days seemed endlessly full of light and laughter. Another child was born, a red-haired sprite named Amy.

Reggie had flourished in that time, tagging after his father all around Strickland, playing with his younger brother and sister. And he had buried every memory of the Dark Age that had gone before.

Until today, when the demon of drunkenness had driven him to the edge of injuring another child. His throat and chest ached at the thought, both for William, and for the child he himself had been.

He twisted restlessly, and his gaze fell on a paper pamphlet on the table next to him. Someone, it seemed, had left it for him to read.

Lifting it, he read the title, "The Effects of Ardent Spirits Upon Man." Underneath was printed "Benjamin Rush, Physician, Philadelphia, 1784." He stared at the pamphlet, wondering who had left it for him, before finally turning to the first page.

A dark chill curled around his heart. Inside was the name "Reginald Davenport," written in a bold, masculine hand.

For an instant he wondered if this was something he had bought, then forgotten. Could his memory lapses have gotten that bad? He studied the signature, then released the breath he had been holding. The handwriting was similar to his, but not identical. He had been named for his father, who was the original owner of this tract. It had been waiting in the library for all the intervening years. He began to read.

Time passed as he read and reread, with long spells of sightless staring. The monograph was short, only a few thousand words, yet in it Benjamin Rush had described in great and ominous detail the effects of drunkenness, from *unusual garrulity* to *captiousness and a disposition to quarrel, to immodest actions and a temporary fit of madness*. And everything in between.

The physician called drunkenness *an odious disease* and described the physical effects, both immediate and long term. He'd gone on to say, *It is further remarkable that drunkenness resembles certain hereditary, family, and contagious diseases.* In other words, like father, like son.

Ardent spirits . . . impair the memory, debilitate the understanding, and pervert the moral faculties. Everything that was happening to Reggie.

He glanced once more at the last pages, where Rush

made dire predictions and mournful commentary on the many ways drunkenness destroyed lives. The physician classed death as among the consequences of hard drinking: *But it is not death from the immediate hand of the Deity: it is death from suicide.*

Reggie closed his eyes and heard again that internal voice of warning: *This way of life is killing you.* With the veils ripped from the past, he identified that voice as his father's, the first Reginald Davenport, who had come perilously close to destroying his life, his family, and his first-born son with drinking.

In an odd burst of fancy, Reggie wondered if his father was keeping an eye on his only surviving child, trying to prevent his namesake from repeating the pattern of self-destruction. Improbable though the thought was, it was warming, the only positive reflection he'd had all day.

What was dark and inescapable was the knowledge that Reggie was coursing down the same merciless path his father had followed. Jeremy Stanton had been skeptical of whether it would be possible to moderate his consumption of alcohol, and implied that only quitting entirely would work. The older man's hard-won advice was proving accurate. As soon as Reggie had swallowed the first glass of brandy the night before, judgment and good sense had gone out the window, resulting in the worst drunk—and the worst morning after—of his life.

The weeks of sobriety had done nothing to reduce his drinking. Indeed, he had been worse. If the physician Rush was right that drunkenness was a disease, it must be a progressive one. And the only cure Reggie could imagine was absolute abstinence.

Massaging his temples, he leaned back in his chair, wishing that the ache and the dank, choking depression would go away. Even now, the desire to drink was a hot, siren call. Every fiber of his body was longing, pleading and cajoling, to have just a single glass, a single mouthful. In a bottle lay surcease from pain. It would be so easy to blot out the intolerable memories, the guilt, the hopelessness. . . .

If he was going to kill himself, a pistol would be quicker and cleaner.

Alys had worked with grim determination all day, trying to blot out the memory of her employer's drunken advances and angry attack. His drinking was getting worse. For the sake of the children and herself, they must move out of the house immediately. Dear God, what if he went after Merry? She shuddered at the thought.

It sickened her to remember how Reggie had behaved. What was worse was knowing how much she cared for him, flaws and all.

She stayed out past dinnertime, preferring her own company. By the time she returned, dusty and weary, shadows were lengthening. She walked into the house to find a delegation waiting. Merry was there, her sapphire eyes showing the strain of parting from Julian; William, unnaturally abashed; and Mac Cooper, looking inscrutable. Only Peter, who was on a holiday with a school friend's family, was missing.

Alys glanced at the concerned faces. "Is something wrong?"

"Not a disaster, exactly," Merry replied, "but we're worried about Reggie."

"Has he run off again? He makes something of a habit of that," Alys said with studied neutrality.

Cooper spoke up. "No, he's been in the library all day, since an accident with that black devil's horse of his."

Beginning to be alarmed, Alys listened to William explain how Reggie had turned rescuer again, then had nearly succumbed to an urge to wring William's neck. Alys could understand that impulse, since she had occasionally shared it, but she frowned as the boy described how Reggie had smashed his fist into the wall over and over. Was the man going mad? Perhaps he had been drinking steadily all night and all day.

She glanced at Cooper. "If you're all so concerned, why doesn't someone just go into the library?"

The valet replied, "I was about to, but then you came in. Might be better if you checked on him, Lady Alys." His aitches were firmly in place.

"Why me?" she asked in exasperation, but Cooper returned her gaze with an opaque expression. Wearily she accepted that since she had been running everything and everyone at Strickland for years, she must be the one to ensure that the owner was alive, and as well as could be expected.

Ironic though the thought was, it produced a small stab of anxiety. Surely he would not have done anything foolish? She asked, "Has he eaten anything today?"

Cooper and Merry looked at each other. "Not that I know of," the valet said.

"Have the cook get a tray together with enough food for two people, and a large pot of hot tea," she ordered. "I'll wash up, then take it in to him."

She didn't take the time to bathe and change, but she washed her hands and face and let her hair down, since the long hours in tight braids had given her a headache. After tying her hair back with a ribbon, she went downstairs. She chased the concerned watchers away, saying the man would never come out if he had an audience.

Then she took the prepared tray and entered the library. Reggie was a lean, silent shape slouched in his favorite chair, half turned away from her. The room was too shadowed to see his face, but his clothing was neat. With luck, he had not availed himself of the liquor cabinet. She set the tray on a table to the left of the door and said quietly, "Are you still among the living?"

His head turned in her direction. After a lengthy silence, he said in a slow, rusty voice, "I've read of penguins that jump around on an ice floe, trying to decide if there are sharks in the water. Eventually they push one of their number into the sea. If the sacrifice isn't eaten, they all dive in. You, I assume, are the sacrificial penguin."

She had to smile. Obviously there was some life in the old boy left. "I've been called many things in my life, but never a sacrificial penguin. How did you know there was a committee outside trying to decide what to do about you?"

"Occasionally the door would open, very quietly, then close again."

"After they had determined that the shark was still lurking here." Without asking if he wanted any, she poured two cups of tea, with heavy dollops of milk and sugar in Reggie's cup, then went and put it in his hand. Close up, he looked dreadful, with haunted eyes and a gray tinge to his dark skin. As he stared at the dainty cup, she said helpfully, "It's called tea. People drink it. It's the British cure for whatever ails you."

He smiled faintly, then raised the cup and took a deep swallow. "In that case, you had better order a larger pot."

She winced at the sight of his lacerated knuckles. The result of smashing his fist into the wall. Later those wounds must be tended.

But for now, the physical was less important than the mental. She set the tray next to him and took the opposite chair, then proceeded to select a substantial supper for herself. "Rumor has it that you haven't eaten in twenty-four hours. Food might help. I'm told the roast chicken and the pickled mushrooms are particularly good tonight."

Slowly he filled a plate and began to eat while Alys periodically topped up the teacups. She was just finishing a portion of Ripon pudding when Reggie said abruptly, "How much do I have to apologize for?"

Alys swallowed her pudding. "You don't remember what happened last night?"

"No, but Mac implied rather strongly that I have a lot to answer for where you are concerned."

Alys sipped her tea and considered. Her lingering anger had largely dissipated at the sight of Reggie's haggard face. Clearly he had gone through hell—and she sensed that he had also crossed some kind of significant mental frontier. "You were drunk and amorous," she said at last, deciding on honesty tempered with discretion.

"In vino veritas," he muttered. "That's what I was afraid of. Did . . . did I hurt you?"

"It was a near run thing for a moment," she admitted. "You refused to take no for an answer and cornered me, so I threw a few books at you."

"Bloody hell." His face sank behind one hand. "Thank God you are a most redoubtable female—I have enough to feel guilty about." He sighed heavily. "I seem to spend a lot of my time apologizing to you, Allie. For what it's worth, I regret most deeply what happened."

"I think we're about even," she said pensively. "The volume of French plays that I threw into your stomach didn't do you much good."

He raised his head at that, and in the dusk she could see a faint smile. "Too many French plays could give anyone a bellyache."

She was glad to hear more life in his voice. Reggie without a sense of humor was a terrifying thought.

He lifted a pamphlet that lay on the table on his other side. "Did you find this and leave it out for me as a not-so-subtle hint?"

Peering through the dusk, she could just make out the words "The Effects of Ardent Spirits Upon Man." It looked familiar. She frowned a moment. "I think it tumbled off a shelf when I was grabbing books to throw at you. Mac Cooper probably found it when he was cleaning up. It does seem to the point."

"Doesn't it, just." He laid the pamphlet down again. "It was written by an American physician. He talks about drunkenness as if it's a disease."

An interesting thought. Alys made a mental note to read the pamphlet later.

"As you must have noticed, I had stopped drinking for several weeks. I thought that would be all I need to reestablish my control." He sighed again. "Last night made it clear that approach won't work. I've reached the conclusion that I must stop entirely."

"I don't suppose that will be easy." She knew her words were inadequate, but was unsure what else to say.

"No, I don't expect it will. However, I see no alternative." From the levelness of Reggie's voice, he could be commenting on the weather rather than announcing what must have been a fiercely difficult decision.

"If there is anything I can do to help . . ." she offered tentatively.

"Thank you," he said in a very low voice. "I don't think this is the sort of thing anyone else can help with, but I do appreciate the offer."

On impulse Alys got to her feet. "Come outside for some fresh air. It's a lovely evening." And being holed up like a badger in its sett couldn't be helping his state of mind.

After a pause he said, "Very well."

She led the way out the French doors into the fresh summer evening. The lawn had just been cut, and the sweet green scent enticed the nostrils.

To the west a spectacular sunset flared, with towers of clouds gilded in gold and orange and indigo. It was lighter outside than in the library, and she could see Reggie's face clearly. His expression was stark and he moved slowly, without his usual lithe grace, but he looked composed.

They strolled down to the lake, by unspoken consent settling on one of the benches and watching the colors fade from the sky overhead. Neither talked, but Alys thought her presence was affording Reggie some silent comfort. She hoped so.

When only a golden rim on the horizon remained of the sunset, Reggie said, "It's getting late, and you've had a very long day. I should let you get some rest."

"It's good to take time to be silent now and then. I don't do so often enough." Alys rose. "I want to show you something else on the way back. One of life's very small wonders."

He followed her passively to the wool room. It was a large, clean chamber in one of the more distant barns, and tonight it was nearly full of fresh-cut fleeces. Alys opened the door and picked up one of the rolled fleeces to show Reggie.

There was just enough light left to see a faint mist clouding the pale wool. "See? The fleeces are still warm and alive. As the sun goes down, they cool."

He took the fleece from her, squeezing its springy bulk in his hands. "Interesting. Who would have guessed that fleeces have their own local dew?"

"That's not all. Listen."

They became very still. Inside the wool room was a gentle sound almost like breathing. At Reggie's questioning glance, Alys said, a little shy at what a simple thing it was, "The fleeces will rustle softly like that all night long. The fibers are interlocked and tense, and they shift to get comfortable, like people."

His expression eased. "Life really is full of small wonders. Thank you for showing me this one."

His somber gaze held hers, and she thought his words

were for more than just the rustling fleece. It was one of those moments of inexplicable intimacy that sometimes connected them. In that instant she determined not to move her charges away from Strickland. At least not if he stayed sober. He was going to need people who cared about him nearby.

Reggie returned the fleece to its place, and they started back toward the manor house. They were almost there when Nemesis came galumphing toward them, her clownish white face vivid in the dark. Wagging happily, she reared up and planted her front paws against Reggie in a demand to be caressed.

He caught the collie's head in his hands and tousled her ears, a process that sent her into raptures. "Where have you been, you worthless creature?" He paused, then glanced warily at Alys. "Did something happen with Nemesis last night?"

Reluctantly she said, "You kicked her, but she wasn't really injured. Just startled."

He grimaced and returned the collie's forepaws to earth. "It's a poor sort of man who will kick his own dog."

"Don't worry about it. It's pretty clear that you're forgiven."

"Would that all one's crimes could so easily be set aside." Then, harshly, he said, "I don't know if I can do it, Allie. It was hard to stop drinking when it was temporary. Now to face a lifetime . . ." A thread of despair, of being defeated before he even began, sounded in his deep voice.

Alys tried to imagine herself in his position. What if she had to deny herself her cherished morning cup of coffee? The mere thought of a lifetime of that denial gave her a shiver of empathy. Yet that was only coffee, something she enjoyed, but did not crave. How much worse it must be for Reggie, who had drunk heavily for perhaps twenty years, who suffered from the disease called drunkenness . . .

Her exercise in empathy gave her an idea. "A lifetime is too long a time. Can you refrain from drinking for the rest of tonight?"

He exhaled wearily. "That I think I can manage."

"Then think only of that," she said. "Tomorrow morning, think only of the morning. What is forever but a collection of minutes or hours? Surely you can always refrain for the next five minutes. Or if that is too much, then the next minute."

It was full dark now, and Reggie's face was a pale blur as he turned to her. "Perhaps . . . perhaps I can do it after all." He raised one hand and touched her cheek. "Thank you, Allie, for everything."

She laid her hand over his for a moment of silent promise. Then she turned to enter the house. As she went inside, she thought wryly that it was a sign of her low mind that even as she rejoiced to hear that Reggie would try to stop drinking, that even as she pledged to do whatever she could to help, she felt a stab of deep regret in knowing that when he was sober, he would never kiss her again.

Chapter 19

The Earl of Wargrave was admitted to Ashburton House, and immediately greeted by his host, Lord Michael Kenyon. "Richard, I'm so glad that you happened to be in London." Michael grinned. "Except for my old friend Rafe, we have a small reunion of former officers of the 95th Rifles."

Kenneth Wilding, Viscount Kimball and new husband, stepped forward to shake hands. "Lord, it's been a long time since we've seen each other. Waterloo?"

Richard nodded. "Right. I was brought back to London with a shattered leg, and you went to Paris with the army of occupation. I think you got the better of that duty."

They all laughed. Richard greeted Michael's friend, Rafe, the Duke of Candover, whom he knew from the House of Lords. Then the four of them adjourned to the dining room. They had progressed to casual conversation over the after-dinner port when Michael remarked, "You're unusually silent even by your standards, Richard. Is impending fatherhood weighing that heavily?"

"Sorry, Michael," Richard said apologetically. "Impending fatherhood is splendid. I was just wondering how my black sheep cousin is faring."

His friend raised a sardonic brow. "There are no reports

that Dorsetshire has been destroyed or blown into the sea, so perhaps Reggie is behaving himself."

Richard smiled. "I didn't realize that you knew my cousin."

"He's a legend at Eton. Everyone who attended during the years Reggie was there knew him." Michael slid the decanter of port along the polished mahogany table to Rafe. "To our sorrow."

The duke said mildly, "Reggie wasn't that bad."

Wry humor gleamed in Michael's eyes. "I'll admit bias, since Reggie and I have known each other for nigh onto thirty years, and have rubbed each other wrong the whole time. Rafe got along with him much better."

Kenneth Wilding said curiously, "You wrote me about this cousin, Richard, but apart from mentioning that he's your heir and that you settled an estate on him, you said very little. What makes him so black a sheep? Is he dishonest?"

When Richard cocked an inquiring eye at Michael, that gentleman said, "Reggie Davenport has always defied classification. He's not dishonest—quite the contrary, in his own perverse way he's belligerently honorable—but he can be supremely maddening."

An artist who was always interested in people, Kenneth asked, "In what way?"

"The problem with Reggie is that he always went one step too far," Rafe said reflectively. "The fashionable world is surrounded by an invisible fence. I always knew exactly how far to go without breaking the limits. That made me dashing." He gave a self-mocking smile. "Reggie always chose to be one step outside the line. That made him dangerous."

"Was he always like that?" Richard asked.

"Not really," Michael admitted. "I met Reggie when he had just become his uncle's ward. Since my father and his uncle were friends and the Wargrave estate is more or less on the way from Ashburton to Eton, someone had the brilliant idea of sending us off to school together. The weather was dreadful, which slowed the coach to a crawl, so we had three endless days in a coach to become acquainted." He sipped his port thoughtfully. "Reggie had just lost his whole family and been pitched into one hostile environment, and was now being sent into another. He was like"—Michael searched for a phrase—"like a rabid dog, snarling and snapping in all directions. If I had been older, I would have made more allowances for him, but at that age I was merely angry."

Rafe took up the story. "Reggie was a King's Scholar, what was called a Colleger by the other students." He grimaced. "You all know how savage the English public school system can be. Bad enough to be a regular student, but the Collegers lived in such appalling conditions that even the most neglectful parents hesitated to subject their sons to that. There were always vacant spaces for King's Scholars."

"This despite the fact that Collegers received full scholarships at Eton, automatic admission to King's College at Cambridge, and if they wanted it, an assured, comfortable lifetime as a Fellow of King's," Michael added.

"I see," Richard said slowly. "My grandfather must have put Reggie in for a scholarship as the simplest, cheapest way to settle him in life."

"Simple, but cruel," Rafe said acerbically. "Collegers were treated like animals in a zoo. They got only one meal a day, usually roast mutton and boiled potatoes. They shared a huge room at the top of a drafty stone building that was over three hundred years old. Every evening they were locked in the Long Chamber at eight o'clock and not released until seven the next morning." He shook his head. "The whole lot, all fifty or sixty of them, were left to their own devices without any masters or other adults to keep order. Thank God there was never a fire, or they'd have all burned to death."

Kenneth winced. "And I thought Harrow was bad. What you're describing is law of the jungle."

Rafe took a sip of port, his eyes flinty. "Reggie had the dubious distinction of being the youngest and smallest of the Collegers his first several years. And he was a good-looking boy, which made things worse."

Understanding the implication, Richard's eyes narrowed. "He was abused by the older boys?"

"Not really. That was how your cousin's legend was forged." Michael signaled a servant to refill the decanter. "Reggie fought like a bull terrier. He wouldn't surrender, no matter what was done to him. Once or twice he was beaten unconscious, yet he came up swinging when he woke. Even the worst bullies in the college didn't want to deal with that." He shook his head admiringly. "Damnedest thing you ever saw—sixteen-year-old boys wary of a child half their age and size. It was the same with the masters. No matter how much they birched him, he would never break."

"A pity he didn't go into the army," Kenneth said, compassion in his voice. "He would have made quite a soldier."

"I believe he wanted the army, but his uncle wouldn't buy him a commission." Michael smiled ruefully. "I would have died rather than admit it at the time, but I admired Reggie tremendously. Besides being tougher than an East End stevedore, he was one of the best scholars and best athletes in the school. But he and I had a bad beginning and never overcame it."

"I appreciate your explaining more of my cousin's background," Richard said, his hazel eyes abstracted. "I think I understand him a little better now."

Kenneth grinned. "I hope I have the opportunity to meet this man someday."

"Perhaps I'll pay a call on my cousin later in the summer," Richard said thoughtfully. "I have some business in Hampshire, so I'll be near Strickland."

Privately Michael thought that Richard took his position as head of the Davenport family too seriously. His difficult cousin was unlikely to welcome the earl with common civility, much less open arms.

Yet sometimes men did change for the better. Michael had. As they rose from the table, the part of Michael that had admired the young Reginald Davenport hoped that the blasted man would turn his life around, before it was too late.

Reggie knew he was going to fail, could feel himself slipping inexorably toward disaster like a man on a steeply pitched roof. When he had stopped drinking earlier, it had been very difficult, but at least he had known the deprivation was temporary.

Now, no matter how desperately he followed Allie's suggestion to think in terms of a day, an hour, a minute, he could feel himself sliding toward the moment when his will would break. Such thoughts did not make him an easy companion.

He spent much of his time training his hunters, since he had discovered that mental engagement was a stronger defense than mere physical activity. In the evenings he stayed with the rest of the household, speaking little but listening to the young people's chatter as a way to keep the craving at bay.

At Allie's suggestion Meredith and Peter were working on plans to redecorate the manor house. The project gave Merry something to think about besides Julian's absence, and offered Peter an outlet for his excellent taste in all things visual. The two young Spensers would discuss their ideas with Reggie, since he had the final say. Reggie had to admire the neatness with which Allie had involved all three of them.

He acquired a pipe, both for the smoking and the endless fidgeting it took to keep the damned thing going, and he continued with his compulsive late night swimming. Only Allie and Mac understood what he was trying to do. He could feel both of them watching him while trying to be unobtrusive about it.

When his nerves became dangerously frayed and he was on the verge of defeat, Allie always seemed to be there. Calmly she ignored his flashes of irritation and anchored him to sanity. He supposed that to her he was another project, a piece of property of doubtful value that would benefit by improvement.

Whatever her motives, he was grateful. After the young people went to bed, he and Allie would stay up late talking, their conversations ranging over farming, politics, literature, and a hundred other things. Two topics they never discussed were her past, or his future. More and more he wondered about her life before she had become a governess, but she never mentioned that, and he felt that he had no right to ask.

As the endless days dragged by, few incidents were intense enough to pierce his inner ferment. One event occurred when he and Meredith and Peter went into Dorchester to look at wallpaper and fabric that had just arrived from London. Peter had driven them, proud to demonstrate his growing skill with the ribbons.

Merry's lovely face was serene, but she was too quiet. Allie had privately told Reggie that Julian wrote often, saying how he missed her and declaring his intention of returning to Strickland within a month. However, the fact that he never mentioned how his father had received news of the proposed marriage was ominous.

In Dorchester, Reggie let Peter and Merry off at the shop, then took the barouche around to a livery stable. He was just leaving after bestowing his horses when he came face-to-face with George Blakeford. With an inward groan but determined civility, Reggie said, "Morning, Blakeford."

The other man stopped in his tracks and glared, his thick,

muscular body stiff with anger. "I should call you out for what you did to Stella."

"What did your ladybird say I did to her?" Reggie asked with some curiosity.

"She told me that you ravished her the first evening you met her, and publicly insulted her at that assembly," Blakeford growled.

"I plead innocent to the one charge, and guilty to the other," Reggie said, suddenly bored. Stella was obviously every bit as much a troublemaker as he had suspected. "The insult was very bad of me, but not a dueling matter. Now, if you'll excuse me . . ."

Blakeford's beefy hand shot out and clutched Reggie's arm fiercely. "Don't you brush me off! If you come near Stella again, you're a dead man."

With shocking suddenness their positions changed as Reggie broke the other's grip, then grasped Blakeford's wrist and twisted bone and tendon with a force just short of breaking the joint. "Don't threaten me, Blakeford," he said in a low, menacing voice. "Use that fire and vinegar to give Stella what she needs so she doesn't go around putting her hands in other men's breeches."

"You bastard!" Blakeford turned almost purple with fury as he tried to wrench himself free.

"Don't be fool enough to get into a public brawl about a whore's virtue," Reggie said contemptuously as he released the other man's arm. "If you really believed that I had ravished her, you would have come after me with a horsewhip weeks ago."

His words checked Blakeford. Restraining himself with visible effort, the other man growled, "You'll regret this, Davenport. For too many years you've done what you wanted and not given a damn for anything, but retribution is just around the corner."

"I don't doubt it," Reggie said coolly. "But in the meantime

I have an engagement." He circled around Blakeford and headed toward the High Street with an itchy feeling between his shoulder blades. He had no doubt that if Blakeford had been carrying a pistol, Reggie would have been a dead man.

Gloomily be recognized that it had been a mistake to lose his temper and talk about the little trollop the way that he had. Where women were concerned, men could be very irrational. Reggie had an uneasy feeling that the encounter might have repercussions.

As he entered the draper's shop and was drawn into Peter and Merry's debate on the relative merits of figured, cream-colored satin damask versus blue and dove gray-striped brocade, he shrugged philosophically. His reputation was already so bad that it couldn't be blackened much further.

George Blakeford wanted to crush Davenport's throat with his bare hands—to beat that cool, contemptuous face to a bleeding pulp. Only the memory of his greater goal kept him from indulging his blood lust. It was far more important that Alys Weston die, and in a manner that could not be traced to Blakeford.

A pity that the fire had failed. Though he had racked his brain, he could think of nothing else that would appear so much like an accident. A second fire would be too suspicious. Besides, fire had proved to be an inefficient method for killing.

He was finding it surprisingly difficult to reach someone who spent virtually all her time on an estate where everyone knew her, and where strangers stood out like red flags. What made it even harder was Blakeford's determination that both Alys Weston and Reggie Davenport must be destroyed.

He eventually realized that he would have to arrange an ambush, the sort of thing that could be attributed to a roving band of cutthroats. There were plenty of those since the war

had ended and thousands of soldiers had been turned off to
starve. Still, it was taking time to find men for the task. They
couldn't be local, and they mustn't be connected to Blakeford.

But he had already found two desperate men who would
do anything for money, one of them a former army sharpshooter. When he had located two or three more, all he
would need was an event that would lure his two victims
away from the estate. It might take weeks or months, but he
was prepared to wait as long as necessary to ensure that
there would be no escape.

For now, he would contemplate the sweetness of his victory, and of his revenge.

Alys entered her bedroom, and almost tripped over the
housemaid, Gillie, who was cleaning the room. The girl
bobbed her head. "Excuse me, miss, I'll leave."

"No need. I'm just here to change into a cooler shirt."
Alys went to her dresser and opened a drawer. "It's turned
warmer than I expected. Rain coming, I think."

She pulled out a fresh shirt, and turned just in time to see
Gillie sway and drop Alys's china washbasin, one of the pottery's prettiest products. The maid's face had a distinctly
greenish cast.

Alarmed, Alys caught the girl's arm. "Sit down and put
your head between your knees before you faint." Gillie
dizzily obeyed. Luckily the water-filled pitcher was still
intact, so Alys wet a towel and took it to Gillie after ringing
for the housekeeper.

After having cool water patted on her face and throat, the
girl's color improved. "Thank you, Lady Alys, I'm ever so
sorry," she said feebly as she straightened in her chair. "I'll
clean up the mess right now."

"Sit a little longer," Alys ordered. "In this heat it's easy
to overdo."

Gillie smiled crookedly. "'Tis nought to do with the heat, miss."

Before the conversation could progress further, the housekeeper, May Herald, entered. Taking in the situation at a glance, she said, "Lie down for the rest of the afternoon, Gillie. You should take better care of yourself."

"I want to do as much as I can, ma'am," the maid said, her pretty chin lifting with a touch of stubbornness.

"I know, but don't be a fool, girl. Take advantage of how lucky you are," Mrs. Herald scolded. "Now, off with you."

With a shy bob of her head to Alys, Gillie stood and carefully made her way out.

Alys frowned after the maid closed the door. "Mrs. Herald, is that child increasing?"

"Aye, haven't you heard?" The housekeeper bent and picked up fragments of the broken basin. "Mind, I don't approve in the least, but it's to Mr. Davenport's credit that he didn't just turn her out. Most gentlemen couldn't care less what happens to foolish wenches like that one." Straightening, she added, "I'll send a girl up to finish the cleaning later this afternoon." Then she bustled out.

Alys was left feeling as if she had been punched in the stomach. So Gillie was the maid she had seen sneaking away from Davenport's bedroom, and she was carrying her master's by-blow. Stupid of Alys to be surprised—babies were one of the natural consequences of sex. Anyone who worked on a farm knew that. There was no reason on earth that Alys should feel betrayed.

But what did reason have to do with it? Her mind and fingers numb, she took off her sweat-marked shirt and donned the fresh one. She must compose herself before she went out, or anyone who saw her would know something was wrong.

She sat on the edge of the bed, staring sightlessly ahead and trying to understand why she felt such hurt. And then she knew.

Feeling too fragile to sit upright, she lay back on the bed, her eyes still blindly open. So she was in love with Reggie, with all his careless charm and indisputable weaknesses. Amazing how long she had been able to conceal that fact from herself.

It had been less humiliating to pretend he was merely a convenient object of her fantasies. Yes, he aroused her senses as no other man had, but he had also treated her as an equal. He had respected her judgment, listened to her ideas, teased and stimulated her until long-buried parts of her personality had come to life. He had paid her the rare compliment of treating her as a friend.

What a pathetic picture she presented, the aging spinster for whom friendship was not enough! Her most profound wish was to see a flawed, cynical man magically transformed into Prince Charming. She wanted him to swear love eternal, beg for her hand and heart, and never look at another woman.

Instead he had a pregnant mistress under his roof, and had only ever noticed that Alys was a female when he was drunk. She sat upright, trying to break the despairing circle of her thoughts.

Pride came to her rescue. She could accept being thought mannish and eccentric, but she'd be damned if she would let anyone think she was pathetic—least of all Reggie. He needed a friend far more than he needed another mistress, and because she loved him, she would continue to offer friendship.

Friendship was better than nothing. It was also much more difficult.

The servants' grapevine being what it was, Mac Cooper swiftly learned that Gillie was feeling poorly. Not being busy

at the moment, he went to the garden and picked a handful
of flowers, then carried them up to the attic in a vase.

He'd never seen Gillie's little room before, and he was
glad to find that it had a window that opened and let a bit of
breeze in. She was lying in her narrow bed with her eyes
closed and her soft brown hair in limp tangles. Mac studied
her face as he put the vase on the dresser. Then quietly he
turned to go.

Before he could leave, Gillie's eyes fluttered open. Mac
ached to smooth away the tired lines in her face. But it was
still too soon. Soothingly he said, "Don't worry, I just
brought some flowers. You go back to sleep."

"I wasn't really sleeping." She looked at the flowers,
pleased surprise in her brown eyes. "Thanks ever so, Mr.
Cooper. No one ever brought me flowers before."

He shuffled his feet uncomfortably. "'Tis nothing."

"Yes, it is." Her gaze shifted to his face. "At first when
you asked me to go walking and gave me little presents, I
thought you wanted to tumble me, but you've never even
tried." Her mouth twisted bleakly. "Half the other men on
the estate have. They all know what kind of girl I am."

He had been waiting for a chance like this. He turned the
one wooden chair that the room boasted and straddled the
seat, crossing his arms on the back. "You're wrong. They
don't know the kind of girl you are. I do. That's why I
haven't tried anything."

"I don't understand," she said in her soft Dorset accent.

He frowned. "One mistake doesn't mean you're a short-
heeled wench. I expect you were in love with the fellow. A
pity he was too much of a fool to appreciate it."

Her eyes closed, and tears seeped from under the lids.
She said apologetically, "I'm sorry, I seem to cry all the time
now." She opened her eyes again, the thick lashes clumped
from her tears. "Why are you so nice to me?"

He hesitated, not sure how to answer. "I like you," he said

simply. "And"—this was much harder to say—"I've been thinking it might be time I found me a wife."

The brown pansy eyes widened. "You . . . you want to marry me?"

That much surprise was a little insulting. He said stiffly, "Is it such a ridiculous idea? I'm not so bad a bargain."

Seeing his reaction, she said quickly, "Oh, no, that's not what I meant. 'Tis that, well, you're a London gent, and I'm just a country girl. And you're the master's man, and I'm only a housemaid. A *pregnant* housemaid. Why would you want to marry me? You can do ever so much better."

He hadn't analyzed even to himself the complex blend of tenderness, desire, and protectiveness she roused in him. Choosing his words carefully, he said, "You're a pretty lass, with a good heart and a good mind. I noticed you right from the beginning. And . . . well, you need a man, I think." As her grave eyes regarded him, he added clumsily, "But I wouldn't want you to marry me only because you needed a husband."

His vulnerability touched her. Until now Gillie had seen him as a rather grand London gentleman, far above her touch, who had singled her out for reasons she hadn't understood. Now she looked at him simply as a man, and liked what she saw. He really wasn't old, no more than thirty. Wiry rather than muscular, but she didn't mind that at all. And he liked her.

Smiling shyly, she said, "I wouldn't marry just for a husband."

No more was said on the topic, but when Mac took his leave, he thought they understood each other tolerably well. And when he brushed a light kiss on her lips, she kissed him back.

Chapter 20

That night Reggie went through the motions of dinner with his surrogate family. He played backgammon with William, who had an unnatural talent for the game, and admired Merry's watercolors of how the drawing room would look after redecoration. But all evening he felt as if he were behind a wall of glass, removed from what the others were saying and doing.

Reality was a demon on his shoulder, whispering that sobriety was a dubious goal, hardly worth the effort it was causing him. All men drank, and Reggie had always held his liquor better than most. What, after all, had he done that was so serious, except be tempted to thrash a brat who had seriously misbehaved?

He fought that demon, and another that whispered that he was doomed to fail, so why stretch his failure out any longer? What made him think that he could ever succeed at anything? What had he ever achieved except passing successes at trivial pursuits like cards and racing? Even if he did succeed at sobriety, what would be the point?

He had been fighting the demons for days, but they grew stronger by the hour. In his heart he knew that it was only a matter of time until he slid off the edge of the roof and fell into infinite space. But he wasn't ready to let go yet.

The tea tray came and went, and his companions prepared to retire for the night. His voice amazingly nonchalant to his own ears, he asked, "Allie, would you care for a game of chess? It's early still."

He had assumed she would accept, for she always had in the past. But this time she hesitated, then said, "Not tonight, Reggie. I've a touch of the headache."

Oh, God, she couldn't say no. But she did. As he watched her graceful figure leave the room, he knew that he had reached the edge of the roof, and the precipice yawned evilly beneath him.

Shaking with suppressed violence, he went to the library and read the pamphlet on ardent spirits again. So must his father have read and reread it—the edges of the pages were frayed from handling.

His father had stopped drinking, and so had Jeremy Stanton. If they could, so could he. He had proved his will over and over—in his school days, whenever he had set out to master a new skill, in his endless subterranean struggles with his uncle.

As he crossed to the French doors to go outside, he could feel the bottles in the liquor cabinet as vividly as if they were a bonfire. White heat calling him to be consumed in the flames.

He stopped with one hand on the doorknob, his forehead sheening with sweat and his body flat-out refusing to obey his will. He had deliberately left the liquor cabinet stocked, knowing that for the rest of his life he would be surrounded by drinkers and drinking. Perhaps . . . perhaps he had been asking too much of himself.

He had to get out *now,* before it was too late, before the insatiable hunger within him won. *Can't you stop for the next hour? If that is too long, then for the next minute?*

His hand tightened on the knob, his knuckles whitening as the force of his grip numbed his fingers. *Why bother? What are you trying to prove? And to whom?*

His will broke.

In a few convulsive movements he crossed the room and yanked open the door of the liquor cabinet. Then he grabbed the nearest bottle and wrenched out the cork.

And as a chorus of internal voices deafened him with their cries of triumph or condemnation, he took the drink he had sworn he would not take.

Alys prepared for bed slowly, her fingers abstracted as she unbraided and brushed her hair. She should have stayed downstairs and played chess with Reggie. For all his cool air of control, she knew how difficult the last fortnight had been for him.

She had vowed to be a friend, yet the memory of Gillie, his pregnant mistress, was too fresh. If they had played chess, she would have wondered compulsively if he was still sleeping with the girl, or how many other bastards he'd fathered. Tomorrow she would be able to suppress such thoughts, but tonight her irrational hurt was still too raw.

Frowning, she plaited her hair into a single braid. She shouldn't be here—she should be downstairs. It was wrong to leave Reggie alone when he was in such straits.

She looked at her bed, torn between the fatigue of the day and a growing sense of anxiety. *Something was wrong.* With an intuition too strong to be denied, she abandoned reason and left her chamber, her steps swift and light on the steps as she made her way through the softly lit house to the library.

The words she had been about to utter died on her lips when she opened the library door and saw Reggie. He stood by the liquor cabinet on the far side of the room, a half-empty bottle in one hand, pain and defeat on his face.

His head jerked up when the door opened. Their gazes locked, his bleak beyond words, hers horrified. There was nothing to say, nothing that could be said.

Alys wanted to cry, or scream with rage. Encourage him not to give up, or rail at him that drinking would kill him and she could not bear to think of him dead.

She did none of those things. After an anguished moment that stretched to near-infinity, she whirled and raced from the library, unable to bear the sight of what he was doing to himself.

Reggie watched her go, stricken to the heart by the expression on her face. Allie had believed in him, had helped him in every way possible, and now she saw him for what he was.

There was not yet enough alcohol in his system to blot out the image of her face, so he raised the bottle in his hand and drank as deeply as he could. He was a craven, a weakling, and a fool, and what could be more appropriate than proving it?

But the spirits he drank inflamed as well as soothed; in his hand was not surcease but madness. He stared at the bottle and whispered, "No."

Gripped by despairing fury, he hurled the bottle into the empty fireplace. It shattered against the bricks into tinkling notes and glittering shards.

"No!" It was a scream of desperation, a repudiation of the pain he had experienced and the pain he had given to others.

"No!" Blindly, hopelessly, beyond control, he seized another bottle and sent it flying after the first with the full strength of his powerful body. He grabbed the next, a cut-glass decanter, and hurled it after the others, the glass plug spinning away in midair before the decanter crashed on the hearth and sprayed across the carpet.

The library was redolent with the mingled scents of

brandy, Madeira, and port, sweet sharp aromas that had beguiled him over the decades even as the liquors had stolen his mind and broken his will. There were a dozen more bottles in the cabinet. One by one he smashed them into the fireplace, finding violent satisfaction in their destruction. When all of the bottles were splintered, he threw goblets, not caring that the antique glass had survived a century before this ignominious end.

Breaking every bottle of spirits on earth would not be enough to cure what ailed him, for his soul was in thrall to a deeper destruction than this. For an instant he wanted to hurl himself into the mound of broken glass, to roll and thrash until he bled in a thousand places, until there would be an end to the grief and loss of living.

The desire to feel that easy pain of slash and bleed beckoned, but he was not ready for that, not yet. After teetering on the verge for long moments, he fled through the French doors into the dark velvet night.

It was the night of the new moon, the night of the hunted, when small frail creatures might elude the predators that sought to rend their flesh. Fueled by despair and lit only by the stars, he ran with all the strength and endurance at his command.

Instinctively he turned toward the wild solitude of the downs, his strides long and heedless. When vicious pains in his side slowed his pace, he walked until he had recovered. Then he ran again, knowing in his fractured, desperate heart that it was Death itself he was trying to escape.

Lying across her bed, Alys cried as she hadn't in a dozen years, mourning Reggie as if he were dead. She knew in her bones that if he returned to drinking, it was only a matter of time until an agonized, undignified death claimed him. The thought was anguish.

Damnation, she should have stayed with him. She sat up and pushed her heavy hair back with a hand that trembled. Friendship was for better and for worse every bit as much as marriage was. If she had been there earlier, he might not have begun drinking. If she had stayed, perhaps he would have stopped.

If she could not even try to help, she was unworthy to be anyone's friend.

Her mind a jumble of arguments, pleas, and determination, she returned to the library. Then she halted in the doorway in shock at the sight of the destruction Reggie had wrought. In the shattered glassware, pooling liquor, and alcoholic scents, she could see his desperation.

But of Reggie himself there was no sign. The only movement was the soft rustle of curtains as a breeze curled lightly through the open French doors.

He might be losing the battle, but he wasn't defeated yet. Swiftly she went to her room and changed to her practical masculine clothing, knowing it would be a long, hard search. Then she plunged into the moonless night to find him.

In the heavy darkness he fell more than once, but he ignored the bruises and torn clothing. He pushed his body harder than he ever had in his whole active lifetime, quartering the estate from the high downs to the water meadows, following the hedgerows, fumbling through the shadowed copses by touch. His mind held nothing so clear as thought, only raw emotions, agony as acute as when his family had died, but less pure and honorable than that true grief.

Finally, when every fiber of his body trembled with exhaustion and his very bones ached, he found himself by the lake in his private watching and dreaming spot. There he sank to the ground, numb to the soul. The lake was so still that the stars reflected in the dark mirror of the water.

Perhaps he could find a final peace there. It would be easy to walk in, feeling the calm waters welcome him. So easy . . .

He was too broken even for the simple act of willing his own destruction. He lay back in the soft grass, hearing the silken rustle of the birch leaves. The soil of Strickland welcomed him, as it would receive him into his final resting place.

Then, in the charred embers of crisis, he remembered what Jeremy Stanton had said. *I had tried my damnedest, and I just couldn't do it. So I prayed . . . a desperate lot of drivel asking anyone who might be out there to help me, because I couldn't help myself.*

Reggie had thought himself different from his godfather, tougher and stronger. Yet tonight he had learned that he, too, could not do it alone. Will was not enough.

In his heart, he surrendered. His weary mind jangled with inchoate phrases and broken prayers as he desperately sought for a strength beyond himself.

His anguish was a tidal wave, on the verge of smashing him beyond any hope of healing. But like a tide, a subtle shifting of the current began. Not a great revelation, no soaring trumpets or flame-edged promises. Just a simple knowledge that he was not alone. That he had never been alone, though he had been too blind and self-absorbed to realize it.

Like the tide, the turning point was slow, with no clear moment at which hope took over from despair. Yet hope did come, a wordless promise that gently soothed his lacerated spirit.

He lay staring at the stars, knowing the battle was not yet over. Struggle and dark doubt still lay ahead. But he also knew that when he needed help, it would be at hand.

Not long after he had reached that understanding, Alys found him.

Even in near-total darkness he knew who came. His raw senses were unnaturally receptive, and he recognized not only her step and her scent, but the ineffable feel of her caring. Wordlessly she sat cross-legged beside him, not quite touching, her face a pale blur in the thick velvet dark.

He stretched out his hand. She took it, her fingers far warmer than his, her clasp light and sure. Linking his fingers with hers, he brought their joined hands to his chest, against the beat of his heart. The tide of hope was running stronger now.

Her voice gentle in the night, Allie asked, "How are you doing?"

"Better." His voice sounded harsh to his own ears. He swallowed hard. "Talk to me, Allie. Please."

And so she spoke of Strickland, of the children, of her plans for the pottery, of the promise shown by the students in her school. Passively he listened to the healing flow of words, immersing himself in the details of normal life.

Finally Alys said in her rich voice, "I think I'm getting hoarse. And though I never thought the day would come, I seem to be running out of things to say."

His fingers tightened on hers, and she had a faint impression of his amusement. "You've done well," he said. His voice was closer to normal now. "Now it's my turn."

He began to talk. He told her of his childhood at Strickland, and the shock of remembering his father's near-disastrous drinking. He spoke of the short, idyllic period when he had been part of a happy home.

Softly she asked, "What happened to your family?"

"Smallpox."

She shuddered as the evil word fell between them. No wonder he had been so insistent on vaccination.

He sighed. "Actually, that isn't quite the whole truth. My father was away when the disease broke out. There was a smattering of cases in the village, but the manor was much harder hit. My little sister Amy died first, then my brother."

"Did you catch it, too?" she asked, assuming that he must have escaped.

To her surprise, he said, "Yes. The only time I've ever been sick in my life. Ironic, isn't it? It killed everyone else, and left me without so much as a single scar. I have a magical immunity to disease, or I would have died of something ghastly years ago." His voice faltered. "I was beginning to recover when I woke with the feeling that I must go to my mother. I could barely walk. It was nighttime, and the house was eerily quiet. The only servant who would stay was an old woman who had survived smallpox as a girl, and she had fallen asleep from exhaustion.

"My mother was close to death, but she opened her eyes when I came in. She . . . smiled." Reggie's fingers tightened around Alys's with numbing force. "She said that she was glad one of her children would survive to grow up. She didn't speak again." He took a deep, ragged breath. "My father had been sent a message that his whole family was dead or dying. He was killed in a carriage accident racing to get back to Strickland. I . . . I've sometimes wondered if he would have driven more carefully if he had known that I was going to live."

Alys wanted to weep for the bleakness, but before she could answer, he said bitterly, "A precious poor use I've made of the gift of life."

"Don't blame yourself for surviving," she said gently. "We are not in a position to understand such things."

"Do you believe in God, Allie?"

It was not a question she would have expected from him, but he had always been unexpected. "Not in a way that Junius Harper would approve of," she said slowly. "I believe there is a pattern, an order, to why things happen. I believe my actions matter, even if only in a very small way. If I have an ambition, it's to leave the world a little better than I found it."

"You're a wise and good woman, Allie," he said in a

voice scarcely louder than the sighing wind and rippling leaves. "I've spent my life fighting windmills, trying to change what couldn't be changed, wanting the approval of a selfish old man. I patterned my whole existence around a contest that didn't matter."

"Your uncle?"

"Yes. He sent his secretary to collect me from Strickland. I was frightened and alone, not fully recovered from my illness. When I reached Wargrave Park, for an instant I half believed the earl was my father. There's a strong family resemblance among the Davenports—tall and dark and damn-your-eyes. I went to him, and . . . he stepped back as if I was a plague carrier. Said that since I was my father's son, he couldn't expect much of me, but he hoped I wouldn't disgrace the name any more than absolutely necessary."

Alys ached for the pain of that rejection on a boy so sensitive, who had already suffered so much. He had been scarcely older than William. "So that is when you started being the Despair of the Davenports."

"You're perceptive." He shifted restlessly. "I discovered very soon that there was nothing I could do that would make my uncle approve of me. But I did learn that I could damn well make him notice me. The harder he and everyone else tried to make me behave, the wilder I got."

He gave a rusty chuckle. "At Eton I made a wonderful discovery. Most of the students who were King's Scholars had allowances from their parents to buy extra food, since a goat would starve on what we were fed. I didn't have any money, but from sheer desperation, I bought food on credit from the inn that stood in the middle of the campus. It was called the Christopher and kept many a lad from starvation. Anyhow, I found that while my uncle disliked giving me any money directly, he would pay bills that I incurred.

"From food, I expanded to the draper, the tailor, the

bookseller, and so forth. By the time I went to Cambridge, I was living fairly comfortably, and the pattern was set—Wargrave would pay my debts for the sake of family pride, even though he loathed me."

So Reggie had been a King's Scholar. Amazing. "Did you finish at King's College and become a Fellow?"

"Yes, though few people know or would believe it. After a year, I gave the fellowship up. Lacked the temperament for teaching." Another rusty chuckle. "I wanted to go into the army, but my uncle refused to buy me a pair of colors as long as I was the heir after his own sons. He insisted I stay in London and gave me an allowance, though hardly a generous one. Since two of his sons wouldn't marry and the other had been disowned and left the country, I was his hostage for the future. I found considerable satisfaction in knowing that even though he despised me, I was the Wargrave heir."

"Ignoble, but understandable."

"More than ignoble—it was stupid," he said with patent self-disgust. "I should have said to hell with him and bought myself a commission the first time I had a good run of luck with my gambling."

Hearing the bitterness, Alys asked, "Why didn't you?"

He moved restlessly again. "Because as a member of his family and his ward, I felt that my uncle owed me the commission. Certainly I would have cost him much less in the army than I did on the town, but he preferred thwarting my ambitions. He was a man who had to control everyone around him. In return I tried to punish him by being as difficult and disgraceful as possible. It was like a . . . a covert war between us. In the long run, I thought I would win, if only by outliving the old bandit."

He paused, then said flatly, "But in the end, he won. He

set his lawyer to looking for heirs of his youngest son, and
my cousin Richard was located."

"That must have been hard to accept," she said sympathetically.

With a ghost of acid humor, he said, "It was. I'd had
every intention of shocking everyone senseless by running
the Wargrave estates profitably and well."

"Which you could have done, based on what I've seen of
you here at Strickland."

He squeezed her hand. "Perhaps. I'll admit that after
growing up on the fringes of society, never quite belonging,
I wanted the title and position of an earl. But far more than
that, I wanted"—he searched for the words—"validation
that I mattered. I wanted proof that spending my life locked
in a battle of wills with my uncle had some meaning."

His voice flattened again. "But it didn't. I could have
made a thousand other choices that would have been better
for me, but in my pride and stubbornness, I stayed locked in
a pointless struggle with an evil old man. Without ever consciously choosing it, I spent my life on a fool's throw."

She stretched out in the grass next to him, lying on her
side with her head on his shoulder and her arm across his
chest. His arm curved around her as if she belonged there.
"I know a great deal about pride and stubbornness, Reggie,"
she said quietly. "I made a hash of my own life for similar
reasons. But I decided that something could be salvaged
from the wreckage, and that's what I'm doing now."

He brushed his cheek against the top of her head. "But
you're wiser than I, Allie." He laughed suddenly. "Not that
that's a decent reason. I'm going to be thirty-eight on All
Hallows' Eve, and by my age, innocence and ignorance are
not valid excuses. If one makes a hash of things, one is
either stupid or guilty."

She smiled, knowing that if laughter had returned, he had
survived this crisis. Then she pressed more closely against

his lean body. There was nothing the least erotic about this embrace, but it felt wonderfully right. "You were really born on Halloween?"

"Yes, and you needn't comment on how some demon must have been substituted for me as a child," he said dryly. "The possibility has been mentioned before."

"That is not what I had in mind," she said with dignity. "Halloween is a perfectly respectable day to be born. I know because it's *my* birthday, too."

"Honestly?" he asked, amused. "You mean we actually have something in common besides Strickland?"

She chuckled and slid her arm around his waist. "Apparently."

As Allie lay quietly in his arms, Reggie felt closer to her than he ever had to any other woman, even in the most passionate sexual intimacy. Despite his teasing words, he knew they had a great deal in common. The significant difference was that Allie used her intensity and will more productively than he ever had. In a way, they were opposite sides of the same coin: the rake and the reformer, both stubborn and proud. One a destroyer, one a builder. One a cynic, one a dreamer.

And, of course, one a man, the other a woman.

As he inhaled the fresh herbal scent of her hair, Reggie realized that his feelings for Allie had gone far beyond respect, liking, and even the sheer, rampaging lust she roused in him. He might have made it through this night without her, but her presence and generous spirit had joined with the tide of hope to heal him, to make it possible to face the rest of his life with more wisdom and grace than he had shown in the past.

He was not ready yet to put a name to how he felt, but someday, when he was whole, when he was sure and sober, he would. Then, perhaps, if Allie was willing . . .

They dozed together, sharing their warmth as the night

cooled and dew dampened their clothing. The sky was beginning to lighten when Reggie came awake. Allie stirred as he did, and they both pushed themselves to sitting positions.

"I'm definitely too old to be sleeping on the ground," he said ruefully.

He got to his feet, feeling the aches from last night's frantic running and falls as well as from the cold earth. Allie rose smoothly with the help of his hand. They walked in silence back to the manor house, his hand lightly touching the back of her waist.

They entered through the library doors, and found that all trace of last night's orgy of destruction had vanished. Only a lingering scent of liquor remained as proof of what had happened. "I guess Mac has been here," Reggie said. "He's always made it easy for me to keep on doing what I've been doing. It's a mixed blessing."

If Mac hadn't been there to put the pieces back together after every debauch, might Reggie have hit the breaking point sooner? Hard to say, but it was possible that Mac's unswerving loyalty had had the destructive consequence of helping Reggie avoid the fruits of his folly.

Too tired for abstractions, Reggie followed Allie upstairs. Outside her door he pulled her into a hug, feeling her slim body along the length of his. Desire was no longer dormant, but this was not the place, and certainly not the time, to travel that road.

He stroked her back, feeling the heavy silk of her hair against his face. "Thank you, Allie," he whispered. "I think the tide has turned now."

"I know," she replied, her voice equally soft. "I sensed that something was different when I found you."

Perceptive as well as kind, generous, and beddable. He wanted to kiss her, but refrained. Instead he let her go, then turned and went to his own bed.

Today he must begin the business of living wisely.

Chapter 21

The summer of 1817 became the happiest time of Alys's life. After his dark night of the soul, Reggie was a different man. He laughed and talked easily, his desperation a thing of the past and drink no longer an irresistible craving. He and Alys often sat up late and talked, but it was no longer because he needed her as a distraction. Now they were simply friends, and never ran out of things to say to each other.

Alas, as she had feared, there was nothing the least lover-like about him. But as a companion he was superlative, his wide-ranging mind and quirky opinions meshing with hers as no one else's ever had.

Reggie still worked long hours, both in the fields and with his horse training, but he now took enjoyment in his labors. The unhealthy color that had underlain his skin was gone, replaced by a deep tan that made his eyes shine like light, bright aquamarine. Altogether he was a delectable sight; Alys's dreams did not get any less restless. But in spite of her repressed longings, she was happy.

The crown of the summer had passed and the harvest was nearing when Reggie casually mentioned over one of their late-night chess games, "My cousin Wargrave will be visiting in a couple of days."

"Really?" Alys paused with her queen's rook in midair. "Did you invite him?"

"He said he would be nearby and asked permission to call." Reggie grinned. "Of course Richard is checking up on the prodigal, for which one can hardly blame him."

"Do you mind that he's doing that?" She set the rook down, capturing one of Reggie's pawns in the process.

"Actually, I don't. Richard has been amazingly tolerant and fair-minded toward me. When we first met, we shared the same roof for some weeks and he didn't see me sober the whole time. I was in a rather evil mood, too." Reggie tamped fresh tobacco into his meerschaum reflectively. "After a lifetime of burning bridges, it's time I built a few."

Alys propped her elbow on the table and rested her chin on her palm. "I can't wait to see his reaction to learning that I'm the A. E. Weston he offered to find a situation for if matters didn't work out with you."

Reggie laughed, a devilish twinkle in his eyes. "Neither can I, Allie. Neither can I."

In the event, the Earl of Wargrave was not at all what Alys expected. With Reggie's remark that Davenports were all tall, dark, and damn-your-eyes, it was a surprise when she returned to the house in late afternoon at the same time as a dusty rider trotted up to the main entrance. As he dismounted, Alys asked, "Can I help you?"

The new arrival was a pleasant-faced young man of about Alys's height. She gave him credit for not looking startled at the sight of her booted, breeched, and too-tall self.

"I'm looking for my cousin, Reginald Davenport," he said in a soft, mellow baritone. "He's expecting me."

It took a moment for her to make the connection. Then she blurted out, "Good Lord, you must be Wargrave."

His face straight, he replied, "I'm not sure if I'm a good lord, but I do try."

Alys burst out laughing and decided that she approved of Reggie's cousin. Her eyes gleaming with anticipation, she offered her hand. She always did that when wearing male dress, to spare men the confusion of having to decide whether to bow or shake her hand. "I'm A. E. Weston, steward of Strickland."

The hazel eyes were startled for just a moment. Then they filled with amusement. "So you're the financial and agricultural wizard who put the estate back on its feet," he said, shaking her hand firmly. "Is it a fair guess that the sick relative who took you away from Strickland on my first visit was considerably less ill than you thought?"

"A very fair guess," she agreed. "Tell me, my lord, if I had accepted your offer to manage Wargrave Park, would you have withdrawn it when you learned I was female?"

"With your record, I would have felt privileged to have you." He looked hopeful. "Are you interested?"

"No, merely curious."

"A pity," he said with an elaborate sigh.

Alys smiled, thinking that even though the earl's appearance was very different from that of his cousin, there was a similarity in their humor. "I believe Reggie's working back in the paddock. Shall we see if we can find him?"

Wargrave agreed, and they walked his mount back to the stables. After leaving the horse with a groom, they continued on to the paddock. Before Reggie became aware of their presence, they were treated to one of his superb exercises in horsemanship.

"He's every bit as good as I'd heard," Wargrave said quietly.

"And then some," Alys agreed.

Noticing the visitors, Reggie broke off his training exercises and rode over to the fence. Alys sensed tension in Wargrave, and remembered that Reggie had said that relations between the two men had been strained. Having met the earl, it was a fair guess that Reggie had been the source of the problem.

As if there had never been any disagreement, Reggie swung from his horse with a smile and offered his hand. "Welcome to Strickland, Cousin."

Wargrave's expression lit up, and he took the offered hand with genuine pleasure. Alys released the breath she had been holding, and knew that everything was all right.

Blakeford felt an exultation so fierce that he wanted to crow it to the hilltops. Finally, after a whole summer of waiting, conditions were exactly right. He had found his men, carefully cultivated his informants, and the time was at hand. In two days there would be an agricultural show in Dorchester, and Alys Weston and Reginald Davenport were going together. It was harmless information, or so the Strickland servant who had let it slip over a pint of porter had thought.

He'd found a perfect ambush site where the road sank below the verges and trees clustered on both sides. There was plenty of cover for his men to conceal themselves as they fired down onto the quarry. Davenport and Alys Weston wouldn't have a chance. Blakeford would be there himself to ensure that the job was done right. In fact, he intended to perform at least one of the executions. Trying to decide which of the two he most wanted to kill was a pleasing mental exercise.

* * *

The Earl of Wargrave proved an ideal guest, not raising so much as an eyebrow at the unusual household, not even to sitting down to dinner with a group that included a seven-year-old. Nor did he flinch when the younger members of the party smothered him in a combination of awe and questions, though Alys had the impression that he had to work hard to suppress a smile on several occasions.

Peter was cast down on learning that the earl had managed to elude his valet and was traveling very light. Wargrave would not displace Julian Markham as Peter's ideal of a fashionable gentleman.

Though anxious to get back to his wife, the earl had accepted Reggie's invitation to extend his visit to include the agriculture show. He spent part of the intervening day accompanying Alys on her rounds. Mostly Wargrave watched, but he also asked occasional penetrating questions.

At midafternoon, as they rode toward the dairy pastures, Alys said, "For a man who knew nothing about farming a year ago, you've made remarkable progress."

"I've been doing my best." The earl made a sweeping gesture. "None of the other Wargrave properties are as well run as Strickland. If I don't learn to ask the right questions and hire the right people, they never will be."

"You'll manage, my lord," Alys said. "I've no doubt of it."

As they crested a hill, the hazel eyes slanted over to her. "Is it my imagination," he asked tentatively, "or is my cousin a new man?"

The earl was perceptive. "It's not your imagination."

"I suppose it's not my place to thank you," he said quietly, "but I'm grateful for the part you've played in his transformation."

Alys felt her cheeks coloring. "Any part I played was strictly incidental."

"Oh?" The earl invested the syllable with disbelief.

Could Wargrave have guessed her feelings for her employer? Acute perception definitely seemed to run in the Davenport family.

Preferring to change the subject before she gave too much away, Alys pointed to the herd that they were approaching. "Our dairy cows are Guernseys. Their milk is richer than that of other cows, and we've been pleased with the results. If you have a milking herd at Wargrave Park, you may wish to buy some Guernseys yourself."

Cows were always a safe topic.

For three farmers, going to an agricultural show was a holiday. The morning was crystal clear, and Alys felt exuberant as she rode between Reggie and the Earl of Wargrave. In deference to the fact that she was going off the estate, she wore a russet habit and rode sidesaddle, but even that nuisance wasn't enough to lower her spirits.

They were about five miles from Strickland when the road dipped into a shallow defile that ran through a clump of trees. Wargrave pulled back his horse a little, murmuring, "By the pricking of my thumbs . . ."

Reggie glanced at him. "Is something wrong?"

Wargrave hesitated, then shrugged. "Not really. It's only that the road ahead reminds me of the kind of ambush spot I learned to be wary of in Spain. The sight still makes my neck prickle." His voice was casual, but his eyes scanned the woods intently. "Is there a problem with highwaymen in this area?"

Equally casual, Reggie said, "Not that I know of."

Nonetheless, Alys saw that he was also watchful. The roads were never entirely safe, and caution was routine. She herself had a holster built into her sidesaddle and never rode outside the estate unarmed. But though she absently touched

the unobtrusive pistol butt, she couldn't believe the weapon
would ever be needed.

From his vantage point in the trees, Blakeford watched
the approaching figures with a frown. He hadn't counted on
Alys Weston and Reggie Davenport having a companion.
However, the second man didn't look like much of a threat.
Whoever the fellow was, he would have to be killed, too. He
should have picked his friends better.

Excitement sharp within him, Blakeford adjusted a
narrow black mask over his face. Then he raised his light,
accurate sporting carbine and checked that it was ready to
fire. He and his four cohorts were mounted and armed,
ready to close in on the quarry from both ends of the defile.

The last attacker, a former army rifleman, lay on his
stomach, the Baker rifle Blakeford had provided steady in
his hands. The rifleman was a real prize, a trained sharpshooter. Alys Weston should be eliminated with the first
shot. Blakeford would take Davenport himself, and he assumed that at least one of his hired rogues would have the
sense to go for the other man. The sooner this was done,
the better.

As the riders neared the center of the defile, Blakeford
whispered to the rifleman, "Shoot the one in the middle."

The barrel of the rifle swung to the target and stopped.
Then the man jerked his head up. "I won't kill no woman."

Blakeford's jaw dropped with shock. Then he hissed
furiously, "You didn't mention any such scruples when I
hired you. She's the main target of this attack."

The man shook his head stubbornly. "Won't shoot a
woman," he repeated.

Blakeford was enraged, but there was no time for argument. "Then shoot the tall man. I'll take the woman."

The rifleman shifted the barrel of the rifle, starting to

track the taller of the two men. Then he froze as his scan drew his line of sight over the smaller rider. "Christ, it's Captain Dalton!" The rifleman swore and jumped to his feet, yelling to the three travelers, "'Ware ambush!"

Aghast, Blakeford saw his whole scheme teetering on the brink of disaster. He chopped viciously down with the butt of his carbine, cracking the sharpshooter's head before the man could say more. The rifleman went limp and pitched forward, his body and rifle rolling down the steep embankment to the edge of the road.

Knowing there was no time to waste, Blakeford yelled, "Now!" to his other men.

Then he aimed his carbine at Alys Weston's head.

Wargrave's comment about the dangerous look of the sunken road had been offhand, but all three riders had an extra degree of alertness. Even so, it was a shock when an unknown man bellowed, "'Ware ambush!" from the trees just above them.

For an instant Alys froze. Then Reggie barked, "Lie low and ride!"

They all bent over their saddles and kicked their mounts into a gallop. Simultaneously, a man's limp body came crashing down the embankment, and a ragged volley of gunshots blasted with deafening nearness.

The warning had saved Alys and her friends from being struck by the bullets, but their escape was cut off when rough-looking horsemen thundered into the road ahead and behind. With their guns discharged, the attackers were turning to hand-to-hand combat.

Fiercely Alys reined in her horse to avoid a collision with a knife-wielding ruffian. The defile had exploded into a world of shouts and shots and crashing hooves. Beside her, Reggie and Wargrave were each being set upon by two men at once, and the acrid smell of gunpowder was harsh in her nostrils. With stunned disbelief, she realized that this was no ordinary robbery—murder was intended.

Reggie used his powerful horse to drive back an attacker, creating a small gap. Knocking aside the man's knife, Reggie yelled, "Allie, get clear!"

Alys tried to take advantage of the confusion to break free so she would have a chance to use her pistol, but a fifth man, his eyes covered by a narrow black mask, cut her off. As she tried to evade him, he yanked his mount to a standstill, raised the carbine he carried, and aimed it at her from less than a dozen feet.

He would never miss at this range—the deadly black mouth of the gun seemed enormous. Acting on pure reflex, Alys jerked back on her reins, causing her mare to rear and wheel. At the same time, she whipped her pistol from its holster and cocked it.

The man in the black mask fired. The shot was so close that Alys was sure she felt the spatter of burning cordite, but the shot missed. His carbine empty, he was temporarily harmless, so Alys pulled away from him and whirled her horse to see what was happening behind her, praying that her single pistol shot might help her companions.

Behind her a battle was raging, incoherent and cacophonous. Despite their superior numbers and weapons, the attackers were having a hard time destroying two men who were unarmed, but trained and deadly fighters. Alys saw Wargrave duck a saber slash, then ruthlessly wrest control of the sword away, unhorsing his antagonist in the process. Reggie was involved in a tussle with another attacker that ended when he knocked the man from the saddle with a savage blow of his fist.

As a third man raised a pistol on Reggie's back, Alys screamed his name and fired her own weapon at the attacker. An accurate shot was impossible, but by sheer luck her bullet winged the man. Bellowing with pain, he dropped his gun.

Then the masked man came at Alys again, leveling a pistol as he drove his horse at her. Impossible to reload under these conditions. Even as she wondered wildly why he was so intent on murdering her, she drew her arm back and hurled her useless weapon as hard as she could. The empty pistol clipped the man's cheek, causing him to jerk and sending his shot off harmlessly.

"You miserable bitch!" he swore. Grabbing at her bridle, he used his burly strength to immobilize her horse. Then he reached into his boot and pulled out a long, viciously edged knife.

Having discouraged his own adversaries, Reggie looked around in time to see the attack on Alys. With horror he saw that she was trapped in the sidesaddle, unable to evade her attacker. Knowing he was too far away to reach her before the knife would strike home, Reggie leaped from his horse and grabbed the Baker rifle that lay by the edge of the road only two feet from him.

Alys was struggling fiercely with the masked man, trying to prevent him from getting a clear stab at her, but the bastard was large and strong, and she was unable to fight free. To Reggie, the movement seemed ghoulishly slow as her attacker raised his knife high, the thin blade flashing in the morning sun.

Too frightened for prayer, Reggie dropped into approved firing position, one knee on the ground, the other raised to support his elbow and steady his aim. As the lethal knife stabbed downward, he cocked the hammer and squeezed the trigger, praying that the weapon was accurate.

His bullet slammed into the middle of the masked man's chest, knocking him backward off his horse. The knife spun glittering through the air. As the flat crack of the rifle echoed between the trees, a shout went up. The four remaining attackers, now considerably the worse for wear, abandoned the fight. The two that had been unhorsed scrambled onto their mounts and bolted after their fellows as quickly as possible.

The entire skirmish had taken less than two minutes. As the hoofbeats faded in the distance, the little stretch of road was absolutely silent. Even the birds had been shocked out of their songs by the gunfire. The masked man lay motionless on the ground, his clothing saturated with blood, while the man who had fallen down the hill still sprawled unconscious in the ditch.

Wordlessly Reggie crossed to Alys's mount and held his arms up. She slid into his embrace. Though she had fought like a tigress and quite possibly saved his own worthless life, now that the danger was over her slim body trembled violently. He held her with rib-bruising pressure as he offered a passionate mental prayer of thanksgiving that she had been spared.

Wargrave trotted his horse over. "Were either of you injured?" He looked as calm as a man riding in London's Rotten Row, but his rust-brown coat had a black hole scorched along one shoulder.

Easy for Wargrave to be composed; it wasn't his woman that had almost been killed. If Reggie had had any doubts that he wanted Alys Weston to be his woman, they were resolved now. "I think we're both all right. Allie?"

"I'm fine. Sorry to be quaking like a blancmange." A little shakily, she disentangled herself from his embrace.

Wargrave swung down from his horse. "Nerves are permitted. For someone experiencing her first taste of combat, you acquitted yourself very well."

"If you hadn't been here, Richard, the odds would have been hopeless. I'm glad you decided to accompany us today. Thank you." Reggie's voice was detached, but his emotions were not. While he rated his own fighting skills highly, the chances of their escaping this deadly ambush would have been nil if his cousin hadn't been with them, and a trained soldier. Even as it was, the result could easily have gone the other way.

Wargrave said, "It was the army's loss when you couldn't join."

It was a typically elliptical exchange of masculine compliments, but entirely satisfactory. Their gazes met and held for a moment, and Reggie knew that from now on, he and his cousin were friends.

Building bridges was a great improvement on burning them.

As Reggie kept one arm firmly around Alys, the earl knelt and removed the dead man's mask, revealing a heavy face set in angry lines even in death. Alys's gasp was drowned out by Reggie's shocked, "Blakeford!"

Wargrave glanced up. "You know him?"

Alys felt Reggie's rigidity in the arm that circled her. "I know him," he said grimly. "There had been some trouble between us recently, but"—he shook his head in disbelief—"it was a minor matter. Not important enough for him to want to kill me."

"It might not have been important to you, but obviously it was to him." The earl stood. "Don't bother with regrets. They would be wasted on a man who hired a gang of cutthroats to ambush his enemies and anyone else unlucky enough to be in the way."

Despite Wargrave's pragmatic words, Alys felt a chill spreading throughout her body. Reggie might think Blakeford had been out to kill him, but Alys knew better. She was Blakeford's intended victim, and she knew why.

Who would have dreamed that her past would reach out with such violence? A man had died today trying to murder her, and two other men might have died simply for being with her. Grimly she fought the wave of nausea that threatened.

On the other side of the road, the man who had fallen

down the hill and lain unconscious through the fight
moaned and stirred. Then he struggled to a sitting position.
He wore a dark green jacket of military cut that was so
grimy and faded it was hard to discern the original color. As
he raised one hand to his head, his eyes darted nervously
around the three watchers, fear on his thin face.

The earl crossed the road and stood by the man, arms
akimbo. "Was it you who shouted the warning at us?"

The man nodded. "Aye. I wouldn't shoot the lady, and
when I was targeting the tall gent, I recognized you, Captain
Dalton."

"I used to be Captain Dalton. A year ago I learned that my
real family name is Davenport. I'm the Earl of Wargrave
now." His eyes narrowed as he looked at the man's dark green
jacket. "Your face is familiar, but I don't think we ever spoke.
You were in the 95th Rifles. Kenneth Wilding's company?"

"Aye, sir. Corporal Willit, sir. Everyone in the regiment
knew you, and what kind of officer you were." He rubbed
the oozing wound on his head. "I figured that if you was
with these other folk, I was on the wrong side."

Voice edged, the earl asked, "What is a former rifleman
doing with a gang of murderers?"

"Trying to feed his family, sir," Willit said sullenly. "After
years of getting our arses"—his eyes shifted to Alys—
"begging your pardon, ma'am. After years of getting our
backsides shot off by Johnny Crapaud, we come home to no
jobs and no back pay. My wife and our babe had been sleeping in the hedgerows for months when that fellow over there
heard I was a sharpshooter and offered me a job." Willit
gestured at Blakeford. "He was a mean cove, but he was
willing to pay fifty pounds for doing what King George paid
me pennies for."

"The situations are hardly the same, but I can understand
why you accepted." The earl frowned. After a long moment,

he said slowly, "If you're willing to move your family to Gloucestershire, I'll find a decent job for you on my estate."

The rifleman climbed unsteadily to his feet, desperate hope dawning on his face. It was the expression of a man who had learned not to expect justice. "You're not going to turn me over to the constables?"

"You've earned better than that. If you hadn't warned us, we might have all been killed." The earl fixed him with a steely glance. "Just remember to act like a Rifleman in the future, soldier."

Willit straightened and executed a smart salute. "Yes, sir!"

When Julian Markham drove his curricle into the stable yard at Strickland, he felt as if he had come home. The groom who took his horse greeted him like a prodigal son. After saying that Mr. Davenport and Lady Alys had gone to Dorchester for a farm fair, he gave a broad wink and added that Miss Meredith was at home.

Obviously everyone in the place knew what was between him and Merry. Julian wondered if the servants had been laying bets on whether he would return. If only they knew how much he had been longing for this moment!

He took the front steps two at a time, knocking impatiently on the door and being admitted by one of the housemaids. Before he could even ask for Miss Spenser, Merry herself appeared in the entryway from the back of the house, a basket of fresh-cut flowers on her arm. In the moment before she recognized him, he saw the grave sadness in her wide blue eyes. Then her expression changed, her lips parting with shock.

Julian's confidence had taken a beating in the last weeks. A note of uncertainty in his voice, he asked, "Are you glad to see me?"

With a wordless cry of happiness, she sped into his

waiting arms, her flowers going flying in a shower of bright colors. While the housemaid watched with shy approval, Julian and Merry lost themselves in the sweetness of reunion, their voices incoherent, their joy palpable as they tried to hug every bit of each other at once.

When Julian returned to awareness of the outer world, he led Merry into the drawing room. He did not want an audience, even an approving one.

In the bright light he saw tears on her cheeks. He drew out his handkerchief and blotted them tenderly. "What's wrong, Merry? Has something happened here?"

She shook her head energetically and gave him a crooked smile. "I'm sorry to be such a watering pot. It's just that I didn't think I would ever see you again."

He did not reproach her for lack of faith. Instead he settled them on the sofa and put an arm around her. As she pulled her legs up and tucked herself under his arm, he said, "I'm back, but not so good a bargain as I was at the beginning of the summer."

At her questioning glance he continued, "You were right about how the world would see this match. I spent weeks arguing with my father, trying unsuccessfully to talk him around, but he was absolutely adamant."

Julian's mouth tightened as he recalled his father's remarks. Lord Markham had serious financial objections to the match, but much of his obduracy stemmed from the fact that Merry was living under Reginald Davenport's roof. Julian had offered to bring her for a visit so that his father could see her suitability for himself, but the viscount had flatly refused to receive a female that he characterized as "a fortune-hunting hussy."

Merry sat upright, her golden hair haloing her distressed face. "Julian, I can't let you become estranged from your family."

He laid a gentle finger on her lips. "Isn't that a decision

I should make? Believe me, Merry, I know what I'm doing. My father can cut off my allowance, but he can't forbid my marriage. He can't even disinherit me from the title. And he certainly can't change my heart."

He took a deep breath, then plunged into his most important news. "One reason I was away so long was because I was looking for a position. A cousin who never got on with my father helped me find a post in Whitehall. With that and a small legacy I inherited several years ago, I can support you. We won't be rich, but we'll be comfortable. That is," his voice hardened, "if you still want me."

That was the moment when Merry realized that Julian, the confident, handsome man of the world, needed her as much as she needed him. Taking his face between her small hands, she kissed him on the lips, tasting his warmth and tenderness and desire, and matching them with her own. She whispered, "How can you doubt it?"

As Julian pulled her slim body into his arms, he knew that Merry was more than worth what he was giving up.

Whoever said that it never rained but it poured was correct, Alys decided, though coming home to find Julian and Merry cuddled blissfully on the sofa was considerably more pleasant than being attacked by a gang of assassins. She and her companions had spent hours in Dorchester, giving depositions and dealing with the aftermath of the attack. Reggie had been grim, Wargrave philosophical as he commented that it always took more time to clean up after a battle than it had to fight it.

The earl had arranged transport to Glouchestershire for his newly acquired employee and the man's ragged little family. When last seen, the Willits were sitting down to a substantial meal at one of the best inns in Dorchester, still not quite believing their change of fortune.

Since his own and Alys's life had been saved by the man's warning, Reggie had tried to pay the Willits' expenses, but the earl had said crisply that Riflemen always took care of their own, and that was that. With amusement, Alys had decided that in his quiet way, the earl was every bit as stubborn as his cousin.

In her capacity as guardian, Alys sat down with Julian and discussed his changed circumstances. His new position would enable him to support Merry in modest comfort, if not luxury. In the long run Merry would still be a wealthy viscountess, but that hardly mattered. The important thing was that she would be loved by a man who cared so much that he was willing to change his whole life in order to marry her.

In the midst of her happiness on her ward's behalf, Alys felt a pang that there would be no such happily-ever-after for her. She suppressed it ruthlessly. She had long since accepted the sad fact that she was not the stuff of romantic heroines.

Chapter 22

Dinner that night was a joyous affair, celebrating both Merry and Julian's official engagement and the miraculous outcome of that morning's ambush. Champagne had been ordered from the cellars and the happy couple toasted, even William being allowed to drink to his sister's happiness.

Reggie's glass was filled with water. Alys wondered how he felt, knowing there would be a lifetime of not quite sharing such moments. If the thought distressed him, it wasn't apparent. He seemed entirely relaxed and at ease, a genial host surrounded by friends.

Over so much chatter, the arrival of a visitor at the front door was not heard. Only after the man brushed aside the maid and stomped into the dining room was he noticed.

Alys had a clear view of the intruder. He was a solid middle-aged gentleman with a handsome, forceful face, and was clad in a caped greatcoat glistening with raindrops. Julian was seated next to her, and she didn't need to hear him jump to his feet and exclaim, "Father!" to know that Lord Markham had arrived in pursuit of his errant son.

The room fell silent, and everyone at the table turned to look at the newcomer. A ferocious scowl on his face, Lord

Markham barked, "I've come to put a stop to this marriage nonsense once and for all."

Face pale but determined, Julian said, "We have discussed this ad nauseam for weeks, sir, and there is nothing more to be said. I would prefer to be married with your blessing, but the lack of it will not stop me."

"My God, boy, have you no more pride than to marry the cast-off mistress of a drunken rake like Reggie Davenport?" The viscount shot a venomous glance at Reggie, who was sitting at the head of the table, watching with narrow-eyed concentration.

There was a moment of paralyzed silence. Before an infuriated Julian could reply, Peter leaped to his feet. Sounding like a man, not a fifteen-year-old boy, he said grimly, "My lord, you insult my sister. If I thought you would accept a challenge from someone my age, it would be pistols at dawn!"

While Peter's phrasing might be melodramatic, there was no denying his sincerity, or his anger. While the viscount stared in astonishment at the upstart stripling, Reggie drawled, "Really, Markham, do you think I keep my mistresses under my own roof with their younger brothers in attendance? Credit me with some *savoir faire*."

Remembering William's presence, Alys turned her best governess glare at the boy, coupling it with a quick jerk of her head at the door in an order that he leave. William looked rebellious, but knew better than to disobey that particular expression. Reluctantly he withdrew, probably to join a cluster of spying servants outside the door, Alys thought with resignation.

Since the men seemed to have reached an impasse, she said frostily, "You also insult my guardianship, my lord. I assure you, Miss Spenser has been raised to the most rigorous standards of propriety. Only the sad destruction of our own home necessitated our temporary acceptance of Mr. Davenport's generous hospitality."

Markham swung to face her. "And who might you be?"

"I am called Lady Alys Weston," she stated in a voice reeking of grandeur. Though it was seldom necessary, Alys could act the haughty grande dame to perfection. She did so now, tilting her chin and drawing herself up to her full height, though being seated diminished the effect.

More than a little daunted by Alys's chilly dignity, Lord Markham glanced at Reggie's cousin and snapped, "If she's a lady, who are you, the Duke of Wellington?"

Richard stood. "Of course not, I haven't the nose for it. I'm the Earl of Wargrave." He executed a polite half bow. "I understand you've been doing some interesting livestock experiments at Markhamstead."

The viscount was almost distracted by the reference to his beloved pig breeding, but duty held him to his purpose. "What are you doing here? They say that you cut your wastrel cousin off without a penny and told him to get out of London before he disgraced the Davenports any further."

Richard raised his brows. "I can't imagine how such vulgar and inaccurate rumors get started," he said in a voice that could chip ice. "As you can see, my cousin and I are on the best of terms."

Alys choked down a laugh. Obviously the easygoing earl had mastered the lordly manner quite thoroughly.

Beleaguered on all sides, Lord Markham paused uncertainly. Deciding that it was time to take a hand in her own fate, Merry rose and went over to him. Casting a mildly disapproving glance at the diners, she said, "You're all being rather hard on Lord Markham. He's had a difficult journey in the rain, and of course he's concerned with his son's future. What father wouldn't be?"

Turning to the viscount, she said in her sweet voice, "You

must be tired and cold. Would you like something to eat?
And perhaps a glass of wine?"

The viscount wavered. The offer of food and drink was
immensely appealing. This beguiling golden-haired girl was
the only person present who had the least sympathy with his
desire to save his son and heir from a disastrous marriage.
"Are you the chit Julian wants to marry?" he asked stiffly.

She nodded, her lovely face grave. "Yes. Truly, I don't
wish to cause a rift between Julian and his family. I know
how dreadfully difficult it must be for both of you." Her
voice broke. "But Julian and I do love each other so."

Nonplussed, Lord Markham stared down into the great
sapphire eyes, where tears trembled. He had come posting
down to Dorsetshire immediately after learning that Julian
had defied his father's explicit orders to end his foolish in-
volvement with an ineligible female. The viscount had expected a confrontation, but not one quite like this, where he
was feeling like a brute for making this beautiful young
creature cry.

For just a moment, Markham wavered. Then his resolve
firmed. Of course she would be beautiful. Young men
seldom lost their heads over antidotes.

Alys cast a glance at Reggie, wondering how he was
taking this invasion of his home and the insults to his
household. Seeing the glint in his eye, she was not wholly
unprepared when he threw down the gauntlet in his own
particular way.

"For heaven's sake, Markham, don't you lose your head
over a pair of pretty blue eyes, too," he drawled. "With
Julian's prospects, he can wed one of England's greatest
heiresses. You'd be a fool to settle for a chit whose face is
her major dowry."

Everyone turned to stare at him. While Lord Markham
bristled like an angry tomcat, Peter and Merry looked

wounded, Wargrave thoughtful, and Julian utterly shocked and betrayed.

Having seen Reggie's diabolical expression, Alys had a glimmer of understanding of what he might be doing. Under the table she kicked Julian just before he could rip up at his erstwhile friend. When Julian turned to her, she shook her head in quick warning.

As Julian tried to interpret Alys's message, Lord Markham exploded at Reggie, "I would think that even a vulgar care-for-nobody like you would realize that money is not the only, or even the most important, criterion for marriage."

Reggie's dark brows arched superciliously. "Of course not. There is also land, title, and influence."

"That's exactly what a gazetted fortune hunter like you would think," the viscount said scathingly. "People of quality know that a foundation of mutual affection and respect is vital to a successful marriage."

He glanced at Merry, his face softening. "It is far more important that a young woman have good sense and an amiable disposition than that she be rich. In fact, girls of modest fortune are less likely to be extravagant with their husbands' money."

Reggie gave a negligent shrug. "It's as easy to fall in love with a rich girl as a poor one, and young men's affections are notoriously volatile. In a few months the boy will have forgotten what Merry looks like."

At that Merry frowned in puzzlement. Then her brow cleared, and a hint of smile began dancing in her eyes.

"A man of twenty-five years is not a boy," Markham snapped. "Nor is my son a fickle, womanizing rake like you, Davenport. He is a gentleman of principle, the kind of son any man would be proud to have. Julian would never have offered for Miss Spenser unless his affections were seriously engaged."

"You would know your own son best," Reggie said,

boredom written on his dark face. "I've always assumed that
the reason you've kept him on a short leash in London is
that he can't be trusted to run even a small estate properly."

Now Julian's expression also changed, the rigidity fading
and a gleam of unholy amusement showing in his eyes.

"You're as ignorant as you are immoral, Davenport. In
fact, Julian has prepared a brilliant plan for the management
of my estate in Moreton. I have every intention of settling
it on him on the occasion of his marriage."

As Julian's eyes widened, his father glanced at him a
little sheepishly. "I didn't want it to go to your head, my boy,
but I was most impressed with your plans, most impressed.
I think it good for a young man to have a few years of
sowing his wild oats before taking on the responsibilities of
marriage and family. But you've had your fling now." He
shot a venomous glance at Reggie. "And the more I think on
it, the wiser it seems for you to move away from London,
where there is so much bad company."

"I suppose he can't do too much damage to a single
estate, but you'd be a fool to let him get leg-shackled to an
unsuitable bride," Reggie said with his best supercilious air,
which was very supercilious indeed.

Vibrating with fury, Markham took two steps toward
Reggie before stopping, his hands curling into fists. "By
God, if there weren't ladies present . . . !" he snarled. "Don't
you tell me how to treat my own son, and don't tell me what
kind of female is suitable. What would a rake know about
respectable women?" He glanced at Merry again. "Miss
Spenser seems every inch a lady. Her birth and fortune are
respectable, and she is my son's choice. The sooner they are
wed and away from your wicked influence, the better!"

He turned to Julian. "I refuse to stay one moment longer
under this scoundrel's roof. I've already bespoken a room at
the Silent Woman. I shall expect you and your fiancée to call
on me at ten o'clock tomorrow morning. We have much to

discuss." He gave Merry a last warm look. "I wish to become better acquainted with my future daughter-in-law."

The viscount turned in a whirl of capes and marched out of the dining room, slamming the door with a force that shivered the china. Behind him he left profound silence, until the Earl of Wargrave leaned back in his chair and went off into gales of laughter. "Cousin," he gasped, "I wouldn't have missed that for all the sheep in Ireland."

As if his words were a signal, everyone else dissolved into a hilarity that was half relief from tension. Julian came around the table to give Merry an exuberant hug. Alys was tempted to do the same to Reggie, who was leaning back in his chair with a smile lurking in his aquamarine eyes. In five minutes of applied obnoxiousness, he had gotten a result that Julian had been unable to obtain in weeks of impassioned arguments.

Who said that deviltry didn't pay?

News of Lord Markham's visit spread through all levels of the household, producing much merriment and pride in the master's resourcefulness. The housemaid Gillie, who had secretly watched the drama through a crack in the door, sought out Mac Cooper and regaled him with the tale when her duties were done. It had become natural to look for Mac when she had something to share. Telling him made a good story better.

Since a cold rain was falling and Gillie tired easily these days, they walked only as far as the barn. There they reclined cozily in a pile of hay while she did her best to remember word for word what Mr. Davenport had said to the Viscount Markham. Mac laughed uproariously, saying that it was one of Reggie's finest moments. Then he regaled Gillie with several carefully expurgated stories of his master's outrageousness.

After they were both weak with laughter, the valet rolled over and placed a kiss on the maid's pert nose. "It seems like marriage is in the air. What do you say, Gillie girl, shall we do the deed also?"

Suddenly sober, Gillie searched his face, which was shadowed in the dim light. While their friendship had been quietly growing and deepening, he had not mentioned marriage since that time in her attic room. She found herself shy again. Unconsciously putting her hand on her burgeoning belly, she said, "I'd like to marry you, Mac, more than I ever wanted to marry Billy. But . . ." she faltered a little, trying for words to express her anxiety, "I worry about whether you might resent the babe for not being yours."

Mac laid his hand over hers. Though it was intended as a friendly gesture, he looked down with pleased surprise. "The baby just kicked. Lively little devil, ain't he?"

His expression changed. "My ma was a housemaid like you. My father was a fine London gentleman she told me, a lord, no less. Some gentleman!" His laughter was bitter. "After he got her in the family way, he turned her out of the house with ten quid. It . . . it would have been nice if there had been a man around willing to take care of her and me. A child needs a father." He was silent for half a dozen heart-beats. "She did her best to raise me right, but she died, worn out working the streets, when I was six years old."

Gillie's heart ached for that desperate girl, and for the lonely, abandoned boy Mac had been. Her fears that he might resent her baby dissolved. She might be just a coun-try girl, but she could see how much he wanted a family of his own to love and cherish. And how much he needed to be loved in return. Marrying her would be a way of mending the past.

Trusting him now, she laid one hand on his cheek. "If you really want to marry me, Mac," she said softly, "I'll be proud, and honored, and happy to accept."

He leaned over and kissed her very gently, but the embrace rapidly developed into something far more exciting. Gillie was delighted to learn that a London man of the world knew a lot more about kissing than country Billy ever had.

As events progressed toward their natural conclusion, Mac suddenly pulled away, his breath coming hard. "I'm sorry, Gillie girl, I don't want you to think that I'm one of those men who tells lies to get a tumble. I'm willing to wait until we're properly wed."

"I'm not!" she exclaimed, her face flushed and hay in her hair. Her lips curved in a smile. "We might as well, since there's no danger I'll catch a babe out of doing it."

Mac laughed, looking like the young man he was rather than the toughened cockney who had escaped one of London's worst stews. Then, very carefully, he proceeded to pleasure his lady in the sweet green warmth of the hay.

The Earl of Wargrave left, and life returned to normal. Julian and Merry also left for the Markham family seat for a fortnight's visit. His lordship had swiftly succumbed to the girl's charm, and was well on his way to forgetting that he had ever opposed the match. An autumn wedding was planned so that Alys would be finished with the harvest and free to play the role of mother of the bride.

The news spread through the household that the master's fine London valet was going to marry the maid Gillie. Tight-lipped, Alys told herself that it was absurd to think the business so distasteful. Such arrangements were the way of the world. Reggie was freed of a nuisance, and Mac Cooper doubtless was being compensated handsomely for taking a pregnant mistress off his master's hands.

The day after Julian and Merry left, Alys and Reggie were enjoying one of their lazy late evening visits after the boys had gone to bed. She wore her comfortable golden robe, and her hair was tied back with a matching ribbon. For Alys, it was the best time of the day. Her reservations about her employer's scandalous conduct always melted in his presence.

They were in the library, the only place in the house where Reggie smoked. He puffed on one of his vile cheroots as Nemesis and Attila snoozed near their respective masters. Even the pets had declared a truce, largely because the cat found the dog too easily intimidated to be a challenge.

"Why not have some brandy?" Reggie suggested after exhaling a wisp of smoke. "I restocked the liquor cabinet while Richard was visiting."

After a moment's hesitation, Alys went to the cabinet and poured herself a small drink. "It doesn't bother you to have spirits here?"

"Believe it or not, no. I missed the drinking for the first three or four weeks, but not now." He shrugged. "Looking back, I realized that I hadn't really enjoyed alcohol in years. I drank because I didn't know how not to. Now that I'm sober, I haven't the least desire to go back to having my life ruled by a damned bottle."

His gaze went to Alys. "Life is infinitely more enjoyable now."

The warmth in his eyes very nearly made Alys blush as she curled up in the wing chair again, her legs tucked under her. At times like this it was hard to recognize Reggie as the abrupt, sarcastic rake who had first come to Strickland. Even then he'd had humor, intelligence, and deep integrity, but such positive traits were not the most visible part of him. Now, as his cousin had noted, Reggie was a different man—relaxed, mentally and physically healthy, and irresistibly attractive.

Diverting her thoughts, Alys asked, "I was amazed that Lord Markham didn't realize how you were manipulating him. Do you have some kind of history with him?"

Reggie grinned, his intensity vanishing. "Some years back we had a little contretemps over a woman, the lady in question preferred me, and Markham has neither forgiven nor forgotten. It was a good bet that his loathing was so profound that he would do the exact opposite of anything I suggested."

"It's always a woman, isn't it?" Alys's voice was sharper than she had intended.

Reggie's expression closed. "Unfortunately, yes." Half to himself, he said, "If I'd had the sense to stay clear of Blakeford's mistress, the man would be alive now."

"A simple squabble over a female doesn't turn most men into murderers." Alys toyed with the stem of her goblet, uncomfortable with her private knowledge. "You can't blame yourself for how Blakeford reacted."

"No?" Reggie raised his dark brows sardonically. "Blakeford always had an odd kick to his gallop, but the fact remains that it was my actions that pushed him over the edge."

"Maybe his mistress wasn't the reason he arranged that ambush," she said, hoping she could relieve Reggie's mind without having to reveal the truth.

"Can you think of another reason?" His long face twisted with self-disgust. "I can't imagine anyone wanting to kill you or Richard, but there are any number of people who would be happy to dance on my grave. Blakeford was certainly one of them."

Alys hated to see his guilt, especially now when he had reformed his way of life. Especially since he was wrong. Deciding to tell him part of the truth, she said, "Blakeford may have looked on killing you as a pleasant bonus, but I guarantee that I was the prime target. He and I have a . . . a history."

She was about to spin a tale she'd invented to support her

remark when Reggie exclaimed, "*You* were involved with Blakeford?"

The harshness of his tone was an insult that struck Alys with numbing force. She had wanted to make Reggie feel better. Instead she had provoked a reaction that shattered her defenses.

For months she had lived in the closest proximity with a man whom she desired and had come to love, bleeding inside every time he casually referred to an old mistress, or got into trouble over a woman, or impregnated a maid. And Reggie, damn him, sat there looking astounded at the mere suggestion that a man could want her.

A physical chill spread through her as the old, unhealed grief about Randolph erupted and fed the anguish of her hopeless passion for her employer. Trembling violently, Alys set down her glass and stood, overwhelmed by the agonizing knowledge of her undesirability. "Of course you're surprised. How could I have forgotten that no man will touch me unless he's foxed or going to receive a fortune in return for the sacrifice of taking me to wife?" Her voice broke. "Considerate of you to remind me what a pathetic excuse for a woman I am. Even you, who have bedded half the women in England, could only bear to kiss me when you were drunk."

She was horror-struck by her own words. Exposing herself so thoroughly to Reggie was the ultimate humiliation. Eyes blind with tears, Alys fled for the door, knowing that his pity would be more than she could bear.

She was halfway to the door when Nemesis, true to her name, padded amiably in front of her. Unable to dodge in time, Alys tripped over the collie and fell clumsily, her palms and knees bruising on the Oriental carpet. "*Damn* this dog!" she cried, nearly weeping.

Reggie stared at her, aghast. Her statement implying that

she had once been Blakeford's mistress had produced a blast of jealousy as intense as it was irrational. Obviously she had interpreted his reaction as contempt. Her emotional disintegration made it shockingly clear that he had opened a wound that ran to the very roots of her being.

Allie had always been so strong, so balanced, even when Reggie was teetering on the edge of self-destruction. It had been easy to forget that she must have vulnerabilities of her own. From her agonized expression, Alys's Achilles' heel was a belief that no man could want her as a woman. For someone of her passionate nature to feel utterly undesirable was tragic.

And the fact that he, who was usually so acute at understanding others, should be so criminally insensitive was unforgivable. He leaped from his chair and knelt beside her. She was struggling to get up, but her legs were tangled in the voluminous folds of her robe. Laying a hand on her shoulder, he said, "Allie, it wasn't surprise I felt at the idea that Blakeford could want you. It was jealousy."

She stared at him, incredulous. "You thought I'd had an affair with *Blakeford?* You're an even bigger fool than I thought."

He felt a rush of relief at her unmistakable revulsion. Catching her gaze, he said intensely, "And you're a fool for thinking yourself unattractive. God knows that I've desired you from the first moment we met."

"Don't lie to me!" She jerked from his grasp and tried to roll away, but he caught her shoulders and turned her to face him.

Her hair had come loose, cascading around her face in a chestnut mass that shone with gold and auburn lights. She was all fire and fury, as irresistible as a goddess. A muscle in his jaw jerked as he clamped down on his response. "I'm not lying. You're a lovely, desirable woman, and it has been the devil of a strain keeping my hands off you."

She turned her head and closed her eyes against him, but could not conceal the tremor in her voice. "What a remarkably fine gentleman you are—I never saw a hint of strain." She twisted sideways in another attempt to pull away.

He tightened his grip on her shoulders. "You seem to think I didn't want to kiss you unless I'd been drinking. In fact, the opposite was true. I wanted to all the time, but only when I was foxed did I forget decent behavior enough to act on my desires."

"*'In vino veritas?'*" Her laughter was bitter. "Rather than 'in wine is truth,' the correct phrase is 'in liquor is lust.' To a man who is jugbitten, any available female will do." She struck at him wildly, frantic to break his grip. "Though even drunken rakes must have some standards, since you never went beyond a kiss. Now, *let me go!*"

Reggie saw that she was too distraught to believe him. This emotional storm had been a long time building, and now a lifetime of pain had broken loose, splintering the calm face she usually showed to the world. His well-intentioned attempts to behave honorably had kindled her deepest self-doubts. He spared a furious curse for how trying to do the right thing had gone so far awry.

So much for honorable intentions. Words would not be enough—he must prove by his actions how utterly desirable she was.

He took her face between both hands to stop her thrashing. Then he kissed the corner of one closed eye, tasting the salt of her tears.

She gasped and became still, her dark lashes lifting. Pupils that were wide and black with the intensity of her emotions made her mismatched eyes almost identical.

Having gotten her attention, he captured her parted lips with the urgency that had been building for months. Her response was instant and fierce. As her arms circled and clung, he bore her down until they lay full-length together on the floor. The feel of her long, lithe body intoxicated him more than brandy ever had.

He loosened her robe. Her lushly curving figure was tantalizingly visible through the fine muslin of her shift. He bent and kissed her breast through the fabric. Her nipple stiffened against his probing tongue and she gasped, her body arching upward.

The sound reminded him of where they were. Reluctantly he lifted himself away and got to his feet. Alys opened her eyes. "Don't stop," she whispered. "Not this time."

"I don't intend to." His breath was as ragged as hers as he scooped her up and set her on her feet. "But you deserve better than the library floor." Then he pulled her to him for another kiss, his mouth demanding, his body hard against hers.

He could have taken her anywhere, and she would not have minded. She had wanted to be swept off her feet and now she was, blind to all consequence, deaf to all reason. Her eyes closed as she opened herself to sensation, to taste and moisture and silky heat, the fevered pulse of his body against hers.

After he had reduced her to the consistency of wax, he lit a night candle in his left hand and looped his right arm around her waist. Then he guided her from the library and up the stairs. Their bodies rubbed with every step, hip to hip, thigh to thigh, with an intimacy that was scorching.

He brought them to her room, closing the door firmly behind. She murmured an involuntary protest when he dropped his arm from her waist and stepped away.

"I'm not going far." His voice came from the darkness, husky with unconcealed desire as he turned the door latch with a metallic snap. "But I intend to see every beautiful inch of you. You and I have waited a long time for this. There will be no hurrying or hiding in the dark."

He ignited more candles until warm light spilled across

the bed and threw the harsh, world-worn planes of his face into bold relief. Then he turned to her. "*All* of you."

He pushed the robe from her shoulders, leaving her covered only by the pale translucent fabric of her shift. She might have been embarrassed that her too tall, too extravagant body was so visible, except for the searing intensity in his eyes.

He undid the drawstring that secured the shift around her shoulders. Then he slowly drew the garment down her body, his callused hands leaving trails of fire in their wake. The tightness of his mouth and the roughness of his breathing told her how much she affected him, how much female power she wielded.

There was a moment of utter stillness when her shift fell about her ankles, leaving her naked to his gaze. Then wordlessly she began unbuttoning his shirt, as hungry for the sight of him as he was for her.

Ah, God, how beautiful he was, from broad shoulders to narrow waist to powerful thighs. He was a sculptor's dream, his rugged athlete's body refined by months of unrelenting physical labor. Hesitantly she stroked the dark hair on his chest, skimming her hand downward, feeling the taut ripple of muscle beneath her palm.

He caught his breath when her hand brushed lightly, ever so lightly, against the hard jut of his erection. Then he bore her backward onto the bed, coming down beside her.

But true to his word, he did not hurry. Under his expert lips and hands, she felt like a flower unfurling into bloom as he learned every secret of her body. Her long-buried fears and doubts melted away as her haunting dreams of passion came to life.

After he had kissed and caressed her into intoxicated life, he guided her in exploring his body. His response to her touch was incontrovertible proof that his desire was as fierce and hungry as her own, and knowing that heightened and deepened her own desire.

When she could bear no more and was on the verge of shattering with urgency, he covered her with his body, kissing deeply as his long, clever fingers prepared her for the final intimacy. Yet he was slow, too slow.

Distantly she realized that he must think she was a virgin, so he was moving with the care such a state deserved. Impatient of waiting and beyond explanation, she thrust her hips against his, whispering, "Now, please."

She felt the hot throb of male flesh with scalding intimacy. Then, with a groan, he yielded to her impatience, possessing her fully with one long shuddering thrust.

She cried out as they came together into an ecstasy of closeness beyond her most fevered dreams. There was an instant of stillness after he buried himself in her, and she sensed his surprise at how easily they had joined.

Then he was in command of himself, and her, once again. With passion and patience and fierce tenderness, he used a lifetime's trove of erotic skill to deepen and prolong the pleasure for both of them.

Until, at the end, he was no more in control than she, and they found boundless joy in each other.

Chapter 23

Shared passion had more than fulfilled her expectations. What Alys had not expected was the sweet languor of lying woven together afterward. Reggie shifted, and for a moment she feared that he intended to leave. Instead he settled on his side, his arm drawing her close so that she was tucked comfortably against him. In this, as in every other aspect of making love, she thought rather sadly, he was an expert.

He slid his hand into her tangled hair, his warm palm cradling her nape. "I want to dismiss once and for all your belief that you're undesirable," he murmured.

She could feel herself stiffening, and so could he. Gently he thumbed the rim of her ear. "I could spend a lifetime making demonstrations of this nature, Allie, but my guess is that some particular incident first gave you the absurd idea that men wouldn't want you. What happened?"

She shifted restlessly, uncomfortable with how well he could read her. "Isn't it enough that I'm too tall, too masculine, too bossy, and odd-eyed?" She tried to make her tone light, but it came out brittle and defensive.

"Yes, you're tall, but Mary, Queen of Scots was a couple of inches taller than you, and she was a great beauty." He stroked the length of her back, lingeringly. "If you were shorter, your legs would not be as gloriously, maddeningly beautiful. You are perfectly and exquisitely proportioned, exactly the best height for kissing, and even an inch less would be regrettable."

He gave her derrière an appreciative squeeze. "Sometimes I thought the sight of you in those pantaloons was more than I could bear."

"Really?" She met his gaze, not at all displeased at his words. "I dress that way merely because it is practical."

"Of course," he agreed. "The fact that you look ravishing is strictly secondary. But surely you must have noticed how every man at Strickland looks at you."

"I'm their supervisor," she said reasonably. "Of course they notice me."

"I own the estate and pay their wages, but they don't look at me that way." There was laughter in his voice. "As for your belief that you are too masculine—whatever that means—no one who has ever looked at you could possibly think you masculine. Every gorgeous inch of you is pure woman." He cupped her breasts and rubbed his face in the cleft between, the sensual rasp of his whiskers sending tingles through her entire body.

"As for being too bossy . . ." He raised his head and considered. "That's absolutely true, but it doesn't make you any less desirable." Laughing, he dodged the playful swat she aimed at him and continued, "Last but not least, your eyes are beautiful."

Now sure that she was being teased, she tried to scowl at him, though her sense of well-being was too great to manage much of a glare. "You're being ridiculous. Now I can't believe anything else you said."

"You should—it's all gospel truth." He raised himself on one elbow and kissed the tip of her nose. "Besides having lashes a yard long, you have one lovely warm brown eye and one lovely, changeable gray eye. Where is it written that eyes must match?"

She dissolved into laughter at his absurdity. Humor was something else that she had not expected to find with a lover.

He finished triumphantly, "And your dimples drive me absolutely wild," before proceeding to kiss them as well.

From there he nibbled down her throat to her breasts. After several minutes he rolled away. "I keep getting distracted, but there's much that needs to be said."

He propped his head on one elbow, his expression serious. "Allie, sex is a very basic part of the human animal, and it's a great tragedy that men and women almost never talk freely about it. Respectable women are taught that ignorance and distaste are signs of refinement. Heaven knows how you survived that kind of upbringing with your passion intact, but don't ever be ashamed of what you are, or what you feel."

She swallowed hard. "I . . . I'll try not to be."

"Sex is an area where everyone is vulnerable in some way." He absently twined a strand of her hair around his finger. "A fundamental difference between the genders is that women worry about their desirability, while men worry about their performance."

She had thought herself alone in her fears, uniquely unalluring. "Really?"

He nodded. "Your self-doubt runs far deeper than most women's, and I intend to find out why, but I have never known a woman, even the most acclaimed of beauties, who did not worry about her attractiveness to men. In fact, the beauties worry the most because so much of their confidence is bound up in their appearance, and time will inevitably rob them. Even women who dislike the actual experience of intercourse usually want to be desired, because it gives them power over men."

Alys stared pensively at the shadowed ceiling as she thought about his words. There was so much she didn't understand about men and women. Her gaze went to Reggie. "I have trouble believing that you worry much about your performance."

He grinned. "Less than most, perhaps, but believe me, it is a subject all men take very seriously." Sobering, he said, "Allie, what happened that made you incapable of looking in a mirror and seeing what you are?"

She shrugged and looked away uncomfortably. "Meredith is my ideal of perfect female beauty. Obviously I fall far short of that."

"Merry is graceful and golden and very pretty indeed, and I'm sure that to Julian she is the most beautiful woman in the world. But beauty comes in many forms that have nothing to do with mere prettiness." Lightly he traced the lines of her cheekbones and jaw. "You have beauty in the bones, and that will never fade."

She closed her eyes, relaxing under his touch like a petted cat until, implacably, he said, "What happened, Allie? I am going to keep asking until you answer."

Even as happy as she was now, remembering caused a sting of tears under her lids. "It would be impossible to explain that without telling you most of my life story."

"Then you'd better start now, because I'm staying here until I hear it." His deep voice was warm and encouraging.

How many men knew or cared how a woman's mind worked? Suddenly she wanted to tell him her story, not the identifying details, but the essence that had brought her to where she was today. "I was the only child of a . . . rather prosperous family. My mother died when I was young and my father never remarried, so I was treated much like a son. That's how I learned so much about farming. My father and I were very close. He's a ferocious, domineering autocrat, and we had battles that threatened to blow the roof off Car . . . off the house, but . . . we understood each other very well.

"When I was eighteen, I became betrothed. It was a perfect match. I adored Randolph, my father approved of him, and Randolph pretended to be in love with me." Her throat closed, and her voice choked off.

"Pretended?"

Reggie's even question helped her to go on. "His protestations of love were all lies. A few weeks before the wedding, he and a friend called unexpectedly. I was out riding, but I saw them drive up to the house and came rushing back." Counting the days until her marriage, she had been overjoyed at the unexpected visit. "I knew he and his friend would be in the morning room, which had French doors, so I went directly there. I was just outside and the doors were open."

Even now she could see the softly waving blue damask draperies that concealed her from the men inside. She could hear the cool, contemptuous voices. "They couldn't see me. The friend asked how Randolph could consider marrying a . . . a bossy Long Meg like me. Ten feet tall and all bones, not the sort to warm a man at night, and with managing ways that would keep him under the cat's paw. That was bad enough."

She shuddered over her whole body, "Far worse was being such a fool that I expected Randolph to defend me. He'd said often enough that he loved me. Instead he said . . . he said that he was marrying me for money, of course. That once he had control of my fortune, he'd rule the roost." The acutely remembered hurt was the source of her nightmares, and saying it aloud was like twisting a knife in her midriff.

Then, miraculously, Reggie laid his hand on her solar plexus, right where the pain was centered. "Steady, Allie," he said quietly. Warmth radiated from his palm, soothing her turbulent emotions.

When she had mastered herself, she opened her eyes and said with more calm than she would have believed possible an hour earlier, "I daresay it sounds trivial, doesn't it? You have survived far worse."

"Don't discount your own pain," Reggie said, his voice rough. "No matter how large or small the cause may appear, the only true measure of an injury is how deeply it hurts you. To be betrayed by the man you had trusted with your love— to have your very femininity disparaged—these are profound and terrible wounds."

She rolled over, burying her face against his shoulder. As she felt the knot of old pain slowly unwind and dissipate, she knew in her bones that while there would always be a scar, this part of her past no longer had power over her.

Reggie said no more, only held her, sharing his warmth and stillness. How could he understand so much about pain and healing? A foolish question. She knew enough of his past to understand what a hard school he had learned in.

Feeling lighter and freer than she had since her girlhood, Alys rolled onto her back and managed a creditable smile. "Thank you."

"Feel better now?" he asked gently, his eyes very warm. When she nodded, he asked, "What happened after you overheard those two young oafs?"

Some of her well-being ebbed away. "I retrieved my horse and rode to the farthest end of the estate, not returning until long after dark. Randolph and his friend had left, since I couldn't be found. When I came home, I marched in to my father and said I wouldn't marry Randolph if he were Adam and the only other choice was the serpent."

Her body began to tighten again. Reggie pulled the covers up and tucked them around her shoulders. She took a deep breath. "We had a battle royal. When I wouldn't give him a reason for changing my mind, he thought I was being foolish and missish. But I couldn't talk about what had happened. I *couldn't*."

"Understandable," Reggie said mildly.

Once more his comprehension relaxed her. "My father got all medieval and swore that I was no daughter of his, and that he would disinherit me if I didn't go through with the marriage. Then he locked me in my room."

"Bread and water?"

She smiled wryly. "I didn't stay around long enough to find out. I put on my breeches and packed what money I had and what clothes could be carried easily. At midnight I climbed down a rope of knotted sheets in the approved romantic fashion. Except that I wasn't running to a man, but *from* one."

"Not one, but two. If your father had been more understanding, would you have left?" Reggie said quietly.

"No." Her voice was deeply sad. "Many women have had broken hearts and survived. Being betrayed by my father was far worse because he had been the center and foundation of my life." She could not think of it, because that wound would never heal. "After I ran away, matters became rather sordid," she said without inflection. "You know that I wasn't a virgin."

His hand skimmed up her body until it rested over her heart. "Allie, you don't have to explain anything to me. The woman you have become is a result of all the choices and mistakes you have made through the years. Don't apologize for your past."

"But I want to tell you. I don't understand myself why I did what I did then. Perhaps you will." She closed her eyes, her face tight. "Two nights later I was staying at an inn, dressed like a female again. I was going down the hall to my room when I met a merchant who was staying there. He was drunk as a wheelbarrow, and he . . . he made an advance." She bit her lip, then forced herself to say, "And I accepted."

The merchant's breath had been sour, his hands clumsy. He neither knew nor cared that she was a virgin. And she had lain there and allowed him to violate her.

Alys swallowed, her mouth bitter with the taste of self-loathing. "I must have been insane. It was over quickly. He was too drunk to know or remember what happened, I think."

"Shall I find him and kill him for you?" Reggie said with deceptive gentleness.

"No!" Alys felt a bubble of semi-hysterical laughter. Perhaps that was what Reggie had intended. "He didn't force me. The fault was mine alone."

He pulled her closer. Her skin was warm, soft satin. "That must have been a very poor introduction to the delights of the flesh."

"It was. Worse, I despised myself afterward." She looked at him, her eyes wide and pleading. "Can you tell me why I did such a revolting thing?"

"Having suffered a devastating blow to your womanhood, you wanted to prove to yourself in the most basic way that a man could want you," he said immediately. "At the same time, it was one in the eye to your father and the repellent Randolph, the kind of action that would most infuriate them if they knew." His mouth twisted. "Unfortunately, it also left you with the idea that only a drunkard could want you."

After a long silence, she said, "Reggie, how do you know so much about people?"

"I started studying humankind when I was very young. Not to mention the fact that I'm something of an expert in the theory and practice of self-destruction," he said dryly. "I presume that after the episode with the drunk, you renounced men and lovemaking in favor of penitence and good works, but you couldn't make your natural passion vanish."

She gave a crooked smile. "Right again. I've always adored men, but after that night, I knew I'd doomed myself to spinsterhood. The man I loved had rejected me, and I couldn't imagine anyone else ever wanting me after what I had done. For a few hours I was on the verge of destroying myself, no matter what the cost to my immortal soul. I even chopped off my hair and burned it." She shivered and burrowed closer to him, taking comfort in the feel of lean muscles and hard bone.

"What brought you back from the brink?" he prompted.

"The next day my groom found me. He'd seen me after I'd overheard Randolph, and knew something was terribly wrong. The next morning he discovered that my horse was gone, and came after me without telling anyone. I think he hoped that if he caught me soon enough, he could persuade me to come back before there was a scandal. But it took him several days to find me, and when he did, I refused to return. He said he wouldn't force me, but he wouldn't leave me unprotected, either."

Reggie inhaled, enlightenment dawning. "Don't tell me—Jamie Palmer."

"Exactly. We had always been friends. He had no family and no reason to go back to my father's estate, so he stayed with me. I was grateful to have someone nearby who cared what became of me." She smiled fondly. "My first position was as history and Latin mistress at a small school near here. Jamie found work in the stables. Later I became a governess with Mrs. Spenser, and he moved along and found another position. When I started the pottery and needed someone I could trust to supervise, he took it on even though he prefers horses. He's been a good friend."

"Is he in love with you?" Reggie asked, trying not to sound jealous again.

She shook her head, not without some regret. "He never thought of me that way. To him I was the young mistress, far above his touch, even when I became a working woman. Several years ago he married one of the Herald girls. She's sweet and much more his style." Alys exhaled roughly. "The rest of the story you know."

"Have you ever thought of going back to your father?"

"Never." The single word was flat and uncompromising.

"It would be one thing if you hate him, but from what you said, that isn't the case," Reggie pointed out. "Don't you want to make peace with him? He won't live forever—he might have died already."

"He isn't dead."

"How can you be sure?"

"I would have heard."

Alys in this mood could give lessons to an oyster on staying mum, but Reggie persisted. It was one of the things he did best. "Allie, take it from someone who knows—living with anger is bad for the soul."

"Which interests you more, my soul or my potential fortune?" she snapped.

He refused to be drawn. "Give me some credit. Lord Markham might have called me a fortune hunter, but if I had ever wished to marry an heiress, I assure you I would have been successful in my quest."

She smiled apologetically. "Sorry. I shouldn't have said what I did. But I can't go back, not ever."

"Because your father will never forgive you?"

She stared at the ceiling. "That's half the reason. The other is that *I* can't forgive *him*. The one time above all others that I needed him to understand, to show that he cared, he failed me." Her voice broke. "Call it pride or stubbornness or sheer bloody-mindedness, but I will never return and ask for his forgiveness. Not now, not even if I knew he would restore me as his heir. Even when he dies, I won't go back."

Sheer bloody-mindedness was another thing that Reggie was an expert on, but he wasn't quite ready to drop the topic. "Would you return if he asked you to?"

Her tone was sad and tired. "My father has never admitted a mistake or made an apology in his life. He would never ask me back."

There was another kind of pain in her voice now. "A pity that you don't hate your father," he said softly. "That would make this easier for you."

Her expression hardened. "I don't need my father or his money. I haven't done badly on my own."

"No, you haven't," Reggie agreed, tenderly brushing the hair from her face. Beautiful, stubborn, honorable Lady Alys, whose veins pulsed with matchless passion. Their lovemaking had been extraordinary, and not only because it had been months since he'd lain with a woman.

He thought back, and winced inwardly when he remembered that the last occasion had been that coarse, mindless coupling with Stella. He hated even to think of that when he was holding Alys in his arms. There had been wonder in their joining, a sense of discovery that took him back decades to the day when he'd lost his virginity with a lusty, good-natured dairymaid. He suppressed that thought as well. The only woman in the world who mattered now was Alys.

Was this the right time to ask her to marry him? The idea had been growing in the back of his mind for weeks. He had intended to wait longer, to prove to her—and him—that he was sober and would remain that way. But tonight had changed everything. There was no way they could live under the same roof and not continue as lovers.

He was reasonably confident that she would accept. Allie was not indifferent to him, she loved Strickland, and she wanted children of her own.

And he loved her. Strange that he hadn't realized before. At some point in the last weeks, lust and respect and companionship and gratitude had fused, and the result far transcended the sum of the parts. In an utterly conventional way, he wanted her to be his woman, forsaking all others, until death did them part.

He had never made such a declaration, but he opened his mouth, hoping that sincerity would compensate for lack of style. Then, before he could speak, the part of his mind that never rested began assembling random pieces of information into a new and stunning picture.

His hand stilled, coming to rest on one of her lovely breasts. Julian had told him of the missing heir to the Duke of Durweston, a girl who had been betrothed to the younger son of the Marquess of Kinross. The marquess's younger son was Lord Randolph Lennox. Reggie knew him slightly. He was a handsome man a few years Reggie's junior, a paragon of gentlemanly virtues. The ideal mate for a girl who would one day be a duchess in her own right. Then Durweston's daughter had allegedly run off with her groom—a dozen years earlier, when the girl was eighteen.

Reggie felt a chill that began deep inside, curling icy tendrils around his heart. His Allie had to be the missing heiress—the two stories fitted together too well. Dear God, she was the only child of a duke.

And Blakeford had been next in line to inherit. Alys had said Blakeford had reason to kill her, and she was right. The duchy and fortune of Durweston would have tempted a better man than George Blakeford. And damnably, Reggie's own careless words had brought Blakeford to Dorsetshire, intent on murder. Though it was impossible to prove, Reggie would wager a thousand pounds that the fire that destroyed Rose Hall had been set by Alys's cousin.

Her husky voice interrupted his thoughts. "Why are you looking so serious?"

He focused his attention on her. The Despair of the Davenports was sharing a bed with the greatest heiress in England. When she'd had her come-out Season in London, he would not have been allowed under the same roof with her.

No wonder command came naturally to Allie—she had been raised to be ruler of the small kingdom of Durweston. She'd said that Lady Alys was an ironic nickname, but he suspected that it had started when Jamie Palmer absent-mindedly used her title.

If only she hated her father, but it was obvious that she cared deeply about their estrangement. And though she might think the duke would never welcome back a prodigal daughter, Reggie knew better.

In sixty seconds everything had changed. With a sickening sense of inevitability, he accepted what must be done. Then, invoking the control of a lifetime, he found a smile. "I was trying to calculate how many more times tonight I can make love to you before I must leave so your reputation won't be in shreds."

She gave him a slow, devilish smile. "You'll never find out by just thinking."

"You're right. There have been enough words." He kissed her hard, a sense of doom increasing his urgency. How could he have believed there might be a happy ending for him?

But for tonight, at least, she was his. And he would ensure that it was a night neither of them ever forgot.

The hours of darkness spun past with a thousand small discoveries, with passion and laughter and the mingling of quiet breath. The more he gave her, the more she was able to give back. Alys knew that if she died tomorrow, she would be content that she had been well and truly loved.

Surely such fulfillment could not be only a fortunate conjunction of bodies. She wanted to say aloud that she loved him, that no other man had ever touched her heart or spirit or body as he did, that none ever could. But she kept silent, not wanting to mar this perfect night.

Besides the mysteries of the senses, the darkness held another revelation. As Alys lay across Reggie's chest in a calm between tempests, she murmured, thinking aloud, "Besides Gillie's baby, how many other children do you have?"

He raised his head. "What are you talking about?"

Unable to withdraw her words, she stumbled forward. "About natural children, like the one Gillie is going to have in a few months. Surely over the years there must have been others."

"Why do you think I fathered her child?" he asked, more curious than angry.

Alys said awkwardly, "I saw her leave your room one night. And you allowed her to stay on here. May Herald said there weren't many men who would be so tolerant."

"I see," he said, his amusement obvious. "However, I deny all charges. I guarantee that her baby will arrive fewer than nine months after I came to Strickland." He went on to explain Gillie's desperate attempt to involve him in her pregnancy.

Alys was startled, and overwhelmingly relieved. "You didn't pay Mac Cooper to take her off your hands?"

"Don't suggest that to Mac, or he might forget that you're a lady," Reggie warned. "Getting married was his own idea, and he's very pleased with himself about it."

"Oh." Alys felt clumsy and not very bright.

The silence stretched, until he abruptly answered her earlier question. "Over the years I have been careful not to sow bastards. I would not want a child of mine growing up an outcast. But there may be one."

The last candle was burned almost to the socket, and its dying flicker showed Alys his impassive profile. "You don't know for sure?" she asked softly.

"I had an affair with one of the aristocratic Whig ladies whose life is as liberal as her politics. Her first two children were by her husband. After that, I think she took pride in making sure that each was fathered by another man." His words were clipped. "Years later, I saw her in the park driving with several of her children. There was a girl who looked a little like me, poor wight. I made inquiries. The child is the right age."

"The lady won't tell you?"

He shrugged. "She may not know. And if the girl is mine, what could I do about it? She's being raised with more than I could give her. Her parents are good people in their way. It would be no kindness to disrupt her life."

The harshness of his tone revealed how much he cared about that child who was lost to him. Would his ache be less if he had another child, one he could raise himself and guide through life's tribulations, as he had not been guided?

Alys had always wanted children, but now, with a ferocity that astonished her, she wanted them to be *his* children. Though she had not dared dream for years, for an instant, she contemplated a lifetime at Strickland, raising tall children with Reggie, sharing laughter and friendship and occasional explosions. And most of all, with thousands of nights like this one, when their spirits were as intimate as their bodies.

It was too soon to dream. But he liked and desired her. Perhaps in time he would come to care more deeply. She would do her damnedest to win him, and what better way to woo a rake than through passion?

So as roseate dawn softened the darkness, Alys set out to demonstrate to her beloved what she had learned in one night, making love to him with as much intensity as he had made love to her. And as they reached new heights of joy, it was easy to believe that love bound them.

Chapter 24

Reggie left Alys with a kiss just before the household began stirring. She luxuriated in happiness for the minutes before a maid appeared with her coffee. She had not known there was such bliss in the world. Though she should be exhausted after such an energetic night, she felt that today she could move mountains single-handed.

After her coffee arrived, she rose and dressed. It was a shock to glance in the mirror. For just a moment, she saw the beautiful woman Reggie claimed that she was.

Then reality set in and she was simply Alys, albeit a bright-eyed, glowing Alys. But for an instant, she had been beautiful.

She went outside, whistling. A pity that she would be spending the whole day at the far end of the estate. She wouldn't see Reggie again until dinner. Habit got her through her duties, but she kept finding herself staring blankly into space with a smile tugging at her lips and the delicious sensation of melting.

Late in the afternoon Alys returned to her office. She felt a swift curdle of panic when she saw the letter that awaited her, addressed in Reggie's bold hand. Could last night's passion have resulted in a letter of dismissal? She stared at the creamy paper for long minutes before daring to open it.

Lips tight, she broke the wafer. The terse but not unfriendly message was a relief. Reggie had unexpectedly been called away. Might be gone for as long as a fortnight, though probably less. Sorry to leave so abruptly. Fondly, R.

She stared at the note. Fondly? Was that a mark of affection, or indifference? She read and reread his words, trying to find deeper meanings without success.

Carefully she refolded the paper, her eyes fixed sightlessly across the room. Every time there had been any intimacy between them in the past, he had run away, but he had always come back.

She must remember that he always came back.

In London Reggie called on Julian's great-aunt, a redoubtable dowager with a passion for gossip and a weakness for rogues. Over a pot of tea he learned that the long-lost Durweston heir was Lady Alyson Elizabeth Sophronia Weston Blakeford, called Lady Alys. She'd had one London Season, was extremely tall and rather shy, but with a great deal of countenance. There had been general approval of her engagement to her father's choice, Lord Randolph Lennox, a handsome and honorable young man with no need to marry for money.

Finally, and damningly, the dowager mentioned that Lady Alyson Blakeford had mismatched eyes.

It took three days to reach Carleon Castle, the great seat of the Durwestons. Carleon encompassed a large part of the county of Cheshire, and it took Reggie half an hour just to ride up the avenue of elms from gatehouse to castle.

His practiced eye evaluated the estate, and found it vast

and prosperous. Strickland could be lost here a dozen times over. Carleon had begun life as a castle, and over the centuries the building had grown and changed to reflect the power and wealth of its owners. The ruler of England would not be shamed to live within these golden stone walls, and kings and queens had visited here.

The closer he came to the heart of the estate, the angrier Reggie became. That Alys had left this for a life of uncertainty and poverty was a measure of how deeply she had been wounded. If offered the chance, he would have cheerfully cut out the heart of Lord Randolph Lennox and of the Most Noble, the Duke of Durweston, and the anonymous drunken merchant, and every other man who had ever hurt Allie. He took grim satisfaction in the knowledge that he actually had killed George Blakeford.

The entry hall soared thirty feet high, its proportions designed to put mortals in their places. Reggie was greeted by a butler with more dignity than the Archbishop of Canterbury. His chilly eyes flicked over the visitor's travel-stained clothing. "The Duke of Durweston is not receiving."

Reggie pulled out one of his cards and scrawled in pencil *I know where your daughter is.* "Give him this," he told the butler curtly. Durweston would not be far away; it was said that the duke had not left his estate in a decade.

The butler glanced contemptuously at the card. His face grew stiffer, if that was possible. Wordlessly he turned and vanished into the castle depths. He returned within five minutes. "His Grace will see you."

The butler turned and led the way through a series of passages that made Reggie wish he had emulated Theseus and brought a ball of string. Eventually they reached the duke's private audience room, another lofty chamber decorated with a royal ransom in furniture and art.

Durweston himself was seated behind an ornate gilded desk. Any faint hope Reggie had that his Allie was not Lady

Alyson Blakeford died at the sight of that handsome hawk face. This man had to be her father. The duke looked to be in his late sixties, tall and lean and fierce, with a shock of white hair and the expression of a man who is never opposed. He neither rose nor greeted his visitor, merely scanned him with gray-green orbs the exact shade of Allie's right eye.

Refusing to be intimidated, Reggie inclined his head once, then stared back, making his expression faintly bored as he waited for the other man to speak.

The duke's gaze fell to the card on the desk. "Reginald Davenport. I've heard of you. You're a rake, a wastrel, and scoundrel, a disgrace to a fine old family. You learned that my heir George Blakeford died and decided there was an opportunity for profit." The wintry gaze went to Reggie again. "Now you're here like a vulture with a trumped-up tale about my daughter. I am no lamb for the fleecing. My daughter is dead. Get out."

Reggie's anger was tinged with compassion. Over the last dozen years, there would have been others who had come with spurious tales of the missing heiress. Durweston's hopes must have been raised and dashed more than once, making him bitter and wary. But he must still have hope that his daughter was alive, or he would not have admitted a stranger. The duke craved news of his only child; he wanted to be proved wrong.

Equally cool, Reggie said, "You're right that I know of George Blakeford's death. In fact, I shot him myself, with a Baker rifle. One bullet through the heart."

"Good God, you're the one who killed him?" Durweston stared at him in amazement, his composure pierced. "It came as no surprise to hear that George died in a brawl, but I have trouble believing that even a man like you would come here to boast about it. You're either a murderer or a madman, Davenport." A strong, bony hand reached for the bell cord. "Probably both."

"I killed Blakeford because he was doing his level best to put a knife in a woman called Alys Weston," Reggie said tersely. "He seemed to think Alys is your daughter."

The duke's hand halted in midair. Then, a tremor in the long fingers, his hand returned to the desk. "Tell me about this Alys Weston."

"She's the steward of my estate, Strickland, which lies between Dorchester and Shaftesbury," Reggie said crisply. "She's a couple of inches under six feet tall and has bright brown hair, improbable dimples, and a figure like Diana the Huntress. She is thirty years old, was born on All Hallows Eve, and she has the stubborn pride of Lucifer."

With clinical detachment Reggie watched the duke's craggy face quiver, as if from an internal earthquake, then added the clincher. "Her eyes are two different colors, the left one brown, the right gray-green."

"My daughter is dead." Blue veins stood out on the backs of Durweston's hands as his grip tightened on the tooled leather surface of the desk. "Don't think you can pass off an imposter. I would know instantly."

"And Great Britain is overrun with six-foot tall females with mismatched eyes," Reggie said ironically. "Very well, if you don't want her, I'll keep her for myself." He pivoted on his heel and headed toward the massive door.

"Wait!"

Reggie hesitated, then turned back. Having decided to come here, he must finish what he had begun.

Durweston had risen to his feet, his face working convulsively. "Alyson never would have stayed away so long."

"Then you can't have known her very well," Reggie said coolly. "When she wanted to end her betrothal, you refused to support her. You said she was no daughter of yours, and locked her in her room. Not surprisingly, she felt that you had betrayed her. That you wouldn't want her to come back."

White-faced, Durweston sagged back into his chair. "Only she and I knew what happened that night," he whispered. He waved at a chair with a shaking hand. "Sit down. Please."

The duke looked so stricken that Reggie wondered if he should ring for help, but after a minute the old man's color improved. "Do you know why she refused to marry Lord Randolph?"

"Yes, but if you want to learn the reason, you'll have to ask her yourself."

Durweston nodded, accepting that. "You say she's your steward, of all the outlandish things. How did that come to happen? She ran off with her groom."

"She ran off alone," Reggie corrected. "Her groom, Jamie Palmer, followed her to make sure that she took no harm."

Briefly he explained how Alys had taught, then governessed, and finally chanced into the position of steward. He also mentioned the radical reforms that she had instituted on his estate, and that she was guardian of three young people.

As Reggie spoke, disbelief melted away in the duke's face. He must know his daughter well enough to believe that not another woman in England would have behaved in quite the same way.

Silence followed Reggie's explanation, until Durweston asked, "Is she a good steward?"

"The best."

A flicker of smile lightened the duke's face before he returned to brooding. "Why didn't she come home?" he asked. "She knows I don't mean half of what I say when I'm angry." Vulnerability sat oddly on that arrogant face.

"She was badly hurt," Reggie said quietly. "After that, pride took over. I daresay you can understand that."

Durweston gave an infinitesimal nod. "Will . . . will she come home?"

"I think so, but you must go to her. She will never come to you."

The duke's face hardened. "Does she expect me to crawl to her?"

Suddenly weary of a man whose pride stood in the way even now, Reggie snapped, "She expects nothing. She doesn't even know I'm here." He stood. "Allie said that her father never apologized or admitted fault. Obviously she knew her man. It was a mistake to come."

"Davenport." Durweston spoke gruffly, hating the truth in his visitor's words. "You say that she's at your estate, Strickland. That's in Dorsetshire?"

Davenport nodded. Durweston said, "I'll be there in four days. How much do you want for your information?"

Davenport's cool blue eyes could have chipped flint. "Keep your money. Just treat Allie better in the future than you have in the past."

Durweston hated Davenport at that moment, hated him for being strong and virile, in the prime of life, hated him for having had Alyson's company when her own father had been alone in his luxurious mausoleum.

More than any of that, the duke hated himself for having driven her away. "What is my daughter to you, Davenport?" he said harshly. "Your mistress, and now you've tired of her?"

No longer cool, Davenport's eyes blazed with fury, his body taut and dangerous. In a remote corner of his brain, the Duke of Durweston knew that he stood closer to death than at any time since his own wild, risk-filled youth. His visitor looked ready to cross the room and do murder with his bare hands.

Instead, after a Herculean effort to control himself, Davenport said in a soft, whip-edged voice, "Your daughter is what she has always been. A lady."

Then he turned and walked out the door.

Hard at work in her office and not expecting Reggie back for days, Alys paid no attention to the sound of a single horse cantering into the yard. She was vaguely aware of the booming hooves of a team pulling a vehicle several hours later, but dismissed that as a loaded dray, since a delivery of timber was expected for the cottage construction.

Hence it was a complete surprise when her office door opened, and she looked up to see Reggie's unmistakable form outlined against the early afternoon sunlight. Her heart leaped with delight, then paused when there was no sign of welcome in his posture.

When he entered, her gaze was so intent on him that she did not even see the man at his heels, not until Reggie said flatly, "You have a visitor."

Alys glanced over to the tall old man, and froze. Throat tight, she whispered, "Father?" not believing the message of her own eyes.

His hair had become pure white, and there were new, harsh lines in his face, but his height and upright carriage had not changed. Eyes suspiciously bright, he said in a voice on the edge of breaking, "Isn't it about time you came home, girl?"

Then she believed. She stumbled to her feet, knocking over her chair in her haste, and hurled herself into her father's embrace. She barely noticed when Reggie faded out of the office, giving father and daughter privacy for their reunion.

Alys wept as her father held her, whispering, "I'm sorry, child, so sorry." No more apology was needed, on either side.

The next half hour was a jumble of confused impressions and babble, where pieces of the past were fitted together, until the duke said, "If we leave in the next hour, we can be in London tomorrow evening."

"London?" Alys repeated, not understanding.

"I assume you prefer to visit there before returning to Carleon." Her father's gaze touched the plain gown she wore for a day in the office. "You'll want a proper wardrobe, and I want to show my daughter off. A pity it's summer— company in town will be rather thin. But we can come back later for the Little Season."

She stared at him. "But Strickland is my home. I have a position here, responsibilities."

"Good God, do you think work for hire is proper for the next Duchess of Durweston?" He waved his hand at her office. "If you want to run an estate, there's all of Carleon to manage. I'll not stand in your way or countermand your orders." A slight smile hovered. "At least, I'll try not to."

Alys would have laughed at his afterthought if her emotions were not in such turmoil. Leave Strickland and the life she had built for herself? Leave Reggie? "But there are the boys," she faltered. "And I have a contract. I can't just walk away."

"That's all taken care of," the duke said impatiently. "Naturally, your wards come with us. I understand there are only two boys now that you managed to catch Lord Markham's heir for the girl. Quite a feat of generalship, girl. You're wasted here. You need a wider field of endeavor." He shook his head admiringly. "As for your contract, Davenport has already released you from all obligations."

Her father paused, then said grudgingly, "Hate to admit it, but I misjudged the man. When he came to Carleon, I thought he was running a rig, but he wouldn't take a penny. He's behaved just as he ought."

The duke stopped speaking abruptly. He had a lively suspicion that Davenport had not always behaved just as he ought to Lady Alyson Blakeford, but it was a topic best left alone. No matter what she had done in the last dozen years, no one in the *ton* would dare cut the heir to Durweston.

Alys was still trying to assimilate her father's words. "Reggie went to Carleon? That's how you found me?" When her father nodded, she asked in bewilderment, "How did he discover who I was?"

"I have no idea." Durweston eyed her narrowly and decided to hurry her along. Though Davenport had behaved like a gentleman so far, the duke had a lively distrust of the man's influence over his daughter. "Best get to your packing."

Alys stood. "I must talk to Reggie myself."

"Davenport thought you'd say that. He's in the house."

Outside, Peter and William had been drawn by the sight of the magnificent Durweston traveling carriage. They stared at her as she crossed the yard. "Are you really the daughter of a duke?" Peter asked incredulously.

The news certainly was spreading fast. "Yes." Correctly interpreting the boys' expressions, she said firmly, "I haven't changed, you know. I'm still your guardian. You still have to do your lessons and"—a speaking glance at William—"wash behind your ears."

William grinned, reassured. He had less understanding of what it meant to be Lady Alyson Blakeford. But Peter knew. Face bleak, he said, "You're leaving us."

Her heart twisted. The boys had lost too many people in their life. Peter was looking at her as if she was gone already. "Absolutely not." She put a hand on his shoulder. "I don't know quite what is going to happen, but I promise that if I go, you and William go with me."

If I go . . . But she didn't want to leave! Swallowing hard, she continued, "You've always wanted to see London. Wouldn't you like that?"

Convinced that he was not going to be abandoned, a wide smile crossed Peter's face. "That would be smashing!"

William looked less convinced, but before he could speak, Alys said again, "I must speak with Reggie." Her father had come up behind her, so she introduced him to the boys and escaped to the manor house while the males were sizing each other up.

Mrs. Herald met her in the front hall, staring as if Alys had suddenly sprouted purple feathers. "Is it true, Lady Alys?" she asked, round-eyed. "That you really *are* Lady Alys, I mean?"

"Yes, it's true," she said impatiently. "Where is Mr. Davenport?"

"In the library, your ladyship." It would be inaccurate to say that May Herald was awed—she was not a woman easily awed—but she was impressed. The daughter of a duke, and a female that would be a duchess in her own right! It was a story Strickland would never forget.

To the housekeeper, Lady Alyson Blakeford was already history.

Of course he would be in the library, scene of so many high and low points in their relationship. That is, if they had a relationship. Her face stiff, Alys entered to find Reggie sitting in his favorite chair, cleaning his pipe.

He glanced up as Nemesis trotted over to greet Alys. The collie sniffed her cold hand, then gave it a sympathetic lick. Her fingers curled involuntarily.

There was a long silence as they stared at each other. She searched his face for some sign that he wanted her, that he even remembered that night of shared loving, but his long face was expressionless.

Tightly she asked, "How did you find out who I was?"

"When you told me about your past, it jogged some things I had heard about Durweston's missing heir." He shrugged. "It wasn't hard to put the pieces together."

So her own confidences had led to this. Passionately she wished that she had said nothing, no matter how much relief confession had given her.

But if he really wanted to get rid of her, he could have found other ways. This just happened to be convenient. Though she tried to speak evenly, her voice broke as she asked, "Do you want me to go?"

"You don't belong here." Neither his face nor his voice showed a shred of emotion.

She couldn't believe it, could not accept that what was between them had been purely physical. That since he'd had her once, he did not want her near him.

But what did she know of such things? Her judgment about men in the past had been dreadful. It was right in keeping for her to couple with an avowed rake who went through women like a dandy used starched cravats, then be fool enough to dream of love.

As she watched blindly, he stood and crossed to the French doors. With one hand on the knob, he turned to her, a tall, lean silhouette, his features invisible as he stood in front of the light. "Good-bye, Allie. Don't ever be ashamed of what you are."

"Reggie!" It was a cry from the heart, but he was already gone. She stared at the glass doors in disbelief before numbly crossing to look after him. He stopped by the carriage and talked to the boys for a few moments before shaking Peter's hand. Less inhibited, William gave him a fierce hug. Then Reggie walked away, and she could see no more.

You don't belong here. If he didn't want her, there was no point in staying, no way she *could* stay. But how could she leave when the very thought sent a knife thrust of anguish through her? Alys gulped for breath, fighting the grief that threatened to break in wrenching, uncontrollable sobs.

The pride that had kept her going through long, lonely years came to her rescue. She was Lady Alyson Blakeford.

Someday she would be the fifth Duchess of Durweston. She would not stay where she was not wanted, nor would she cry. *She would not cry.*

Outside the library she met Mrs. Herald and gave crisp orders to pack everything belonging to her, Merry, and the boys. Then she went outside and informed Peter and William that they were leaving for London immediately.

It was frighteningly simple to pack up a whole life. In the weeks since the fire, there had been no time to accumulate belongings. She considered going to her office, where account books were still lying open on her desk, but dismissed the thought. Reggie said he didn't need her, so he could damn well sort everything out on his own.

Depressingly, she knew that he would have no problems, apart from having less time for his horses. Her records were always ordered, and by this time he knew almost as much about Strickland as she did. The bailiff was reliable for supervising the field hands. Even the pottery was running smoothly and starting to show a profit.

She only said one good-bye, and that was to Jamie Palmer. She found him in the barn, repairing harness. Unsurprised, he glanced up. "So you're going home, Lady Alys. It's time."

She looked at him, so solid and kind, and wanted to climb in his lap and cry. He was the one friend she had always been able to count on. "Do you want to go back to Carleon, Jamie?"

He shook his head. "Annie wouldn't like it. Her family is here, and now it's my home, too. You don't need me anymore."

She almost did cry then, but didn't, since it would have distressed Jamie no end. He had never seen her cry. "Thank you, Jamie, from the bottom of my heart. For everything. I'll never have a better friend." She offered her hand. "You'll keep an eye on the pottery and let me know if there are any problems?"

"Aye." He bobbed his head gravely before shaking her hand. "You'll not be coming back for a visit?"

Her mouth tightened to a thin line. "I don't think so."

Half an hour later they left in a rumble of wheels and hooves while a hastily gathered crowd bid her good-bye. As they headed north toward the Shaftesbury road, she did not look back.

He posted himself in a clump of beeches on a hill overlooking the long drive. In no time at all, the splendid carriage was rattling down the tree-lined road, raising a cloud of dust in the dry afternoon. William's pony and Alys's mare trotted behind on their tethers. He stared at the carriage avidly, wishing he could see her just once more, and knowing what a stupid, futile wish it was.

The carriage curved around the bend and out of sight, and suddenly he was running down the hill, crashing through the underbrush, racing at full speed until he reached a place where he could see the next loop of road. He made it barely in time, his limbs trembling with fatigue and his breath burning in his lungs. The gleaming black carriage was visible for one last instant before disappearing around the bend.

She was gone.

Numbly he turned and began walking in no particular direction, unready to return to the empty house. She was gone, and it was entirely his choice. He could have stayed silent and kept her if he'd wanted to. All it would have meant was separating her from her heritage, her father, and her fortune.

Why the hell did sobriety have to make him so damned noble?

It was after dark when he wearily returned to the manor house. Attila was in the front hall, prowling back and forth in agitation. Mrs. Herald heard Reggie enter and came to greet him. "Attila was nowhere to be found when they left. Lady Alys asked that you make sure he's cared for."

"Of course," Reggie said woodenly.

As he went upstairs to change, Attila darted past in a flash of fur, then came to a halt outside the room that had been Alys's. Reggie opened the door. The cat went in, whiskers and nose twitching as he sniffed about looking for some sign of his vanished mistress. Finally he jumped on the bare bed and yowled plaintively.

"I know exactly how you feel, old boy," Reggie muttered. Then he headed toward his own room. He would simply have to learn to live without her.

Surely there must be a way.

Chapter 25

Lady Alyson Blakeford could do no wrong. Head high and all banners flying, she did not flinch from being noticed. Alys found a certain ironic amusement in her change in status. In Dorset, she had been respected. In London, she was very nearly worshipped.

Town was quiet, with most of the *beau monde* in Brighton or other fashionable resorts. The arrival of the long-secluded Duke of Durweston and his prodigal daughter caught the attention of everyone who was left. In fact some members of the *ton*, scenting excitement, hastened back to London. Intimate little gatherings were held to reintroduce her ladyship to People Who Mattered.

A lavish new wardrobe was ordered and delivered almost overnight since the modiste wasn't busy at this season. Duty calls were paid on ancient Durweston connections, who greeted Alys and professed themselves delighted to see the gel again. She could almost hear the sounds of mental wheels spinning as they examined her and speculated on possible marriage partners. Despite her advanced years, she was still—again—the greatest heiress in England.

The magnificent pile known as Durweston House was opened for the first time in a decade. It looked exactly as it had a dozen years earlier when Alys had her Season; apparently nothing so plebian as dust was allowed within those august precincts.

But she had changed. Lord, how she had changed! She no longer cared what a lot of fashionable fribbles thought of her. When she swept confidently into a room, splendidly gowned and the tallest woman present, she held every eye.

It was all monstrously dull.

The only real pleasure came in expeditions with the boys to the Tower, Astley's Circus, and other such vulgar amusements. To everyone's surprise, the duke accompanied them and showed every evidence of enjoyment.

With a faint pang of unworthy jealousy, Alys watched her father's growing friendships with Peter and William. The duke had always wanted a son. She had never managed to be that, though heaven knew she had tried.

But there was no question that her father was overjoyed to be reunited with his daughter. They cautiously began to reestablish much of their old closeness. As they did, an ache that had been part of Alys for so long that she no longer consciously noticed it finally went away.

Not even that was worth the loss of Reggie.

Strickland was staggeringly empty, ten times as empty as it had been when Reggie had first returned. Amazing how quickly he had become used to having other people there. He missed the young Spensers and their laughter and occasional squabbles, but mostly he missed Allie.

Fortunately the harvest had begun. That kept him busy, even though the excellent bailiff supervised routine work. There were invitations from the local gentry who wanted to hear firsthand of Alys's ascension to a higher place. It was all rather biblical.

Reggie accepted some invitations, mostly to fill up

empty hours of the evenings when he missed her most sharply. Once those hours would have been filled with liquor, but he was determined not to go back to that, no matter how desperately lonely he was.

Much of his evening time was spent playing the piano-forte. He regained his youthful skill and went beyond, which was a source of great satisfaction. And the concentration needed acted as a kind of drug for forgetting.

Attila and Nemesis had taken to sleeping on Reggie's bed. He supposed that his acquiescence was a sign of his de-clining standards. Irritable at Alys's continuing absence, Attila would occasionally pick a fight with Nemesis by biting the collie's tail or sinking a pawful of claws into her tender nose. Nemesis would yelp reproachfully and go to sleep again.

Even when irritable, Attila knew better than to bite Reggie.

A week after their arrival in London, the duke took the boys to Tattersall's. Females were not welcome within the holy sanctuary of horse selling, so Alys took the opportunity to write letters.

She was puzzled when the butler entered her sitting room with an engraved card on a silver salver. It was too early in the day for formal calls. She glanced at the card. *Lord Randolph Lennox.*

A tidal wave of panic and insecurity swept over her. She had known that sooner or later their paths would cross, since Lord Randolph and her father were friends. But not *this* soon. She wasn't ready yet!

She would never be ready to face Randolph again. For a moment she considered refusing to see him. Then she squared her shoulders. Hadn't she decided that his rejection no longer had the power to hurt her? She was no longer so sure, but it was essential to face him.

Nervously she checked her appearance in a pier glass. She wore a rich, terra-cotta–colored morning gown that flattered her figure with demure provocation. The severe coronet was gone, replaced by a fashionable tumble of curls and waves. After a critical appraisal, Alys decided that she was creditably attractive. But not beautiful. Only once, the morning after she had made love with Reggie, had she been beautiful.

Randolph was waiting in the gold parlor. She paused in the doorway and they studied each other, neither of them speaking.

Her former fiancé stood an inch or so taller than Alys, with hair like dark burnished gold and the beautifully proportioned face and figure found in classical sculpture. He was impeccably dressed, and the years had only improved his looks, adding maturity to the handsomeness he'd had a dozen years earlier.

With a small shock, Alys realized that he had been only twenty-one when they were betrothed, just a boy. She had never thought of him as young.

"Alyson?"

His soft voice had a questioning note, and it broke Alys's abstraction. "Hello, Randolph." She smiled and offered her hand, determined to carry this off in a civilized fashion, as if a dozen years of anguish didn't lie between them. "Am I so changed that you can't recognize me?"

Randolph returned her smile with relief, and she realized that he was as nervous as she. How strange.

He crossed the room and kissed her hand, then continued to hold it as he straightened up. "You look marvelous, Alyson. It's wonderful to see you again."

Alys pulled her hand away. "What, a Long Meg like me, ten feet tall, all bones and bossy? Of course, there is still the fortune." Then she winced, aghast. So much for being civilized. She had not meant to say those brittle, angry words, and now they hung in the air like the stench of burned flesh.

Randolph shut his eyes, a spasm of emotion crossing his face. More to himself than her, he whispered, "God help me, that was the reason."

He drew in a deep breath and opened his eyes again. "For the last dozen years I've racked my brain, trying to understand why you ran away. Since your father said you had wanted to break our betrothal just before you left, I feared that you might have heard those words, but I prayed that I was wrong."

For years Lord Randolph had loomed in Alys's mind as a cynical, mocking betrayer. That image crumbled at the sight of his stricken face. She said coolly, "Perhaps we should sit down. It seems that we have matters to discuss."

They chose facing chairs. Alys explained, "I had returned from riding and was just outside the French doors, and heard what your friend said. And I heard your answer." Once more she saw the fluttering draperies and felt the twist of shock in her solar plexus, yet it was all very distant. What she felt now was not pain, but the memory of pain.

Randolph's face tightened. "Of course you thought I agreed with what he said."

"How could I not?" she asked dryly. "I heard you with my own ears. After your claims of love undying, it was rather—unpleasant—to learn that my fortune was my principal attraction."

"It wasn't, you know," he said quietly. "The truth was that I loved you, more than I had ever put into words."

"Ah, yes, who could not love all that beautiful money?" she murmured, an edge of bitterness in her voice. Randolph had a very respectable fortune of his own, or he would never have been acceptable to her father. But her fortune was many times the size of his, and it was often the rich who are the greediest.

He gave a quick, sharp shake of the head. "Alyson, I am a wealthy man in my own right. Oh, no one objects to more money, but I had no reason to marry a girl unless I cared for her deeply. As I did you. You were unlike anyone I'd ever met. Intelligent, enthusiastic, caring about those less fortunate. Amusing, sometimes imperious, more often oblivious to dignity. And so lovely that I could hardly keep my hands off you."

She flushed. "Don't mock me, Randolph. I prefer honest insults to false compliments."

His slate-blue eyes met hers with patent sincerity. "Alyson, I never lied to you. The only dishonest thing you ever heard me say was my answer to Fogarty's stupid question that day."

She took an unsteady breath. Oddly, she believed him. "If you really did care for me, how could you say what you did?" she said in a low voice. She was discovering that remembered pain could still hurt.

He sighed. "I don't know if you can understand this, but young men don't admit to having deep feelings. Lust perhaps, but never love. Most of my friends were amazed that I wanted to get married rather than drown myself in opera dancers. They could have understood better if you had been a conventional golden-haired china doll, but you were different."

Her mouth twisted. "So we're back to ten feet tall, all bones, and unable to keep a man warm at night."

He winced. "You were like a young foal, all legs and great eyes, not yet having found your balance, not at all in the common way," he said, choosing his words carefully. "But to me you were beautiful. I knew that as time passed, you would only become more beautiful. As you have."

Sudden tears stung Alys's eyes. She closed them sharply.

"Are you all right?" Randolph said, concerned.

"I'm fine." She bit her lip, then opened her eyes. "You're

very convincing. But, then"—her tone hardened—"you always were."

A muscle jerked in his handsome jaw. "I suppose I deserve that."

Nervously she brushed back her hair. "Why, Randolph? Why did you tell your friend you were marrying me for money when he asked why you were doing it?"

"Because it was a reason he could understand." He sighed. "Fogarty would have laughed at me if I had tried to explain how I felt about you. Love makes one vulnerable. It was hard enough to tell you about my deepest feelings. Revealing them to a doltish male friend was impossible."

Alys regarded him with wonder. "It was as simple as that?"

"As simple as that," he agreed with a smile that held no humor.

Alys stared unseeing across the chamber. It was impossible to disbelieve Randolph. Even though a dozen years had passed, it couldn't have been easy for him to come here and expose himself in this way. "I don't know whether this is tragedy or farce. My whole life was changed by hearing an insult that wasn't even intended."

"You spent a dozen years in exile because in a moment of weakness, I denied my own heart," Randolph said, his expression bleak. "I'll never forgive myself for that. Nor do I expect you to forgive me. All of these years I've feared that it was my words that sent you away. It's almost a relief to know the worst."

He got to his feet. "I can't imagine that you'll want to see me again. I spend much of my time in the country, so I should be able to stay out of your path. I'm sorry, Alyson. That's hardly adequate for having ruined your life, but . . . it's the best I can do."

Alys stood also. "Don't run away. Have some tea."

Before he could object, she rang for refreshments, then

waved him back to the chair. As she assimilated Randolph's words, her predominant emotions were relief and an up-swelling of confidence. One man finding her lovely and desirable could be attributable to insanity or perverse taste, but two men had made such statements recently. She couldn't believe they were both mad. Between them, they were healing the crippling blow to her self-esteem that had occurred a dozen years earlier.

She seated herself again. "You were not solely responsible for me haring off the way I did. My father is at least as much to blame. And looking back, it was rather bird-witted of me to run away." She gave him a rueful grin. "Once I did, the pride of the Blakefords took over. I would have died rather than come back and admit that I was wrong. If a . . . friend hadn't interceded, I would not be here today."

The tea arrived. She paused to pour them each a cup and offer a plate of delicate pastries to Randolph, who was much more at ease than when he had arrived. After a blissful bite—her father kept the best chefs in Britain—she said, "You can also disabuse yourself of the notion that you ruined my life. Mind you, I have no desire to go back to being a history mistress, but experiencing the world outside the golden bars of Carleon has vastly improved me."

He regarded her gravely. "Are you saying that just to make me feel better?"

"Not in the least." Alys reached for another pastry, then decided against it. She was going to have to be careful about such things now that she wasn't as active. She gave him a mischievous smile. "Do I look ruined?"

He gave a long, slow smile. "You look splendid, and you have grown into the remarkable woman I always knew you would be."

If Alys had been the sort of female who could toss her head coquettishly, she would have done so. Regretfully she decided that it simply wasn't her style. She would have to learn how to accept compliments with dignity. She poured more tea. "Now that all that ancient history has been disposed of, tell me about yourself, Randolph. Surely you are married now, with a family."

"No. For years I hoped that you would return. I couldn't really look at another woman." A shadow crossed his face. "I finally gave up and married four years ago. She died in childbirth."

"I'm so sorry," Alys said with compassion. Perhaps Randolph's momentary lapse had ruined his life more than hers. She changed the subject, and they drifted into easy conversation, with Alys describing some of the more amusing aspects of her working career. Randolph made an appreciative and admiring audience.

When he finally took his leave, he paused at the door, his handsome face intent. "I don't suppose that it is possible to begin again."

He had kind eyes. Alys studied him for a moment, then shook her head. "It would have worked then, but not now."

He nodded, kissed her hand with regret, and left.

Filled with gentle nostalgia, Alys went up to her chamber. Randolph was a thoroughly nice gentleman who was born to make some lucky woman a good and loving husband. She hoped that his luck would improve in the future.

Of one thing she was sure: he would be wasted on a woman who had a regrettable preference for rakes.

Alys was brushing out her hair in preparation for going to bed when she heard a tap on the door. Guessing that it was her eldest ward, who had just returned from visiting her future in-laws, she called, "Come in, Merry."

Meredith, exquisite in a blue velvet dressing gown, entered and made herself comfortable in the wing chair. "I had a good visit with the Markhams, but it's nice to be home."

She smiled mischievously. "Home is defined by where you are, since I never set foot in Durweston House before today. Or dreamed of doing so, either!"

Alys smiled, touched by her ward's definition of home. "Would you like to be married from here? That should impress Julian's family."

"It's definitely worth considering. I'll write Julian and see what he thinks." Merry made a face. "But much as I look forward to marriage, I'm going to miss our talks."

Alys would, too. So much of her life had changed, and so quickly. With a sigh she perched on the bed and began braiding her hair. "Tell me more about your visit."

Merry obliged. She and Julian had also visited the estate at Moreton, where they would live after their marriage, and she was bubbling with ideas for what they would do there. All Alys had to do was nod and make an occasional comment, until Merry asked, "When are you going back to Strickland?"

Alys drew her long legs up and wrapped her arms around her knees in an unconscious reaction to the question. "I'm not going back."

"Of course you're going back," Merry retorted. "What will Reggie do without you?"

"He doesn't want me there." Alys tried to sound casual, but her voice broke on the words. "He made that quite clear."

Merry looked at her guardian in astonishment. "And you *believed* him?"

"What else could I do?" Alys asked stiffly. "He never wanted to have a female steward in the first place. He's quite capable of running the estate himself."

Merry gave her a pitying look. "What has that to do with it? The man is mad about you. He may not need you as a steward, but he certainly does as a woman."

Alys's emotions were very raw, and to her horror she found herself on the edge of tears. As she bowed her head,

Merry moved to the bed and put a comforting arm around her guardian—something of a stretch—in a reversal of their usual roles.

"If he needs me that much," Alys managed to say, "why did he tell me I didn't belong there?"

"Misplaced nobility," Merry said calmly.

When Alys raised her head in surprise, the younger woman continued, "Alys, you are the cleverest, most capable woman I've ever met, but your judgment about men is lamentable. Because Reggie really cares about you, he is bending over backward to do the right thing. Given his lurid reputation and your exalted breeding, that translates into removing himself from the picture so you can find a mate more worthy of you."

"Nonsense," Alys snapped.

"Oh? Think about it."

Alys opened her mouth to protest again, then stopped. Actually, her instincts had said that she and Reggie shared something magical, and that the caring was not only on her side. Then she'd revealed enough for him to guess her identity, and everything had changed. Given her terrible doubts about her desirability, she had dismissed her instincts as wrong.

She frowned. Would he really think himself unworthy of her? She considered how the world would view such a match, and decided that it was entirely possible. Perhaps she had been too easily persuaded to leave.

She turned to her ward, eyes narrowed. "Are you really, really sure that Reggie cares about me as . . . as more than just a friend?"

"I guarantee it. As you've said more than once, I was born understanding men. The way he looked at you when you were absorbed in other things . . ." Merry shook her head. "It was like you were his last hope of heaven."

"Really?" Alys asked in amazement.

"As God is my witness," Merry said solemnly. "When you were around, there was a kind of . . . intentness, as if half of his attention was always turned to you. To be honest, I always felt that he was only a step away from sweeping you up to his room and locking the door for a week."

Alys blushed. Reggie had said as much himself. "You shouldn't be speaking of such things," she said automatically as she struggled with her thoughts.

"I'm on the verge of marriage," Merry pointed out. "I'm practicing how to sound like a wicked wife."

Alys had to smile, but it faded quickly. Good heavens, if Merry was right, what about Reggie's drinking? If he was lonely and miserable, might he return to it? It didn't bear thinking about, not after what he had suffered to stop. She jumped from the bed and went to her clothespress.

As she opened a drawer, Merry said, "What on earth are you doing?"

"Packing to go back to Strickland."

Laughing affectionately, Merry said, "You can't leave in the middle of the night."

Alys paused. "I could, but I suppose I shouldn't. I must talk to my father, among other things. Tomorrow morning should be soon enough." She prayed that it would be.

Meredith rolled onto her stomach and rested her chin on her folded hands, now more the tomboy than the young lady. "Do I need to give you any hints on how to persuade Reggie to a proper acceptance of the inevitable?"

Alys smiled. "No need. If you're sure he really wants me, I have a few methods of persuasion myself."

Meredith nodded with approval. Now that Alys had been put on the scent, Reggie hadn't a chance of escape. Not that he would want to.

* * *

The Duke of Durweston was not pleased by his daughter's announcement that she was returning to Strickland for a visit of indefinite length. "It's Davenport, isn't it?" he asked gruffly. They were meeting in his office, a chamber that the Sun King himself would have felt at home in.

"Yes. I left much too abruptly." Alys paced across her father's office, impatient to be on her way. "Reggie and I have unfinished business."

"How can you throw yourself at a rake, Alyson, a man with the most sordid of reputations?" the duke snapped. "Have you no pride?"

She considered. "In general, yes. Where Reggie is concerned, not much."

His mouth thinned into a hard line. "Will he marry you?"

She pulled on her gloves. "I hope so, but I wouldn't insist on it."

Perhaps that was too much candor; her father turned the color of aged port wine. "I can disinherit you, you know," he growled. "The title and entail only go to a daughter if her father thinks her worthy of receiving it. I always thought George Blakeford's younger brother would make a decent duke, and he is next in line."

"Choosing an heir is your affair." She met his gray-green eyes with her own steely gaze. "I walked away from all this"—she waved her hand at the luxury around them—"once before. I've proved I am capable of supporting myself comfortably. Do you really think I am more likely to bow to your will at thirty than I was at eighteen?"

Her father's face was a study in conflicting emotions. Taking pity on him, she went to his chair and kissed him lightly on the forehead. "Father, don't let us become estranged over this. I have missed you too much."

He blinked rapidly. "I've missed you, too, girl. But why can't you marry someone like Lord Randolph? He's a fine man, and he'd renew his proposal in a minute if you were willing."

"I know, but he's much too nice for me." She gave a teasing smile. "I'd keep him under the cat's paw for sure."

"He wouldn't mind."

"No, but I would. I don't want a husband I can dominate, any more than I want one who will try to bully me." She looked at her father sternly. "You just don't like Reggie because he's too much like you. I've heard the stories about your wild youth. Except for the difference of a million pounds or so, you two are like peas in a pod."

"Don't try to turn me up sweet, girl." The duke snorted and tried with limited success to suppress a smile. "And a million pounds is a substantial difference."

"*Substantial*, yes," she admitted, "but not *significant*."

She gave her father a good-bye kiss, then sailed out. She wasn't going to let it be significant, and that was that.

Chapter 26

Going without Allie was rather like stopping drinking, only worse. The pleasures of the bottle had been limited, the punishment almost immediate. With Allie, the pleasures had been infinitely varied, from the rarified to the earthily sensual, and if there was a negative aspect, he hadn't discovered it.

Reggie was dining alone, and even a hard day of physical labor didn't give him much appetite for the roast fowl. Pushing his plate aside, he absently began to eat a dish of raspberry fool. He was going to have to do better with his eating, or the cook would be insulted. Feeding two boys who approached every meal like a biblical plague of locusts had spoiled her.

He smiled a little at the thought, but levity immediately vanished, replaced by a great heaviness of spirit. Helping Allie heal the breach with her father was one of the few entirely unselfish things he had ever done. He hoped that virtue would prove to be its own reward, because there weren't any others.

Abandoning his dinner, he headed for the music room. Playing the piano was usually a good distraction. He reminded himself that the first few weeks of sobriety had been the worst, but after that things had become easier. Surely in time Allie's loss would also become easier to bear.

It hadn't yet.

After two days rattling around the inside of the coach, Alys was tired and rumpled and questioning the wisdom of this mad trip. She stopped at the Silent Woman and booked the best room so she could rest and freshen up. Though she had flatly refused her father's offer of outriders, the crested Durweston traveling carriage was still the grandest equipage ever seen at the modest inn. She was recognized, of course, and time was wasted in greeting people, since she didn't want to appear too proud to talk to old friends.

After a short nap and a light meal, she prepared to go to Strickland. It was nearly dark, and a respectable female would have waited until morning, but she was in the process of abandoning all claims to respectability. Besides, her sense of urgency was too great. She could never have rested knowing that Reggie was only a few miles away.

Since she was acting like a scarlet woman, she had decided to dress like one. She'd brought her newly acquired French maid, who was a skilled hairstylist, and her carefully chosen gown was bittersweet red, a rich, subtle color that made her skin and hair glow. After donning the gown, she examined herself in the mirror.

"Madame looks *magnifique,*" her maid said admiringly.

"Madame looks like a strumpet," Alys said dryly.

"*Oui,* but a lady at the same time," the maid said, eyes twinkling. "Only the finest of modistes can do both in one garment."

The maid was right—the gown was a triumph of the art of provocation. The silk was simply cut, clinging and swirling over the curves of breast and hip and thigh. Not only was the neckline extremely low, but Alys had ordered the modiste to put a knee-high slit in one side seam. She had been thinking of Reggie when she ordered the dress. Duke's daughter or not, she wasn't sure she was brave enough to wear such a revealing gown in public. It made her figure, never demure, look positively indecent.

Alys inhaled deeply and wriggled a bit, then nodded in satisfaction at the result. She looked her best. If Reggie thought her half as attractive as he claimed, he would never be able to resist her in the red dress. And if he could resist . . . well, she would take stronger measures.

An hour of Mozart did nothing to quiet Reggie's restlessness. Impatient and irritable, he closed the pianoforte and stalked off to the library.

The evening was unusually chilly, so he knelt at the hearth and methodically built a fire. Most Britons would be aghast at having a fire before November, no matter what the temperature, but he could afford it. Small indulgences were compensation for what he didn't have. A very feeble compensation.

He tried to lose himself in *The Aeneid*—he'd always rather identified with the roguish Aeneas—but tonight none of the usual distractions helped. The lonely, empty hours stretched endlessly in front of him. Tomorrow would be just the same, unless it was worse.

What was the point? *What was the bloody point?* He ran his hands through his hair, then pulled his coat off and tossed it aside, edgy and uncomfortable in his own skin. A glass or two of brandy would help him through the night.

It wouldn't stop with a glass or two.

So what if it didn't? So what if he did drink himself to death? Who would be hurt? There was no Alys here to injure, or look stricken at what he was doing to himself. And one of the housemaids, Daisy or some such, had been eyeing him with interest. She was rather tall and had brown hair. If he was drunk enough, perhaps he could imagine, at least for a few moments, that she was Allie. . . .

Oh, God, Allie . . .

A shudder went through him, chilling him to the bone. Then he pushed himself violently from his chair and stalked to the liquor cabinet. Not allowing himself to think about what he was doing, he lifted the Venetian glass decanter that replaced the one he had broken and poured a generous four fingers of brandy. Then he tilted the goblet and watched the play of light through the amber fluid as he prolonged the anticipation. The brandy glowed like topaz. Sweet poison. Sweet surcease.

As he lifted the goblet, Nemesis raised her head and whimpered from her station by his chair. "What's the matter, don't you approve?" He tilted the glass toward the collie in a mocking salute. "Here's to all well-intentioned females, and the men who aren't good enough for them."

Then he raised the glass to his lips.

Having left her maid at the inn and her carriage and coachman in the stables, Alys quailed at the prospect of marching up to the front door. In spite of her boldness in coming here, she found that her new confidence was a fragile growth.

It would be best to check and see what Reggie was doing. It was full dark now, and the best lit room in the house was the library. Perhaps he had company. Perhaps he had another woman there—Cousin George's Stella must be in need of a new protector. Maybe Reggie had imported a whole damned harem. Even if he missed her, she doubted that monastic suffering was his style.

Walking softly around the house, she went to the library

French doors. Luckily, the draperies hadn't been drawn, so she could see inside.

Reggie was there, alone. For a moment she simply admired the sight of him as he leaned against the mantel. He had removed coat and cravat and was in his shirtsleeves, all lithe power and dark male beauty.

Then he raised his arm. With a chill that iced her bones, she realized that his long fingers were wrapped around a goblet filled with a liquid the unmistakable color of brandy.

The cool touch of glass on his lips revived his common sense. Sweet Jesus, what was he doing?

Reggie lowered the goblet and stared at it. Anyone with the sense God gave a goose should know that drinking from loneliness would be a mistake of major proportions. He hadn't gotten sober for Allie's sake, or to live up to his parents' hopes, or for anyone else. He had done it for himself, for his own pride and dignity.

No, it hadn't been for pride. Pride was how one behaved when others were watching. Honor was what a man did when there was no one else to see. If he knew that he was going to die tomorrow, he would still not seek oblivion in drink. Whatever his life might hold in the future, for the sake of honor he would see it through sane and sober. And though he missed Allie hideously, he was not truly alone, had not been so since that night he had broken and been reborn.

With a fierce twist of his wrist, he tossed the brandy into the fire. Blue flames blazed up from the liquor. Then he carefully placed the empty goblet on the mantel. There would be no more smashed glassware; there had been enough high drama in his life. He was an honorable country gentleman, no more, and he intended to be no less.

As he watched the flames flicker and die, he heard a small sound from the direction of the French doors. He looked up. Then his jaw dropped, and he stared in stunned disbelief as Lady Alyson Blakeford swept into the library.

She was pale, but she offered a cheerful smile. "I'm so glad you threw that brandy away. It's always much easier to talk to you when you're sober."

Attila streaked across the room and began banging against her ankles, making excited yowling noises. She bent over and scratched the tomcat's head affectionately. "I'm glad someone is pleased to see me."

She straightened and removed her dark velvet cloak, laying it over a chair. Underneath she wore a shimmering dark red dress that showed an amazing amount of her splendid figure, and lovingly caressed the rest. Reggie felt himself tense all over. "What are you doing here?" he said harshly.

She strolled over to join him by the fireplace, leaning against the mantel with elaborate casualness. Her shining hair was pulled up loosely in a riot of curls that threatened to come tumbling down at a touch. She was like a grand and delectable confection suitable for a king. She looked like a duchess, not a steward.

Things had been much easier when she'd had hay in her hair.

Realizing that he was staring all too obviously at her lush body, he raised his gaze to her face. Her wide eyes sparkled with mischief, but underneath was uncertainty. "I have a contract with Strickland," she said lightly. "It was very bad of me to go on holiday during the harvest." She reached out and drew a slim finger across the back of his hand, where it lay on the mantelpiece.

Even that light touch almost destroyed his control. He snatched his hand away from her and retreated along the mantel. Building a fire had been a mistake; it was far too hot in the library. In fact, he was ready to go up in flames. "I released you from your contract. For God's sake, Allie, get back to London and live the life you were born to."

"To release me without my consent and without cause is illegal," she said blithely.

She was wearing some subtle cosmetic that made her lips look particularly ripe and kissable. He stared at her mouth, his breathing heavy and irregular. "In that case, you're fired. I'll pay your salary until the contract expires. Now, *go!*"

She dropped all pretense of lightness. "That's not the life I want, Reggie. I would much rather be here at Strickland." She drew a deep breath, which did dramatic things to the minimal bodice of her dress, and still more dramatic things to his loins. "And even more than Strickland, I want you."

He flung away from the fireplace, wishing she had had the grace to stay away rather than come here and make everything so much harder. When he'd put a safe distance between them, he turned to face her.

"Allie, you have a position and fortune that allow you more freedom than any other woman in England. You can do almost anything you want. You can have any man—or as *many* men—as you want," he said bluntly. "You're just on the verge of taking wing and enjoying that freedom. The fact that I gave you your first real lesson on the delights of the flesh doesn't mean you have to spend the rest of your life with me. There is so much more for you to discover."

She cocked her head to one side. "Do you mean that making love can be better than what we did?" she asked with disbelief.

Reggie's face tightened as vivid memories of that night eroded his will even further. "I can't speak for you, but from my point of view, it has never been better," he said quietly. "But it wasn't only sex I was talking about. You can use your fortune and influence to help people on a scale impossible here at Strickland. You can rub elbows with the Prince Regent, or the prime minister or the poet laureate if you choose."

"I can do that no matter where I make my home. Are those the only reasons you went to my father and told him where to find me?" She shifted her stance, and her silk gown flowed across her willowy body, revealing an enticing length of long, shapely leg.

He had known that she had a sensual nature, but now that she no longer believed herself hopelessly unattractive, she could teach Delilah a thing or two. Trying to steady his breathing, Reggie said quietly, "When you spoke of your father, I heard echoes of myself in you. I wasted many of the best years of my life locked in a meaningless feud with a man I hated. I didn't like seeing you do the same with a man you loved."

Alys was deeply moved by his perception and generosity. She was also giddy with relief as she realized that Meredith was right: Reggie was being noble. Surely he could be cured of that.

"You're right. I was letting my life be shaped by anger and pride, and I didn't know myself just how much it was hurting me until the breach with my father was healed. It is far better to live a life shaped by love." Brazen though she might be, it was almost impossible to say the next words. "That's why I'm here," she said haltingly. "Because I love you."

He stood halfway across the room, tall and unyielding. "Don't confuse desire with love. You're a woman of rare passion, and for years that nature has been denied. Don't throw yourself away on me merely because I was the one who helped you find yourself. How long would it be before you became curious about greener pastures? I won't bind you to promises that you won't want to keep."

He was thinking in terms of promises? This was definitely progress. She began walking across the room toward him, her steps slow and provocative. "I am no green girl, Reggie. I don't have to sleep with half the rakes in England before I can properly appreciate what you and I have. Would you be talking this fustian if I were still Alys Weston?"

He was silent for a long moment. "I was on the verge of asking Alys Weston to marry me when I deduced who you really were. But there is an enormous difference between Mr. and Mrs. Davenport, and the Duchess of Durweston and her commoner husband, Mr. Davenport. You can't turn away from your heritage again, Lady Alyson. That cat's out of the bag and won't go back in."

In fact, the cat was still stropping her ankles, Alys realized absently. So Reggie had actually wanted to marry her. How could she get him back to that point? "Is all this nobility because you have too much pride to take a wife who is wealthier than you?"

"That's one factor," he admitted, "but there are others. Good God, Allie, think of what everyone would say! That you were seduced by a fortune hunter who took advantage of your isolation and inexperience to trap you into a disgraceful marriage."

"That might be said," she agreed, "but, in fact, you're the only man I can really trust, because you were interested in me when I wasn't an heiress." She smiled. "Whose reputation are you most concerned about, yours or mine?"

"I'm concerned for both of us, blast it!"

As she covered the last few paces, she shook her head sorrowfully. "I'm disappointed in you, Reggie. What kind of a rake cares what anyone else thinks?"

She stopped directly in front of him and looked up into his aquamarine eyes. "Will you be more agreeable if my father disinherits me? He half threatened to when I said I was coming here."

He stared down at her, raw emotion in his eyes. "Could you bear it if he does disinherit you?"

"Yes," she said flatly. "Could you bear it if he doesn't?"

He let his breath out in an explosive sigh. "I don't know."

Too much money was a problem that could be solved,

she thought. On the more important questions, it was time for a new tack. "Reggie, I am quite ridiculously in love with you." She slowly scanned him, admiring every lean, muscular inch. "And not just for your body, beautiful though that is. I love your honesty and your deplorable humor and the sense of honor you pretend not to have."

She raised her gaze to his, and asked the hardest question of all. "Do you love me?"

He took a shuddering breath. "Of course I do. That's why I don't want to see you make a decision you'll regret."

He didn't move, but his whole body radiated tension, and in his eyes she saw a love and craving as intense as her own. Reggie had always walked a lonely road, living by his own iron code, sustained by pride. Now that pride divided them. Also, perhaps, the small boy who had been shunted aside and taught that his wishes were of no account could not believe it possible that he was loved.

Her heart ached for him. For both of their sakes, she must convince him they belonged together. To overcome the barriers of pride and self-denial, she must return the humor and passion he had given her, as well as offering her own love.

She reached out and deftly unbuttoned his waistcoat, then began on his shirt.

He grabbed her hands between his and held them away from him. "Good God, Allie, what are you doing?"

"Trying to compromise you," she explained. "Then you'll have to marry me, or not have a shred of reputation left."

For a moment he stared. Then his tension dissolved into laughter, his blue eyes brimming with warmth. "You are the most impossible woman I've ever met, and far too much like me for my peace of mind."

Since he had released her, she neatly undid some more buttons, then laid her hand inside his shirt against his chest. His skin burned beneath her touch.

He gasped and trapped her hand against his chest. "My capacity to be noble is limited," he said, deadly serious. "If you don't leave here in the next ten seconds, I am never going to let you go again. The infinity of choices that you have now will be reduced to only those that include me."

"Splendid," she whispered as she tugged his shirt loose with her free hand. "That is exactly what I want."

He held her gaze for one taut, endless moment more. Then he surrendered, crushing her to him as their mouths met with savage hunger.

No longer denied by logic or propriety, the desire that had bound them from the start flared into consuming fire. She gloried in the remembered feel of hard muscle and bone, fierce strength and aching tenderness. There was none of the hesitance of new lovers, but rather an absolute recognition of kindred spirit and yearning flesh, as if they'd known each other for a thousand lifetimes.

Their clothing came off in a tangle of crushed and ripped fabric. Then they lay down together before the fire, and she learned that lovemaking could indeed be better than what they had already shared. Flame and sweetness, gift and demand, they joined with a searing emotional resonance that spiraled them up to new heights and depths and widths of loving.

And when he whispered ragged words of love, the greatest joy of all was knowing that they both had found their homes in the shelter of each other.

Much later they lay drowsing together in front of the fire, covered by her velvet cloak. She smiled dreamily. The first night they had made love, Reggie had said that she deserved better than the library floor, but actually the library floor was an absolutely marvelous place. Attila was curled up against her right side, and from the sound of canine breathing, she guessed that Nemesis was lying by Reggie. A scene of perfect domestic bliss.

Her bittersweet red silk dress would never be the same, not after the way Reggie had torn it off. Well, she was an heiress, and she couldn't think of a better self-indulgence than buying gowns that the man she loved wanted to tear off.

She chuckled at the thought, then explained when Reggie asked what she found so amusing. He laughed, his hand moving in a lazy caress down her body. "For a woman who was convinced that no man could want her a fortnight ago, you have come an incredible distance."

That distance had been the first steps on a journey that would last a lifetime. She studied the relaxed expression on his face, the strong bones sculpted by firelight, and thought that she would dissolve with tenderness. "That's because you make me feel that I am the most beautiful, desirable woman in the world."

"You are." He leaned forward and kissed her, very gently, his lips warm and firm against hers. "And, my beloved, you have performed the miracle of your reforming career in changing me from a care-for-nobody rakehell into a faithful, adoring husband."

He traced the edge of her ear with his tongue, than moved downward. She arched against him like a cat. With a soft puff of breath that caressed her throat, he murmured, "Don't complain that I've become too boring and proper, because it's entirely your fault."

It was a freely given pledge of fidelity. For the first time in her life, she believed the old saying that a reformed rake made the best husband, believed it with visceral knowledge and trust. He had just given her a gift worth more than all the treasures of Durweston. She wanted to weep with joy.

Then his lips moved to her breast and his hand lightly feathered across her abdomen, stirring embers into fire. Catching her breath at the wonder and excitement of him, she gasped, "You, boring?"

He raised his head with a deliciously wicked smile, and she pulled him to her for a proper kiss. As they went tumbling once more into delight, she whispered huskily, "Somehow, I don't think there is any danger of that."

Epilogue

News of the marriage of the greatest heiress in England and the Despair of the Davenports was received with mixed reactions. A red-haired tart named Stella shrieked and hurled a hairbrush across her bedroom, smashing a mirror. A dignified madame called Chessie whooped with delight when she read Reggie's letter, then drank a toast to the lady who had tamed him.

Junius Harper grieved. If he had known that Alys Weston was the heiress of Durweston, and that she was so desperate to marry that she would accept *Davenport,* he would have courted her more assiduously instead of secretly hankering after Miss Spenser. Gloomily he wrote letters to all his grand relations and told them to find him a different living, and the sooner, the better.

As Caroline, Countess of Wargrave, happily told her husband, it proved that miracles did happen. Looking no further than his wife, Richard fondly agreed.

Lord Michael Kenyon, who had once secretly admired the outrageous young Reginald Davenport, smiled at the news, and wondered if there was any chance that he and a sober Reggie might become friends. He would make a point of finding that out.

Jeremy and Elizabeth Stanton rejoiced. Anne's son was now back where he belonged, and behaving exactly as he ought. Their duty as godparents was finally discharged.

Mac Cooper thought it perfectly reasonable that a future duchess had the discernment to appreciate his master. As he cuddled Gillie in their cozy stone cottage, Mac told her rather complacently that a man needed a wife. She couldn't have agreed more.

Peter and William had the best of both worlds. They were back among their friends at Strickland, but they now had holidays in London and Cheshire. As William said, the Duke of Durweston was quite a good old bird. It was as well, perhaps, that his grace never heard the compliment.

Merry agreed, regretfully, that it would not be politic to have Reggie give her away at her wedding, but she and Julian made sure the Blakeford-Davenports were the first guests invited to the Markhams' new home at Moreton.

The Duke of Durweston grumbled when his only daughter married by special license, though he knew it would have been ridiculous for Davenport to formally ask for the girl's hand when the rogue already had the rest of her. Hot irons could not have persuaded him to admit it, but as he came to know his son-in-law better, the duke had to admit that he rather liked the impertinent rogue.

Evicted from the master's bed, Nemesis and Attila took to sleeping together in one entwined mass of fur. Occasionally the tomcat would nip the collie, but apart from a more-in-sorrow-than-in-anger yip, Nemesis never retaliated.

Reggie claimed that the collie was a born victim, but in her secret romantic heart, Alys thought they were seeing an unlikely love between two improbable creatures. She herself knew quite a bit about such things.

Dear Readers,

Of all the books I've written, this one is closest to my heart. Reggie Davenport started as a minor character in my very first Regency, *The Diabolical Baron*. He was, frankly, an obnoxious jerk, rude and selfish and usually drunk. But at the end of the book, he surprised me by showing intriguing glimpses of humor and honor. I started wondering who Reggie was, and what made him behave as he did.

The result was *The Rake and the Reformer*, a Super Regency written in the purest burst of creativity I've ever experienced. Naturally I was pleased when the book became an instant classic and won numerous awards, including a RITA from the Romance Writers of America. But what meant far more were the letters from readers who told me how profoundly the book had moved them.

Now I'm delighted that this story is again available to the historical-romance audience. The title was changed to *The Rake* and I did some polishing, but the essence of the story is exactly the same: It's about Reggie Davenport, a self-destructive man, leavened by wit and humor and painful honesty, who is making one last, desperate bid to change his life. And it's equally about Alys Weston, a strong, independent woman who is far better at giving love than receiving it. Together they discover laughter and healing, and a passionate love that transforms them forever.

I don't pretend to be objective about *The Rake*. I simply hope that Reggie and Alys touched your heart as they have touched mine.

Sincerely,

Mary Jo Putney

Have you tried the first three books in the
Lost Lords series?

It starts with LOVING A LOST LORD . . .

In the first of a dazzling series, Mary Jo Putney introduces
the Lost Lords—maverick childhood friends with a flair for
defying convention. Each is about to discover the woman
who is his perfect match—but perfection doesn't come
easily, even for the noble Duke of Ashton . . .

Battered by the sea, Adam remembers nothing of his past,
his ducal rank, nor of the shipwreck that almost claimed his
life. However, he's delighted to hear that the golden-haired
vision tending his wounds is his wife. Mariah's name and
face may not be familiar, but her touch, her warmth, feel
deliciously right . . .

When Mariah Clarke prayed for a way to deter a bullying
suitor, she didn't imagine she'd find the answer washed
ashore on a desolate beach. Convincing Adam that he is
her husband is surprisingly easy. Resisting the temptation to
act his wife, in every way, will prove anything but. And now
a passion begun in fantasy has become dangerously real—
and completely irresistible . . .

And continues with
NEVER LESS THAN A LADY . . .

New York Times bestselling author Mary Jo Putney continues her stunning Lost Lords series with this stirring, sensual story of a rebellious nobleman drawn to a lovely widow with a shocking past.

As the sole remaining heir to the Earl of Daventry, Alexander Randall knows his duty: find a wife and sire a son of his own. The perfect bride for a man in his position would be a biddable young girl of good breeding. But the woman who haunts his imagination is Julia Bancroft—a village midwife with a dark secret that thrusts her into Randall's protection.

Within the space of a day, Julia has been abducted by her first husband's cronies, rescued, and proposed to by a man she scarcely knows. Stranger still is her urge to say yes. A union with Alexander Randall could benefit them both, but Julia doubts she can ever trust her heart again, or the fervent desire Randall ignites. Yet perhaps only a Lost Lord can show a woman like Julia everything a true marriage can be . . .

Followed by
NOWHERE NEAR RESPECTABLE . . .

Mary Jo Putney's riveting Lost Lords series unleashes a high stakes royal plot—which may prove easier for Damian Mackenzie to handle than his own unruly desire . . .

He's a bastard and a gambler and society's favorite reprobate. But to Lady Kiri Lawford he's a hero—braver than the smugglers he rescues her from, more honorable than any lord she's ever met, and far more attractive than any man has a right to be. How can she not fall in love . . . ?

But Damian Mackenzie has secrets that leave no room in his life for courting high-born young ladies—especially not the sister of one of his oldest friends. Yet when Kiri's quick thinking reveals a deadly threat to England's crown, Damian learns that she is nowhere near as prim and respectable as he first assumed . . . and the lady is far more alluring than any man can resist . . .

Don't miss the next title in the Lost Lords series,
NO LONGER A GENTLEMAN,
coming in May 2012!

Grey Sommers, Lord Wyndham, never met a predicament he couldn't charm his way out of. Then a tryst with a government official's wife during a bit of casual espionage in France condemns him to a decade in a dungeon, leaving him a shadow of his former self. Yet his greatest challenge may be the enigmatic spy sent to free his body—the only woman who might heal his soul.

Cassie Fox lost everything in the chaos of revolution, leaving only a determination to help destroy Napoleon's empire through her perilous calling. Rescuing Grey is merely one more mission. She hadn't counted on a man with the stark beauty of a ravaged angel, whose desperate courage and vulnerability thaw her frozen heart. But a spy and a lord are divided by an impassable gulf even if they manage to survive one last, terrifying mission . . .

London, January 1813

Time to dance with the devil again. Cassie wielded Kirkland House's dragon head knocker, wondering what mission awaited her this time.

The door opened. Recognizing her, the butler bowed her inside. "His lordship is in his study, Miss Fox."

"No need to show me the way." Cassie headed to the rear of the house, thinking that it was about time Kirkland sent her back to France. For years, she had moved secretly between England and France, spying and acting as a courier at Kirkland's direction. The work was dangerous and grimly satisfying.

Outwardly a frivolous gentleman of leisure, in private Kirkland was a master of intelligence gathering and analysis. He'd kept her in London longer than usual this time as part of a team working desperately to uncover a plot against the royal family. They had succeeded, a wedding and Christmas had been celebrated, and now Cassie was restless. Working to undermine Napoleon's regime gave her life purpose.

She knocked at the door of the study and entered at his call. Kirkland sat behind his desk, as well tailored as always. He rose courteously as she entered.

With his dark hair, broad shoulders, and classic features, the man could never be less than handsome, but today his face was etched with strain despite his smile. "You're looking more anonymous than usual, Cassie. How do you manage to be so forgettable?"

"Talent and practice, since anonymity is so useful for a spy," she retorted as she chose a chair opposite him. "But you, sir, look like the death in the afternoon. If you don't take better care of yourself, you'll be down with another attack of fever and we'll find out if you're indispensable or not."

"No one is indispensable," he said as he resumed his seat. "Rob Carmichael could do my job if necessary."

"He could, but he wouldn't want to. Rob much prefers being out on the streets cracking heads." Rob had said as much to Cassie since they were close friends, and occasionally more than friends.

"And he is so very good at it," Kirkland agreed. "But I'm not about to fall off the perch any time soon." He began toying with his quill pen.

"It isn't like you to fidget," Cassie said. "Have you found a more than usually perilous mission for me?"

His mouth quirked humorlessly. "Sending agents into France is always dangerous. My qualms increase when the mission is more personal than of vital interest to Britain."

"Your friend Wyndham," she said immediately. "Bury your qualms. As heir to the Earl of Costain, he'd be worth a few risks even if he weren't your friend."

"I should have known you'd guess." He set the quill neatly in its stand. "How many times have you followed possible leads about Wyndham?"

"Two or three, with a singular lack of success." Nor was Cassie the only agent to look for proof that the long vanished Wyndham was either alive or dead. Kirkland would never give up until there was evidence of one or the other.

"I haven't wanted to admit it, but I've feared that he was killed when the Peace of Amiens ended and all Englishmen were interned so they couldn't return to England." Kirkland sighed. "Wyndham wouldn't have gone tamely. He might well have been killed resisting arrest. He hasn't been heard from since May 1803, when the war resumed."

"Since he isn't in Verdun with the rest of the detainees and no other trace of him has turned up, that's the most likely explanation," Cassie agreed. "But this is the first time I've heard you admit the possibility."

"Wyndham was always so full of life," Kirkland said musingly. "It didn't seem possible that he could be killed senselessly. I know better, of course. But it felt as if saying the words out loud would make them true."

It was a surprising admission coming from Kirkland, whose brain was legendarily sharp and objective. The man really did have emotions. "Tell me about Wyndham," she said. "Not his rank and wealth, but what he was like as a person."

Kirkland's expression eased. "He was a golden haired charmer who could beguile the scales off a snake. Mischievous, but no malice in him. Lord Costain sent him to the Westerfield Academy in the hope that Lady Agnes would be able to handle Wyndham without succumbing to the charm."

"Did it work?" Cassie asked. She'd met the formidable headmistress and thought she could handle anyone.

"Reasonably well. Lady Agnes was fond of him. Everyone was. But she wouldn't let him get away with outrageous behavior."

"You must have a new lead or you wouldn't be talking to me now."

Kirkland began fidgeting with his quill again. "Remember the French spy we uncovered when investigating the plot against the royal family?"

"Paul Clement." Cassie knew the man slightly because of her ties to the French émigré community. "Has he provided information about Wyndham?"

"Clement had heard rumors that just as the truce ended, a young English nobleman ran afoul of a government official named Claude Durand," Kirkland replied. "I know the name, but little more. Have you heard of him?"

Cassie nodded. "He's from a minor branch of a French

noble family. When the revolution came, he turned radical and denounced his cousin, the count, and watched while the man was guillotined. As a reward, Durand acquired the family castle and a good bit of the wealth. Now he's in the Ministry of Police. He has a reputation for brutality and unswerving loyalty to Bonaparte, so he'd be a dangerous man to cross."

Kirkland winced. "Wyndham might not have survived angering a man like that. But Clement had heard that Durand locked the English lord up in his own private dungeon. If that was Wyndham, there's a chance he might be alive."

Cassie didn't need to point out that it was a slim chance. "You wish me to investigate Clement's information?"

"Yes, but don't take any risks." Kirkland regarded her sternly. "I worry about you. You don't fear death enough."

She shrugged. "I don't seek it. Animal instinct keeps me from doing anything foolish. It shouldn't be hard to locate Durand's castle and learn from the locals if he has a blond English prisoner."

Kirkland nodded. "Dungeons aren't designed for long-term survival, but with luck, you'll be able to learn if Wyndham was imprisoned there."

"Did he have the strength to survive years of captivity?" she asked. "Not just physical strength, but mental. Dungeons can drive men mad, especially if they're kept in solitary confinement."

"I never knew what kind of internal resources Wyndham had. Everything came so easily to him. Sports, studies, friendships, admiring females. He was never challenged. He might have unexpected resilience. Or—he might have broken under the first real pressure he'd ever faced." After a long pause, Kirkland said quietly, "I don't think he would have endured imprisonment well. It might have been better if he was killed quickly."

"Truth can be difficult, but better to know what happened and accept the loss than be gnawed by uncertainty forever,"

Cassie pointed out. "There can't be many English lords who offended powerful officials and were locked in private prisons. If he is or was at Castle Durand, it shouldn't be difficult to learn his fate."

"Hard to believe we may have an answer soon," Kirkland mused. "If he's actually there and alive, see what must be done to get him out."

"I'll leave by the end of the week." Cassie rose, thinking of the preparations she must make. She felt compelled to add, "Even if by some miracle he's alive and you can bring him home, he will have changed greatly after all these years."

Kirkland sighed wearily. "Haven't we all?"

Paris, May 1803

"Time to wake, my beautiful golden boy," the husky temptress voice murmured. "My husband will return soon."

Grey Sommers opened his eyes and smiled lazily at his bedmate. If spying was always this enjoyable, he'd make it a career rather than merely dabbling. "'Boy,' Camille? I thought I'd proved otherwise."

She laughed and shook back a tangle of dark hair. "Indeed you did. I must call you my beautiful golden man. Alas, it is time for you to go."

Grey might have done so if her stroking hand hadn't become teasing, driving common sense from his head. So far, he'd acquired little information from the luscious Madame Camille Durand, but he had increased his knowledge of the amatory arts.

Her husband was a high official in the Ministry of Justice and Grey had hoped the man might have spoken of secret matters to his wife. In particular, had Durand discussed the Truce of Amiens ending and war resuming again? But Camille had no interest in politics. Her talents lay elsewhere, and he was more than willing to sample them again.

Once more indulging lust led to drowsing off. He awoke when the door slammed open and a furious man stormed in, a pistol in his hand and two armed guards behind him. Camille shrieked and sat up in bed. "Durand!"

Grey slid off the four poster on the side opposite her husband, thinking sickly that this was like a theater farce. But that pistol was all too real.

"Don't kill him!" Camille begged, her dark hair falling over her breasts. "He is an English milord, and shooting him will cause trouble!"

"An English lord? This must be the foolish Lord Wyndham. I have read the police reports on your movements since your arrival in France. You aren't much of a spy, boy." Durand's thin lips twisted nastily as he cocked the hammer of his pistol. "It no longer matters what the English think."

Grey straightened to his full height as he recognized that there was not a single damned thing he could do to save his life. His friends would laugh if they knew he met his end naked in the bedchamber of another man's wife.

No. They wouldn't laugh.

An eerie calm settled over him. He wondered if all men felt this way when death was inevitable. Lucky that he had a younger brother to inherit the earldom. "I have wronged you, Citoyen Durand." He was proud of the steadiness of his voice. "No one will deny that you have just cause to shoot me."

Something shifted in Durand's dark eyes from murderous rage to cold cruelty. "Oh, no," he said in a soft voice. "Killing you would be far too merciful."